Certain Girls

Certain Girls

a novel

JENNIFER WEINER

ATRIA BOOKS

New York   London   Toronto   Sydney

ATRIA BOOKS

A Division of Simon & Schuster, Inc.
1230 Avenue of the Americas
New York, NY 10020

First Atria Books hardcover edition April 2008

ATRIA BOOKS and colophon are trademarks of Simon & Schuster, Inc.

For information about special discounts for bulk purchases,
please contact Simon & Schuster Special Sales at
1-800-456-6798 or business@simonandschuster.com

Designed by Davina Mock-Maniscalco

Manufactured in the United States of America

1   3   5   7   9   10   8   6   4   2

Library of Congress Cataloging-in-Publication Data

Weiner, Jennifer.
Certain girls : a novel / by Jennifer Weiner.
p.   cm.
Sequel to: Good in bed.
1. Single mothers—Fiction.   2. Jewish women—Fiction.
3. Child rearing—Fiction.   4. Mothers and daughters—Fiction.
5. Philadelphia (Pa.)—Fiction.   I. Title.
PS3573.E3935C47   2008
813'.54—dc22   2007038373

ISBN-13: 978-0-7432-9425-6
ISBN-10:   0-7432-9425-4

For my family

Some say a parent should teach a child to swim.
—The Talmud

PART ONE

Everybody Knows

ONE

When I was a kid, our small-town paper published wedding announcements, with descriptions of the ceremonies and dresses and pictures of the brides. Two of the disc jockeys at one of the local radio stations would spend Monday morning picking through the photographs and nominating the Bow-Wow Bride, the woman they deemed the ugliest of all the ladies who'd taken their vows in the Philadelphia region over the weekend. The grand prize was a case of Alpo.

I heard the disc jockeys doing this on my way to school one morning—"Uh-oh, bottom of page J-6, and yes . . . *yes,* I think we have a contender!" Jockey One said, and his companion snickered and replied, "There's not a veil big enough to hide *that* mess." "Wide bride! Wide bride!" Jockey One chanted before my mother changed the station back to NPR with an angry flick of her wrist. After that, I became more than a little obsessed with the contest. I would pore over the black-and-white head shots each Sunday morning as if I'd be quizzed on them later. Was the one in the middle ugly? Worse than the one in the upper-right-hand corner? Were the blondes always prettier than the brunettes? Did being fat automatically mean you were ugly? I'd rate the pictures and fume about how unfair it was, how just being born with a certain face or body could turn you into a punch line. Then I'd worry for the winner. Was the dog food actually delivered to the couple's door? Would they return from the honeymoon and find it there, or would a well-meaning parent or friend try to hide it? How would the bride feel when she saw that she'd won? How would her husband feel, knowing that he'd chosen the ugliest girl in Philadelphia on any given weekend, to love and to cherish, until death did them part?

I wasn't sure of much back then, but I knew that when—if— I got married, there was no way I'd put a picture in the paper. I was pretty certain, at thirteen, that I had more in common with the bow-wows than the beautiful brides, and I was positive that the worst thing that could happen to any woman would be winning that contest.

Now, of course, I know better. The worst thing would not be a couple of superannuated pranksters on a ratings-challenged radio station oinking at your picture and depositing dog food at your door. The worst thing would be if they did it to your daughter.

I'm exaggerating, of course. And I'm not really worried. I looked across the room at the dance floor, just beginning to get crowded as the b'nai mitzvah guests dropped off their coats, feeling my heart lift at the sight of my daughter, my beautiful girl, dancing the hora in a circle of her friends. Joy will turn thirteen in May and is, in my own modest and completely unbiased opinion, the loveliest girl ever born. She inherited the best things I had to offer—my olive skin, which stays tan from early spring straight through December, and my green eyes. Then she got my ex-boyfriend's good looks: his straight nose and full lips, his dirty-blond hair, which, on Joy, came out as ringlets the deep gold of clover honey. My chest plus Bruce's skinny hips and lean legs combined to create the kind of body I always figured was available only thanks to divine or surgical intervention.

I walked to one of the three bars set along the edges of the room and ordered a vodka and cranberry juice from the bartender, a handsome young man looking miserable in a ruffled pale blue polyester tuxedo shirt and bell-bottoms. At least he didn't look as tormented as the waitress beside him, in a mermaid costume, with seashells and fake kelp in her hair. Todd had wanted a retro seventies theme for the party celebrating his entry into Jewish adulthood. His twin sister, Tamsin, an aspiring marine biologist, hadn't wanted a theme at all and had grudgingly muttered the word "ocean" the eleventh time her mother had asked her. In between pre-party visits to Dr. Hammermesh to have her breasts enlarged, her thighs reduced, and the millimeters of excess flesh beneath her eyes eliminated, Shari Marmer, the twins' mom, had come up with a compromise. On this icy night in January, Shari and her husband, Scott, were hosting three hundred of their nearest and dearest at the National Constitution Center to celebrate at Studio 54 Under the Sea.

I passed beneath a doorway draped with fake seaweed and strands of dark blue beads and wandered toward the table at the room's entrance. My place card had my name stenciled in elaborate script on the back of a scallop shell. Said shell contained a T&T medallion, for Tamsin and Todd. I squinted at the shell and learned that my husband, Peter, and I would be sitting at Donna Summer. Joy hadn't picked up her shell yet. I peered at the whirling mass of coltish girls until I saw Joy in her knee-length dark blue dress, performing some kind of complicated line dance, hands clapping, hips rocking. As I watched, a boy detached himself from a cluster of his friends, crossed the room with his hands shoved in his pockets, and said something to my daughter. Joy nodded and let him take her hand as he led her underneath the strobe that cast cool bubbles of bluish light.

My Joy, I thought as the boy shifted his weight from foot to foot, looking like he was in desperate need of the bathroom. It isn't politically correct to say so, but in the real world, good looks function as a get-out-of-everything-free card. Beauty clears your path, it smooths the way, it holds the doors open, it makes people forgive you when your homework's late or you bring the car home with the gas gauge on E. Joy's adolescence would be so much easier than mine. Except . . . except. On her last report card, she'd gotten one A, two B's, and two C's instead of her usual A's and B's (and worlds away from the straight A's I'd gotten when I was her age and had more brains than friends). "She just doesn't seem as engaged, as present," her teacher had said when Peter and I had gone in for our parent-teacher conference. "Is there anything unusual going on at home?"

Peter and I had shaken our heads, unable to think of a thing—no divorce, certainly, no moves, no deaths, no disruptions. When the teacher had folded her eyeglasses on her desk and asked about boyfriends, I'd said, "She's *twelve.*" The teacher's smile had been more than a little pitying. "You'd be surprised," she said.

Except I wouldn't. Other mothers, maybe, but not me. I kept a close watch on my daughter (too close, she'd probably say). I knew her teachers, the names of her friends, the horrible, whiny boy singer she likes, the brand of twenty-bucks-a-bottle shampoo on which she blows the bulk of her allowance. I know the way she struggles with reading and is a whiz at math, and that her favorite thing in the world to do is swim in the ocean. I know that apricots are her favorite fruit, that Tamsin and Todd are her best friends, that she worships my little sister and is terrified of needles and bees. I'd know if anything had changed, and Joy's life, I explained, was the same as it had ever been. Her teacher had smiled and patted my knee. "We see it a lot with girls her age," she'd said, putting her glasses back on and glancing at the clock. "Their worlds just get bigger. I'm sure she'll be fine. She's got involved parents and a good head on her shoulders. We'll just keep an eye on things."

As if I don't do that already, I'd thought. But I'd smiled and thanked Mrs. McMillan and promised to call with any concerns. Of course, thirty minutes later, when I'd gone straight to the source and asked Joy whether anything was wrong, my interrogation had been met with the shrug/eye-roll combination that is the hallmark of adolescent girls everywhere. When I'd said, "That's not an answer," she'd replied, "Seventh grade's harder than sixth," and opened her math book to let me know definitively that the conversation was over.

I'd wanted to call her pediatrician, a psychologist, her old speech therapist, at the very least the school's principal and guidance counselor. I'd made a list of possibilities: tutoring centers and homework-help websites, support groups for parents of premature children or kids with hearing loss. Peter had talked me out of it. "It's one quarter of seventh grade," he'd argued. "All she needs is time."

Time, I thought now. I sipped my drink and shoved the worries away. I've gotten good at that. At the age of forty-two, I've decided, ruefully, that I'm slightly inclined toward melancholy. I don't trust happiness. I turn it over as if it were a glass at a flea market or a rug at a souk, looking for chipped rims or loose threads.

But not Joy, I thought as I watched my daughter shuffle back and forth with the boy's hands on her hips, laughing at something he'd said. Joy is fine. Joy is lovely and lucky. And in the manner of almost-thirteen-year-olds everywhere, my daughter has no idea how lovely, or how lucky, she is.

"Cannie!" Shari Marmer's voice cut across the crowded atrium of the Constitution Center, where guests were clustered, waiting to take their seats for dinner. I clutched my shell and my drink and gave a halfhearted wave as she hustled over, all bright red lips and blepharoplasty, a new diamond solitaire trapped in the Grand Canyon of her cleavage. "Yoo-hoo! Can-nie!" Shari singsonged. I groaned inwardly as she grabbed my arm with her French manicure. When I tried to pull away, her hand came with me and ended up lodged beneath my right breast. My embarrassment was instant and excruciating. Shari didn't appear to notice.

"You and Peter are sitting with us," she said. She swept me into the dining room, where I saw thirty tables for ten draped in aquamarine tablecloths with seashell centerpieces, topped with glittering disco balls.

"Great!" I said. *Why?* I wondered. Shari and Scott had relatives, grandparents, actual friends who should have been sitting with them. And it wasn't as if Shari and I needed to catch up. Our kids were best friends, and even though we'd never become friends ourselves, we had years of shared history and saw each other plenty. Just last month we'd spent an entire day together, rehashing our latest reality-TV fixation and grating thirty pounds of potatoes for our synagogue's annual preschool Latkefest. Peter and I could've been over at Gloria Gaynor with the Callahans, or at Barry Gibb with Marisol Chang, whom I'd loved since I'd met her ten years ago in Music Together class.

"What do you think?" Shari asked me, waving her toned, sculpted, and possibly lipo'd arm at the room as we made our way toward the head table.

"It's fantastic," I said loyally. "And Tamsin and Todd did a wonderful job."

She tightened her grip on my arm. "Do you really think so?"

"They were great. You look amazing." That, at least, was the undisputable truth. Eight years older than me, Shari had been in advertising in New York before marriage and motherhood. Her job now was self-maintenance, and she worked at it harder than I'd worked at any paid employment I'd ever had. Frying potato pancakes in the synagogue's kitchen, I'd listened, awestruck and exhausted, as Shari had described her rounds: the personal trainer, the yoga and pilates, the facials, the waxing, the laser treatments and the eyelash tinting, the low-cal, low-carb meals delivered each morning to her door. It was, perhaps, the one good thing about never having been beautiful—you didn't have to kill yourself trying to hold on to something you'd never had in the first place.

"And the party?" Shari fretted. "It's not too much?"

"Not at all!" I lied.

Shari sighed as a gold-medallioned, Jheri-curled DJ who was a dead ringer for a pre-incarceration Rick James led her parents to the front of the room for the blessing over the bread. "Tamsin's furious. She says that marine biology is a serious science, and that I'm . . ." Her bejeweled fingers hooked into air quotes. " 'Trivializing her ambitions' with seashell centerpieces and mermaid costumes." She blinked at me with her newly widened eyes. "I think the waitresses look cute!"

"Adorable," I said.

"They should," Shari muttered. "I had to pay them extra to wear bikinis. Something about the health code." She towed me through the crowd, past the tables draped in ocean-blue tablecloths, and over to Donna Summer. Of the ten people at the table, six were family, two were me and Peter, and numbers nine and ten were the programming director of the city's public radio station and his wife. I waved at my husband, who was standing in the corner, deep in conversation with a gastroenterologist of our acquaintance. *Better Peter than me,* I thought, and sank into my seat.

The elderly woman to my left peered at my place card, then at my face. My heart sank. I knew what was coming. "Candace Shapiro? Not Candace Shapiro the writer?"

"Former," I said, trying to smile as I spread my napkin over my lap. Suddenly the gastroenterologist wasn't looking so bad. Ah well. I supposed I should be flattered that Shari still thought my name was worth dropping. I'd written one novel under my own name almost ten years ago and, since then, had produced a steady stream of science fiction under a pseudonym. The pay for sci fi was a lot worse, but anonymity turned out to suit me much better than my fifteen minutes of fame had.

My seatmate placed one spotted, shaking hand on my forearm. "You know, dear, I've had a book inside me for the longest time."

"My husband's a doctor," I told her gravely. "I'm sure he could help you get it out."

A puzzled look crossed the aged party's face.

"Sorry," I said. "What's your idea?"

"Well, it's about a woman who gets divorced after many years of marriage . . ."

I smiled, sipped my drink, and tried to turn her synopsis into a pleasant blur of sound. A minute later, Peter appeared at my side. I shot him a grateful smile as he took my hand.

"Excuse me," he said to the woman. "They're playing our song. Cannie?"

I got to my feet and followed him to the dance floor, where a few grown-up couples had worked their way in among the kids. I waved at Joy, stretched up to plant a quick kiss on the dimple in Peter's chin, and leaned in to his tuxedoed chest. It took me a minute to recognize the music. " 'Do It Till You're Raw' is our song?"

"I had to get you out of there, so it is now," he said.

"And here I was, hoping for something romantic." I sighed. "You know. 'I Had His Baby, But You Have My Heart.' " I rested my cheek on his shoulder, then waved at Shari and Scott Marmer as they fox-trotted past us. Scott looked euphoric, puffed up and proud of his children. His round brown eyes and his bald spot gleamed under the disco lights, along with his cummerbund, made of the same red satin as Shari's gown. "Can you believe that's going to be us this fall? I looked at Shari more closely. "Except I probably won't be getting my implants refreshed beforehand."

"No need," Peter said, and dipped me. When the song was over, I raised my hands to my hair, which felt fine, then dropped them to my hips, encased in black velvet. I thought I looked all right. No less an authority than my daughter had signed off on my ensemble. True, she'd done so with a less than enthusiastic *I guess it's okay,* and told me on our way into the building that if I took my shoes off at any point in the evening and wandered around like a homeless person, she would legally emancipate herself, which children were allowed to do these days.

I wondered, the way I always did on occasions like this, what people thought when they saw me and Peter together, and whether it was some incredulous version of *He's married to her?* Unlike poor, paunchy, balding Scott, Peter was tall and lean, and had only gotten better-looking as the years had progressed. Sadly, unlike the surgically improved Shari Marmer, the same could not be said of me. *Ah, well,* I thought. *I should look on the bright side.* Maybe they all assumed that I had the flexibility of a nineteen-year-old Romanian gymnast and the imagination of a porn star and could do all manner of crazy stuff in bed.

I squared my shoulders and lifted my head as the DJ played "Lady in Red" and Peter took me in his arms again. I was determined to be a good role model, to set a good example for my daughter, to be judged on the content of my character as opposed to the size of my thighs. And if I was going to be judged by the size of my thighs, let the word go out that I was actually an impressive seven pounds thinner than I was when I'd gotten married, thanks to an indescribably hellish six weeks on the Atkins Diet. Plus, except for a touch of arthritis and the occasional back spasm, I was disgustingly healthy, while Peter was the one who'd inherited a cholesterol problem that he had to treat with three separate medications.

I looked up to find him staring at me, his forehead slightly furrowed, eyes intent.

"What is it?" I asked hopefully. "Do you wanna go make out in a stairwell?"

"Let's take a walk." He snagged a few beef satay sticks and a plate from a passing waiter, added some raw vegetables and crackers, and led me up the staircase to the Signers' Hall, with life-size statues of the men who'd signed the Constitution.

I leaned against Ben Franklin and took a look around. "You know what? Our country was founded by a bunch of short, short men."

"Better nutrition these days," said Peter, setting his plate on a cocktail table by the railing and giving John Witherspoon a friendly slap on the back. "It's the secret to everything. And you're wearing heels."

I pointed at George Washington. "Well, so is he. Hey, did Ben Franklin have VD, or was that someone else?"

"Cannie," Peter said soberly. "We are in the presence of great men. Molded bronze replicas of great men. And you have to bring up venereal disease?"

I squinted at Ben's biography, on a small rectangular plaque on the back of his chair. It made no mention of any nasty souvenirs he might have picked up during his years in Paris. History was a whitewash, I thought, crossing the floor and leaning over the railing to look down at the hired dancers, gyrating wildly as a specially constructed Studio 54 emblem descended from the ceiling (instead of sniffing cocaine, the man on the moon appeared to be reading from the Torah). "This party is insane," I said.

"I've been thinking about something," Peter said, looking at me steadily over George Washington's wig.

I hoisted myself up onto the stool in front of our cocktail table. "Joy's party?" Our daughter's bat mitzvah, and the party that would follow, were many months away but had already emerged as a hot topic around our house.

"Not that." He took the seat across from me and looked at me sweetly, almost shyly, from underneath his long eyelashes.

"Are you dying?" I inquired. Then I asked, "Can I have your beef stick?"

Peter exhaled. His brown eyes crinkled in the corners and his teeth flashed briefly as he struggled not to smile.

"Those weren't related questions. I'm very sympathetic," I assured him. "I'm just also very hungry. But don't worry. I'll do the whole devoted-wife-of-many-years thing. Hold your hand, sleep by your bedside, have your body stuffed and mounted, whatever you like."

"Viking funeral," Peter said. "You know I want a Viking funeral. With flaming arrows and Wyclef Jean singing 'Many Rivers to Cross.' "

"Right right right," I said. I had an entire file on my laptop labeled "Peter's Demise." "If Wyclef's busy, should I try for Pras?"

Peter shrugged. "He could use the work, I guess."

"Well, you think it over. I really don't want you haunting me from beyond the grave because I hired the wrong Fugee. And do you want the music before or after they set your corpse on fire?"

"Before," he said, reclaiming his plate. "Once you light a corpse on fire, it's all downhill from there." He munched ruminatively on a carrot stick. "Maybe I could lie in state at the Apollo. Like James Brown."

"You might have to release an album first, but I'll see what I can do. I know people. So what's up?" I raised my eyebrow in a knowing manner. "Do you want a threesome?"

"No, I don't want a threesome!" he boomed. Peter has a very deep voice. It tends to carry. The three women in strapless gowns who'd wandered into the hall, presumably for some fresh air, stared at us. I gave them a sympathetic shrug and mouthed, *Sorry.*

"I want . . ." He lowered his voice and stared at me, his dark brown eyes intent. Even with all the little businesses of ten years of marriage between us, the conversations about when to get the roof fixed and where to send Joy for summer camp, his gaze could still melt me and make me wish we were somewhere all alone . . . and that I really was as limber as a Romanian gymnast.

"I want to have a baby," Peter said.

"You want . . ." I felt my heart start pounding, and my velvet dress suddenly felt too tight. "Huh. Didn't see that coming. Really?"

He nodded. "I want us to have a baby together."

"Okay," I said slowly. This was not the first time the possibility of a baby had come up over the course of our marriage. There'd be a story about some talk-show host or country singer on the news, the proud mother of twins or triplets "born with the help of a surrogate," an expression that always made me roll my eyes. It would be like me saying that the oil in my car had been "changed with the help of a mechanic," as if I had something to do with it other than paying the bill. But if we were going to have a baby who was biologically our own, there'd need to be a third party involved. Joy had been born two months early, via emergency C-section, which had been followed by an emergency hysterectomy. There'd be no more babies for me. Peter knew this, of course, and even though he'd pointed out the pieces about surrogates, he'd never pushed it.

Now, though, it looked like he was ready to push. "I'm fifty-four," he said.

I turned away and read out loud from James McHenry's plaque: " 'Physician, military aide, and politician.' And a very sharp dresser."

Peter ignored me. "I'm getting older. Joy's growing up. And there might be possibilities. You might have viable eggs."

I batted my eyelashes. "That is, hands down, the most romantic thing you've ever said to me."

Peter took my hand, and his face was so open, so hopeful, so familiar and dear that I was sick with regret that my one shot at natural motherhood had come via my stoned jerk of an ex-boyfriend instead of with my husband. "Don't you ever think about it?" he asked.

My eyelids started to prickle. "Well . . ." I shook my head and swallowed hard. "You know. Sometimes." Obviously I'd wondered. I'd daydreamed about a baby we'd make together, a sober little boy who'd look like Peter, with flashes of his dry humor, like heat lightning in the summer sky; one perfect little boy to go along with my perfect girl. But it was like dreaming about being in the Supremes, or winning a marathon, or, in my case, running a marathon: a fantasy for a lazy afternoon in the hammock, something to mull over while stuck on a runway or driving on the turnpike, nothing that would ever really happen.

"We're so happy now," I said. "We have each other. We have Joy. And Joy needs us."

"She's growing up," he said gently. "Our job now is to let her go."

I freed my hand and turned away. Technically, it was true. With any other going-on-thirteen-year-old, I'd agree unconditionally. But Joy was a different story. She needed special attention because of who she was, the things she struggled with—her hearing, her reading— and because of who I'd been.

"Our lives are wonderful, but everything's the same," he continued. "We live in the same house, we see the same people, we go to the Jersey shore every summer—"

"You like it there!"

"Things are good," he said. "But maybe they could be even better. It wouldn't kill us to try something new."

"Back to threesomes," I said, half to myself.

"I think we should at least take a look. See what's what." He pulled a business card out of his wallet and handed it to me. Dr. Stanley Neville, reproductive endocrinologist, offices on Spruce Street—in the same building, I noted ruefully, as the doctor who treated my recently diagnosed arthritis. "He can do an ultrasound of your ovaries."

"Good times," I said, and gave him back the card. I thought of our lives, perfectly arranged, the three of us safe, cocooned from the world. My garden, after ten years of attention, was in full flower, with espaliered roses climbing the brick walls, hydrangeas with blue and violet blossoms as big as babies' heads. My house was just the way I'd always wanted it. Last month, seven years of searching had finally yielded the perfect green-and-gold antique grandfather clock that sat on top of the staircase and melodically bing-bonged the hours. Everything except for the tiny and no doubt fixable matter of Joy's grades was perfect.

Peter touched my shoulder. "Whatever happens, whether this works out or not, our life is good just the way it is. I'm happy. You know that, don't you?"

Beneath us, a parade of waiters and waitresses, in their bodysuits and bikinis, exited the kitchen bearing salad plates. I nodded. My eyelids were still burning, and there was a lump in my throat, but I wasn't about to start bawling in the middle of the Constitution Center. I could only imagine the gossip that would start if Shari got wind of it. "Okay," I said.

"Candace," he said fondly. "Please don't look so worried."

"I'm not worried," I lied. He handed me his plate, but for one of the rare times in recent memory, I wasn't hungry at all. So I set it back on the table and followed him down the stairs, past the windows and the moon hanging high in the sky, flooding the lawn with its silvery light.

Two

Todd plopped himself down on my bed and stared at me eagerly. "So what were you guys doing in there?" he asked.

I pulled the bobby pins out of my hair, letting my curls tumble around my shoulders, smiling without saying a word.

"We're your best friends," Todd pleaded. "James is our cousin. We can give you inside information. I think he's a hottie."

Tamsin, in her sleeping bag on the floor, pursed her lips and noisily flipped the page of her book. Todd was still wearing his suit, but his sister had gotten out of her dress the minute my bedroom door was closed, and looked much happier in her *Lord of the Rings* nightshirt and her sweatpants, with her face scrubbed clean of the makeup her mother had made her wear and her freckles back in full force on her nose.

"We didn't do anything," I lied as Frenchelle, my dog, hopped onto my bed and curled up like a Danish at my feet. The truth was, I'd danced with Todd and Tamsin's fifteen-year-old cousin, James, three times. Then James had offered me a sip of his drink, which had turned out to be a whiskey sour that his older brother had given him, and I'd said okay to that, too. Then he'd taken me into the darkened auditorium where they do the "Freedom Rising" multimedia presentation and pressed me against the carpeted wall, and we'd stood there in the darkness, him in his shirt and tie and me with his jacket draped over my shoulders, kissing like something

16

out of a movie, or at least a music video. I'd worried a little when he started rubbing himself up and down against me, but when he put his hand on my breast, I just moved it away, and when he didn't put it back, I let myself relax. It was so dark in the auditorium that I could pretend he was anybody. At first I'd pretended that he was Dustin Tull the singer, and that had been good, and then I'd pretended that he was Duncan Brodkey, my crush from school, and that was even better, standing there in the darkness with James's thin lips pressing against mine so hard that I could feel the bumps of his teeth.

You're so hot, he'd murmured in my ear, and that was the best thing of all, because I thought he believed it: that in that dress, for that night, it might actually have been true. Then one of James's hands had slid back to my chest, and he'd pinched me too hard. I'd pushed him away and said, *I don't think so,* in a scornful, almost snotty voice, and I had sounded exactly like Taryn Tupping, who is actually hot and the star of *The Girls' Room* on TV. It was just the kind of thing she'd say to a boy who'd gone too far, the exact words and tone that a real hot girl would use. James had stepped away from me immediately, and I thought he'd look angry, but he just looked as if it was what he expected—as if that was how hot girls were supposed to behave.

"Spill, spill!" Todd chanted. I blushed, remembering it: the feeling of James's lips and his hands, and that respectful look on his face. But I didn't want to say anything because Tamsin hadn't kissed anyone yet, and if I did tell, Todd would pass the story along to everyone, probably starting with his mother.

Frenchelle turned in a circle, then curled up again and started snoring as my mother made her way slowly up the stairs. I rolled over, hiding my face in my pillow as she paused, the way she always did, to admire the clock at the top of the staircase. "Shh," I said. "It's her."

The three of us lay there, the silence broken only by the sound of Tamsin clicking her retainer in and out of her mouth, until I heard my mother turn around and head toward her bedroom. I rolled onto my back, stared at the ceiling, and began my litany. "Reasons I cannot stand my mother: one through ten."

"Here we go," Tamsin muttered.

" 'Scuse me," said Todd, carrying his pajamas to the bathroom.

I ignored them both. "One: her boobs."

"They're not that bad," Tamsin said without looking up from the copy of *Ghost World* I'd gotten her for Chanukah, to replace the one she'd read until it had fallen apart. Todd came back in, barefoot in striped seersucker pajamas, smelling like benzoyl peroxide and mint toothpaste, his dark brown hair brushed up from his forehead, his lips and nose and the arch of his eyebrows identical to his sister's. Even though he's not into girls except as friends, this would probably be the last time Todd would be allowed to sleep over—*Today I am a man,* he'd said, making a face—but there was going to be a brunch at the Marmers' house the next morning. The caterers would arrive at six, and Mrs. Marmer had decided that the benefits of the twins getting a good night's rest outweighed the risks of a mixed-sex sleepover. "They're just . . . you know." Tamsin rolled onto her side. "Big."

I sighed. Todd and Tamsin have been my best friends since kindergarten. We met the day Matthew Swatner started teasing me because of my hearing aids and calling me Machinehead. The two of them had plopped themselves down beside me at the sand table—Tamsin with her hair in pigtails tied with red ribbons, Todd in a red baseball cap—and told Matthew to leave me alone. Then Todd had given me his baseball cap to wear, and Tamsin had tied one of her ribbons around my wrist, and at snack time they'd sat on either side of me, glaring at Matthew, at anyone who stared. *Your own personal Fruits of Islam,* my mother had said when she'd seen them. I still don't know what she meant by that, but I know for sure that even after all our years together, Tamsin and Todd still don't get the deal of my mom.

"Her chest is ridiculous," I said. "Do you know what size bra she wears? Thirty-six G."

"G?" Todd repeated. "Is that a real size?"

"Sort of. She has to order them online because the regular store doesn't have them."

"Wow," said Tamsin, but she sounded respectful, not horrified, the way I'd been when I'd seen the tag on my mother's bra.

"And she always wears clothes where you can see her chest!" I shook my head. "But that's probably not her fault. I mean, what's she going to wear so you can't see her chest?" I stared at the ceiling and told my friends the worst part. "And now I'm getting them, too."

"You're lucky," Tamsin said, looking up from her book to gaze unhappily at her own chest. "Guys love big boobs."

"Which is why our mom bought hers," Todd said.

"She says I can get implants, too, when I'm sixteen," said Tamsin. "As if."

I flushed, thinking of James again, who hadn't seemed bothered by my chest. "Amber Gross doesn't have big boobs," I said. "Amber Gross barely has any boobs at all."

"Yeah, but she's Amber Gross." Out loud, it sounded stupid, but I knew exactly what Tamsin meant. In spite of her last name, which you'd think would be an automatic disqualifier, Amber Gross is the most popular girl in our grade. Amber Gross has chestnut-brown hair, straight and shiny as a satin curtain, and a twinkly smile that would make you think her braces are jewelry she had commissioned for her teeth. No zit would ever dare deface her skin. Her body is tiny and perfect, and her clothes are tiny and perfect, and she is going out with Martin Baker, who's on the J.V. soccer team even though he's only a seventh-grader. Best of all, most important, Amber can talk to anybody, parents or teachers or boys, and everything that comes out of her mouth—the words and the sound of the words—is always just right.

I am the anti-Amber, the girl whose face you'd skip right over, the one who stands in the back row of class pictures, slouching, looking away; the one who smiles and nods at things she can't quite hear and hopes that will be good enough. I never know the right thing to say, not even in my own head, and half the time, if I do manage to say something, people ask me to speak up or repeat myself, because my voice is so low and gravelly and strange-sounding that they can't hear me or understand what I'm saying.

I used to think that I was special—special in a good way, like my mother used to tell me. I remember being maybe three or four, in my speech therapist's office, feeling my mother's fingers against my chin as she gently moved my face so I was looking at her lips in the mirror. *Watch me, Joy.* I was born premature, with mild hearing loss in one ear and moderate loss in the other, so it took me longer to talk than most kids. In nursery school, I'd get frustrated when people couldn't understand me. I'd scream, throw things, hurl myself onto the ABC carpet and pound it with my feet and fists. My mother came to school with me every day. She never got mad at me or lost her patience. She'd wait until I stopped crying. She'd wipe my face and give me apple juice in a sippie cup and lead me over to the easels or the Story Corner, where she'd settle me in her lap and read me a book. At home, we'd practice in front of the mirror, her eyes on my eyes and her fingers on my chin. *You're doing so well! You're doing just great! Say "mmm."* She'd sit with me in her lap, pressing one of my hands against my throat so I could feel the sound's vibration, and my other hand on my lips, so I could feel the air streaming out of my nose. *Say "mmm." Say "mmm." Say "Mama."*

We'd walk home together at lunchtime, and if it had been a hard day, I would get a treat. We'd go to Pearl Art Supplies for watercolor paint or new buttons, or to Rita's for water ice when it was warm, and my mother would scoop me into her arms and say that she was so proud, that I was so special. It has taken me all of this time to learn that I'm really not. The only reason anyone in the real world thinks I'm special is because of my hearing aids and my weird voice and because once, a long time ago, my mother wrote a book.

"Can I go now?" asked Tamsin. She had one hand curled around *Ghost World,* her finger marking her place.

"I'm only on two. Two," I said. "She and my father are disgusting." They laugh together all the time. They kiss when they think I'm not watching. They speak a private language, one made up of all the movies and TV shows they've seen and the magazines they've read. One of them will say something like "Can't we all just get along?" or "Lewis Lapham has gone too far this time," and the other one will start laughing. "Who is Lewis Lapham? What's so funny about a sweatshirt that just says 'College'?" I'll ask, and they'll try to explain, but it's like when I was little again: Even though I can hear the words, they don't come together in a way that makes sense.

"My turn," said Tamsin. She sat up and piled her hair into a knot on top of her head. "Um . . ."

I turned away. If Tamsin could find even one thing she didn't like about her mother, I would be shocked. Mrs. Marmer has a normal-size chest—or at least she did before the implants. Tamsin and Todd's father is her husband, not an old boyfriend who got Mrs. Marmer pregnant and never even married her.

But the best thing about Mrs. Marmer is that she leaves her kids alone. Last month she was twenty minutes late to the all-school holiday musical. Tamsin, who was sitting next to me and checking the time on her cell phone every thirty seconds, glared as her mom came tiptoeing in right in the middle of Todd's first solo, one hand pressed to her mouth, flimsy rubber flip-flops slapping against the auditorium floor. *Traffic,* she mouthed, easing herself into the seat next to Tamsin. "I'm so sorry, baby, did I miss much?" My mom was sitting on my other side, and I saw her lips tighten as she took in Mrs. Marmer's flip-flops and bright coral toenails. My mom's face relaxed when she saw me looking, and she shrugged. "Things happen," she whispered while Tamsin flipped her cell phone shut, pressing her lips together.

I thought that I'd never been so jealous of my friends. My mother would never, ever forget me. Not even for twenty minutes. Probably not even for twenty seconds. I am the main topic of interest in her life. She drops me off at school every morning (every other kid in my class walks or takes the bus), and every afternoon, as soon as the last bell rings, her minivan (chosen because *Consumers Digest* rated it the safest car on the market) is first in line to pick me up. When I have swim practice or show choir rehearsal, she waits for me, sitting in the bleachers or the auditorium, knitting or tapping away on her laptop. She's the president of the home/school association, and my room mother, and she's always the first one to volunteer to bring the cut-up fruit and sports drink to the meets, or host the cast parties after the shows, or push a book into my hand, something about Terabithia or Narnia, something by Philip Pullman or Roald Dahl. *Ooh, Joy, you're going to love this one; it was my favorite when I was your age!*

She's with me almost every minute of the day when I'm not in class, watching me like she's waiting for me to throw my sippie cup across the floor and start kicking the carpet, to need her again, the way I did when I was three. And when she's not with me, she's thinking about me, planning some kind of mother-daughter activity or knitting me something I don't need (another scarf, another sweater, another pair of mittens), buying me yet another book that I'll just leave on my bookshelf or installing special safety locks on my bedroom window because once, before I was born, some rock star's kid fell out of a window (I looked it up online and found out that the window was on the fifty-third floor of a high-rise in New York City, and the kid was four, but even after I'd explained all of that to my mother, she still had the safety locks installed).

"Our mom makes terrible school lunches," Tamsin finally managed.

"The worst," Todd said, nodding. I tried to sound sympathetic, but I was thinking that I'd trade a soggy cream-cheese-and-olive sandwich or a leftover low-carb burrito any day of the week if I'd get Mrs. Marmer instead of a mother who never left me alone. She doesn't hold my chin anymore, but sometimes I think I can still feel her fingers on my face. As soon as I get into the car after school, it starts: *How was your day? How was school? Can I get you a snack? Want to help me make dinner? Can I pick you up anything at the supermarket? Do you need any help with your homework?* until I just want to scream, *Leave me alone, leave me alone, I can't breathe with you this close to me!,* but I can't, because if I do, she will look at me like I slapped her or stuck a knife in her tire or did something else on purpose, just to hurt her.

I adjusted my pillow, half listening to Tamsin and Todd describe the latest horror they'd pulled out of their lunch bags ("She thought she was being this great mother for buying the all-natural peanut butter that's all oily on top, but I don't even like peanut butter, and then she didn't even stir it, so I was, like, eating a grease sandwich"), staring at the glow-in-the-dark stars my mother and I had pasted to the ceiling when I was little, a long time ago.

"Shh," I said as I heard my mother's footsteps approaching. I turned out the lights, and the three of us lay in the darkness. Tamsin clicked her retainer in and out of her mouth and picked up her book and tried to read it by the light of the digital clock, and I whispered for her to be quiet and put it away. Frenchie grumbled in her sleep. The numbers on the clock changed from 12:45 to 12:46.

"Why does she do this?" Todd wondered.

"She just loves me so much," I said. I'd meant for it to come out sarcastic, but instead it just sounded pathetic, and weak, and worst of all, true.

At 12:57, the door creaked open. I made sure my hair was over my ears so that my mom wouldn't see my hearing aids and know that we'd been talking, and I held my breath, hoping that Tamsin wouldn't start with her retainer and give us away. My mother approached the bed and stood there for a moment, not touching me but looking down, the way she did every single night of my life, standing in the dark, listening to me breathe. When she turned toward the window, I opened my eyes a crack, and I could see her in the lamplight, her secret face, the one she shows only to me.

THREE

"He wants . . . to have . . . a baby."

"That bastard," said Samantha from the yoga mat beside me. "Okay, wait. Who are we talking about?"

I smiled. My best friend had been having a rough few months, guywise, that had culminated in a painful breakup with her latest beau. During what Sam delicately called "an intimate moment," he'd grabbed some lotion from the bedside table and wound up slathering her breasts and his business with her five-hundred-dollar-an-ounce anti-wrinkle cream. Sam had been furious, and her gentleman caller had been furious that she'd been furious ("What? You're saying I'm not worth it!" he'd shouted, and she'd informed him that no man was worth five hundred dollars per session, plus the time she'd have to spend on the Cellex-C waiting list to get more).

"Peter. My husband," I said. "Guy I married? Tall, dark hair? Bought me a Roomba for my birthday?" I lowered my voice. Linda Larson was two rows ahead of us; Linda, with the body of a nineteen-year-old starlet and the ears of a CIA snoop. "My husband, Peter, wants to have a baby."

"Oh my," Samantha said. She shook her rich, glossy hair and adjusted her headband, then her pigeon pose.

I gave up on my own pigeon and rolled from my hands and knees onto the forgiving floor. Sam, meanwhile, had eased into downward dog, then, in one ridiculously fluid movement, rolled into a shoulder

25

stand. It was six o'clock on Tuesday night, and we were at Yoga Child on South Street for Over Forty Yoga. I'd signed us up in September, optimistically picturing a class full of stooped-over grannies with walkers and osteoporosis who'd complain about their hot flashes in between the chants. How wrong I'd been. Our group was comprised of eight fit, firm babes in black stretchy yoga pants, none of whom—Sam and Linda included—appeared to be over thirty-five, and me, in extra-large blue sweatpants and a Philadelphia Academy T-shirt, looking every year of my age, trying, and mostly failing, to keep up.

"So what are you going to do?" asked Sam.

"Hang . . . on," I huffed, heaving myself into an epically clumsy downward dog. The room smelled like oranges and beeswax candles and competing perfumes. Sam flipped onto her belly, pushed up into a baby cobra, and swiveled her long neck so she could look at me.

"Peter made me an appointment. I'm supposed to find out if I have viable eggs," I whispered. "And then find a surrogate, I guess."

Sam looked horrified. "Cannie, I love you like a sister, but I hope you're not going to ask me what I think you're going to ask me. Get your mind off my vagina!"

"It'd be your uterus, actually," I whispered back.

"Either way, it ain't happening."

Ashleigh, our instructor, looked at us sternly. "Let's all move into happy baby," she said in her low, soothing voice.

"God, I hate it when yoga becomes ironic," I muttered as we shifted onto our backs and grabbed our feet, pulling our knees to our chests.

"Do you even want another baby?" Sam asked.

"Not sure." Babies. How could I think about babies when Joy was already talking about her bat mitzvah party, and I was buying my Tylenol in the easy-to-open bottles with the warning printed in big, easy-to-read letters on the side? "I'm old."

"Oh, you are not," said Sam loyally (and a bit defensively—she's six months older than I am).

"Forty-two is too old to be doing three A.M. feedings."

"Madonna did it," Sam offered.

"Madonna isn't human," I replied.

At Ashleigh's instructions, we lowered our legs to the floor, let our arms fall heavily to our sides, breathed through five minutes of shivasana, then sat cross-legged for the final meditation.

"You could hire someone," Sam offered. "Like a wet nurse." Ashleigh frowned at us again. "Wet nurse" didn't sound even vaguely like *om shanti shanti.* Sam pressed her hands together in front of her chest. "They're bound to come back. Everything else has. Anyhow, wet nurses aren't the point. The point is, do you really want another baby?"

I sat up, pressed my clasped hands against my heart, and nodded *namasté* at Ashleigh. "It's something I'm not unwilling to consider," I finally said.

"You've been hanging around too many lawyers," Sam said.

I shook my head. "Only you. And it might not even matter. My eggs are probably funky."

We rolled up our mats while Ashleigh stood at the doorway, bidding each of us a serene Zen farewell. We dropped our blocks and straps into the basket by the door, then sat on the futon in the foyer to pull on our boots and our jackets. I was wearing a wool hat with earflaps that I'd knitted myself, a matching scarf, and a puffy fuchsia down coat that made me, by my own charitable assessment, about the size of a compact car. Sam had on a gorgeous red cashmere poncho, trimmed with red and orange angora pom-poms. *If I wore that,* I thought, *I'd look like an erupting volcano.*

We crossed snow-lined South Street to the coffee shop, where it had become our tradition to follow yoga class with double-shot lattes. Inside, I hung my coat on the back of a chair while Sam doctored her drink with cinnamon and nutmeg. *A little brother or sister for Joy,* I thought. A baby with Peter's brown hair and his dark eyes, his slow, thoughtful manner, and nothing at all of my ex-boyfriend,

Bruce Guberman, who'd celebrated Joy's birth by taking a two-year vacation to Amsterdam, where, I can only assume, he devoted himself to the noble goal of smoking his body weight in marijuana.

I grow old, I grow old, I thought as Sam sat down with a chocolate-dipped biscotti in her hand and a wicked gleam in her eye.

"The thing is, Joy's in trouble," I blurted.

Sam looked surprised. "What?"

"She got a C in English."

Sam's expression shifted from surprise to bemusement.

"Okay, I know, no big deal, but every time I ask her about it, she ignores me. She talks to me like she's being charged by the word, and she looks at me like I smell bad."

"Puberty," Sam pronounced, dipping her biscotti into her latte.

"Already?" I thought back to Joy's teacher asking if she had a boyfriend, and how swiftly I'd dismissed the very notion.

"It's the hormones in the milk," Sam said. "*60 Minutes* did a special. Little eight-year-olds in Texas with tampons in their lunch boxes."

I shuddered. "Joy hasn't gotten her period." At least she hadn't said anything about it. And if she had gotten her period, she'd have told me, I thought—even as a twinge of unease worked its way up my spine and I wondered whether it was true. "And what about her grades?"

"I wouldn't worry too much," Sam said. "It's not like she's flunking out, and it's seventh grade, not high school. She's probably got a crush or something."

"It's a phase, right?" I fretted. "I hated my mother. You hated your mother."

"Still do," Sam said cheerfully. "Which leads us to this week's adventures." She reached into her crocodile bowling bag and extracted a manila folder. "Okay," she said, passing the first page across the table. I looked down at the face of a middle-aged man with thick glasses and thinning hair. His eyes were a watery blue. His smile was an anxious grimace. His biography said that he was forty-seven, divorced, a Reform Jew who attended synagogue on the high holidays, the noncustodial parent of a fifteen-year-old, with a master's degree in urban planning and a penchant for sushi and sunsets. His online handle was Mark the Mensch.

"Mark the Mensch?" I tried to keep my tone neutral, but my face must have revealed my horror. "He looks . . ." I studied his picture, his biography, the parameters he'd set for his ideal date. "I don't know. Maybe not a good match for you?"

"I am not looking for perfect," said Sam, sliding another sheaf of papers across the table. "I'm looking for acceptable." She sighed. "Actually I would take a Jew with a pulse at this point."

"The wedding?" I asked.

"What else?"

Sam's brother, who'd been born Alan and now called himself Avram, was marrying Hannah, born Heather, in August in an Orthodox ceremony in Pittsburgh ("August in Pittsburgh," said Sam. "It's just like April in Paris. Only not"). Upon receiving the news, Samantha—who'd endured so many disastrous blind dates, first dates, group dates, and speed dates that she'd finally bought herself a state-of-the-art vibrator and sworn off men forever—had gone running straight to the Internet, investing five hundred dollars in a Star of David–level membership at AJew4U.com and spending hours downloading profiles of the as-yet-unchosen Chosen People. Never mind that, as I'd pointed out, at an Orthodox wedding the men and women wouldn't even get to dance together and would most likely spend the service and most of the reception in separate rooms. "I'm not looking for love," Sam told me. "I'm not looking for a relationship. I just need one man, for one night, so my mother won't hassle me. Is that so hard?"

Turns out, it was. Or at least AJew4U.com had failed to yield any prospects so far. But Sam wasn't giving up.

"What about this guy?" I said, flipping past Mark to the next prospect.

Sam barely spared him a glance. "Forget it," she said. "He's Canadian."

I studied the profile. "He lives in Collingswood, New Jersey."

"Born in Manitoba," Sam said, pointing at the bio. "Once a Canadian, always a Canadian."

"Now, Samantha," I said. "I went there on my book tour, remember? It's a lovely country, and everyone was very friendly. There's nothing wrong with—"

"Fake country," she interrupted. "Fake country with fake holidays. Do you really want me to have to celebrate Thanksgiving three weeks after everybody else?"

"I think it'd actually be six weeks before."

"Canadian Thanksgiving," she sneered. "They didn't even have pilgrims and Indians there. Whatever. Here," she said, leaning across the table so that one of her pom-poms dangled dangerously close to my coffee. "Look at him."

I looked. The man in the picture was bald and beaming, and . . . "Seventy?" I squinted at the small print, certain that I'd read it wrong, then at Sam, who shrugged.

"Seventy's the new sixty. Sixty's the new forty-five. There was a story about it in the *Times*."

"Gah!"

"Oh, don't be ageist," she snapped.

"He's old enough to be your father!" I crumpled up the page, but not before accidentally learning that Grandpa's screen name was Sexy Septuagenarian. "Gah!" I said again.

"You know what would be weird?" Sam asked. "What if your father showed up on one of these websites?"

"Gah!" I said for the third time—only this time my horror wasn't feigned. "Anyhow, he's married."

"Oh," said Sam, "and these guys aren't?"

I shook my head. I'd seen my father only twice in the last fourteen years, and as far as I knew, he was still living in Los Angeles, still married to the much younger dental hygienist with whom he'd had two kids (I'd met them all for the first and only time when he brought them to my college graduation, less out of a desire to see me than because of Princeton's proximity to Sesame Place). I try not to think about him. Most of the time I don't. "That would be weirder than you dating a seventy-year-old?"

"Fuck you, Smug Married," she said. "Besides, he told me he wasn't interested."

"Wait. Wait." This was too much. "You propositioned a seventy-year-old?"

"Walter," said Sam.

"And Walter turned you down?"

She sighed, dropped her head, and nodded. When she looked up, her eyes were sparkling, not with excitement but with rage. "Do you think we could figure out a way to short-circuit someone's pacemaker by remote?"

"What'd he say?"

"That he was only dating eights and above, and from my picture, I looked like a seven."

"Oh my God. Are you kidding? What picture are you using?"

"Brooke," said Sam.

I groaned. Sam was beautiful, but as she'd waded into the waters of online dating, she'd become increasingly and alarmingly insecure. After her first nibble-free week on AJew4U, she'd found a candid shot of Brooke Shields exiting a friend's baby shower on *Us* magazine's website. Then, using technologies I had no idea she'd mastered, she downloaded the picture, Photoshopped in her own eyebrows ("So it's not a total lie"), and posted it, without shame or fear of repercussion, underneath her screen name, SassySam.

"Ouch," I said, and shook my head. "Poor Brooke."

"Poor Brooke nothing," Samantha said. "She's married, remember? Married twice. Goddamn double-dipper." She glared at the table. "I hate them worse than Canadians."

"Can I ask you a question?" I waited for her nod, then said, "What are you going to do when one of these guys meets you and notices that you're, um . . ." There was no delicate way to put it. "Not Brooke Shields?"

"I'll tell them it's an old picture," Sam said.

"But . . ." Sam's hair was darker than Brooke's. Her eyes were brown, not blue. Her face was a different shape, and Brooke Shields was probably three inches taller, fifteen pounds thinner, and not even remotely Semitic. *Let it go,* I thought. "Why don't you just take Peter to the wedding?"

Sam broke off a chunk of biscotti and bounced her water bottle against her thigh. "I'm touched that you'd offer, but my mother's met him, remember?"

"Oh, right." Sam's mother had joined us a few years ago for Thanksgiving. She'd swept into our house in a floor-length mink, frowned at the turkey as if it had insulted her, eaten precisely one spoonful of cranberry relish, and showered Joy with expensive American Girl dolls and accessories after observing pointedly to no one in particular that she had to spoil little girls when she could, since it was clear that Sam wouldn't be giving her grandchildren of her own. "Well, isn't there anyone from work you could take?"

"The firm directory's online," Sam said. "My mother would look up whoever I brought and figure out that he was just doing me a favor."

"Your mother would do that? She'd Google your date?"

Sam shrugged. "I come by my obsessive personality honestly."

"How about someone from a different firm? Don't you meet people at those Continuing Legal Education things?"

She shook her head. "Married. Gay. Occasionally both."

"Um. You could hire an actor."

"As a last resort," she said. "I've already made a few calls."

"Really?"

"I told them I was casting a low-budget commercial. Do you know what SAG's day rate is?"

"Do I want to?"

"You do not. And it doubles on weekends, and you have to pay extra for travel, so never mind." Sam polished off her biscotti. "You're so lucky. You have no idea."

Then why does Peter want to change everything? I wondered. *And what was going on with Joy?* I didn't say any of it out loud. "Go with God," I said instead, and hugged Samantha goodbye. I retrieved my coat, checked the time, and considered wandering up to Walnut Street for a little window-shopping. But it was almost eight, and Joy might need help with her English homework. I pulled my scarf tight around my neck, tugged my hat over my ears, and started my ten-block walk back home.

I'd lived in the neighborhood long enough to bore friends and acquaintances with my Used-To tour: the Starbucks that used to be a pizza shop where you could buy twists of garlic bread, three for a dollar; the burrito place that used to be a video store; the shoe store that used to sell books.

Tiny white Christmas lights still twinkled from the door of the cheesesteak place, and the bright windows of Whole Foods were papered with hopeful red and pink valentines, but there was no denying that we were between holidays. In the bitter trench of winter, the weather had turned ugly again. A hard-edged wind blew grit and newspapers and someone's discarded weave down South Street, and the bare tree branches shivered in the dark. I fell in behind a pack of girls in rolled-up black jeans and stilettos, snapping pictures of one another with their cell phones. Cold seeped up from the sidewalk through the rubber soles of my boots. *How old are these girls, anyhow?* I wondered as one of them wiggled her tongue between her spread fingers while her friend snapped a picture. Did their mothers know they were out?

You're so lucky, Sam had said. But if our life was so good, why was Peter so eager to shake it all up? A baby, I mused. A baby would change everything. But maybe change was good. Maybe it wasn't that I'd arrived at the safe harbor I'd longed for during my own unhappy childhood. Maybe it was just inertia—or, worse, fear—that was keeping me in the same place, living in the same house, taking the same vacations, never hoping for more than what I had.

Of course, I'd hoped for more once, once upon a time, in my fearless twenties, when I'd sold a screenplay and published a novel and been, very briefly, a strange kind of famous. It hadn't ended well. I pushed down the memories, gave my hat another tug, crossed the street with my breath hanging in front of me in icy white puffs, and hurried back home so fast that anyone watching might have thought I was being chased.

FOUR

On Valentine's Day, the kids at the Philadelphia Academy buy one another sugar cookies shaped like hearts with pink and red frosting, and little cards attached for a message. Each cookie costs a dollar, and all the money goes to the school's building fund.

I've been going to the Philadelphia Academy since kindergarten, and every year I know exactly what I'll find on my desk on February 14: one cookie apiece from Tamsin and Todd, and a cookie from Jeremy Albin, whose mother, like mine, makes him buy cookies for every kid in our class.

I also know that every year at some point during early February, my mother and I will have a fight ("a discussion," she calls it, but it's really a fight) about the cookies. I will tell her that I should just buy them with my own money and give them to my actual friends. She'll reply that I'll have the rest of my life to start excluding people and that seventh grade (or sixth grade, or whatever grade I'm in at the time) is too early to start.

I'll say that if I give cookies to everyone, they don't mean anything. She'll sigh, which will make her boobs shift in a way I can't stand to look at, and say, Yes, they do, they mean "Happy Valentine's Day from Joy," and what if there's a kid who doesn't get any cookies at all? How would that kid feel? And how would I feel, knowing that I could have prevented such a tragedy by spending her money—not even my own money but hers—making sure that everyone gets a cookie?

She kind of has a point. It's true that there are a few kids in my class—Jack Corsey, who has such terrible dandruff that when he wears dark sweaters, it looks like he was out in a snowstorm, and maybe even Tamsin, who can be kind of intense when she starts talking about speculative fiction—who might not get cookies if it wasn't for me and Jeremy Albin.

My problem is with the people who don't deserve extra cookies, like Amber Gross. Amber Gross, as far as I can remember, has never said a single word to me, even though we've been going to regular school and Hebrew school together since we started both. Amber and I were even in the same Little People's Music class when we were two. My mom has pictures, and while there are photographs that show us actually in the same room, we're never in the same part of the room, leading me to believe that Amber was too cool for me even before we could talk. Amber gets tons of cookies. Believe me, she doesn't need mine.

But when I pointed this out to my mother the Friday before Valentine's Day, she got a sour look on her face and unloaded one of her dozen useless phrases: "Joy," she said, "life's too short."

Too short for what? I wanted to ask, but the bell started ringing loudly enough for us to hear through the rolled-up windows. My mom slipped a twenty-dollar bill into my hand. "Do it because it'll make me happy," she said. She tried to hug me, but I slid to the edge of my seat. "Have a great day!" I could hear her calling as I stuffed the money into the pocket of my jeans and walked across the play yard with my head down while the first bell rang.

On February 14, like every school day, I set my alarm for five-forty-five. In the shower, I exfoliated my legs and elbows with the Orange Sugar Energy Scrub that Aunt Elle had given me, and shaved my legs and armpits. I washed my hair with Step One of the Jon Carame Secret Agent Anti-Frizz Protection Program and conditioned with Step Two, then turned the water to cold and stood there shivering while I counted to thirty, so the cold water could seal the cuticles.

By six-fifteen, I was in my towel, teeth flossed and brushed, the next two steps of the Anti-Frizz Protection Program already spritzed (Step Three) and smoothed (Step Four) through my hair. It took me forty-five minutes with a paddle brush and a diffuser to get my hair looking right. It might have taken me less time if I didn't have to keep checking to make sure the door was locked. My mother doesn't believe I should straighten my hair. My mother believes I should embrace my natural beauty. This means I am the only girl in the world who has to hide her straightening iron under her bed like it's a dirty magazine or a gun.

At seven o'clock, my hair was done. I hung up my wet towel, rinsed my mouth again, and stuck a pantiliner on my underwear. My period isn't due for weeks, but I don't take any chances. When you've already got one major thing wrong with you, you can't risk having to run to the nurse's office with a borrowed sweater flopping around your waist and everyone staring at you, knowing exactly what's happened.

I wiped off the sink and counter with toilet paper, put my night-gown back on, and slid back into bed. Five minutes later, my mother knocked on the door.

"Rise and shine," she said. Her own hair was shoved back from her face in a sloppy half bun, half ponytail, and she was wearing my dad's bathrobe, with her glasses sticking out of the V of the chest. "Do you want eggs or oatmeal?"

I haven't eaten eggs or oatmeal for breakfast all year. What I eat for breakfast is three-quarters of a cup of high-fiber protein-enriched bran flakes, a half cup of organic skim milk, and six raw almonds. This does not stop my mother from asking if I want eggs or oatmeal every morning. "No, thanks. I'll just have cereal." I threw back the covers and went to the bathroom like I hadn't already been in there for over an hour. I brushed my teeth again, pulled on my jeans and boots and a pink sweater, tucked my mascara and lip gloss into my pocket, and went downstairs to the kitchen, where I found my mother holding the red kettle in her hands like it was some kind of magical object she'd never seen before. I counted out my almonds. She didn't move. "Mom?" I finally asked.

She set the kettle on the burner and clicked on the flame. "Sorry, honey." She sat down at the table across from me and sighed before patting her scrunched-up hair, as if that would help (it didn't). "Just thinking."

"About what?"

She fussed with her hair some more and smiled kind of sadly. "Oh, you know. Grown-up stuff." Which was, I thought, exactly what a mother would say to her daughter. If her daughter were four.

She dropped me off, as usual, outside of the chain-link fence that separates the empty play yard from the sidewalk. I stopped in the empty first-floor girls' room, where I pulled my lip gloss out of my pocket and smoothed some onto my lips. Then I unzipped my backpack and pulled out my lunch, which was stored in a zippered, insulated pink bag with my name monogrammed on the front. I transferred the food out of the horrible pink bag and into a plain plastic bag from the grocery store, which is what every other kid uses.

At last I reached behind my straightened hair, pulled out my hearing aids, and slipped them into my pocket. It's not like this is going to fool anyone. Almost every kid in my class remembers how I started kindergarten with the big, square, horrible behind-the-ear hearing aids. Up until third grade, my teachers would wear wireless microphones, and I would wear earphones, like the ones from an iPod, so I could hear them. I'd try to fluff out my crazy, frizzy nest of hair so nobody could see the hearing aids or the headphones, but everyone knew they were there. Which wasn't entirely bad: The one spell of popularity I'd ever had occurred after Mrs. Mears left her microphone on when she went to the teachers' lounge and the entire class huddled around my earphones to listen (the next day, instead of discussing photosynthesis, Mrs. Mears's lecture was "Irritable Bowel Syndrome: It Is Not a Joke").

In sixth grade, I graduated to the kind of hearing aids that sit inside my ears. I'm supposed to wear them every day and sit in the front row. But last summer Aunt Elle came to the beach for a week's visit with the tiniest black bikini I'd ever seen and a canvas tote bag full of *Elle* and *Vogue* and *In Touch* and *InStyle*. My mother shook her head as Aunt Elle stacked the glossy magazines next to her chair and started smearing oil over her shoulders. We don't have magazines like that in our house. My mother thinks they're a bad influence. "Those are manipulated images," my mom said, frowning at the beautiful, long-limbed models on the covers, explaining how the pictures are specially lit and airbrushed and edited. She even downloaded pictures on the computer to show me how the editors smoothed out wrinkles and slimmed down backs and arms and thighs and, in one case, even erased a model's hand and made her arm longer.

"For God's sake, Cannister, it's a frickin' magazine," Elle had said, and she'd slipped me copies when my mother wasn't looking. After seven days straight of reading *Vogue* and watching my aunt, I'd decided that this year, seventh grade, would be when I would change. I'd ditch my hearing aids and my special seat. I'd straighten my hair and wear makeup and tuck in my shirts. Then people would see me differently from the way they always had; they'd see that I wasn't the geeky girl with only two friends and crazy hair and a mother who treated her like a baby.

So far, it hadn't worked, but when I walked into homeroom that morning I had my first glimmer of hope that things might be changing. The first thing I saw was Tamsin and Todd huddled in the corner, whispering. A second later, I saw what they were whispering about: twelve frosted sugar hearts heaped on my desk. It was unbelievable. Not even Amber Gross had more.

I checked to make sure I was in the right classroom. Then I counted to make sure I was looking at the right desk, the third from the front. I picked up one of the cookies, waiting for someone to say something, to tap me on the shoulder and say, "Um, sorry, that's actually mine."

TO: Joy. FROM: Martin. MESSAGE: *Happy Valentine's Day!*

The only Martin in our school is Martin Baker, Amber's boy-friend, who always wears his cleats to class so there's no chance of you forgetting that he's on the soccer team. I turned the cookie over in my hands, holding it carefully. "Gentle touches!" my preschool teacher would say during show-and-tell when we'd pass around the toy the kid of the day had brought to share. "Gentle touches" meant you could hold it, but it wasn't really yours.

I picked up another cookie. TO: Joy. FROM: A Secret Admirer. MESSAGE: *I think you're sweet.*

My cheeks flushed. *A Secret Admirer.* I had a secret admirer. I looked at the cookie, then, quickly, at Duncan Brodkey. Just as fast, I looked away.

I shuffled slowly through the rest of the cookies until I came to one that made my heart stop thudding and skitter to a stop. TO: Joy. FROM: Amber Gross. MESSAGE: *Happy V Day!*

Amber Gross. Amber Gross sent me a cookie. Amber Gross wants me to have a happy V Day. At any minute, the world will spin off its axis, hell will freeze over, and monkeys will fly out of my ears from where my hearing aids should be.

Just when I was sure that the day couldn't get any weirder, when I was positive that it was all a dream and I was going to wake up in my room underneath my flowered comforter and the stuck-on stars with my mother standing at the door asking about oatmeal, Amber Gross herself sauntered toward me with her thumbs hooked into the belt loops of her ultra-low-rise jeans. ("No, I am not buying you those," my mother said when I pointed out a pair at the mall. "Why?" I'd been dumb enough to ask. "Because they're obscene," said my mother. "And you'd need all new underwear.")

"Hi, Joy," she said. *Hi, Joy.* Like we were actually friends. Like we IM'ed each other every night and sat together on the bus in the mornings.

"Thanks for the cookie!" I squeaked in what I hoped was a

normal-girl voice. I couldn't believe she'd said my name. I wasn't even sure she knew it.

"No prob," she said. Her braces glittered as she smiled. "Hey, do you want to sit with us at lunch?"

"Oh. Um. Sure, I guess," I said. I thought that even if my voice sounded weird, my words sounded right. Very casual.

"Cool!" she said, and walked back to her seat.

Tamsin whirled around, wide-eyed. "What was that about?" she whispered, exaggerating the syllables and adding a big shrug so there'd be no chance I'd miss her meaning.

I'd just opened my mouth to say something—what, I wasn't exactly sure—when Mr. Shoup dropped his briefcase on his desk. "Settle down," he said. At least I thought that was what he said. Mr. Shoup had a mustache, and the longer it grew, the harder my life got.

He turned toward the blackboard, and I bent my head, hoping nobody else could hear the way my heart was pounding.

"You're not really going to sit with them, are you?" Tamsin said directly into my right ear four endless periods later, as I was collecting my lunch from my locker.

I ducked my head and mumbled, "Dunno."

"She's just using you," said Tamsin. To make sure I'd heard, she shoved up the sleeves of her gray sweatshirt, stepped in front of me, and signed the words: "Using you!" (American Sign Language is one of the languages offered at the Philadelphia Academy, along with Spanish, French, and Latin. Tamsin has taken all four.)

"Using her for what, though?" Todd said as he caught up to us in the hall. He was in his usual school uniform of crisp khakis and a button-down shirt that he'd ironed himself. His handsomeness and his height make him stand out among the boys in our grade, but because he'd rather sing show tunes than kick a soccer ball, his good looks don't matter. Last October the boys on the lacrosse team wrote

FAG on his locker, which meant that everyone in the school got stuck in an all-day seminar with a psychologist about the Importance of Tolerance and Understanding. *It could have been worse,* Todd said. *It got us out of algebra.*

"Maybe she wants to copy my homework?" It wasn't a very good guess, but, in four periods' worth of thinking, it was the best I'd come up with—even though my grades had gotten so bad that Amber would have to be completely stupid to want to copy my work.

Todd considered this. "Maybe," he said, after what was, in my opinion, a way-too-long pause. "But I'm the best in English, and Tamsin's best in math."

"Actually, I'm best in everything," Tamsin said.

"Well, maybe she wants to copy off someone who gets something wrong once in a while," I snapped.

"You won't come back," said Tamsin. "Remember Amanda Reilly?"

Of course I did. Every girl in our grade remembered Amanda Reilly. She'd been just a *kind of* girl—kind of smart, kind of cute, kind of a lot of things. Then—shazam!—Gregory Bowen asked her to go to his high school's homecoming with him. Suddenly, Amanda Reilly, or Manda, as she started calling herself, was installed at Amber Gross's table. Aside from the new nickname, she hadn't changed at all. No new haircut, no new clothes. Gregory Bowen's attention was the magic pixie dust that had let her fly from being a *kind of* girl to a popular girl. I tried to remember if Manda had sent me a cookie.

"I am not Amanda Reilly," I said. I squared my shoulders and straightened the straps of my backpack as we entered the lunchroom. "I'll be back."

First I walked past the table full of the kids who don't really fit in anywhere else, the place I'd sit if I didn't have Tamsin and Todd. Jack Corsey and his dandruff sit there, and so does Sally Cullin, who's fat, and Alice Blankenship, who got sent home from school for a week last year after her English project turned out to be a bunch of poems about suicide.

Next to the misfits are the boy jocks, the soccer and lacrosse players, then the girl jocks, the ones who tie their colored rubber mouth
guards to shoelaces and wear them like necklaces around their necks.
Then there's a table of drama/music types who wear leg warmers and
leotards and act like they're in *High School Musical VI* and try to dance
in the lunch line. Todd and Tamsin and I normally sit at the end of
that table: Todd's a legitimate drama type, and Tamsin and I don't
really belong anywhere else.

I held my breath as I passed the drama table, then walked by the
hippie kids who smell like incense and play Hacky Sack and wear
their hair in dreadlocks whether they're black or white. I passed the
grinds, the ones who will probably leave the Philadelphia Academy
in ninth grade and go to Masterman, the city's magnet high school,
and on to the Ivy League.

At the center of the room sit those certain girls, the girls who are
jocks, or arty, or hippies, or smart, but first and foremost they
are . . . easy, I guess. Not "easy" like "sex," but as in everything they
do comes easily to them, whether it's wearing the right thing or saying the right thing or knowing the right thing to do. Amber Gross is
their queen. She can even tease Mr. Shoup about his clothes. "Great
tie," she said once. "Did your kid knit it for you?" Which sounded
really mean, except Mr. Shoup laughed. I'd said "Great tie" to him
once, when he'd been wearing the same tie, but he'd just looked
puzzled.

I carried my lunch over to their table, a row of girls in pastel
button-downs and low-rise pants and boys in rugby shirts and jeans,
holding my breath again, half believing that Amber would laugh
and say, "You didn't think I was serious!"

Instead, she smiled at me. "We saved you a seat!" she said, and
squinched herself over to make room.

I put my plastic lunch bag on the table, slid my backpack to the
floor, and eased myself onto the bench, with Amber on my left side
and Duncan Brodkey on my right. I felt myself flush as our shoulders
touched. I'd never imagined actually being this close to him, close

enough that I could smell his shampoo and see gold hairs glinting on his forearms, above the rolled-up sleeves of his shirt.

I pulled out my sandwich, sneaking little looks: his shaggy brown hair and light gray eyes and ears that are somehow more appealing than everyone else's. Once, in gym class, he wouldn't put his shorts on. "I'm a conscientious objector," he told Mr. Huff, and I'd thought that was the funniest thing I'd ever heard, even though I'd never been able to figure out exactly what made it funny.

"So what's up?" said Amber. She wore a slim silver bracelet on her left wrist, a necklace with a silver heart around her neck, a pink shirt, and jeans. Her hair was dark brown with lighter brown streaks. *Highlights,* I thought, and wondered if my mom would let me get some, then instantly decided that she wouldn't. "Did you get a date?" she asked.

I knew immediately what she was talking about; she didn't mean "date" as in "boy" but "date" as in "bat mitzvah." "Next October. How about you?"

"June," she said. "Do you have a theme?"

I squirmed on the narrow seat. "I don't think I'm going to have a theme." In fact, I was positive I wouldn't. The one time I'd asked my mother about it, she'd raised her eyebrows and said in a very snotty and unhelpful tone, *Um, God?*

Amber looked shocked. "No theme?"

I shook my head.

"Huh. Weird. Mine's Hollywood. Hey, do you want to come?"

Did I want to come to Amber Gross's Hollywood-themed bat mitzvah? Was a bean green? "Sure," I blurted.

"Cool," she said. I noticed Manda Reilly squirting her hands with disinfectant gel. My mom puts that in my lunch bag, and I usually ignore it, but today I pulled it out and squirted my hands, too. I ate quietly and watched people's hands and faces as the conversation swirled around me. High, twittery girls' voices talked about home-work, soccer tournaments, babysitting jobs, a sweater at Banana Re-public that would be on sale soon. Deeper boys' voices rumbled replies. I was polishing my apple on my sleeve, feeling my skin flare every time Duncan shifted or took a bite of his pizza. My own voice sounded so different from these girls' voices. Maybe that was my real problem: No matter how I dressed or how carefully I straightened my hair, I could never sound like them, and everyone would know I was an imposter as soon as I opened my mouth.

Amber tapped my shoulder. "Hey," she said. I wondered how long she'd been talking to me, how long it had taken her to realize that I needed to see her in order to know she was talking to me. I watched her sparkly pink lips form the words "Is Maxi Ryder coming to your bat mitzvah?"

The breath I hadn't realized I was holding whooshed out of me. *So this is it.* Mystery solved.

"I don't know," I said slowly. "She's busy. She's shooting a TV miniseries this summer, so she might be on location."

"Oh, sure," said Amber, helping herself to one of my blue-cheese olives. (She had a French manicure. I made a note to figure out how to give myself one.) "But she's, like, a friend of the family, right?" I must have looked confused, because she said, "She's in your mom's book. In the acknowledgments." She pursed her lips and stared at me. "You've read it, right?"

Before I could answer, Duncan Brodkey put down his pizza. "Your mom wrote a book?" His body was so close to mine, his mouth so close to my ear, that I could feel the words more than hear them.

I nodded again, then looked down at my apple. The table had gone silent. Every eye was on me. The truth was, my mother had written a bunch of books, science fiction adventures in the StarGirl series, but those were under a pen name. The book that they had to be talking about was the only one written under her own name. It had been published when I was three. "It was a long time ago."

I watched everyone's eyes move across the table as Sasha Swerdlow started talking. "It's called *Big Girls Don't Cry,*" Sasha said. "You guys have all totally seen it. It's got, like, gigantic boobs on the

cover." She held her hands out way in front of her own not inconsid-
erable chest. "And a hot-fudge sundae, and the cherry from the
sundae's sliding down the cleavage, and anyway, it's about this girl
who's in love with a guy, but he dumps her, and they have all this
sex, and she's got this terrible father who's, like, incredibly mean to
her, and then she finds out her mom is gay . . ."

Duncan looked impressed. "Hot stuff." I winced and looked
away. Woman with enormous bosom and a gay mom. That certainly
sounded familiar.

Sasha kept talking so loudly that I heard every word. "And then,"
she continued, "she goes on, like, this quest to Los Angeles, and she
meets a duchess in a casino and finds out she's pregnant—"

"The duchess?" asked Duncan.

Duchess? I thought. The cramp of panic inside my chest eased a
bit. My mom didn't know any duchesses, and as far as I knew she had
never been to Los Angeles. Maybe the book was nothing for me to
worry about.

Sasha giggled. "No, silly. Allie. The heroine. And she's totally
insecure about her weight and how she looks and everything, because
the baby's father dumped her when she was pregnant, but then she
falls in love with this guy back in Philadelphia . . ."

I stuffed the rest of my lunch into my plastic bag, forcing myself
to smile, trying, even though it was hopeless, to look like the rest of
the girls. Dumped her when she was pregnant. That sounded familiar, too. The truth was, I'd never read any of my mother's books—not
the StarGirl ones that were published under the name J. N. Locksley,
and definitely not *Big Girls Don't Cry.* I'd seen it, of course. There
were different versions of it lined up on the top shelf of my mom's
study, hardcovers and paperbacks and versions in foreign languages.
It's for adults, my mom had told me once, a long time ago, and I'd
never been curious enough to read it. Maybe because Bruce, my biological father, had given me a copy of his book, which was published
by an academic press and was all about post-apocalyptic imagery in
Doctor Who. It was full of big words like "semiotics" and "synecdoche,"

with some pages that were one-third filled by footnotes. I'd always figured my mother's book was just as bad.

"Do you see Maxi a lot?" Amber asked.

Part of me wanted to pick up my bag, get up from the table, and go. Tamsin was right. They were using me, and they weren't even being subtle about it.

But another part of me kind of liked sitting there, at the center of the table that might as well have been at the center of the world, with Duncan Brodkey, who had his eyebrows raised, like he was saying, *Do go on.*

I shook out my hair and turned to Amber. "My mom and I were out in L.A. in December," I said.

Amber grinned at me. There was a piece of olive caught in her braces. "I saw pictures of her house in *InStyle*. Does she really have eight hundred pairs of shoes?"

I nodded, and when I talked, I concentrated on making my voice sound high and light, just like theirs. "At least. But she keeps most of them in storage."

Tara Carnahan leaned toward me, her eyes sparkling. "Did she really date Brad Pitt?" she asked. "And what about that stunt man?"

Cadence Tallafiero got up from her seat and wedged herself next to Tara. "I heard she had his name tattooed on her arm."

"On her *butt*." Amber giggled in my ear.

"She's got a tattoo, but it's half lasered off. On her ankle. It used to say *Scott,* but she changed it to a heart with wings." I sat back, feeling pleased and slightly nauseated as Tara and Sasha and Amber clamored for more details.

When the lunch bell trilled, I realized there wasn't time for me to go back to Todd and Tamsin, the way I'd promised. I swung one leg over the bench, wishing I had twinkly braces, too, forcing myself to smile. "Gotta go!" I said, and hurried across the lunch room, trying to make it to my friends before the bell rang again.

FIVE

At two o'clock on a slushy gray February afternoon, Dr. Stanley Neville's waiting room was full of pregnant women. Pregnant women with their bellies bulging under loose smocked tops or encased in skintight Lycra, pregnant women with their husbands' hands resting on their bumps, pregnant women by themselves, working their BlackBerries while they waited. I could look at them only with fast glances—too long, and I'd find myself staring in a way that had to be a little creepy.

"Do you think they're shills?" I whispered to Peter after we'd taken our seats underneath a reproduction of a Mary Cassatt portrait of a mother and child. If I were a reproductive endocrinologist trying to pique the curiosity and pry open the checkbooks of over-forty hopefuls, I'd stock my waiting room with expectant ladies. Or maybe I'd hire actresses. Stick them in pregnancy pillows, have them sit in the chairs, maybe rub their backs every once in a while and groan convincingly.

I looked away from the knocked-up chorus line and turned my attention to the forms in my lap. Age. Address. Height. Weight. *Ugh.* Previous pregnancies. I wrote, *One.* Previous surgeries. I wrote, *C-section* and *hysterectomy,* and the date: Joy's birthday.

"Mrs. Krushelevansky?"

I got to my feet and proceeded to the exam room, where I stripped from the waist down, draped myself in three different cotton robes (one to cover my front, one to cover my back, and one on top of those two in case there was any stray flesh peeking out), and arranged myself on the examination table, my legs in stirrups. I lay back, eyes closed, and practiced my pranayama breathing. I breathed in, and Joy appeared before me, eyes averted, face cast down, hands shoved in her pockets and shoulders hunched as if steeled for a blow, hurrying across the school yard. I breathed out, imagining my reaching for her, feeling my hand on the soft wool of her sweater. *Baby, what's wrong? Tell me. I'll help you. I'll fix it.* Breathe in, and the image dissolved. Breathe out. I should call that child psychologist, the one the synagogue brought in last month to talk about the overscheduled child, the stress of pre-adolescence. Breathe in. If she'd just talk to me. Breathe out. Where had I put my copy of *Reviving Ophelia?* Breathe in. Maybe there was an explanation for her behavior other than "throes of adolescence." Maybe she actually did have a crush on some boy who'd spurned her. Breathe out. I could help with that. I'd take her out somewhere special: maybe the chocolate buffet at the Ritz-Carlton. I'd sit her down and tell her that having your heart broken is a part of growing up. I'd share with her some of the less lurid examples from my own life, and then I'd point to Peter and tell her that everything happens for a reason, that every heartbreak serves a purpose, and that it all works out in the end.

There was a brisk knock, then the door swung open. "Hello there!" said Dr. Neville, who turned out to be a black man in his sixties, with close-cropped iron-gray hair. Peter wheeled over a stool and sat by my side as Dr. Neville stood at the counter with his back to me, squirting gel from a squeeze bottle onto . . . oh my God.

"Is that . . . are you . . ." I gestured vaguely at the probe in his hands, which bore a disturbing resemblance to the item Sam had given me for my bachelorette party. "Shouldn't you at least buy me dinner first?"

Peter and Dr. Neville shared a collegial chuckle. As they "ho ho ho'd," I closed my eyes and tried to relax. The nurse dimmed the lights and tilted the monitor so that I could see it. I sucked in my breath as the probe slid inside of me.

"And . . . look! There we are."

I turned my head toward the screen and saw a swirling mass of gray—and then, against it, tiny circles like glowing nickels, like little moons.

"Those are your eggs," Dr. Neville said, all hearty and congratulatory, as if I was personally responsible for their presence. He nodded, satisfied, pulled out the probe, and handed it off to his nurse. Peter squeezed my shoulder as the doctor offered a solemn high five and said, "Congratulations, guys. We're in business!"

After I'd gotten dressed, I met Peter in the doctor's wood-paneled office, where everything from the business-card holder to the mouse pad was emblazoned with the name of a different pharmaceutical company, and the walls were papered with pictures of babies. Dr. Neville led us through the particulars of the process: the half-dozen drugs I'd have to take to override my natural cycle, ripen the largest possible number of eggs, and set the optimal conditions for the harvest—"a simple procedure, really," Dr. Neville assured me, that would be performed in the hospital, under sedation, not even anesthesia.

"And this is all safe? The surgery? All those hormones?" More doctorly chuckling between the men with MDs before I got my answer, which came down to: *Yes, we think so, but the technology's relatively new. However, long-term longitudinal studies seem to reveal . . .*

I tuned out the tech-speak and stared at the walls. All those happy families. Moms and dads, siblings and grandparents, and their brand-new babies, pink and serene as miniature Buddhas or screaming from underneath their pink-and-blue caps with their eyes shut and their toothless mouths open wide.

Six

When I put my hearing aids back in my ears in the locker room after swim practice, I feel like I'm coming up from underwater again. Down in the deep end of the school's swimming pool, or bodysurfing the waves in the summertime on the beach in Avalon, every sound is faint and muffled. You have to work harder than normal to make sense of them, and what you feel is the water itself, heavy against the bones of your face. Breaking the surface of the pool is a relief and a disappointment. For me, it's like leaving a secret world where everyone's equal, where everyone hears the same way as me, and where our coach yells and signs instructions so that I get them at the same time as everyone else.

I slid the little pink knobs inside my ears and took a breath, hearing the sound of my own exhalation, the water dripping from the shower onto the tiled floor, the echo of my teammates' voices. Then I pulled on my coat and fleece hat and walked out to the curb, where my mother was waiting, same as always. "How was school?" she asked, and I said, "Fine," which was what I always said. It's strange, but she had no idea how much everything had changed. She didn't know that I'd had lunch with Amber Gross and her popular friends, that I maybe could be one of those girls.

At home, my mother made me a snack and sat down at the table with me, leaning forward expectantly, as if we were going to have some big heart-to-heart. "I'm going to Tamsin and Todd's to do my homework," I said.

Disappointment flickered across her face, but her voice was chirpy as ever. "Home for dinner, right?"

"Sure," I said. Twenty minutes later, Tamsin and Todd and I were walking down Bainbridge Street, toward the used bookstore on the corner.

"I don't know if this is such a good idea," Todd said. I kept walking. It felt as if all of my senses had gotten sharper since I'd left the house. I could see every bit of grime on the curbs, every piece of trash blowing down the sidewalk, the words FUCK YOU inked across the yellow metal box stuffed full of free newspapers; I could feel the damp breeze on my cheek, could smell frying onions from the cheesesteak place a block away.

"Why is it a bad idea?" I asked. "You guys have read it, haven't you?"

"Um," said Todd. Tamsin shot him a look. Then neither one of them said anything else as the bookstore door swung open. Todd followed me through the stacks, and Tamsin drifted off toward the comics.

It took me only a minute of wandering the dusty aisle to find *Big Girls Don't Cry*. There were five copies: three big paperbacks and two chunky smaller ones, with the words THE SMASH HIT WORLDWIDE BESTSELLER written in gold foil underneath the title. I picked one of the small paperbacks because it was the cheapest.

"Ah, an oldie but a goodie," said the clerk, sliding the book into a brown paper bag. "You know, the author used to live in Philadelphia."

I didn't answer. It was strange to hear my mother referred to in the past tense, as if she'd moved away or died.

I tucked the bag into my coat pocket, and Tamsin and Todd and I walked to Three Bears Park, where we'd played when we were little. Weak sunshine was starting to filter through the clouds; it had warmed up enough for the kids to take off their jackets. Toddler-sized coats in bright yellows and soft pinks were piled on one of the benches, and kids chased one another around the big circular planter that was still filled with mounds of half-melted snow.

I sat on a bench, flipped the book open at random, and read out loud. *"Baby," Drew gasped, and eased one sweat-sticky hand down my panties.*

Todd was watching the kids on the slide. Tamsin pulled a book out of her own shopping bag. I gulped and kept reading to myself. *I wriggled out of my bra and straddled his lap, careful to distribute my weight so that I wouldn't leave bruises. If I was bigger than other girls who'd been there before, he didn't seem to mind, as he gasped my name and licked my . . .* "You know what? This isn't fair. It's a sex scene. I mean . . ." I flipped the book open to another page and started reading that. *"It's tiny," I told Sarah. "Teeny-tiny! Like the end of one of those pencils they give you at the miniature golf course. I didn't know whether he was trying to fuck me or erase me!"* "Okay," I said, slamming the book shut. "Is this entire thing just people having sex?"

Todd shrugged.

"It's not all sex scenes," said Tamsin, slipping her own book back into her bag. "There's stuff about your family, too. I mean," she added quickly, "the heroine's family."

I turned the book over. My mom's picture was on the back cover, beaming at me from ten years ago. Her hair was longer and curled, like she was auditioning to be a newscaster, and her lipstick was the exact same shade as the stuff I'd just wiped off my mouth in the school bathroom. "Has everyone in our grade read this?" I asked.

"No idea," Todd said too fast. I flipped through the pages slowly, letting them fan against my fingers. Words and phrases jumped out. "Fat . . . his fingers caressed my lardy, dimpled thighs . . . the lavender mafia rides to the rescue . . . my father, the Bad Dad . . ."

I closed the book carefully. I yanked my hair down tight against my cheeks, something I did when I was nervous, to make sure nobody could see my hearing aids. Then I wrapped my arms around myself. "This is awful."

Todd said nothing. Tamsin pressed her lips together without

meeting my eyes. Little kids raced around our bench, screeching and waving plastic wands, filling the air with iridescent soap bubbles.

"It's not that bad," Todd finally said. "It's not about you."

Except, as I found out when I read all 372 pages of *Big Girls Don't Cry,* it kind of was.

I once heard a story about a man in Dallas who ate a 747. *How,* asked the interviewer, *did you manage to eat an entire airplane?* The man—he sounded like a very normal man—said, *One bite at a time.* I read my mother's book the same way, one bite at a time. It took me over three weeks of late-night reading: three weeks when I sat with Amber every day for lunch, and every afternoon when my mother asked how school was, I always answered "fine." The days went by just like normal—swim practice and homework and getting up early to style my hair—except it felt as though there was another life, a secret life, unfolding at the same time. It was almost like my real life felt fake—the life of school and homework and swimming and listening to my parents trying to figure out whether to rent the same beach house for two weeks that summer. The world that was happening on the pages seemed somehow more real and more true.

By the middle of March, I had choked down every word, from the dedication on the first page ("For my Joy") to the Interview with the Author in the back. "Why did you write *Big Girls Don't Cry?*" was the first question. "In part, there was an impulse to rewrite elements of my own life story, to take them apart and put them back together, to make them work," my mom said. Which meant what, exactly? That the book was true? Made up? That there were elements of truth, only scrambled, rearranged? And if this book was an improved version of life, how bad had her real life been?

I felt as though every page of the book was now permanently engraved on my brain: the part about how my mom's ("Allie's") father forced her to stand on a scale in front of her entire family every time she came home from prep school for vacation, the part where she tells how her boyfriend ("Drew") had a penis that looked like a malnourished gherkin. *That small or that green?* I'd wondered, and put the book aside, even though I'd read only seven pages that night.

What I learned by the time I finished was that my mother, or "Allie," the heroine of the book, weighed more than the average football player by the time she was in high school, where she had more sex than every girl I knew combined. She may be a nymphomaniac—and if the last part of the book is true, or based on truth, or even only sort of true, I was definitely an accident.

Of course, this was not what she'd told me about how I was born. *I always wanted a baby,* she'd said to me about a million times, pulling me onto her lap or smoothing my hair, her eyes misty with tears. *I was so happy when I found out . . . and even though it was kind of a surprise, Bruce was happy, too. We were both so happy to have you. I am so happy you're here.*

When I was little, that didn't sound much different from any other kid's story. *We wanted a baby so much* is what parents who adopted or used donor sperm or donor eggs or had a baby some other way always say. *You were all we ever wanted. We were so happy.* I knew kids with moms and dads, and moms and moms, and dads and dads, and single mothers who'd been divorced, and single mothers who'd gone to gay friends or to sperm banks to get pregnant, or to China or Guatemala to adopt, and every story was a version of the same thing: *I wanted a baby, and then I got you.*

Except if what she'd written in her book was true, my mother hadn't wanted me, or any baby at all. I flipped to page 178 and reread the passage I'd already memorized: *I hold the stick, still drippy with pee, between two fingers. Heads, I win; tails, I lose. One line, please God, one line, and if I ever have sex again, I'll get two IUDs and a prescription for the pill, I'll make him wear a condom and pull out before he comes. "One line, one line, one line," I chanted. "One line, I'm saved; two lines, my life is over."*

"Fuck," I whispered, sitting cross-legged in my pink bed underneath the fake stars. I swallowed hard, queasy with shame. I'd been fooled. I'd been lied to. No matter how much she said she loves me, no matter how careful she was, the truth, in black and white, was that my grandmother was a lesbian, my grandfather was a jerk, and my parents hadn't wanted me at all. Worse than that, everyone who read the book knew it: everyone in my school, everyone in my life, everyone in the world, maybe. Everybody knows.

My hands clenched into fists. I stomped down the stairs to my mother's office and snatched a black Sharpie from the mug on her desk. Back on my bed, I dragged the marker over page 178, erasing the pee-drippy pregnancy test and all of Allie's "fucks," running the black tip back and forth until the ink bled onto the page underneath and I'd obliterated every single letter of every shameful word.

When we got home from school the day after I'd finished the book, my mom went to the kitchen and started unloading the dishwasher. "You got a letter," she said casually.

"Oh yeah?" The mail was stacked on the kitchen counter, and on top of the stack was a giant glossy black envelope with my name— MISS JOY SHAPIRO KRUSHELEVANSKY—written on the front in fancy silver script.

I stared at it. "What is it?"

My mother poked at the envelope with a spatula, making it scoot along the countertop. "I don't know," she said.

The envelope, which was the size of one of my school folders, felt like it was made of thin glass or plastic, not paper. The return address—written on the back, in the same calligraphy as my name and address—was from the Pokitilow family in Cedar Hill, New Jersey. *Tyler's bar mitzvah,* I thought, and tore the envelope open. A piece of cream-colored paper with a silver border that looked like a cross between a diploma and a diner menu slid into my hands. Black and silver ribbons were laced through the top of the invitation, and they fell against the printed part in long curls, like pigtails.

WITH GREAT HAPPINESS,
BONNIE AND BOB POKITILOW INVITE YOU

TO ATTEND THE BAR MITZVAH
OF THEIR SON TYLER BENJAMIN ON SATURDAY,
APRIL 21, AT TEN O'CLOCK IN THE MORNING
TEMPLE BETH ISRAEL, SHORT HILLS, NEW JERSEY
LUNCHEON AND DANCING TO FOLLOW
SHORT HILLS COUNTRY CLUB.

"Huh," said my mom, who'd sneaked up behind me and was reading over my shoulder. I turned away fast, picked up the giant envelope, and shook it gently. More pieces of paper rained down onto the counter: a small envelope with another card that fit inside of it (THE COURTESY OF A REPLY IS REQUESTED BY APRIL FIFTH), a map of how to get to the temple and the country club, another little card on which I could check off my selection of beef or salmon for lunch. All the pieces of the invitation also had the address of Tyler's bar mitzvah website at the bottom. As I smoothed the ribbons, my mother read it out loud: " 'www.Tylersbigbash.com.' Well. Hmm." She ducked her head, and I could tell she was trying not to say something, or laugh. She turned away to pick the kettle up from the stove and fill it at the sink. "Want some tea?"

I shook my head, went to the refrigerator, and poured myself more juice. She flicked the burner on and put the kettle down. It hissed as the flame burned away the water that had collected on the bottom. "Your April's pretty free," she said.

I sipped my juice and thought it over. Bonnie Pokitilow was Bruce's first cousin. She had pale, freckly skin and curly hair like mine, only hers was a brown so dark it was almost black. I see her, and her husband, and my cousin Tyler, who's about my age, at my grandma Audrey's house for Passover and at the birthday parties Grandma Audrey used to have for me when I was little. Tyler and I don't really have much in common. Last Passover, he spent the entire night in Grandma Audrey's living room reading Harry Potter and watching old professional wrestling matches on his handheld.

I wondered who I'd know there. Then, as if reading my mind, my mom said, "Bruce would be there, with, um, Emily, and their kids, and your grandma Audrey. If you wanted, I could give you a ride."

I hoisted myself onto one of the stools at the breakfast bar. I didn't want her doing me any favors. As far as I was concerned, she'd done enough to me already.

My mother squirted honey into her tea and shook some Wheat Thins onto a yellow plate. "You'd probably sit at the kids' table, with Tyler and his friends, and his sister, um . . ."

"Ruth," I said. My tone made it clear that my family, my biological family, Bruce's side of the family, was also none of her business. But either she didn't catch my dirty look or she decided to ignore it.

"Ruth. Right. It might be fun," she said in a perfectly neutral voice.

I shrugged again and arranged the pieces of the invitation in a neat stack.

My mom looked at me. "You know that your invitations won't be quite as . . ." She paused, and I could tell she was picking out her next word carefully. "Elaborate as Tyler's," she finished.

I shrugged. "Tyler's kind of a geek."

"Well, it's up to you. Just let me know." Her voice was still neutral, but I could tell from the look on her face that she was pleased, as if I'd passed some kind of test. I wished I'd told her that I wanted to go, that what I wanted more than anything was to be a part of Bruce's normal family.

I braced myself, waiting for her to say something or ask me what I was thinking. But she surprised me and managed to restrain herself, leaving me in the kitchen as she carried her tea into the office. After a minute, I heard the familiar sound of her fingers rattling across the keyboard.

I looked down at the invitation, then slid all of the pieces except for the reply card back into the oversize envelope, which I left on top of the recycling bin, where my mother would be sure to see it. I stuck the reply card in my back pocket. After dinner, when my mom was watching one of her reality-TV shows and my father was editing some medical-journal article, I pulled it out and carefully wrote, *Miss Joy Shapiro Krushelevansky will be pleased to attend.* Then I slipped the card underneath a stack of underwear in my top dresser drawer, thinking, *Maybe. Maybe not.*

Seven

"All right!" I said as we piled out of the minivan, doing my best to sound upbeat and cheerful, as opposed to desperate and panicky. "Who wants to start?" It was a sunny March morning, the weather warming, the sky a clear blue, the air soft and scented with honeysuckle. The trees were beginning to bud, and the path along Forbidden Drive was only slightly muddy. My plan was to go for a family hike—two miles up, then two miles back, with a stop to feed the ducks in between. Then we'd drive to Manayunk for brunch and hammer out the plans for Joy's bat mitzvah along the way.

My daughter slammed her car door and stood in her familiar posture: chin tucked against her chest, shoulders drawn up toward her ears. Her long legs were encased in tight jeans that she'd topped with a fleece jacket that matched her bright blue fleece headband. Frenchelle's leash was wrapped around her right wrist, and her left hand was shoved into her pocket, presumably beside the fleece hat I'd made her take (I'd also told her she might want to bring a scarf, but she'd glared at me as if I'd proposed she wear a petticoat, so I'd just wrapped an extra around my own neck).

While Peter rummaged in the glove compartment for the energy bar he was certain he'd left there, Joy started walking, head down, fists clenched, looking like she expected to find gates reading ARBEIT MACHT FREI at the top of the path, instead of a stand that sells sports drinks and ice-cream bars in the summertime. I resisted the urge to chase her, to run up the path and walk with her until she tells me what is wrong.

"Joy," I called. She didn't turn. "Joy!" I said.

She stopped ten yards ahead of us. Her entire body seemed to sigh as she let me catch up.

"Joy," I said, panting slightly. "Slow your roll. Bat mitzvah. Ideas."

She shrugged. "Well, I guess I'm having one, right?"

I bit back the half-dozen replies that instantly occurred to me. "Yes," I said pleasantly to my daughter's back. "You're having a bat mitzvah. A fate worse than death, I know, but somehow you'll have to endure. Your father and I were thinking about a Saturday-morning service and a luncheon afterward."

This earned me another shrug, coupled with a contemptuous look at my hiking gear: sweatpants, sneakers, a long-sleeved T-shirt with a short-sleeved V-neck on top. Was that so bad? Judging from her face, it was. *Probably the two scarves,* I thought.

"Well, if you've already decided, what do you need me for?" Joy asked.

I stopped walking, frozen in place on the damp dirt of the path, staring at my daughter and imagining my hands on her shoulders, digging into the fleece and the flesh underneath as I gave her the brisk, corrective shake that she so desperately deserved. Last year at this time, before her jeans got tight and her grades and attitude got rotten, she'd have been delighted to spend an afternoon with Peter and me on an adventure: a hike or a bike ride or a trip to the antique shops in Lancaster. We'd done this same walk a dozen times with my sister or Samantha or my mom, and Joy had never objected, never behaved like this. I gave Peter what was quickly becoming my own patented look of desperation: the *I can't talk to her; you take it from here.* Maybe it was being older, or a man, that made him so patient. Or maybe, I'd think sometimes, and instantly feel guilty for thinking it, it was because she wasn't really his. He was less invested; he could afford to keep his cool.

"How about colors?" Peter asked Joy, catching up with us effortlessly. "Is pink still your favorite?"

"Pink," Joy said icily, "was never my favorite."

Peter looked back at me. I shrugged. Pink had definitely been her favorite when she was eight years old. We'd spent a whole afternoon at the paint store, and we'd brushed patches of the three different shades we'd chosen on her bedroom wall and observed them in the morning, afternoon, and evening light to determine the perfect pink.

"Do you want favors?" Peter continued. "We could have a photo booth, like Tamsin and Todd did."

Shrug. "Whatever."

"Monogrammed clamshells?" I inquired, unable to keep from sounding frustrated. "Fake gold bling? Do you need me to get implants ahead of time? Because, sweetheart, if that's important to you—"

"Like anyone would ever give you implants," Joy said, her tone matching mine.

"Joy, did I ever show you my bar mitzvah party pictures?" Peter asked. His face was calm and his voice untroubled enough to suggest that we'd been having a cordial conversation.

Joy shrugged, but it was a slightly less hostile shrug than what we'd previously enjoyed.

"We partied at the Pound Ridge Country Club," said Peter. "My theme was *Star Wars*. Cocktail hour featured a Death Star constructed entirely from chopped liver."

The faintest smile flickered across Joy's face. "No way."

"Way. Did you ever see pictures of my grandfather? By the time he was ninety, the man was a dead ringer for Yoda. Wise he was," Peter said, shaking his head sadly.

I gave him a grateful look, knowing that he was lying: *Star Wars* wouldn't have come out until after Peter's bar mitzvah; the senior

Krushelevanskys hadn't been what you'd call whimsical folks; and his grandfather Irv hadn't even slightly resembled Yoda.

"We had inflatable light sabers for favors," Peter continued.

"Even the girls?" Joy asked.

"Hmm," Peter rumbled. "Maybe they got something different." He walked, lanky and loose-limbed in his khakis and sweatshirt. "Fake Princess Leia hair?"

"Ha ha ha," said Joy.

"I remember that my uncle Herman made the kiddush, and after he was done with the blessing, he told all my friends to stand up and reach under their seats. He'd taped dollar bills under every seat at the kids' table—"

"A dollar was a lot of money in those days," I interjected, which earned me, inevitably, another eye roll from Joy.

"And he said," Peter continued, "that the most important lesson of adulthood he could give us was 'Get off your ass and you'll make a buck.' "

I laughed. Joy's mouth lifted slightly. "Do I know Uncle Herman?" she asked.

"He's gone to the great Borscht Belt in the sky," Peter said.

"But he was at your father's bar mitzvah, and that was important. Having family there . . . making memories . . ." I said.

Joy muttered something under her breath that sounded like *Oh, please.*

"Have you thought about what you want?" Peter prompted her.

"How about *Grease?*" Joy said.

"How about no?" I snapped. The two of them stared at me. I shrugged. "Well, what's *Grease* about? High school delinquents. Unplanned pregnancy. Cliques. Smoking!"

"Smoking," Peter mused, his voice filled with ersatz sorrow. I gave him a look of *Back me up here, please.* He nodded soberly. Only someone who'd known him as long as I had could have understood how hard he was struggling not to laugh.

"What did you have, a *Sound of Music* theme?" Joy asked me, her lips curling as she named my all-time favorite musical (needless to say, she hated it, refused to watch it with me, and had referred to it more than once as "that thing about the Nazis"). "Was there, like, yodeling?"

"I didn't really have a party," I said shortly. *I didn't have a party because my father was crazy,* I didn't add. Crazy and cheap and something of a hypocrite. As the only son of an upper-middle-class family, he'd had a big bar mitzvah—a few hundred people at a black-tie dinner in the synagogue, with Super 8 movies to prove it. But by the time his kids reached the age of Jewish adulthood it was the eighties, and the bar and bat mitzvah bashes were starting to get seriously out of hand. We'd attended four of my cousins' fetes in Ohio before my thirteenth birthday. Each one had been grander than the last (one, I remember, had a circus theme, complete with a troupe of performers on stilts and fire-eaters between courses). On the long car rides back to Pennsylvania, with my mother sitting silently beside him, my father had complained bitterly about the ostentation, the expense, the superficiality, the conspicuous consumption, the way my mother's sister and her husband—a hapless accountant named Phil—had used a religious occasion to spend thousands of dollars to impress friends and relations with the fact that they had thousands of dollars to spend, how none of it had anything to do with God.

So, unlike my Cleveland cousins and my Hebrew-school classmates, I hadn't had a catered luncheon at the country club or a dinner with dancing on a Saturday night. No disc jockey, no hired entertainers, no fancy favors with my name embossed on a T-shirt or stitched onto a baseball cap. I'd been bat mitzvahed on a Friday night in a ruffled, flounced Gunne Sax dress that my mother had bought off the clearance rack at Marshall's. Two months before the big day, my father had presented me with a box of stationery and his Mont Blanc pen; he'd given me a speech about how the invitations would mean more if they came from me, personally. Every night when I finished my homework, I wrote out invitations: to grandparents and great-grandparents; aunts and uncles and cousins; the three friends I had at the time, inviting them to join me as I became a daughter of the Commandments.

My mother's mother, full of head shakes and disapproving looks but too cowed by my dad's temper to say anything, had come a week early and spent seven days making rugelach and mandel bread and delicate, scallop-edged butter cookies, so we'd at least have fancy baked goods at the *oneg,* the reception after Shabbat services. Sprinkling the dough with nuts and sweet wine, my grandmother regaled Elle and Josh and me with details of my cousins' receptions, as if we hadn't been there to witness each blowout: the bands and the food and the favors, how the pastry chef had spelled out our cousins' names in icing on the petit fours.

So on a Friday night I celebrated with a slightly amplified post-Shabbat reception in the synagogue's social hall. There was no music, no dancing, and no professional photographer, which was probably a good thing, given how awful I'd looked in my ruffled, beribboned dress that I'd realized, too late, looked much better on the models in *Seventeen,* or my pretty cousins, than it ever would on me. At thirteen, I was all boobs and braces, a too big nose and too short hair. Fifty people came: the Friday-night regulars, my friends, a dozen relatives. My mother told me she loved me. My father kissed my cheek and said that he was proud. My grandmother snapped pictures with her little Instamatic and cried.

But it hadn't been a disaster. I'd wound up feeling perversely good about my low-budget DIY affair, believing, as my father had instructed, that I was participating in a ceremony that meant something, instead of just an excuse for a big show-off party. After I'd finished my Torah portion with hardly a stumble, I'd bent to touch the spine of my prayer book to the scroll, then lifted it to my lips. My father's hand was a heavy, warm weight on my shoulder. *I'm proud of you,* he'd said, his voice rumbling through me, his brown eyes soft behind his glasses—and at that minute, standing on the bimah in my all-wrong dress, I felt proud of myself. I felt smart, radiant, even a little bit pretty. I felt vastly superior to my cousins from Ohio, with their fancy parties and the same photographer who'd always made all of the boys stand in a row and pretend to gape at a *Playboy* centerfold for their picture.

More than anything, I wanted Joy to have that feeling: of pride, of accomplishment, of actually having done something more than mouthing a little Hebrew and having an over-the-top bash as a reward. There was so much I couldn't give her: my love of books, for one thing; a normal first-comes-love, then-comes-marriage story of her own birth, for another. I just wanted her to feel what I'd felt in front of the congregation at that moment: that she knew who she was, and that it pleased her. I took a deep breath and quickened my pace until I was close enough to hear Frenchelle panting. I reached out my hand for her leash, and Joy handed it over without meeting my eyes.

"How come you didn't have a real party?" asked Joy.

I decided to keep it simple. "My parents didn't really believe in them. They wanted my bat mitzvah to be more about religion than having a big party with a theme. They wanted it to be about religion, and meaning, and adulthood. Growing up."

"Huh." I stopped while Frenchie squatted over a clump of ferns.

"We want your bat mitzvah to be meaningful, too," I said. "Have you thought about your mitzvah project?"

Joy shrugged. Even surly and miserable, she was still so lovely, with her honey-colored hair and her coltish figure. "Maybe something with kids," she said. "Or pets."

Okay, Miss America. "What kind of thing?" I prompted. Another shrug. "Which kids?" I asked. This time she didn't even bother shrugging. She just snatched Frenchelle's leash away from me and started up the path again. "Never mind," Peter said, giving my hand a squeeze. "We've got all morning." I shook my head, staring at my daughter's back as she marched away, head held high, widening the gap with each step.

At the sunny café on Main Street, in Manayunk, Joy drank black coffee and poked at her huevos rancheros, moving beans and eggs and tortillas around the plate without eating much. However, she agreed to step up her search for a mitzvah project that would mean something to her.

In turn, we agreed to a party with music and dancing, and that I wouldn't make her hand-write sixty invitations (nor would I agree to bake platters of sweets for the party). Joy grudgingly consented to the elegant but relatively inexpensive invitations I'd found online, and agreed that a photo booth was a good idea.

"And I want to invite everyone in my Hebrew-school class," she said. "I don't want anyone to feel left out."

"That's really nice," I said, swallowing hard. Here was my good girl, my sweet, serious, considerate Joy who'd tried to give the gold-fish crackers left over from her nursery-school lunch to the homeless people we'd pass on our way home from the park. When I smiled at her, she didn't smile back, but she didn't turn away, either. I leaned forward eagerly, thinking this was progress. I could get her talking, get her excited about her bat mitzvah, get past the coldness in her eyes.

I looked around the restaurant—the yellow walls hung with paintings, the dark wood tables—and breathed in the good smells of coffee and bacon and corn bread. "You know, I used to take you here all the time when you were little," I said. "We used to do Mommy and Me yoga right across the street with—"

"Emmett and Zack and Jack," Joy said in a bored voice. "And then we'd go to Whole Foods, and you would get me chickpeas and tofu from the salad bar, because chickpeas and tofu were my favorites."

"Right," I said. I guessed she'd heard that story once or twice before. When she was little, she'd liked nothing better than to hear me tell stories about when she was a baby, a toddler, the first time she'd said the word "Nifkin," the time I'd put her in her baby backpack and taken her for a walk in the snow. "You always liked that stuff. You ate—"

"—like I was born in the parking lot at a Grateful Dead show," Joy said in that same bored voice. She raised her eyes and glared at me with such a smoking look of fury that I almost gasped. Then it was gone, and it was just Joy again, her lovely face, her look of bored disdain. "Maybe I got that from my father."

Beside me, I imagined I could feel Peter flinch. Joy didn't mention Bruce to me too often, and she hardly ever mentioned him in front of Peter. "I don't think you got that much from him," I said. It was equal parts statement and prayer. *Please, God,* I thought, *let the only thing she got from him be her good looks and not his predilection for parental handouts and pot.*

"Is he invited?" Joy asked.

I scooped a stack of sugar packets, desperate to have something to do with my hands. "Bruce? Of course Bruce is invited."

"Good." She pushed herself away from the table, stuck her thumbs in the pockets of her jeans, and sauntered off toward the bathroom with her hips and ponytail swinging, drawing appreciative glances from the busboys in her wake.

I looked at Peter helplessly. "What did I do?" I asked, spreading my hands, palms to the sky. "Did I run over her dog? Steal her boyfriend? My God. Did you see the way she looked at me? It was like"— I gulped—"like she hates me."

Peter took my hand and pried the sugar packets free. "She's just thirteen."

"She's not thirteen yet." I ripped off the top of a creamer. "I wasn't like that at thirteen." Cream splashed into my coffee cup. "Maybe sixteen." I searched for my spoon. "Maybe not ever."

"So she's precocious," he said. "Take it easy. Give her time." I poked at my eggs again. *You get what you get* had been one of the refrains at Joy's nursery school. If a kid started crying because the snack was pretzels instead of crackers, or the book at story time was *George and Martha* instead of *Charlie and Lola,* one of the teachers would swoop in and say, "You get what you get, and you don't get upset!" It was true for the three-year-olds, and maybe true for the mothers of thirteen-year-olds, too. *You get what you get,* I thought. I'd learned that, and Joy would, too. I leaned sideways until my weight was resting against Peter, and just for a minute, I closed my eyes.

EIGHT

Wednesday afternoon is the one day of the week that my mother doesn't pick me up from school. I'm allowed to take the bus down Pine Street, past the boutiques and the galleries and the big brownstones, then walk over one block to Hebrew school at the Center City Synagogue on Spruce Street, along with Tamsin and Todd and Amber Gross and Sasha Swerdlow and the other Jewish kids in our grade.

From four until four-forty-five, we chant prayers and blessings: the one that says we believe in only one God; the ones that promise to love God "with all your heart, with all your soul, with all your being," the prayer for mourners, exalting the name of God. Then we have half an hour for individual work on our Torah and haftorah portions, the ones we'll chant at our bar and bat mitzvahs. The Torah is the Old Testament, only in Hebrew, and the haftorah is from Prophets. The portion you're assigned depends on your bar or bat mitzvah date. Most kids have the cantor sing their portions into their iPods and just learn them phonetically, but because my mom believes in the deep meaning of everything and exists for the purpose of making my life difficult, she wants me to actually learn the words I'm chanting. She thinks this is going to make it easier for me to write my d'var Torah—the speech I'll have to give in which I explain what my portions are about. My Torah portion's about Jacob and Esau and the story of how Jacob stole the birthright of his older brother, Esau, by dressing up like him and fooling their blind, dying father, which is something you learn in first grade. My haftorah is about how many sheaves of wheat the ancient Israelites had to pay for crimes such as livestock theft. I have no idea how I'm supposed to relate these stories to current events and modern times, unless there are people wandering around Philadelphia stealing each other's birthrights. Or goats.

But this Wednesday, normal classes were canceled because of a special presentation: "B'nai Mitzvah and the Blended Family." Parents were invited, so of course my mom was there, dressed in jeans and a long purple sweater she'd knitted herself. My mom has lots of nice clothes, all in dry cleaner's plastic at the back of her closet, left over from her book tours. Even though they're old, they're still pretty. If she'd wear those clothes, do her hair, and get that laser-vision surgery and maybe a breast reduction, she'd be fine. Ordinary. Like every other mom. Or at least she'd look that way.

When I walked into the sanctuary, my mom was talking with Rabbi Grussgott, her body angled toward the door, watching for me, as usual. As soon as she saw me, she started waving, sawing the air with big back-and-forths of her arm. The ruffled sleeves of her sweater fluttered as I made my way over slowly. "Shalom," said the rabbi, and I said hello back, wondering whether she'd read *Big Girls Don't Cry* and what her religious opinion about it was.

"Where's Tamsin?" asked my mom, plopping down in her seat and patting the cushion beside her, the way you would if you were trying to get a puppy to hop onto a couch. Her chest bounced, and I imagined the other parents whispering, *That's her. She's the one who wrote that book;* staring at my mother with her clogs and her tote bag full of knitting and a first-aid kit, a smaller sibling of the one she keeps in our minivan. Phrases from *Big Girls Don't Cry* popped into my head: *blow-job queen* and *sand-scratchy beach-blanket fucking* and *I wept until I thought I'd turn myself inside out.*

"Library," I said. That was where the kids who'd had their bar or bat mitzvahs already or whose parents were together had been sent.

"Ah," said my mother. The truth was, things between me and

Tamsin had been weird since I'd started sitting with Amber. I split my time: one day at Amber's table, one day with the drama kids and Tamsin and Todd. I thought it was kind of a biblical solution, at least a fair one, except Amber and her friends hardly seemed to notice when I was gone, and Tamsin didn't seem happy when I was with her. For a minute I thought about telling my mother what was going on, seeing if she had any suggestions. Then someone called my name.

"Hey, Joy."

I looked up and smiled. Walking down the aisle toward us, in a suit and a tie, his sandy hair falling over his forehead and his briefcase dangling from one hand, was Bruce Guberman.

"Hi, Bruce!" I said, and slid over to make room. My mother stared at me with a look that clearly said, *What is he doing here?* I pretended I didn't see it. I'd e-mailed Bruce the invitation to the seminar, with a note on top reading *Hope you can come,* and he'd written back saying that he thought he could rearrange his class schedule to be there.

My mother sat up straight with her tote bag in her lap, holding herself stiffly. Bruce sat down and spread his legs wide, cracked his knuckles, then crossed his ankles and leaned forward, while I tried to look cheerful and not picture the dozens and dozens of disgusting sex scenes in which he—or "Drew"—had starred in *Big Girls Don't Cry.*

Bruce is a professor of popular culture at Rutgers and, according to the inside flap of his book, one of the world's leading experts on myth and allegory in *Battlestar Galactica* and *Doctor Who.* This means he gets to give lots of speeches to groups of people where at least half of them will be wearing pointy plastic ears or blue body paint. When I was six, he took me to a convention in Philadelphia, only we got separated after his speech, and I had kind of a freak-out after a really tall guy with a plastic sword tried to direct me to the lost-and-found table in Klingon. In the old pictures I've seen, he had a ponytail and a goatee, but they're both gone now. His hair is the same color as mine and his eyes are the same shape.

"Candace," he said coolly to my mother.

She let go of her bag's straps long enough to yank at the hem of her sweater. "Bruce," she said back. The two of them are always super-polite to each other. They say *please* and *thank you* and *oh, of course, that will be fine.* I suppose it could be worse. Last year Tara Carnahan's mother called her father a rat bastard during parent/teacher conferences, then threw her cell phone at his head, which was a double offense because at the Philadelphia Academy we're supposed to use respectful language at all times, and cell phones aren't allowed.

"Thanks for coming," I said to Bruce loudly enough for my mother to hear.

"Sure thing," he said, and blinked at me. That was the thing about Bruce—he blinked too often and too hard. Especially when he was around my mother.

The rabbi stood at the front of the room and introduced Deirdre Weiss, a national expert on the topic of divorce and b'nai mitzvot.

"What," Deirdre Weiss began, "does 'bar mitzvah' mean?"

Someone—it sounded like Amber Gross—groaned. Deirdre's butt jiggled underneath her tight purple skirt as she wrote on the blackboard. "It means, literally, to become a son or daughter of the Commandments. To be an adult in the eyes of Judaism. To read from the Torah, the Word of God, for the first time . . . to be counted as part of the minyan, the number of Jewish adults necessary for a prayer service to take place. Becoming a bar or bat mitzvah means participating in a lifetime of Jewish values: to study the Torah, to do deeds of charity and loving-kindness, to strive for *tikkun olam,* the repair of the world." She swept the crowd with her eyes, trying to single out each potential bar or bat mitzvah. "Last but not least, it means that each one of you will be your own responsibility, not your parents' anymore." She looked at us again. We just stared back at her. Did she think we didn't know all of this already?

She turned back to the blackboard and began writing words like "inclusion" and "respectful listening," her charm bracelet rattling with each letter. I sneaked a look sideways and saw that my mother was writing "inclusion" in a notebook that said *Joy's Bat Mitzvah* on the cover.

"When planning the service, and the party, everyone needs to make sure that his or her voice is being heard," said Deirdre.

I gave my mother a significant look that she ignored.

"The beauty of the modern-day ceremony is that there's a role for everyone," Deirdre said cheerfully. "Aliyahs, participating in the candle-lighting, dressing and undressing the Torah . . ."

While my mother took notes, Bruce stared straight ahead at Deirdre. I let my gaze wander around the sanctuary, with its high-backed wooden pews and the words KNOW BEFORE WHOM YOU STAND written in Hebrew above the ark. Amber Gross waved at me. Had I known her parents were divorced? I wasn't sure. I kept scanning the aisles. Boy I didn't know, boy I didn't know, girl I didn't know . . . and Duncan Brodkey, sitting at the end of an aisle with a woman in red pants and silver hoop earrings. She was probably his mother. I felt my face heat up as I turned away. Maybe he'd gone looking for my mother's book the same way I had. I squirmed in my seat, wishing Bruce hadn't come, because what if Duncan looked at him and saw "Drew"?

"One of the places I've found that can cause the most contention at the party is the candle-lighting ceremony," said Deirdre Weiss. "Frequently, the custodial parents feel that their relatives should have more opportunities to light candles than the noncustodial parent, which gets tricky."

My mother's shoulders stiffened. Bruce blinked four times fast. Deirdre kept scribbling more words on the board: "party" versus "service." "Parity" versus "equity." "*Tikkun olam*" versus "*shalom ha' beit*": healing the world versus peace in the house. "Now I'd like to do an exercise," she said, passing around pencils and blank pieces of paper. "I'd like everyone here to write down the words that come to mind when picturing an ideal bar or bat mitzvah."

I stared at my blank page, thinking. *Everybody happy,* I wrote.

Then *Broadway theme.* And *CD favors with music from* Grease. I looked at my mother's paper and saw that she'd written *Judaism* and *tradition* and *God.* Bruce's page had no words. It did have a drawing of a man in a spacesuit firing a gun at a bunch of one-eyed aliens. Splats of blood flew out of the aliens' heads to puddle on the ground underneath them.

I looked up to see my mother staring at Bruce's paper. Bruce looked at her, shrugged, and picked up his pen. The next alien he drew looked a little like my mother. I snorted. Bruce grinned at me. My mother drew herself up straight and pulled her tote bag tight against her chest.

"Now let's compare!" Deirdre sang out. "I think you'll all be pleasantly surprised to find out how much you have in common!"

Bruce ducked his head and folded his page in half. Too late.

"Oh, come on," said my mother. "Who wouldn't want a *Doctor Who* alien invader bloodbath bat mitzvah?"

Bruce blinked, blinked, blinked. "I'm sure whatever Joy wants will be fine," he said.

"I want *Grease,*" I said quickly.

"You're not getting *Grease,*" said my mother.

"What's wrong with *Grease?*" asked Bruce.

"She thinks it promotes teenage delinquency and smoking," I said without looking at Bruce, because at that particular moment I was finding it hard not to picture him naked, rolling around on top of my mother in the backseat of his parents' car.

Bruce smirked. "When did you turn into the church lady?" he asked my mother.

My mother's face turned pink, but she ignored him, taking a deep breath. "If you want a theme, I understand. I'm a fan of narrative, too."

I rolled my eyes. Whatever.

"You could have *Hairspray,*" she said. "What about *Hairspray?*"

I pressed my lips together. Sure, it was a huge leap for her to even suggest that I could have any theme at all, but of course she'd want the theme to be the musical where the fat girl gets the hot guy. Like that ever happens in real life.

"Or *Wicked*. We loved *Wicked*, remember?"

I rolled my eyes again. Obviously, she'd loved *Wicked*. In that one, it's the girl with green skin who gets the guy. If someone were to ever write a musical in which the fat green girl gets the guy, my mother would probably die of happiness on the spot.

"Questions!" called Deirdre.

A woman with short pink nails raised her hand. "My ex-husband is remarried to a woman who isn't Jewish, and they aren't raising their children as Jewish, but they're still Zoe's half sister and half brother. What role should they have in the service?"

Deirdre talked about a blessing for children. My mom leaned forward, hanging on every word. Bruce drew more bullets spraying from the spaceman's gun. I scanned the room again. Amber was fidgeting in her seat, crossing and recrossing her legs, perfect as always in her boots and V-neck and jeans, not too dark and not too light, not too loose and not too tight.

A small, dark-haired man in the front row caught Deirdre's eye. "I don't know if you can help me with this," he began.

Deirdre smiled widely. "Try me," she said. "I've heard it all."

The small man snatched at his yarmulke before it slid off his bald spot and onto the floor. "Well, my oldest son is nineteen. He's undergoing gender reassignment surgery. You know, a sex change?"

Deirdre's smile wobbled. I guessed that maybe this was something she hadn't heard before.

"He's been taking the hormones and had the laser treatments, but he hasn't had the, um . . ." He raised two fingers in a snipping gesture. Bruce winced and crossed his legs. "He dresses as a woman. He considers himself female now. He—well, she—she'll have an aliyah at my daughter's bat mitzvah, but she wants to be called by her new name. Naomi *bat* Peninah." He fumbled with his yarmulke again. "Naomi, daughter of Peninah. And our rabbi won't do it because technically he's still a he."

Deirdre's bracelet jangled as she raked one hand through her hair. "Well," she said. "Have you considered a role where your, um, child's name wouldn't come into question? Maybe dressing the Torah?"

Right, I thought. *Because she'll be so good with clothes now.*

"But even though that gets us out of using the Hebrew name, what's the rabbi supposed to say? That Maddy's sibling will come to help dress the Torah? He won't say 'sister.' "

"Maybe if the rabbi won't say it, your daughter can."

The small man thought this over. "Maybe," he agreed.

Deirdre sighed in satisfaction, or possibly relief. "Other questions?"

My mother raised her hand. I cringed and inched away from her. "I understand what you've said about inclusion and respect," my mom began. "But in cases where you can't agree, who gets to make the decision?"

"Are we talking about a disagreement between parents? Or between a parent and a child?"

"All of the above," said my mom. I groaned softly. "Theoretically," she added.

"Well," said Deirdre, "I think it's important that each member of the family gives his or her input, but ultimately it's best to hammer out some kind of compromise where everyone feels respected."

My mom raised her hand into the air again. "But what if you can't?" she asked.

Deirdre's smile faltered.

My mom went on. "What if, for example, the parents want a simple, meaningful, religious celebration that addresses the Jewish values that you talked about, and the child wants dancers in Spandex to do some routine to the remix of 'Promiscuous Girl'?"

Bruce looked at me. " 'Promiscuous Girl'?" he asked.

"I don't know what she's talking about," I muttered. "I don't want oldies."

"Did you hire the dancers yet?" another mother asked my mom. "When's your date?"

"October," she said.

"If you want dancers, you better hurry," said the other mom, leaning forward with a hot pink day planner clutched in her hand.

"We don't want dancers!" my mother said. "She wants dancers." She pointed at me. I slumped in my seat, wishing I could disappear.

"Oh," said the other mother, leaning back in her own seat. "That's good, because you can't get dancers now anyhow. They're all completely booked. Believe me, I've tried. I know."

"Have you looked in New York?" asked another mother. "North Jersey? You may have to import, but they're available."

Deirdre Weiss clapped her hands. "Compromise!" she said. Her bright smile was back, but it looked a little shaky. "Have you given any thought to a separate party for the kids? You could have age-appropriate activities there, music and dancers and what have you . . ."

"I just don't think that kind of party is consonant with what a bat mitzvah means," my mom said.

"We're doing a separate kids' party," said somebody's dad. "Service in the morning, luncheon for the grown-ups, party for the kids at a nightclub Saturday night."

"Forget it," said the first woman who'd spoken. "Every decent place is booked."

"And the indecent places," said another mom. "Did you hear about the bar mitzvah boy who had his party at Delilah's Den?"

"That has to be an urban legend," said my mother. "No responsible parent would throw a party at a strip club."

"No, it actually happened," said the other mom. "My acupuncturist used to date the disc jockey. I've seen pictures."

Bruce bent his head over his folded sheet of paper. He wasn't making any noise, but I could see his shoulders shaking.

A minute later, two rows' worth of mothers, plus the sex-change dad, were having a noisy conversation about kosher caterers, and about some lady from Malvern who'd booked the Four Seasons two years ago for a June wedding, even though she didn't have a fiancé or an engagement ring, or even a boyfriend, and now was refusing to give up the date. "Dog in the manger, that's what I call it," one of the mothers said. "Hope springs eternal, I guess," said someone else.

Deirdre Weiss was clapping her hands. "Parents!" she said. "Children!" Her charm bracelet jangled. Everyone ignored her. "EVERYONE!" she yelped. "Let's . . . let's take a little break, all right? Fifteen minutes? And then we'll reconvene, maybe parents only?"

I slid off my seat and hurried out of the sanctuary with my hands in my pockets and my head down. Tamsin waved at me from the doorway of the library. "Hey, what's Bruce doing here?" she asked. I was just about to answer when Amber Gross grabbed my hand.

"Let's ditch," she said.

"Huh?"

"Come on," she said, and tugged me toward the door. I looked over my shoulder. Tamsin was still standing there with her lips pressed together. *Sorry,* I mouthed. Tamsin narrowed her eyes, spun on her heel, and stomped toward the library. Amber yanked me through the synagogue's front doors. Sasha Swerdlow was sitting on a bench by the front of the white marble building with her legs crossed, jiggling her feet. "Are you ready?" she asked, bouncing up.

"Lock and load," Amber said.

"We can leave?" I stammered.

"Who's going to stop us?" Amber said. She raised her hand and instantly a cab screeched to a stop at the curb in front of us, which I guess is what happens when you're Amber Gross.

"Where are we going?" I asked as the three of us piled into the squishy backseat.

"Surprise!" said Amber. I watched through the scratched windshield as we sped up Spruce Street, dodging potholes and buses and bikes, past Pennsylvania Hospital, then across Thirteenth Street, the restaurants with their tables set out on the sidewalks, the boutiques that sold fancy dog beds and dresses and baby clothes.

The cab stopped at Eighteenth and Walnut. Amber peeled a ten-dollar bill out of her brown-and-gold leather wallet, and I followed her out of the cab and into the Kiehl's store on the corner.

"What are we—" I started.

"Just come on!" Sasha hissed.

Amber grabbed my arm and pulled me along. "Hey, who's the hottie?" she said, giggling, and I felt slightly sick, with scenes from my mom's book dancing in my head, as I said, "That's my dad. My real one."

The shop was small and crowded, with high glass windows on one side and shelves and shelves of tubes and jars and bottles on the other. There were three women with glossy hair and white coats and name tags. One was behind the cash register, one was talking to an old lady in a fur coat. Amber walked confidently over to the third lady. "Hello," she said. "I'm looking for something for my dry, itchy scalp?"

Sasha, over by the lip gloss, grinned. Even though I had my hearing aids in, I was positive I'd heard wrong. Amber Gross had a dry, itchy scalp? While Amber talked to the saleslady, I looked up and saw Sasha picking up a bottle of sunscreen from the counter and slipping it in her pocket. She caught my eye, winked at me, and made a big show of putting some of the sample lip gloss on the back of her hand. Her lips formed the words *try it* as she walked by. And I knew she wasn't talking about the lip gloss.

I moved down the counter slowly, my heart hammering, picking up containers of sunscreen and Silk Groom, then putting them back down. There was a detangling conditioner that I bet would work for my hair, and a cuticle cream in a black-and-white tube. I looked at the door to make sure there weren't any sensors, then checked to make sure the salesladies weren't watching. Two of the white-coated salesladies were having an earnest conversation with Amber, one of them lifting a lock of Amber's hair between her fingers. "The flat iron's, like, killing me!" Amber said, and the salesladies smiled. Sasha was still browsing. *No,* I told myself, watching her hand dip into her pocket again, *Sasha is still stealing.* She turned and raised her eyebrows, looking at me as if to say *Get on with it.* I grabbed an amber-colored glass pot of something and dropped it in my coat pocket, where it sat like a grenade. *I haven't done anything wrong,* I told myself. *Not yet.* Until I walked out the door, I could still say that I'd meant to pay for it, that I'd just put it in my pocket to keep my hands free.

The clerk was piling samples into a brown paper bag for Amber: makeup remover and concealer and hand cream. Probably they'd never suspect that Amber was the kind of girl who would steal anything. A pretty girl like her, with the shiny hair and the sparkly braces and the just-right clothes, didn't look the part.

"You guys are the greatest!" Amber told the salesladies. I managed a weak smile and promised myself that as soon as I got back to temple, I'd give the cream to Tamsin and tell her that I was sorry for ditching her. Then Sasha grabbed one of my arms and Amber grabbed the other and the three of us tumbled out of the store and onto the sidewalk, with the bell on the shop door tinkling behind us.

"What'd you get?" Sasha asked. Her lips were shiny with gloss.

I pulled the glass jar out of my pocket and showed it to both of them. "Anti-aging cream?" said Sasha. Her forehead puckered.

I could have told her, *You'll need it if you keep scrunching your face up like that.* Instead I just said, "It's never too early to start a good anti-aging regimen," which was something I'd heard Aunt Elle say more than once.

"Huh," said Sasha. She unscrewed the lid, dipped her finger into the pot, and smoothed some lotion on her cheeks.

Amber pulled a cell phone out of her pocket and flicked it open to look at the time. "C'mon, if we hurry, we can hit Anthropologie."

"You guys go ahead," I mumbled. "My mom will freak out if I'm late."

The two of them looked at me curiously. Then they headed across the street, arms linked, laughing, with their coats unzipped and hoods bouncing on their backs, boots clicking on the pavement, two girls out walking on a spring day, two pretty not-quite-teenagers who would, of course, pay for everything they took. I stood there for a minute, my cheeks burning in spite of the chilly wind. What was the

penalty for a thief? How many goats or oxen would I have had to sac-
rifice if I'd lived back then?

I turned the little jar of cream over in my hand. Then I pushed it
deep into my pocket and hailed a cab on Walnut Street and rode back
to the synagogue, where my mother would be waiting, the way she
always was.

NINE

I walked home from synagogue flushed and furious and trying hard to hide it from Joy, who sauntered alongside me like she didn't have a care in the world. Bruce Guberman! In our synagogue! In the sanctuary! By my daughter's invitation!

My voice was level as I asked Joy what Bruce was doing there. Hers was just as reasonable as she hurried down the sidewalk and explained that it was an event for blended families, and Bruce was part of hers.

"Why didn't you tell me you'd invited him?" I asked.

She shrugged. "I just figured you knew he'd be there, because he's part of my family." Her logic was unassailable. I couldn't argue. Instead, I seethed, and fretted, and, as we turned onto Third Street, mentally reviewed the contents of my kitchen for possible succor. There was a quart of mint chocolate cookie ice cream that I'd stashed in the back of the freezer for an occasion just such as this. I'd take out the ice cream, let it soften, set the table, have a glass of wine . . .

I'd just set my purse down on the half-moon table by our front door when Peter came over and kissed me hello. "Get out your checkbook," he murmured into my ear. I pulled off my coat and sniffed the air. I could smell pot roast in the Crock-Pot where I'd left it, its rich scent of garlic and onions mixing with the distinctive tang of Fracas perfume and liquor.

"Cannie!" My little sister was wearing her red leather cowboy boots, glossy hair piled on top of her head, and leather pants cut low enough to display a few inches of supple midriff and jutting hip bone. There was a wineglass in her hand. From her flushed cheeks and glazed eyes, I guessed it wasn't her first beverage of the evening.

"Aunt Elle!" said my daughter.

"Joy!" Elle cooed, and smacked Joy's cheek, sloshing wine on the floor. Her Louis Vuitton weekend bag was by the door, along with her purse. She'd already plugged in her cell-phone charger and set her phone, blinking, next to the blue-and-white pottery bowl where I kept my keys, bus tokens, and spare change. I hugged my sister hello, mentally forgoing the drink I'd been planning on and doubling the portion of ice cream.

My sister was born Lucy Beth Shapiro, but she shed the name years ago. Although she claims to be "thirty-two and holding," she's actually eighteen months younger than I am, but she'll be the first to tell you that she doesn't look a day over twenty-five. For the past eight of her thirty-second birthdays, she's lived in New York City, supporting herself as a bartender, a waitress, an occasional extra in whatever soap opera or HBO drama is filming in her neighborhood, and, every December, doing a two-week stint behind the cosmetics counter at Bergdorf's (which entitles her to a year-round discount).

"I didn't know you were in town," I said, moving her sunglasses aside so I could plug in my own phone.

"Well," Elle began. I followed her into the kitchen, where she perched her admirable bottom on one of my bar stools, unfolding a not unfamiliar tale of woe involving a misplaced rent check and an irate landlord ending with a request to "just chill with you guys for a couple of days, if that's okay."

Peter, retrieving a beer from the refrigerator, made a face. I frowned at him. "Of course it's okay!"

"You're always welcome," said Peter in a voice a few degrees cooler than my own. Elle either didn't notice or pretended not to.

Joy perched on the seat beside Elle's while I whisked vinaigrette, and the two of them bent their heads together, giggling, with

Frenchie happily snorting at their feet. I got a dish towel and went back to the entryway, where I mopped wine off the hardwood. Back in the kitchen, I set the table with my favorite plates, glazed pumpkin and goldenrod yellow, and the napkins that matched. I put out bread and butter, salad and the dressing, a pitcher of water and the half-empty bottle of wine, and called everyone in for dinner.

"Yay pot roast!" cheered Elle as she sashayed into her seat. "So *homey!*" She sat expectantly while I set the pot roast and potatoes on the table. Peter, who'd emerged from the office, filled our water glasses and offered both of us wine. "So sweet!" my sister said, giggling, as Joy stared at her worshipfully and Frenchelle eschewed her dog bed to curl at my sister's feet.

After dinner Peter and I cleared the dishes. I wiped off the counters and recentered a vase of lilies and gerbera daisies on the dining room table while he loaded the dishwasher. Then he took his crossword puzzle and was heading up to our bedroom when Joy and Elle breezed in for dessert. "Any ice cream?" my sister asked innocently. I pulled out my brand-new quart of mint chocolate cookie ice cream and opened it to discover that someone had meticulously removed each chocolate chunk, leaving behind a pockmarked mass of green. I tried not to make a face, found a quart of vanilla, and handed it over, along with slices of the sugar-dusted pound cake I'd baked the night before.

Elle took her bowl and pulled a stack of magazines out of her purse. "We're going to look at bat mitzvah dresses!" she said.

"Great." My heart sank. God only knew what Elle would think was an appropriate dress for a thirteen-year-old. By the time my sister was through with her, Joy would probably be demanding a pimps and hos party complete with monogrammed condoms in the gift bags.

Joy and Elle went back to the living room. I reopened the denuded mint ice cream and stabbed at it with my spoon, bracing myself for the argument Peter and I would be having in bed, the one I already knew by heart, the one that had once ended so badly that I'd tuned the TV set to the LUV channel (which plays only Hallmark Hall of Fame movies), packed the remote controls in my suitcase, and gone to Samantha's for the night.

"You can't keep bailing her out," Peter will tell me—his inevitable opening gambit. "You're enabling her."

I will squirm guiltily and recite my lines: There will always be a gap between what Elle is capable of and what the world in general and her landlord specifically require, and it's my job, as her sister, to bridge it. He'll repeat the word "enabling." I will tell him loftily that I prefer to think of it as generosity, or as *tzedakah,* if I'm feeling particularly religious or especially obnoxious. He'll roll to the very edge of the bed and stay there until I fit myself against him, kissing the back of his neck and saying that if he had a ne'er-do-well brother or illegitimate child, I would be the very picture of generosity and compassion.

Then he'll make himself scarce for the remainder of my sister's stay, and I'll take pains to hide my checkbook and ATM receipts so that he'll never figure out the full impact of her tenure, while quietly thanking God that we never merged our finances. I'm sure there are marriage counselors who would recoil in horror at the notion of such duplicity, but, as possibly the only woman alive who's read Erica Jong's memoirs as both cautionary tales and financial-planning primers, I firmly believe that the path to lifelong love is paved with separate checking accounts and that foolish is the woman who does not keep her investments in her own name.

I stomped into the living room with my needles and yarn and plopped myself onto the couch. Elle and Joy had the TV tuned to the Fashion Channel, and they'd spread their material out on the floor: I saw *Vogue* and *Elle* and *Prom!* and even, God help me, a bridal magazine. Elle looked up, wide-eyed. "Everything all right?"

"Fine," I said, trying for a smile. Peter came back downstairs, probably for his nightly cup of tea. On his way back from the kitchen, he draped an afghan over my shoulders and retrieved my empty ice-cream mug from the table. When he kissed my forehead, Joy winced, and Elle gave us a sappy smile. "Look at you two," she cooed. "Ward and June."

I spread the green-and-gold afghan, one I'd knitted when Joy was tiny, over my legs, and wondered whether my sister had ever guessed at the truth, which was that Peter and I almost never got married at all.

Things came to a head on a hot August night. Peter and I were in the car, parked on the street in front of my apartment, while Joy, who had just turned one that April, dozed in the backseat. Peter's face was lit by the streetlamp. His hands were clenched on the wheel.

"Why does it matter?" I asked. "We're together. Why do we need to go stand in front of some rabbi and spend all our money on a party? What will it change?"

"I want a real wedding," he said in his deep voice. "It matters to me."

I sighed. We'd spent the day at Fairmount Park, at a barbecue for the weight and eating disorders department, where the diet doctors and nurses and support staff played horseshoes and vigorous rounds of volleyball, and the burgers came in your choice of soy or turkey. Peter wore khaki shorts and a dark blue polo shirt with a stethoscope where the alligator would have been. I'd chosen a thin cotton sundress paired with the new miracle panties guaranteed to slim my hips, lift my butt, and prevent the dreaded thigh chafe. They worked, but underneath my dress, I could see the dents in my thighs where the spandex ended and I began . . . and I assumed, sadly, that if I could see them, everyone at the barbecue could, too.

After dinner, Peter and I drove home, sunburned and sated, with Joy dozing in her car seat. Everything was fine until we swung by Rittenhouse Square, where there was a wedding in progress.

We were stopped behind a trash truck, which gave us plenty of time to check out the bride and her attendants posing in front of the fountain in the twilight. Her bare shoulders gleamed against the silk of her dress. She had pearls twined in her updo, and one of her attendants was fanning her with a program.

"Nice," said Peter.

"Pret-ty," Joy said sleepily from the backseat before her eyes slid shut again.

I sighed, knowing what was coming, knowing there was no way to avoid it. Peter had proposed on New Year's Eve, eight months before, and I'd said yes tearfully, joyfully, gratefully. I'd been wearing his ring ever since, while craftily avoiding the question of when we'd actually get hitched. That night I sat in silence as Peter pulled the car up to the curb and asked, "So when is that going to be us?"

I bit my lip and shrugged. That bride was beautiful, elegant, and slender. Both of her parents were there, the mother glowing in a blue dress, the father puffed up and proud in his tuxedo, directing the photographer.

"Give me a reason," Peter said. "One good reason why not."

Because I'm scared, I thought. But I couldn't say that. Peter had given me no reason to be afraid. I just couldn't imagine actually going through with it: walking down an aisle, taking the vows. Years ago, before Joy, I'd imagined marrying Bruce Guberman in the synagogue where he'd been bar mitzvahed. I could picture myself standing under the chuppah with his family on one side and mine on the other. In my vision, Bruce had cut off his ponytail, and I'd been radiant in the fitted white gown that I somehow, magically, would have lost enough weight to wear, and my father would have reappeared in time and apologized sufficiently for me to allow him to walk me down the aisle. Our wedding announcement would appear in the *Times* (sans photograph, of course), and Bruce and I would buy a house in a leafy suburb convenient to both of our jobs, where we'd have two babies with his metabolism and my work ethic, and live happily ever after.

And what had those dreams gotten me? An illegitimate baby whose premature birth had come, I was convinced, courtesy of Bruce's new girlfriend, who'd shoved me into a sink when we'd met by chance in the ladies' room of the Newark airport. The Pusher, I called her, even though my doctors in the hospital and, later on, my shrink, had told me that my mispositioned placenta would have caused problems whether my belly had met the porcelain or not. So: one premature baby. One hysterectomy. An ex-boyfriend who'd left the country, who had wanted nothing to do with his daughter. His mother sent me five-hundred-dollar checks each month—drawn, I'd noticed, on her account, not Bruce's.

The whole thing had left me angry. Actually, that was an understatement. It had left me filled with rage that was constantly bubbling just beneath my skin, and I knew that wasn't a typical way for a bride to feel. Things that would have annoyed a normal person—that would have been worth at most maybe a minute or two of pique— would cause me to literally see red, to shake with anger, to have visions of doing grievous bodily harm to my oppressor, and then to Bruce Guberman, every lazy, stoned, faithless, gone-to-Amsterdam inch of him. The driver of the sportscar that cut me off along I-76; a cop giving me a parking ticket when I double-parked to haul Joy's stroller out of the trunk; the nurse at the allergist's office who'd stuck Joy three times, making her cry, before finding a good vein: I could picture myself stomping on the gas and forcing the car onto the Schuylkill; lifting the diaper bag and swinging it, hard, at the cop's head; grabbing the syringe and jabbing the nurse in her pale, freckled arm. I knew it wasn't normal, and I couldn't tell Peter about it. Being as big as I was made me enough of a freak in his world, especially compared to the hard-bodied residents and interns who'd played volleyball all afternoon while I'd sat in the shade at a picnic table, sipping lemonade, watching Joy shovel sand into a bucket and giving my spandex panties the occasional surreptitious tug. He didn't need to know that I was not just fat but possibly also insane.

Luckily, I had my excuses ready. "First of all, you should know that if we do get married, I'm totally letting myself go," I began.

Peter crossed his legs underneath the steering wheel and looked at me expectantly.

"I know what you're thinking," I said. "But the truth is, even staying this size requires a Herculean effort that will end the minute I take my vows. My plan is to spend the next thirty years or so sitting on the couch, watching TV, and eating sugary cereal with my hands."

"No spoon?"

I shook my head. "Too much effort. By the time I'm forty, I'm gonna look like Jabba the Hutt. You'll have to move me from room to room with a reinforced wheelbarrow. For exercise, every once in a while, I'll lean over in the direction where I think you are and yell, 'Sucker!' "

Peter lifted one of my hands from my lap and kissed my palm. His forearm was dusted with grains of sand—from the volleyball court, I guessed. "Do you think I won't love you if you gain weight?" he asked.

I felt my throat close as I shook my head. I could remember my own parents. My mom would go all the way to New York for her clothes, brightly colored, beautifully made outfits, tunics and caftans and wide-legged pants. *You look beautiful,* I'd tell her when she came down the stairs, but I could see from the way my father turned his face away, from the way he looked too long at the other doctors' thinner wives, that he didn't agree. Another nail in the marriage coffin.

"And let's not forget the curse of the *InStyle* wedding," I said.

"What," Peter rumbled, "is the curse of the *InStyle* wedding?"

"Come on. I know I've told you about this. Every couple who's ever appeared in *InStyle* has gotten divorced, like, ten minutes later. Sometimes before the issue's even on the stands."

"So we won't let *InStyle* write about our wedding," he said.

"Too late," I said, sighing. "I already did that freelance piece for them about spring's new lipsticks. I'm cursed by extension. And what about my parents?"

Peter dropped my hand and turned to look out the dust-streaked windshield at the empty sidewalk. "We've been over this. I am not your father."

"And let's not forget the gays," I continued. "Until the gays can marry, I think it's unfair for heterosexuals to exercise the privilege. I mean, think of my mother and Tanya!"

Peter glared at me. "Your mother and Tanya *had* a commitment ceremony last year. We were there. You read from *Jonathan Livingston Seagull*."

I bit my lip. He was being too kind. I'd tried to read, per Tanya's request, from *Jonathan Livingston Seagull,* but I'd wound up laughing too hard to get the words out, so my sister had taken over, reciting with many dramatic hand gestures a passage about the importance of freeing yourself from the flock.

"Reason four," I continued. "I like sex, and I have read in many credible publications that married people don't have sex anymore."

I leaned over to kiss him. He turned his head away so that my lips landed on his ear. "That's not going to fix things," he said. "I want to get married. I don't want to be engaged for the rest of my life. And if you can't—or won't—"

"I wouldn't be a good wife," I blurted. The words seemed to hang in the air longer than they should have, and I could almost see the words I was thinking hanging alongside them: *I would have been a good wife to Bruce, before all of this happened. I can't be a good wife to anyone anymore.*

But maybe that was wrong. Maybe I could be a good wife. Maybe I could love Peter the way he deserved to be loved. Maybe I could believe, the way I did on good days, that Peter loved me. What I couldn't do was get past the mental block of a wedding: the white dress, the walk down the aisle. My ex-boyfriend hadn't loved me enough to stand by me when I'd had a baby. My own father hadn't loved me enough to acknowledge me when I'd found him in Los Angeles. Peter deserved better than that: someone who attracted love rather than repelling it. Someone who wasn't bitter, or broken, or carrying the baggage of a flamboyantly failed relationship. *A beautiful bride.*

Peter lifted his chin without looking at me, almost as if he'd sensed the spectral presence of other men in our car. "If you can't, or won't, then I think we should . . ." His throat worked. I watched as he pulled his keys out of the ignition, opened the door, unfolded his long legs, and let the door slam shut. Joy woke up, startled, and began crying.

"Peter," I said. "Peter, wait!" He didn't hear me through the glass, over the sound of Joy's wails. I flinched as the car roof shuddered while he pounded it with his fist. Finally, he bent down and yanked his door open.

"This isn't fair," he said.

I kept my eyes on my lap. "I know."

"It's not fair," he said fiercely. His cheeks had gotten sunburned, and I could already tell that his nose was going to peel.

I lifted my hands helplessly and watched them fall into my lap. "I'm a mess," I said, twisting around and trying to unstrap a shrieking Joy from her car seat.

"Candace—"

"You deserve better," I said as one of my daughter's tiny fists caught me on my right cheek. Tears came to my eyes. I blinked them away. "You're right. You do."

"I want you to be happy," he said doggedly. "But I've done everything I can, everything I can think of, to show you that I love you, that I'll always be here for you and for Joy."

The tears were rolling down my face, plopping onto my bisected thighs. I was getting dumped. Right here, right now. "Wait," I croaked, and reached for Peter's hand. "Wait."

He stared down at me for a long, long moment before he shook his head. "I'm sorry, but I'm done waiting," he said, and turned and walked away.

I hauled myself out of the car and onto the heat-sticky sidewalk. I slung my purse and Joy's diaper bag over my shoulder, put my key ring in my teeth, eased Joy's writhing weight into my arms, nudged the car door shut with my hip, pulled the keys out of my mouth, unlocked the front door, and carried my sleeping daughter up three flights of stairs to my apartment. My legs were numb; my hands, as I unlocked the door, looked like they belonged to someone else. I forced myself to keep moving. I sponged off Joy's face and hands with a warm washcloth, changed her, put her in pajamas, and settled her into her crib. *Baa baa, black sheep, have you any wool?* I sang over and over, until she yawned and her eyelids got heavy, then fell shut. I turned on the baby monitor, shoved the receiver into my bra, hooked my little terrier, Nifkin, to his leash, dashed back down the stairs, pulled the stroller out of the backseat of the car, and let Nifkin pee at the fire hydrant while listening to the monitor, hoping Joy would stay asleep, before hauling the dog and the stroller up the stairs. The apartment was so quiet I imagined I could hear it echoing. *Alone,* whispered the floorboards, and the water heater, and the walls. *Alone, alone, alone.* I should have been crying, but I just felt numb as I slipped Peter's engagement ring off my finger and put it in my jewelry box alongside my one pair of good earrings, a heart-shaped locket Bruce had given me once for my birthday, and a spare key for my bicycle lock.

I'm so grateful, one of the mothers in my premature-baby-mama support group said every week. She was a tiny thing, with Alice-in-Wonderland blond hair and a high, soft voice. *I'm grateful she's alive,* she'd say, wide-eyed, sweet-voiced. *I'm grateful I'm all right.* After six months of listening to her protestations of gratitude, I'd gotten the guts to approach her at the coffee urn and ask for her secret, half hoping she'd give me the name of some magical antidepressant or maybe just confess that she'd been hitting the crack pipe while her kid did hydrotherapy. *Oh,* she'd said, swirling a wooden stirrer in her cup. *Well, my husband helps me. My church. And I write in a journal. That helps, too.*

I didn't have a husband, or a church, or a journal. I didn't have a job, either. I'd been living off the money I'd gotten for selling my screenplay, and, as with most of the things that got sold to Hollywood, it didn't look like the screenplay would ever be made into a movie. Both of the executives who'd acquired the project had moved on to other studios, and the big-deal director who'd been attached was currently on a sabbatical of unspecified length, hiking along the

Annapurna trail (she'd taken to answering my increasingly pointed e-mails about when and whether things would ever move forward with a breezy "Insha'Allah," which my computer told me means "God willing," and was neither encouraging nor helpful). So I had what was left of that option payment, plus paychecks from my monthly freelance gig writing about single motherhood for *Moxie,* and the occasional trend piece or profile I wrote for my pre-baby full-time employer, *The Philadelphia Examiner.* How long would that keep us afloat? I pushed the thoughts away, walked to the kitchen, and started digging through the junk drawer.

I'd tried keeping a diary once, when I was twelve or so, but my sister had found it and read out loud from it over dinner, and my father had laughed nastily at the parts about my crush on football captain Scott Spender, his lips curling as he said the word "cliché." I did, however, have a reporter's notebook in my junk drawer—an old one, I figured, judging from the pages filled with my notes about the 1996 Miss America pageant. I ripped out pages of Miss Tennessee's deep thoughts on world peace and stared down at the blank page. Then I found a pen, crept into Joy's room, sat in the rocker, and wrote, *Of all the men who've fucked me up and let me down, my father was the first and worst.* I sat back and considered the words in the pink glow of my daughter's Cinderella night-light, with Nifkin curled up in the Moses basket my daughter had finally outgrown. Joy loved her night-light, a gift from my sister. Even though I was trying to keep Joy away from the commodified, phallocentric, "someday my prince will come" world of the Disney princesses, my daughter was so enraptured that I'd broken down and plugged in Cindy. For the past six months, the queen of happily-ever-afters had danced across Joy's wall, her skirts daintily lifted, her tiny feet flashing in their glass slippers, her painted eyes dreamy beneath her taffy swirl of golden hair, and my daughter now refused to sleep without her.

I read the words over, sniffling, and wiped my nose on a burp cloth. *Write what you know,* my tenth-grade English teacher had once told me. So I could write a story about a girl who was a lot like me;

her ex-boyfriend, who was a lot like Satan, with a twitchy eyelid and a penis the size of a worn-down nub of eraser; and the happy ending I could barely let myself hope for. I bent down over my notebook and started to write.

That night I left Joy and Elle with their magazines at ten o'clock. I emptied the dishwasher, checked the locks, and went upstairs to where my husband was sleeping. Peter rolled over when I eased myself into bed beside him, and opened his eyes. "How long this time?" he grumbled.

"A few days," I said. "And it's not that bad. Joy talks to Elle, and Elle talks to me, so it's almost like Joy's speaking to me again." I massaged hand cream onto my palms and wrists, smeared anti-aging goop onto my cheeks, then lay down and spooned my body against his back. "You're a good sport," I said.

"It's why you married me," he said, his voice muffled by the pillow. "Eventually."

"That," I said, sliding my hands around to the waistband of his pajamas. "And this," I went on, reaching over his body toward his wallet, which he'd left on the bedside table. "Let's be honest—in the end, it was your health insurance that won my heart." In the faint light from the hallway, I could see his smile as he rolled over and kissed me.

TEN

On Monday morning, with my backpack over my shoulders and a mug of steaming coffee in my hands, I knocked on the guest-room door. No response. I took a deep breath and knocked harder and finally heard a faint groan.

"Aunt Elle?" I whispered, easing the door open until I saw her lying on the bed with the Amish quilt pulled up to her chin, earplugs stuffed in her ears, and a rhinestone-trimmed satin sleep mask that read ROCK STAR covering her eyes. The top of her yellow silk pajamas peeked out from underneath the covers, and the bright tangle of her hair fanned out on the satin pillowcase that she'd brought with her from New York. "Aunt Elle?" I whispered again. "Are you awake?"

Frenchelle hopped onto the bed and applied her flat nose and wrinkled face to my aunt's cheek. "Sweetie," my aunt mumbled, batting the dog away. "Coffee."

"Aunt Elle," I said again, waving the mug so she'd smell it.

She yawned and sat up, shoving the eye mask onto her forehead. "Oh," she said, blinking. Last night's eyeliner and mascara had smudged into blurry circles around her eyes. "Whattimeizzit?"

"Early," I whispered. "Early" was not when I'd be getting my aunt at her best, but it was the only time we'd get some privacy and be able to talk without my mother sticking her head in, asking if we wanted eggs. "I want to talk to you about something."

She yawned again. "Go for it."

I hopped onto her bed and sat cross-legged with my backpack on my lap. Aunt Elle sat up and smiled. I adore Aunt Elle. She's the one who hooked me up with the Jon Carame straightening products and one of her old flat irons. She bought me a black lace bra for my twelfth birthday and snapped, "Lighten up!" when my mother made a face. She tells me all the details of her dates. She does ninety minutes of cardio four days a week and goes tanning on her days off from the gym. My mother wears cotton high-waisted briefs that she buys three in a package at Target. Aunt Elle wears lacy tangerine and turquoise thongs she orders from Frederick's of Hollywood online. That, in my mind, kind of sums up the entire situation.

"Listen," I began. "You know my mom's book." She squinted at me. I unzipped my backpack and pulled out my marked-up copy of *Big Girls Don't Cry,* in case Aunt Elle needed a visual aid.

"Oh, you read it?" she said, covering her mouth as she yawned. I nodded a little reluctantly. A long time ago, Elle had told me not to read the book. "It has mature content," she'd said, and when I'd asked what that meant, she said, "Old people."

"It was awful!" I blurted. "It was disgusting! All of that sex stuff!"

"Hey, don't knock it," said Aunt Elle. "All of that sex stuff paid for your summer vacations." She sat up. "And my recent series of oxygen facials." She patted her cheeks fondly. "My personal opinion," she continued, "is that the little sister is the most interesting character in the whole story. I told your mother that the whole book should have been about her."

I smiled. Dorrie, the little sister in *Big Girls Don't Cry,* had a lot in common with Elle. She was beautiful, and wild, and secretly working as an escort doing outcalls in a Catholic schoolgirl's uniform. When Dorrie's mother asked where she was getting all of her money, Dorrie answered, "Babysitting."

"So let me have it. What do you want to know?" asked Elle.

"Is it true?" I blurted. "About Allie and Drew." I swallowed hard. "About how my mom got pregnant."

"Hmm." She pulled her mask up over her forehead. "This is, like, ancient history, and I wasn't around for most of it."

I nodded. I knew that when she was in her twenties, Aunt Elle moved to Alaska for a year ("where the odds are good, but the goods are odd") and lived with a boyfriend in a cabin that he'd built himself. Which, she said, sounded a lot more romantic than it turned out to be. Also, she'd confided, parkas and lace-up fur-lined boots were not that good of a year-round look for anyone.

"Okay, let's see, let's see." She slurped from her mug, her features softened with sleep and the effort of remembering. "Bruce Guberman and Candace Shapiro dated for almost three years, and if I remember, your mother was the one who wanted time off. Then your father wrote that article in *Moxie,* and your mother was furious, but then Bruce's dad died—"

"Wait. What article?" I asked. Elle frowned at me. "Oh, right," I said, doing my best to act like I knew what I was talking about. "That article."

She turned her mug slowly in her hands. "You know what? Maybe you should ask your mom about this."

"You know she won't tell me anything."

Aunt Elle grinned, as if my mother's treating me like an infant were funny. "Good point. Well, I can tell you that it wasn't all bad." She swung her legs onto the floor, then stood at the side of the bed, doing some kind of complicated stretch. "Your dad came back eventually . . ."

Back from where? I wondered. I pressed my lips together, willing myself not to interrupt.

"And your mom showed him." She gave a satisfied nod.

"Showed him what?" Even as I was asking, I thought I knew the answer.

"She got the book out of it, and a ton of money—and you read the book, right? He should have known better. *Never* mess with the Shapiro girls." She scratched the top of her head thoughtfully. "Actually, you could mess with your grandmother if you wanted. She probably wouldn't even notice. I swear to God, the woman's been lobotomized."

"Thanks," I said. I was thinking that trying to get the truth out of my family was like trying to get answers out of a Magic 8-Ball. *Yes. No. Ask again later.*

Aunt Elle walked toward the bathroom. "Don't forget to tell your mom we have to go to New York to look at dresses!" she called over her shoulder. "You'll never find anything decent here!"

The library at the Philadelphia Academy has thirty computers available for students' use, and you can surf the Internet for an hour before school and an hour after, as long as you've got your parents' permission and a password. Needless to say, I have neither. I'm only allowed to use the Internet with either my mom or my dad in the room, and I'm limited to twenty IMs a day.

There's a way around it, though. Aunt Elle says there's a way around anything (she said this on Sunday afternoon, when my parents were taking Frenchelle to the groomers', just before she extracted a MasterCard from my mother's wallet so that we could go to Buddakan for cocktail hour). When I got to the library first thing Monday morning, it was empty except for Mr. Perrin, the librarian, two sixth-graders I didn't recognize, and Duncan Brodkey, in jeans and a green button-down, with his sneakers loosely laced and his hair flopping over his forehead.

"Hey, Joy," he said.

"Hi." I'd sat next to him every other day at lunch for over a month but had barely been able to look at him directly. Today, though, I made myself do it. "Do you have a password?"

"It's . . ." He mumbled something I couldn't hear.

"Sorry, what was that?"

"Oatmealie!" he practically shouted. Then he lowered his voice and spelled it slowly.

"Oh." I typed it in, and the screen bloomed to life. "Do you really like oatmeal or something?"

"Nah. My mom picked it for me. When I was a kid I had a teddy bear called Oatmeal Bear." He shrugged. I was pretty sure he was blushing.

"Moms are weird," I said, which I thought sounded like something Amber would say.

He flopped his hair back off his forehead. "Yeah." He scooted his chair close to my computer. "So what are you working on?"

I fiddled with my hair. I hadn't been counting on Duncan Brodkey at all, let alone Duncan Brodkey with questions. "A research project." Inspiration hit me. "Genealogy. How about you?"

"English homework." He sighed and turned back to his screen. I leaned forward, went to Google, then typed *Moxie* and *magazine,* then *Bruce Guberman.* The words *Loving a Larger Woman* filled the screen. I tilted my body so that Duncan wouldn't be able to see the screen, clicked on the link, and read, *I'll never forget the day I found out my girl-friend weighed more than I did.*

Oh. Ew. I squeezed my eyes shut, then opened them a crack, enough so that only a sentence or a phrase here and there could sneak through. *I knew that C. was a big girl . . . I never thought of myself as a chubby chaser . . . her luscious, zaftig heft.*

Oh . . . my . . . God, I thought. What was wrong with them? Why was I descended from a pair of sex maniacs? I must have groaned out loud because Duncan looked over at me, looking worried. "Are you okay? Did you just find out that you're related to Jeffrey Dahmer or something?"

I wish. "I'm fine," I said, and smiled weakly. I flipped open my tattered, dog-eared copy of *Big Girls* and wrote in tiny letters on the inside of the back cover *Loving a Larger Woman,* and the date it had been published. Then I counted backward on my fingers. My mom had gotten pregnant with me after this article was written, after she'd already read it, after she and the entire world knew that he'd tried to buy her lingerie and found out that the sizes stopped before she started. It made no sense, but there it was.

In a flash of inspiration, I went back to Google and typed in *Moxie* and *magazine* and my mother's name. Nothing came up under Cannie, so I tried Candace and found that she'd written twelve articles for them. I scrolled through the titles and clicked on the one called "Gone, Daddy, Gone."

> *We go around the circle at the premature moms' support group, saying our name, our child's name, our child's diagnosis, our husband's name. Some of the women are so broken up or sleep-deprived that they can barely form a word. Some are so sad that they can barely choke out the names they've chosen for their children. But everyone has a name and a diagnosis, and all of the women have husbands. Everyone but me. I have a sperm donor. Sperm Donor is currently, as far as I know, in Amsterdam. Sperm Donor has met his daughter precisely once, has contributed exactly nothing to her support, and at least once a day (or, if I'm being honest, once an hour), I entertain a brief but vivid fantasy of cramming pannenkoeken down his throat until his face turns purple.*

I squinted. The screen had gotten blurry. I brushed at my eyes, and then, because I couldn't think of what else to do, typed *pannenkoeken* into Wikipedia. *Dutch pancakes, yet unlike the usual American pancake, pannenkoeken are usually larger and thinner and sometimes incorporate slices of smoked bacon or apple and raisins.* Great. Maybe I'd make them for World Celebration Day next September.

I sat there, counting the months again. When my mother wrote that article, I was one year old, and Bruce was gone.

Your, um, Bruce. That was what my mother always called him, and I couldn't remember a time in my life when he wasn't around to visit every other Sunday, to take me to one of the same places he always took me—the Franklin Institute, the Please Touch Museum, the

Camden Aquarium, or the zoo. When I was little, I thought that every kid had an "um, Bruce," a kind of a backup father, the same way you'd have a flashlight and batteries in a drawer in the kitchen in case the power went out, a spare dad to buy you too-big clothes for your birthday, to take you out for pizza and ask you stupid questions about school and homework. When I got old enough to realize that maybe this wasn't normal, my mother told me that they'd been boyfriend and girlfriend, and that even though they'd never gotten married, they'd both wanted me, both loved me, loved me so much.

But here was the truth in black and white, on the Internet, for the entire world to see. She'd been fat—not that that wasn't obvious. He'd run away, which no one had ever told me. She hadn't wanted me, which I'd figured out from her book. And he'd run away to Amsterdam, which meant that neither one of them had really wanted me at all.

"Hey, Joy?"

I looked up. Duncan was standing right behind me, reading over my shoulder. I logged off fast.

"The bell rang. Didn't you hear it?" he asked.

I shook my head. I didn't trust my voice yet.

"Come on." Duncan bent down and scooped up my backpack from under the desk. "Can't be late for Mr. Shoup." He looked at me again as I walked down the hall on legs that felt like they'd been cut off a dead person and stitched onto my hips. "Do you have any big spring-break plans?"

"Not really," I said, and pasted Amber Gross's smile on my face and walked down the hallway wishing there were an Amsterdam for almost-thirteen-year-old girls, a place I could run to and eat pancakes with apples and raisins, a place where I could go, and change my name to Annika, and never come home again.

Eleven

Peter kissed me goodbye and dropped us off at Thirtieth Street Station on his way to work Thursday morning. Inside the cavernous, echoing, high-ceilinged chamber, I slid my credit card into the automatic ticket machine. Once it spat out three tickets, I bought a large iced coffee, two muffins (one blueberry, one corn), and the latest *Us* and *InStyle* and *People*. At ten-fifteen Joy and Elle and I boarded the Acela, which would get me to New York City in plenty of time for my one o'clock lunch with my agent and publisher, and for Joy (currently on spring break) and Elle (currently on a hiatus of unspecified duration) to spend the afternoon shopping.

The two of them took seats side by side, turned down my muffins, and spent the hour and fifteen minutes of the trip with their heads bent over *Women's Wear Daily* and *Vogue,* whispering to each other, marking the pages with Post-it notes and occasionally looking sideways at me and giggling. I was too preoccupied to care.

Normally when I went to my publisher's, my editor, Peyson Horowitz, called in for sandwiches, and we bought sodas from the vending machine down the hall. Today, though, I'd be dining with my agent at Michael's, unofficial cafeteria of the media world. It would be the two of us, she'd told me, plus Patsy Philippi, the publisher of Valor Press, which had published all the sci fi I'd written for the last ten years, along with *Big Girls Don't Cry.*

I said goodbye to my sister and daughter at Penn Station, and I walked slowly to the restaurant, knowing that even if I dawdled, I'd be embarrassingly early. I browsed at a newsstand, had another iced coffee, and marveled at the women passing by, all gym-tight bodies and perfect hair. In the coffee shop bathroom, I washed my hands and studied myself in the mirror, wishing that I'd swiped Joy's straightening iron, the one I'm not supposed to know about, or that I'd borrowed her lipstick (not supposed to know about that, either), or that I'd accepted Elle's offer of some help with my makeup and outfit selection, because the clothes that had looked perfectly acceptable that morning in Philadelphia—the straight black skirt and low black heels, the gray cotton shirt and the necklace of faceted jet-black beads—now seemed dowdy and dull.

My agent, Larissa, waved to me from beside the maître d's stand and kissed me on both cheeks, a recent affectation, I assumed. I airkissed back, trying not to stare at the elderly lady broadcaster ensconced at a table for four by the window, whose famous face had been lifted so many times that her eyebrows and her hairline were more or less in the same place. "And you remember Patsy, of course," Larissa said.

I nodded and submitted to Patsy's double kiss. I'd met Patsy only once, when Valor had held a champagne-and-cake reception to celebrate *Big Girls*'s sixth month on the best-seller list. Patsy was short and plump and looked vaguely like Mrs. Claus, with her white curls and twinkling gold-rimmed glasses. Looking at her, you'd never guess that she'd earned her Ph.D. in comparative literature by twenty-three, or that beneath her sugar-cookie exterior she was scarysmart (and sometimes, I'd read, just plain scary).

Larissa removed her coat, revealing one of what I'd once joked were her two hundred identical black pantsuits. Over her arm, she carried what looked like a bowling-ball bag made of green leather, ornamented with all manner of fringes and tassels plus a heavy brass padlock—the kind of thing my sister would have been able to identify by name, designer, and price tag on sight.

Finding Larissa had been a happy accident. After I'd written my book, I'd gotten in touch with Violet, the agent who'd sold my screenplay.

"A novel?" she'd repeated dubiously.

"You know," I'd said. "The things that screenplays are sometimes based on?"

"Can't help you, lovey. I— *Hey, fuck you, asshat!*"

I'd grinned. Violet looked like a Girl Scout and cursed like Chris Rock. "You okay?"

"Yeah, yeah. Some douche-sip took my parking spot. Listen, I'll shoot you the names of some book agents. How's New York?"

"Philadelphia," I'd reminded her. She'd apologized and sent me ten names within the hour. Larissa had been the first one on the list to request the entire manuscript, and she'd called me on a Saturday to tell me, in her tiny, squeaky voice, how much she'd loved the book, how it had spoken to her (at the time, I distinctly remember thinking, *How?*).

The hostess led us across the sunny restaurant, through the maze of tightly packed tables set along white walls filled with bright modern art, past editors and agents lunching on salads and grilled fish, to a prime table for four. A waiter passed out oversize menus and offered sparkling, tap, or still water. We made small talk about my train trip, the renovations of Patsy's flat in London, and Larissa's new assistant, who'd put herself through college working weekends in her family's nail salon and insisted, each week, on giving her boss a pedicure. Patsy's dress was navy, and when I looked more closely, I saw that Larissa's black suit was actually a very dark blue. *Navy,* I thought regretfully. Navy was the new black. How had I missed that? Why couldn't I have been a tenth as obsessed with high heels and high fashion as the *Big Girls Don't Cry* critics had once claimed? Ah, well. *Content of my character,* I thought, and *Seven pounds thinner.*

After a few more minutes of small talk, the waiter returned. "Ready to order?" he asked.

I requested a Cobb salad. "Dressing on the side?" he asked.

"Oh. Sure." Silly me. I hadn't realized that the object of the game was to order a Cobb salad with so many things omitted that you'd be left with basically a twenty-four-dollar pile of lettuce leaves and to-matoes. Larissa asked for a Cobb salad without bacon, dressing on the side. Patsy ordered hers without bacon or avocado, or any dress-ing at all.

Yummy, I thought. I slipped my feet out of my shoes and set them on the carpet, which I could feel literally buzzing beneath me. *The electric energy of New York,* I thought a little romantically. Then I real-ized that what I was feeling was the reverb from a dozen cell phones and handhelds and BlackBerries set on vibrate and humming away from a dozen different expensive purses on the floor.

I smiled at Patsy as she sat back and said, "So!" Then I reached into my own pedigree-free bag. I'd brought the latest Lyla Dare man-uscript, completed just the night before. I slid the pages across the table.

Patsy shook her head. "Actually, we didn't ask you here to talk Lyla. Although you've been doing an excellent job," she added.

I slipped the manuscript back into my purse. "Okay." I was start-ing, very belatedly, to get an idea about why they'd asked me to New York instead of sending me the usual edit memo by e-mail; about why I was nibbling lettuce in the plush front room of Michael's, sit-ting on bentwood chairs at a linen-draped table within earshot of an executive editor at *Allure,* seeing and being seen, instead of in Peyson's tiny windowless office, eating corned beef off of wax paper.

Patsy steepled her chubby fingers underneath her chin and leaned forward, blue eyes saucer-wide. "As you know," she began, "the tenth anniversary of *Big Girls Don't Cry* is coming up this fall."

I nodded. My knees were already starting to shake, and my hands, when I wiped them on my napkin, were slimy.

"We'd like to do a special rerelease," said Patsy. "New cover, new packaging, a beautiful new author photo, a whole new publicity campaign."

"That sounds amazing," said Larissa. I nodded numbly. Well, they owned the rights to the thing. It wasn't as if I could stop them.

"We were hoping," Patsy continued, "that you'd be available to help us promote it. We were thinking about a sixteen-city tour."

"Oh, I can't." I tried to sound apologetic rather than insane. Judging from the looks I was getting, I didn't think I'd been entirely successful. I lifted my water glass with a trembling hand and took a sip. "I'm sorry," I said. "But I just don't think I can leave home anytime soon. Joy's bat mitzvah's this fall, too, and there's a lot of planning to do."

"Of course," said Patsy. Perhaps sensing my discomfort, she reached across the table and patted my icy hand with her warm one. "Maybe just a satellite-radio tour, some TV bookings. And a reading here in New York, of course. It could be fantastic."

I nodded, thinking I'd get out of that when the time came. There were excuses I could make, illnesses I could feign. Actually, I probably wouldn't even need to fake it. Just the thought of having to sit on a couch with some newscaster and relive that part of my past made me want to heave.

Patsy tugged at one of her white corkscrew curls and resettled her napkin on her lap. At the table beside us, a young woman in navy (of course) was settling into the chair the waiter had pulled out. "My agent will be joining me," she said proudly. I turned away.

"And," Patsy continued, "with the tenth anniversary of publication this spring, everyone at this table, all of us at Valor"—she favored me with her warmest smile—"and the millions of *Big Girl* fans, of course . . ."

I smiled weakly, bracing myself.

Patsy went on. ". . . we're all wondering whether you've given any thought to another novel." She beamed at me as if she'd just set a beautifully wrapped gift on the table.

"It's very flattering. I'll, um, think about it," I stammered.

"We don't need a whole book right now," said Patsy in her softest and most soothing tone. "It doesn't have to be a sequel, either. If there's just an idea you've had kicking around . . ."

"Will you excuse me?" I pushed myself up and out of my chair.

My water glass shivered as I turned around fast, almost crashing into the waiter, who was carrying our denuded salads to the table. "Excuse me," I said again, and hurried around the corner to the ladies' room, where I sat in the tiny marble stall with my head in my hands.

A dream come true. Cliché city, right? Yet no fewer than twenty newspaper articles about the surprising success of *Big Girls Don't Cry* had quoted me saying exactly that. *It is a dream come true.* It certainly looked that way: unlucky-in-love, oppressed-at-the-office, unhappy-in-her-own-skin big girl from broken home gets love, and a man, and a beautiful baby, and a best-seller. Not necessarily in that order, but still, an undeniable happy ending.

Twelve years ago, I'd written *Big Girls* in my spare bedroom, banging out five hundred pages in six months of white-hot fury. The manuscript was a sprawling, profane picaresque about a fat, funny, furious girl, the father who'd abandoned her, the boyfriend who'd broken her heart, and the girl's fitful journey toward love and happiness, with many (entirely fictional) stops in many (equally fictional) boys' beds along the way. In a fit of literary pretension, I called the book *Nought.* Would I be open to a title change? Larissa had asked. I'd told her I would be open to a sex change if she thought she could sell the book and give me enough of a cushion to pay for health insurance and maybe put a down payment on a condo.

Three weeks later the book was revised, cut down from its original 500 pages to a much more manageable 370, and renamed *Big Girls Don't Cry.* A week after that, Larissa sold the book to Valor for an amount of money that alternately thrilled or terrified me, depending on my mood.

The first thing I did as soon as the check for the first chunk of the advance cleared was to make a down payment on a row house around the corner from my apartment, a redbrick building with four good-size bedrooms spread over the top two floors. The house had a postage-stamp garden in the backyard, with southern and eastern exposures, and a weeping cherry tree standing shoulder-high in one corner, along with wooden half-barrels where I could grow herbs and tomatoes. After I'd moved Nifkin and Joy and all of my earthly possessions into our new digs, I rented a house by the beach in Avalon for two weeks.

I drove Joy to the shore on a Friday afternoon in August. I'd treated us to fried clams and crabcakes for dinner, and made it to the rented house as the sun set. I gave Joy a bath in the deep claw-footed tub, tucked her in to the bedroom next to mine, and plugged her Cinderella night-light into the wall. *"Knuffle Bunny,"* she demanded. I read her the story of how Trixie's daddy loses her favorite toy at the Laundromat, until Joy yawned and popped her thumb into her mouth.

"Love you, boots," I said, cracking open her bedroom window. The house still smelled faintly musty, but mostly of the salty breeze. I could hear the waves from every room.

"You're my mommy," Joy said sleepily. Bundled under the covers, she still looked tiny, baby-size, even though she was two. *She'll grow out of it,* her pediatrician assured me, explaining that she was just the right size for her gestational age. *Eventually, she'll catch up to the rest of the kids. You'll look at her, and you won't even see a difference.* Except I knew I'd always see.

"That's right," I assured her. Nifkin came clicking into the room and settled himself in Joy's suitcase, rooting around until he'd made a nest on top of her shorts and shirts.

Joy sat up in bed and looked at me. "Who is my daddy?"

"Um . . ." I leaned against the doorjamb. I'd known this question would be coming, but I'd thought I'd have more time to figure out my answer. "Yes. Well. About that . . ."

"Pe-tah." She nodded, looking satisfied.

My breath caught in my throat. It had been a year since that August night in the car, the night when he'd told me he wouldn't keep waiting. I'd thought of him every day and every night, but I wasn't sure Joy even remembered Peter. "You see, honey, the thing of it is—"

She waved one fist at me—Joy-speak for *Quiet, you, I'm*

thinking!—and stared at me with her lips pursed. "Granny Annie is your mommy," she said.

Okay. Terra firma again. "That's right."

"Who is your daddy?"

My hand closed convulsively on the light switch, and the room was plunged into darkness except for Cinderella in her ballgown, dancing just above Joy's pillow, head lifted, as ever, in expectation of the prince's kiss. "I . . ." I took a slow breath and swallowed. "Well, his name is Larry."

"Arry," Joy repeated sleepily. I leaned against the wall. If I wasn't ready for questions about her father, I was doubly unprepared for questions about mine. My father had left when I was a teenager, married a much younger woman, and had two kids. I hadn't seen or heard from him since our single encounter in Los Angeles, when I'd shown up at his office pregnant, wearing a gold wedding ring I'd bought for myself, hoping for something I couldn't name—that, at twenty-eight, single and knocked up, I could be his little girl, his princess; that he would think me beautiful.

It hadn't happened. He'd turned away, his expression somewhere between disinterested and disgusted, and I'd remembered with a pain that felt like a cramp, like something tearing inside of me, a bit of graffiti I'd seen once in the ladies' room at the Vince Lombardi Service Area on the New Jersey Turnpike, written in tiny black letters on the scarred green metal door: *I never knew my father / it doesn't really matter / that's all there is to that.*

That's all there is to that, I'd thought. I'd walked out of his office, and I hadn't seen him since. I hadn't planned on Joy even noticing that she was down a grandpa for years. I'd thought I would have time to prepare: read the right books, figure out the right thing to say.

I stood there in the darkness, looking down at her, wondering whether she'd think that people—no, not people, parents—could just drop out of your life like loose teeth. Peter had. Bruce had. My father had. She'd probably think that everyone could or would. Maybe she'd think that someday I would leave, too.

There was only one telephone in the rented beach house, an old rotary model made of black plastic on the kitchen counter right beside the sink. Peter answered on the first ring, as if he'd been walking around the way I had, with his phone stuck in his pocket, or as if he'd been sitting beside it, waiting. Not that I believed he'd been waiting. He'd probably met someone already. She was probably right there beside him on the bed, and if she knew about me at all, she was probably thinking I was the biggest idiot who'd ever lived. She was probably right.

"Peter? It's Cannie. I wrote a book," I blurted.

His voice was neutral. "Oh."

"It . . . if you'd read it, it explains . . ." I slumped into the chair in front of the telephone, thinking how ridiculous I must sound. "About Bruce and my father and what happened to me. About why I can't be a good wife." I gulped. "Peter, I'm sorry. I am." Tears were running down my face, and words were spilling out of my mouth. "Joy misses you. Tonight she said that you're her father, and I think . . ." I gulped again and wiped my eyes. "I wish . . . I mean, she's had enough people leave, and I thought maybe if you would read the book . . . I could give you a copy. It's not coming out until next spring, and they changed the title, but I could print it out and give it to you . . ."

His tone was fractionally warmer, the bedside-manner voice he'd used with me when I was at my lowest, the voice you'd use to tell a patient that yes, her condition was terminal and you'd try to keep her comfortable. So maybe he was alone. Or maybe it was just that his new girlfriend had gone to the bathroom to slip out of her lace merry widow and into her leopard-print thong. "Where are you?" he asked.

"New Jersey. I took Joy on vacation. I'm sorry to bother you. I'll be okay. I should have . . ." I made myself stop talking. "Well, anyhow. I'm sorry I bothered you."

Now he sounded amused. "Where in New Jersey?"

"Avalon. The beach. I got some money for my advance, and I thought we should go to the beach. Get some sun. Walk on the sand. Joy's therapist said it's good for her to walk on the sand."

"What's the address?"

My heart rose, and I bit down hard, not letting myself hope. "Hang on." I told him where I was, and we said goodbye. Then I climbed up to the widow's walk off the master bedroom, with the door open, listening to the hushing sound of the waves rolling onto the shore, laughter from the bar down the block, and the voices of people playing cards on the porch of the house next to mine. I let the summertime smells swirl around me, salt water and the smoke from somebody's charcoal grill, until headlights washed over the walls and Peter walked unerringly up the stairs and out to the deck and took me in his arms.

Later, on a mattress that sagged in the middle, in a room where the walls were glazed with moonlight, it occurred to me that writing my book had been something like an exorcism. I'd written it all down, every angry, hateful, vengeful thought, every sorrow and insecurity, my bad romances, my messed-up family and lousy self-esteem. I'd embroidered the truth with the gaudy gold thread of sex, and a lot of it, letting my heroine work out her anger in a variety of far-fetched and acrobatic encounters, giving her everything I'd ever wanted, and now I was free—or as free as I could ever be. I nestled against Peter's chest, imagining that the bed was a boat and the two of us were adrift on a gentle sea, floating far, far away from my unhappy history, everything and everyone who had ever caused me pain.

His hand was in my hair, and my cheek was warm against his chest. "I'll marry you," I said. "If you still want me."

He chuckled. "Isn't that obvious?"

I twined my legs between his. "The only thing is, no big party. I don't want a spectacle."

"No spectacle," he repeated.

I kissed him sleepily. "Also, I really don't want a wedding dress. They're a huge waste of money. I mean, two thousand dollars on something I'll wear only once!"

"No dress," Peter agreed.

"Joy should be the flower girl." I closed my eyes, picturing it. "Can Nifkin be the ring bearer?"

"Whatever you want." I could feel his lips curve into a smile against my cheek. "No party. No dress. Taint carrying rings. Excellent."

"Don't call him Taint."

"Means the same thing as Nifkin," he said, yawning.

True enough. "Oh, and I can't have my picture in the paper."

Peter sighed. "Do I want to ask why not?"

I shook my head. I'd used that scene in the book, a page right out of my own life. Once, my father had found me at the dining room table, poring over the wedding listings, studying the pictures. He'd squinted at the page, checking out the brides like he'd never seen one before. Maybe he hadn't: "Fish wrap" was one of his kinder terms for our local paper. He stuck to the *Times.* "Why so interested?" he'd asked. I'd told him about the Bow-Wow Bride contest. "Can you believe it?" I'd asked, my voice rising indignantly. "Can you believe people would be so mean?"

He'd glared at me. His face was flushed, and there'd been a tumbler of Scotch in his hands. "Do you worry about the bride?" he'd asked. He spoke slowly, and the words were a little blurred around the edges, but I could still understand each one. "Or are you really worried about yourself?"

"Larry," my mother had said from the sink, where she was washing the dinner dishes. Her voice rose, wavery and weak, above the sound of the running water. "Larry, please."

In bed with Peter, I took a deep breath, pushing away the memory. "It's a long story," I said. "You can read it"—I yawned and snuggled against him, warm and sated and content—"in my book." Eventually, he did. Him and everyone else. The consequences had been, in my biased opinion, close to disastrous. And here was my publisher, wanting me to wade back into the fray and do it again.

"Cannie?"

I saw the tips of Larissa's glossy navy patent-leather shoes peeking underneath the bathroom stall.

"Are you all right?" she asked.

"Fine," I said.

The shoes didn't move. "I'm sorry," said Larissa. "I should have seen that coming, but when I called Patsy to ask what lunch was about, she said she wanted to surprise you."

"Well, I'm surprised," I said lightly, getting to my feet. "The thing is, I'm really happy doing what I'm doing now. I like Lyla Dare. I like having a pen name. I'm happy."

"But you'll think about it?" Larissa's voice was high and hopeful. I opened the stall door and walked to the sink.

"Sure." I knew the word was a lie as soon as it was out of my mouth, but it was a harmless one, I figured. I'd tell Larissa what she wanted to hear; she'd tell Patsy what she wanted to hear; and I'd go back to Philadelphia, plan my daughter's bat mitzvah, knit another sweater, and screen my calls until the whole thing had blown over.

Larissa beamed at me. "Do you mean it? I can't even tell you how thrilled they'd be. If you've got a new idea—if you could write me up an outline, or maybe even just a paragraph . . ."

For an instant my reluctance gave way to amazement. "You could sell a paragraph?"

"From you? I could sell a sentence. I could sell a burp."

I dried my hands with my mouth closed tight. No way was I giving her anything to go on.

"Come on," she said. She linked her arm through mine and uttered a sentence I seriously doubted had ever been said out loud in this particular ladies' room: "Let's send back our salads and order dessert."

TWELVE

"The most important rule of fashion," Aunt Elle instructed as she led me through the doors of Bergdorf Goodman, "is 'Know yourself.' "

"Know yourself," I repeated. I felt as if I should be taking notes.

"Are you pear-shaped? An hourglass? Are you short-waisted? Do you have broad shoulders? Good legs? Narrow feet? You have to embrace the thing that makes you you, and make the most of it."

"I . . . uh . . ." I honestly wasn't sure I had a thing that made me me, other than my absolute embarrassment about my mom and the truth of my birth. "I like my hair," I finally said, even though that was true only after I'd spent over an hour on it. Aunt Elle nodded. She had a sparkling sarong—pink silk with silver thread—wrapped around the hips of her jeans, and silver ballet flats and a skinny black top with a plunging neckline. Her hair was tucked underneath a gray tweed cap that she'd decorated with six rhinestone pins of various sizes. She tinkled and jingled with every step, and I felt plain as a pigeon walking next to her in my khakis and the sneakers that my mother had forced me to wear. ("You're going to be on your feet all day, Joy; you will thank me for this later.")

"Before you buy even a pair of panties, you need to know what you're working with," Elle said. She hopped off the escalator and put her hands on my shoulders, holding me in place. I tugged my hair over my hearing aids, sucked in my stomach, and straightened my

115

shoulders, frozen in place as crowds of well-dressed women walked past us. Elle touched my head briefly, ran her hand down my hair, walked around me in a circle, then smiled, satisfied, and led me onto the next escalator.

"I'd say you're a four or a six. Good proportions. *Great* complexion. I'm thinking pink," she said. "Not yellow. Definitely not red or blue. A little pair of sandals, an updo . . ." She reached forward, gathering my hair into a twist. "I saw this beaded Proenza Schouler? Killer. Just killer."

"Um . . . the thing is . . ." I wasn't sure where to start, but I was positive that "beaded Proenza Schouler" was incompatible with "Don't spend over three hundred dollars," which was the last thing my mother had said to me after she'd given me her credit card at the train station. It had been preceded by "Don't talk to strangers" and "Don't lose that credit card" and "Did you remember to bring the snack I packed?" at which point I'd been forced to remind her that I was going shopping, not to Amsterdam. A shadow had crossed her face when I'd said "Amsterdam," but she'd just kissed me and wished me good luck. "You know I have a budget, right?"

"I did hear that rumor," Aunt Elle said. "How much are we supposed to be spending?"

"Three hundred dollars?" I said. Aunt Elle's expression was so shocked I might as well have slapped her. "For two dresses?" I said even more quietly.

Aunt Elle shook her head, looking disgusted. "And where," she asked, "are we supposed to procure a gown for a hundred and fifty dollars? H&M?"

I bit my lip. My shirt was from H&M.

"Hold my hands," Aunt Elle said as we got off the escalator. She stretched her arms out to me. *Aunt Elle's new-age nonsense,* my mom sometimes said about her sister, but I let her press her palms against mine. "Close your eyes." I did. "See the dress." I tried, but all I saw was darkness. "See the dress," Aunt Elle chanted. "Be the dress." I concentrated hard, and this time I did see a beautiful dress with a tight satin bodice and a flowing tulle skirt. Unfortunately, the girl in the dress wasn't me, it was Amber Gross. Still, I guessed it was a start.

Aunt Elle exhaled slowly and loudly, let go of my hands, and whipped her silver cell phone out of her beaded leather purse, punching what I guessed was my mom's number. "Cannie? Yes. Yes, she's here. Everything's fine." She paused, head cocked. "No, we have not found the dress yet. It's been half an hour! Are you insane?" She rolled her eyes and mouthed the word "crazy." I smiled at her. "We need to talk budget," Elle said. "Yes. Yes, she told me—but Cannie, really. Three hundred dollars?" She paused. "Okay, but do you know what gowns cost?"

Another pause.

"Yes, I said gown. She needs a gown." A short pause. Elle grabbed my elbow and tugged me after her, onto the floor, where the names of designers, written in silver, wrapped around the walls. *Narciso Rodriguez,* I read. *Zac Posen. Armani. Valentino. Marchesa.* I mouthed the words, almost tasting them. "Candelabra, I do not have the time to explain the difference between a dress and a gown to you at this moment," Aunt Elle said as she pulled a one-shouldered white dress off a rack, held it against me, then shook her head and rehung it. "Just trust me. There is one. And three hundred bucks might get you a decent dress somewhere in Philadelphia, but it will not even begin to pay for a gown, which is what the occasion of your only child's bat mitzvah requires." She pulled a pale gold dress with a short, poufy skirt off a rack, held it against herself, smiled, then shook her head sharply, as if to remind herself of our mission. When the phone slipped away from her ear, I could hear my mother's voice, a thin, indignant squawk.

Elle grinned and pulled another dress off another rack. This one was shimmering lavender satin with a pleated, ruched top. I'd seen the actress Taryn Tupping in something exactly like it—maybe even this exact dress—in one of Aunt Elle's magazines. My heartbeat quickened. Taryn Tupping's exact dress! But Aunt Elle shook her head. *Not your color,* she mouthed.

"What?" she said incredulously into the telephone. "No. No. A thousand times no. I am not buying your exquisite daughter, quote-unquote, something with a long skirt and maybe ruffles. God, what is the matter with you? How did you turn out this way?" She pressed the phone to her ear, but I could still hear more squawking. "Listen," she said at last. She waved at a saleslady, who hurried over to help us. "Just because you don't spend money on your clothes doesn't mean that Joy shouldn't. In fact, just because you don't spend money on your clothes means that Joy can afford something really nice." I shyly ran my finger over the bodice of one of the dresses. It was made of bands of green satin, pale as new shoots of grass. I lifted the price tag, then dropped it fast, then picked it up again, thinking that I must have counted in an extra zero. When it was clear that I hadn't, I sidled past the saleswoman, who was practically standing at attention beside Aunt Elle, toward the rack topped with a discreet sign reading SALE.

Elle was listening to my mother, her brow furrowed under the twinkling brim of her cap. When she spoke again, her voice was icy. "Bad values?" she said. I froze, holding my breath. "Because I care about clothing? Because I think Joy should look beautiful on her big day?"

She winked at me again, and I felt myself relax even before she gave me a thumbs-up. "Right. Right. No, no, I hear you. I got it. I'll do my best. I'll let her know. Right. 'Kay. What?" She put the phone against her shoulder. "Your mother wants to know if you used the bathroom."

I rolled my eyes. Aunt Elle rolled hers.

"I'm sure she can take care of herself. Yes. Uh-huh. Call you later. Bye." She flipped her phone shut and put it back in her purse, looking satisfied. "I got her up to five hundred," she said.

I gasped. "Aunt Elle, you're amazing!"

"True," she agreed. "But you've got to pay a hundred dollars of it."

"That's okay," I said. "I'll do errands or babysitting or something. My friend Tamsin babysits, and she gets fifteen dollars an hour."

"Fifteen dollars?" Elle shook her head and plucked a dark blue dress off the rack. "Jeez. I was lucky if I got three. Then again, I wasn't what you'd call attentive. Hey, get away from there!" She grabbed my arm and pulled me past the marked-down dresses with her eyes on the floor. I grinned. I'd forgotten that Aunt Elle believed in the Law of Affinity, which meant that if you wanted nice things, you had to be around them as much as possible. Aunt Elle not only wouldn't buy clothes on sale, she wouldn't even touch them.

"We should probably go to Macy's." She said the word like it tasted bad. "I think I remember where it is. They'll have cute knock-offs, and maybe . . ."

I was following her as she jangled her way through the racks when I saw it: pink, sparkling, beads flashing, thin straps draped over a padded silk hanger. "Aunt Elle."

"What?" she asked. I pointed wordlessly at the dress. "Ooh." She lifted the gown off the rack and shook it gently, making the beads shimmer and the skirt sway. "Nice."

I found my voice. "That's it. That's the dress I want."

She held the dress at arm's length, moving it this way and that. Watching the palettes catch the light, hearing beads on the hem click against each other, I could imagine myself dancing in the dress; could see myself gliding across the floor; could even picture Duncan Brodkey looking at me, his lips pursed in a soundless whistle. Elle's forehead furrowed when she lifted the price tag.

"Bad?" I gasped.

"Well, let's not be hasty. We'll try it on." She tapped one pink-painted nail against her teeth. "I think I've got a gift certificate we can use. And maybe . . ." She slung the dress over her forearm, and I practically skipped after her toward the dressing room.

• • •

"Can I ask you something?"

"Ask away, honeybee," said Aunt Elle. She shook salt onto the puddle of ketchup she'd squirted on her plate, dipped one french fry, and nibbled it daintily. We were in the Brooklyn Diner, in a booth next to the rotating cheesecake display, Aunt Elle on one side of the table, me on the other with my new pink dress beside me. We'd split the price between my mother's credit card, Aunt Elle's debit card, and her gift certificate, and even then we'd gone way over budget, and I didn't have a dress to wear to Amber's bat mitzvah, if she really was going to invite me, but I didn't care. When I'd slid the pink dress over my head and Aunt Elle had pulled up the zipper, I'd never felt so pretty in my life. *You look hot,* I could imagine someone whispering, and the voice had sounded like Duncan Brodkey's, and he'd been saying those words not to Amber but to me.

"I . . ." I pulled the lettuce off my turkey burger, then the round pickle slices. "So I guess Bruce wasn't around much when I was little."

Aunt Elle smirked. "Doing a little fact-checking after the fact?"

I took a bite of my burger. "How long was he in Amsterdam?"

She shrugged. "I don't know. You were so little . . . and by the time you were three or so, he started coming around again." She lifted her fork and speared a lettuce leaf. "Your mother was probably trying to protect you."

"By not telling me that my biological father didn't even meet me until I was three?"

Aunt Elle looked worried, maybe because she was afraid that my mother would be angry at her for spilling the beans. "Well, is it really such a big deal? Can you remember anything from when you were one or two? I mean, you were probably just stuck in a playpen."

I was momentarily confused. "What's a playpen?"

She scowled. "A little baby cage. That's what your grandmother kept us in."

Never mind that for now, I thought. "It is a big deal. It's important. I mean, hello, it's my father!"

"I had a father," Aunt Elle said. "It wasn't such a walk in the park."

"What do you mean?" I knew the basics of my mother's family's story: that her father had left when she'd been a teenager, and married someone much younger and had kids with her, and that my mom and her brother and sister didn't see him anymore.

Elle pressed her lips together and put her fork down. "Just not nice," she said. "He was not a very nice guy."

"What do you mean, not nice? Did he hit you guys?" The father in *Big Girls Don't Cry* hadn't hit his kids; he'd thrown things at them: books, bottles, cordless telephones. "Allie" had a dent in her forehead from the father chucking an ice skate at her when she was nine.

Elle sprinkled more salt into her ketchup. "He never hit us." She was quiet so long that I thought she wasn't going to say anything, and then I'd have to start again with the computer or maybe Grandma Ann, when she said, "He called me names."

"What names?"

Her face was flushed, and her hair, when she raked her hand through it, stood up from her head, making her look disturbingly like my mother. "Dummy. Stupid. Idiot. Moron. You get the idea."

"Wow." I didn't know what to say to that.

"And then he was just . . ." She snapped her hands in the air and exhaled furiously. "Gone. Vanished. Into thin air. He missed Josh's high school graduation. He missed my college graduation."

"You graduated from college?" This was news to me.

"Well, maybe I would have if he'd paid my tuition!" Her voice rose. The two white-haired ladies sharing a slice of cheesecake stared. Aunt Elle smacked the bottom of the ketchup bottle so viciously I was surprised I didn't end up splattered with the stuff. "Anyhow," she said, putting the bottle back down, "you've got a mother and a father and, um, Bruce. You've got a bunch of people who love you. You're practically self-actualized! At your age!"

While Aunt Elle chattered about self-actualization and some seminar she'd recently attended, I let my mind wander. Fact: She and my mom had had a bad father—except he hadn't been bad in exactly the way the father in the book was. I'd already found out the truth of my mother and Bruce. I could find out the truth of this, too. I could continue to play detective, the detective of my life and my whole family's life, reading the books and the articles, interviewing the witnesses, separating what had really happened from what had been invented, finding out all the stuff that nobody ever wanted to tell me. Maybe the truth was something different from what my mother had written, different from what she'd told me. Maybe the way she behaved was the truth, and what she'd written was the lie, and she really had wanted me, and I hadn't ruined her life.

The thought of it made my heart lift. I smiled at Aunt Elle, who smiled back almost gratefully, looking like herself again, all glint and flash and shine. I let my hand drift down to the shiny gray bag beside me and rested my fingers on top of the tissue paper tucked over the dress, as if it could give me strength or good luck.

"No," said my mom. It was four hours later, that night. The three of us had taken the train home, my mother with her novel, Aunt Elle with her cell phone, and me with the bag in my lap, refusing to let my mom take even a peek, making her wait for what Aunt Elle called "the unveiling."

I was standing in her bedroom, in front of her full-length mirror, with the pink dress on and my mother walking in slow circles around me. "I'm sorry, Joy. It's a beautiful, beautiful dress. But it's just not going to work for your bat mitzvah."

"But why not?" I moaned. I'd piled my hair on top of my head and worn the one pair of heels I had, left over from last year's Class Day. The dress fit me perfectly—not too tight on my chest, not too loose on the hips. The skirt brushed softly at the skin just below my knees, and the silver palettes shimmered, making it look as if the dress were actually made of light.

My mom sat down Indian-style on her bed, with her boobs practically resting in her lap. "The synagogue sent guidelines. Nothing strapless or with spaghetti straps."

"But it came with a wrap!" I ran out of the room to get it. When I came back with the silvery fabric flung around my shoulders, Mom was still frowning.

"It's lovely, Joy, it really is, but I think it's just too grown-up for a thirteen-year-old."

Too grown up. Ha. That was a good one for a woman who'd written about losing her virginity on her parents' pullout couch when she was fifteen—unless that was a lie, too. "But I am growing up. That's the whole point of the bat mitzvah! I'm becoming a woman, and I can't wear a little kid's dress!" I wished Aunt Elle were there to defend me, but she'd vanished almost as soon as we'd gotten home, tossing a wave over her shoulder and telling my parents not to wait up.

"No," said my mom.

I looked at her. She looked back at me, her face tense and unreadable. "What are you so worried about? What do you think's going to happen to me if I wear it? Do you think . . ." I shut my mouth. *Do you think I'll have sex with some guy on a pullout couch?* I'd been on the verge of asking. *Do you think I'll get pregnant accidentally, like you?*

"I'm sorry," she said. "But that dress is not going to work for the kind of day your father and I want you to have."

Which father? I almost said. But I could tell from her face it wouldn't do me any good. I knew this expression. It was the same one she'd worn when she'd told me that I couldn't go to an R-rated movie, that I couldn't go to a party unless she'd talked to the parents beforehand, that she didn't care how late everyone else stayed up, my bedtime on a school night was ten o'clock.

I pulled off the dress and tossed it onto my mom's bed, where it lay in a pathetic puddle of pink. "Honey, I'm sorry, but . . ." I didn't

say anything. *Hypocrite,* I thought, forming the syllables on my lips
and teeth and tongue without any breath behind them as I stomped
down the hallway lined with family pictures: me as a baby, me as a
toddler, me on my first day of nursery school and kindergarten and
seventh grade, past the clock my mother was so proud of and the tables with vases of red and pink roses. *Hy-po-crite.* When she was only
a little older than I was, she'd been having sex, actual sex with actual
boys, and now she was worried that I was showing my shoulders?

In my bedroom, I yanked on jeans and a sweatshirt and pulled
the reply card to Tyler's bar mitzvah out of my underwear drawer.
Downstairs, I hooked Frenchie to her leash, walked out into the clear
night and down to the mailbox at the end of our street, and I stood
there listening until I heard my card land at the bottom.

Thirteen

At ten o'clock that night, Peter came home from the game of Quizzo he played once a month with his fellow diet doctors (*Bariatric physicians,* he'd say whenever he heard me call him and his colleagues "diet doctors." *Please!*). He'd barely made it through the door before I grabbed his arm, put my finger to my lips, and dragged him upstairs. We tiptoed past Joy's closed bedroom door, and I flung open the door to our bedroom and pointed dramatically at the silvery pink dress spread out on the bed.

"Do you see this?" I demanded.

He looked at the dress, then at me, then at the dress again. "It's pretty," he finally said. "Is it for you?"

Oh good God. As if I could get the thing over my hips. Over my hip, singular. "It's Badgley Mischka. They don't serve my kind. This," I said dramatically, "is the dress that our daughter wants to wear to her bat mitzvah."

Peter peered at the garment cautiously, as if it might spring up from the duvet cover and strangle him. "It's nice," he said. Then he saw my face. "It's not nice?"

I took a deep yoga breath. "It's all wrong. Completely and totally wrong."

Peter crossed the room, lifted the dress up by its skinny straps, and spread it over the bench at the foot of the bed. Then he lay down with his head on the pillow and one arm folded behind his head. He used the other one to pat the space beside him. Grudgingly, I lay down next to him. Peter nibbled at my earlobe. "You smell nice," he said.

"Stay on topic," I said, shifting so that my head rested on his chest. "We need to discuss this. We need to have a serious . . . adult . . . discussion . . . oh, that tickles!" I started giggling, my breasts quivering against his side, which he didn't seem to mind. "Can I ask you something? Are we doing this all wrong? I mean, I want the day to have meaning—that's the most important thing, that it means something—but maybe we'll look cheap if we just have a DJ. Maybe we should have dancers. Or we could show a movie of Joy's life. Do you think it's too late to get a videographer? And a producer? And buy the rights to some songs?"

"We should stick with the plan," Peter advised, and unfastened all four of my bra's hooks single-handed, a skill he'd perfected over the years that still never failed to impress me. "A disc jockey, a nice lunch, that photo booth for favors. It'll be fine." He curled his fingers under my chin and looked at me. "Now what's really going on?"

I opened my mouth and found that I couldn't tell him. I couldn't say, *Honey, the truth is that our daughter looks like a thirty-year-old in that dress.* I couldn't add that if Joy were a grown-up instead of a girl, the world was going to hurt her, the way it hurt all of us. And I couldn't even whisper the worst part, which was this: If she was a grown-up, then where did that leave me? Sure, I had a career, even if it was a half-assed, mostly hidden one, but my real work for the past ten years had been keeping my daughter safe. Seeing her in that dress was as good as getting a pink slip and a severance check. *Your work here is done,* the dress said. *Too bad, so sad, don't let the door hit your ass on the way out.* I couldn't tell Peter the specifics of the bargain I'd worked out in my head: Give Joy the kind of party she wanted, the kind that her friends and relatives were having, and gratitude would keep her my little girl for a little bit longer.

I pulled Tyler's bar mitzvah invitation out of the drawer of my bedside table, where I'd stashed it for just such a discussion after rescuing it from the recycling bin. "Take a look."

He picked it up. "Big."

"Big," I repeated. "And this is what she thinks is normal. This is what's normal, in her world. So maybe we . . ." Peter kissed me. My eyes slipped shut as he eased my shirt and bra over my head. Then my eyes flew open again.

"Centerpieces. We need to rethink the centerpieces."

"Shh," Peter said, and kissed me again, easing me onto my back and pressing the length of his body against mine. "No talking for ten minutes."

"Ten minutes?" The giggles were back. "Are we going to do it twice?"

"Pipe down," he whispered. His mouth was hot against my cheek, then my neck, and I closed my eyes and let my heart, that eternally clenched fist, relax and spread its fingers open to the sky.

It was actually closer to forty minutes by the time either of us was interested in conversation again. I made my case as we lay together in the dark, a down comforter over our bodies, the sound of passing cars outside our window.

"So let me make sure I understand you," Peter said in his driest and most sober tone. He was still naked, the lean planes of his chest illuminated by the candle flickering on the bedside table. Post-sex, I'd scrambled into pajama bottoms and a University of Philadelphia T-shirt. I tucked my head into the warm hollow between his neck and shoulder and braced myself for the recap.

"You think," he began, "that bar mitzvahs like Tyler's are the reason the world hates America in general, and Jews in particular, and that if we throw Joy a hundred-thousand-dollar party with dancers and video invitations and costume changes, it means that the terrorists have won."

"More or less," I confirmed.

"However," he continued, "you are also racked with anxiety—"

"And guilt!" I added.

"—anxiety and guilt that we haven't planned sufficiently lavish festivities for our daughter, and you would like me to leave the comfort of my warm bed, go online, and find out whether Aretha Franklin is available to perform a four-song set for the party."

"Aretha doesn't fly," I reminded him. "I don't know whether she'd take a train or a bus or what, but make sure to tell her people that we're willing to pay for transportation." I rolled away and forced myself to stretch, breathing deeply, legs pointed toward the corners of the bed, arms raised above my head.

Peter propped himself on his elbow and looked down at me fondly. "You're nuts."

I sighed. "You're right. Joy's probably never even heard of Aretha Franklin. We should get what's-his-face—you know, the one who looks like Leonardo DiCaprio's brain-damaged little brother? Dustin Tull? Joy loves him."

"Cannie," Peter said patiently. "We are not hiring Dustin Tull to entertain at Joy's bat mitzvah."

"Well, we have to do something." I got out of bed and started pacing.

"How about we just be ourselves?" Peter asked.

I flopped back onto the bed and buried my face in a pillow. "I don't think that's good enough." Then I sat up. "Do you think we should get Prince?"

"Candace," said Peter, resting his warm hand between my shoulder blades.

"Nah. Not Prince. He'd say two and show up at eight, and he's got those assless chaps—"

"Cannie," Peter rumbled. "What is going on?"

I got to my feet and gave him the tip of the iceberg, a little taste of the truth. "I told her that dress wouldn't work. She needs something with sleeves. She wasn't very happy." *And the award for understatement of the evening goes to . . .*

"So why don't we let her wear the dress she wants?" said Peter. He blew out the candle. "She could put something on top of it. A shawl or something."

"A shawl?" I repeated. "Is she ninety? Do we live in Anatefka?"

"You know what I mean."

"A wrap," I muttered.

"A wrap," he said agreeably. "It's not a big deal."

"Our daughter looking like a prostitute in shul is not a big deal?"

"She won't"—he covered his mouth and yawned—"look like a prostitute."

"Maybe not a prostitute," I conceded. "Maybe just an escort. You know, where you'd have to pay her extra for the sex stuff."

"Maybe just a teenager," Peter said.

I closed my eyes, wincing, knowing that we were getting to the heart of the thing.

"We need to let this be about what she wants, too."

I nodded. That sounded very fair.

"She's growing up," he said.

I shook my head wordlessly. *All golden lads and lasses must, like chimney-sweepers, come to dust.* It was inevitable, but that didn't mean I had to like it. Just because he was in such a hurry to push Joy out of the nest and have another baby, and my publisher was dying to have me write another novel, didn't mean I had to go along with any of it.

"It happens," he said, and kissed me gently: my cheek, my neck, my forehead. "It's okay."

A tear slid out of my eye, rolled down my cheek, and plopped on the pillow. *My little girl,* I thought, and swiped at my face with my sleeve. My only one.

FOURTEEN

For my birthday every year the past four years, I have celebrated in exactly the same way. The weekend before, my mom and I go to Toppers for manicures and pedicures. On the weekend of my birthday, we go to the Kimmel Center for a musical, and we have tea at the Ritz-Carlton and eat cucumber sandwiches and tiny eclairs. The weekend after my actual birthday, I can invite two friends to sleep over, and my mom will make me anything I want for dinner. My guests have always been Tamsin and Todd, but this year, because Todd became a man and was off-limits, I invited Tamsin and Amber Gross.

Tamsin and I were in the living room the afternoon of the sleepover when the doorbell chimed. "Come on," I said. I got to my feet.

Tamsin just sat there with her book (*Persepolis 2*) in her lap and a sullen look on her face. "You go," she said. I could tell she wasn't happy about Amber coming over, even though when I'd asked her she'd said it was fine. For the past week, Tamsin and Todd had both been sitting at Amber's table with me. I'd thought that Tamsin would be thrilled when Audrey and Sasha scooched over to make room for her, but Tamsin just ate her mother's discarded Zone burritos and read her book and didn't even try to make conversation—although I suspected that even though she looked like she was reading, she was really listening as hard as she could, in the way she always did. I also suspected she wasn't very impressed with what she'd heard, but so far, she hadn't said anything about it to me.

I opened the door, and there was Amber Gross. I still couldn't quite believe it. It was like the president showing up for dinner and a movie. I hoped that other people in the neighborhood were watching out their windows and seeing this: the most popular girl in the Philadelphia Academy at my door.

"Hi!" She had a pink backpack over one shoulder and yellow elastics on her clear braces. I could have stared at her for hours, taking her in piece by piece, trying to figure out how she got it all so right: how her pants were the perfect length, how she knew to turn the cuffs of her shirt up twice so they didn't look too sloppy or too neat.

"Hi. C'mon in," I said, and led her in.

"Wow," she said, looking impressed as she peeked into my mother's office. She eyed the stacks of *Big Girls Don't Cry* in many languages and lifted the framed picture of my mom and Maxi Ryder, all dressed up on the red carpet, that I'd made sure was prominently displayed. "Wow," she said again, and I felt myself relax until Amber ran her finger along the stacks of black-and-green StarGirl books that took up two shelves.

"Your mom reads these?"

My heart started pounding. StarGirl was a secret—one of my mother's many secrets, now that I thought about it—but why was it my job to keep her secrets for her? What had she done for me lately, except tell me no?

"She reads them," I said. "And she writes them, too."

Amber's eyes widened. "For serious?"

"Yep. That's what she does. But it's kind of a secret, so—"

Tamsin stuck her head into the office.

"Hi, Tamsin!" Amber said.

"Hi, Amber!" Tamsin said in Amber's exact same tone of voice.

I shot Tamsin a warning look. She ignored me, and I led everyone to the living room, where Frenchelle was on the couch with her head and half her body inserted into the bowl of popcorn.

"So what's the plan?" Amber asked once I'd shooed the dog back onto the floor and dumped the contaminated popcorn into the trash.

"Um . . ." I'd thought the plan was going to be dinner and going out for ice cream afterward, but maybe that wasn't exciting enough. "We were just watching TV," I said. "I can make more popcorn."

Amber pulled a pink envelope out of her pocket. "Do you guys want to see my bat mitzvah invitations? They just came in this morning."

We both nodded. Well, I nodded. Tamsin just kind of shrugged. Amber pulled a DVD out of the envelope and slipped it into our player. A minute later, the song "Isn't She Lovely" filled the living room, and Amber's face, in black-and-white profile, filled up the screen. " 'Isn't she lovely,' " Stevie Wonder sang. " 'Isn't she won-der-ful . . .' "

"Wow," I breathed.

"Wow," Tamsin said sarcastically. I glared at her. She shrugged and lifted her book again, but I was sure she was still watching. The TV screen filled with shots of Amber dressed up like different movie stars: in hoopskirts descending a staircase as Vivien Leigh in *Gone With the Wind,* in a little black dress and pearls as Audrey Hepburn in *Breakfast at Tiffany's,* posed on the bow of a ship (I recognized the ship from our class's many field trips to the Independence Seaport Museum) as Kate Winslet in *Titanic* ("Who's the guy?" I whispered, pointing at the man with his arms around Amber's waist, and she said it was her stepbrother, and winked, and told me I'd meet him at the bat mitzvah). A deep-voiced announcer who sounded exactly like the guy who did the movie previews said, "On June eighteenth, Philadelphia, Pennsylvania, becomes . . . Amberwood."

"How'd you do that?" Tamsin asked.

"Do what?" asked Amber.

"Get them to change the name of the whole city just for you?"

"Shh," said Amber, jiggling on the balls of her feet so that her hair bounced along her back. "Here comes the best part." There was a montage of people in body paint, men and women whirling across a stage, flipping and tumbling and fighting each other with flaming swords. "Cirque du Soleil!" Amber said. "That's the entertainment!" The invitation ended with a picture of Amber dressed like Anne Hathaway in *The Princess Diaries* after she has her makeover, with her parents and, I guess, a little brother standing behind her and smiling. "Please join our princess," said Amber's mom. "As we celebrate one of the proudest days of our lives," said her dad. Then the screen filled with the URL of the website where you could RSVP "to the Queen Mother," and then big swirly letters in gold spelled out "THE END."

Amber punched the eject button. "My parents practically ruined the whole thing. They can't stand being in the same room with each other, so it took them forever to get their lines right, and my stupid brother is such a spaz."

"It's totally amazing," I said. Even Tamsin, behind her book, looked awestruck.

My mom carried a fresh bowl of popcorn into the room and peered at the TV screen. "What are you guys watching?"

"My bat mitzvah invitation," said Amber. She waved the remote control at the TV set and the whole thing started again.

My mom sat down on the couch to watch. For once in her life, she seemed out of questions. It seemed like words in general had deserted her. "Well," she said, and "Wow," and then "That's very . . ." and "My goodness!" and "Cirque du Soleil!" Once the credits had rolled, she said, "I should make sure nothing's burning," and hurried into the kitchen with her checks flushed and her eyes sparkling, like she was trying as hard as she could not to laugh.

I picked up the remote control from where Amber had dropped it on the couch arm. "You're so lucky," I told Amber. "There's no way they're going to let me have video invitations. Or entertainment."

"Really? You're not even having dancers?" She shook her head, her straight hair swishing. "I thought it was, like, in the Torah some-where that you had to have dancers."

"I didn't have dancers," Tamsin said from behind her book.

"Yes, you did," I said.

She made a face. "*Todd* had dancers. I was just along for the ride."

Amber ignored her. "Maybe if you, like, get really good grades this quarter, your parents will change their mind," she told me.

"Maybe," I said, and shrugged. The only way I could get better grades was if I wore my hearing aids all the time, which I didn't want to do, although if my grades got any worse, my mother would hire the tutor she was already threatening me with, or demand a meeting with all of my teachers, and she would figure out what was going on with my hearing aids, and I'd be grounded for the rest of my life.

Amber adjusted her headband. "No video invites, no theme . . ." I could feel her evaluating me, deciding whether I was cool enough to deal with or whether, in spite of my secondhand connection to Maxi Ryder, I was a hopeless spaz.

"But I'm going to get a really great dress," I said. "In New York."

Amber perked up. "Really? Which store?"

"My personal shopper and I did some scouting at Bergdorf's," I said casually. "But my mom said I couldn't keep the dress I liked. Too adult or something."

"Bummer," said Amber.

"You've got a personal shopper?" Tamsin said.

"Yes," I said, and gave her a very severe look. "I do." She shrugged again and went back to her book.

"You're so lucky," Amber said. "I have to get everything at the stupid King of Prussia mall." She gave what was, to her credit, a very theatrical shudder, just as my mom stuck her head into the room again and announced that dinner was served.

That night, just like on every birthday night I can remember, my mom made my favorites: spa-baked chicken and buttery biscuits flecked with black pepper and cheddar cheese, canned peaches that I'd helped her pick the summer before, and creamed spinach dusted with nutmeg. For dessert, there were my favorite chocolate cupcakes with peanut-butter frosting and silver sprinkles, served on the antique cake stand that Aunt Samantha had given my mom and Peter for their wedding. My mom stuck a candle in mine even though I'd begged her not to, but at least she didn't sing. Amber licked a little frosting off her pink fingernails, took two dainty bites, then set her cupcake aside. I did the same thing. "Aren't you going to eat that?" Tamsin asked, and when I shook my head, she picked up my cupcake and finished it herself.

After dinner, Amber and Tamsin and I walked to the TLA video store and rented *Titanic,* which was Amber's choice, and *Ghost World,* which was Tamsin's ("You've never seen an R movie?" Amber asked me, with her eyes bugging. "Never ever? God. I got the *Wedding Crashers* special edition for, like, my tenth birthday"). We went back down South Street with Amber on one side of me, talking about dresses, and Tamsin on the other side, absolutely silent, except every once in a while I'd catch her humming a little bit of "Isn't She Lovely." We got lemon water ices at Rita's and ate them on our way home. Then we changed into sweatpants and T-shirts, and for a while I thought everything was going to be okay. My mom and dad moved around the kitchen quietly, running the dishwasher, making coffee. Amber and Tamsin ignored each other, but with the movies on, it wasn't even a problem. At eleven o'clock, my mom said lights-out. We went upstairs and brushed our teeth. I stared straight ahead when Tamsin came out of the bathroom in her *Lord of the Rings* night-shirt. "Nice shirt," Amber said in the exact same tone she'd told Mr. Shoup "Nice tie." Amber was dressed in a sleeveless white night-gown with pink lace trim. Tamsin ignored Amber as she took her usual place in her sleeping bag on the floor beside my bed and yanked the zipper up to her chin. Frenchie hopped onto the foot of my bed and curled in a ball.

Amber unrolled her own sleeping bag. "Oh, no," I said. "You can sleep here." I pointed to my bed. "You sure?" said Amber. I nodded as Tamsin's eyes followed me. Amber tucked herself in, and I spread my blanket on the floor on Tamsin's other side. As soon as I'd turned out the lights, Amber pulled her cell phone out of her backpack and flipped it open, filling the room with a bluish glow. Frenchie lifted her head.

"We should buzz some guys," Amber said. Her braces caught the light from the telephone as she leaned toward me.

"Um . . ." I tried not to talk to people I didn't know on the phone. I was never sure whether my voice sounded right. "I don't know."

Tamsin picked up her book and rolled onto her side. Amber whispered something I couldn't hear. I clicked on my bedside lamp so I could see her lips.

"Come on, Joy," Amber said. "I'll call Martin. Who do you want to call?"

Duncan Brodkey was right on the tip of my tongue, but what would I say to him? What if he was sleeping? What if I sounded really weird? What if he thought I was a guy or something? I felt myself starting to blush.

"You don't say anything," Amber said. "You just hang up."

"What's the point of that?" asked Tamsin, turning a page.

"So they know we're thinking about them," Amber said with an extremely disgusted look. "See, if you do a star-sixty-seven, that blocks caller ID, so they can't tell who's calling."

"How do they know who's thinking about them?" Tamsin asked. "It could be anyone. It could be a wrong number."

"Don't you have a book to read?" Amber asked. She rolled her eyes at me. I bit my lip and said nothing. "What a drip," Amber whispered. I ducked my head, tucking my chin into my chest, and pretended that I hadn't heard her say that, even though she probably knew I had. Worse, Tamsin heard it, too.

· · ·

The next morning I woke up at seven-thirty, got dressed quietly, slipped my hearing aids into place, and shook Amber's shoulder as gently as I could.

"Huh?" she said without opening her eyes.

"Can I borrow your phone for a minute?"

"Sure," she said, rolling onto her side.

"Can I call long-distance?"

She yawned. "Unlimited minutes."

I'd been counting on that. I pulled my copy of *Big Girls Don't Cry* out from under my mattress, stuffed it into my backpack, put Frenchie on her leash, and double-checked that Amber's phone was snug in my pocket. I wasn't sure whether my mother checked my phone to see who I'd been calling, but I knew she kept track of my minutes and how many texts I sent, and it was important that she not know about this particular call. I left a note—*Going to get bagels*—on the kitchen counter and slipped out the front door.

The sky was a deep blue, and a sweet-smelling breeze shook the trees, sending showers of blossoms into my hair and onto Frenchie's back, casting wavering shadows on the sidewalk. I slipped off my jacket and tied it around my waist. "Pretty girl, pretty girl," chanted the homeless guy from his wheelchair on the corner, and the man behind the counter at the bagel place smiled at me and slipped an extra French-toast bagel into my bag. I tucked the bagels under my arm and walked three blocks south, then sat down on a bench underneath a towering dogwood tree in Mario Lanza Park. Frenchie trotted along the perimeter of the dog run, ignoring the other dogs, sticking her nose haughtily into the air when they tried to sniff her. I pulled *Big Girls Don't Cry* out of my purse, opened it to the page where I'd stuck a Post-it, and began to read.

> *My official major at the esteemed Larchmont University was*
> *English literature, but by the third week of freshman year, it*
> *became clear that my real subject of concentration would be Rich*

Bitches' Boyfriends. During classes, on tangled sheets where I'd find crumbs and pizza crust (and once an entire slice of stiffened pepperoni), stolen hours that would always end with me traipsing back across Bell Courtyard with a smirk on my face and my XXL panties in my pocket. I was not the kind of girl who slept over. I was not the kind of girl who was even invited over if there was a roommate nearby. I was a guilty pleasure, an indulgence, the girl who'd do anything. Word got around. As did I. I wasn't in it for the sex itself, which ranged from mediocre to merely okay. What I craved were the precious minutes afterward, cradled in the Rich Bitch's Boyfriend's arms, as shafts of dusty sunlight made their way underneath the university-issued green blinds, and I could imagine the words "I love you." Not that Chas or Trip or Trey or Talbot ever said them. They wouldn't even say hello to me if we passed in the courtyard, or ended up sitting next to each other in Freshman Seminar. You could shout about sex from the rooftops if you were having it with one of the anorexic, horse-faced blondes who seemed to comprise half of Larchmont's Class of '91, but sex with a girl like me was a secret . . . and I plowed through those boys like I'd devoured those long-ago Whitman's samplers my father would bring home before he decided that candy, and then his marriage and his family, were a bad idea.

I couldn't imagine my mother doing things like that: my mother, with her knitting and her committees and her minivan and the three kinds of stain remover standing at the ready in our laundry room. But what I knew of *Big Girls Don't Cry* so far had been sort of true. A tweaked version of the truth. True-ish. If my mom had been that much of a slut in college, I figured there was one person who'd be able to tell me about it.

In the book, my mother's roommate at "Larchmont" was called "Baldwin." In real life, her freshman-year roommate was Alden Langley of Richmond, Virginia. I'd found Alden's new last name (Chernowitz, which seemed like a terrible downgrade) on the Princeton alumni website, which I'd accessed by typing in the code on one of my mother's *Princeton Alumni Weekly*s that I'd found in the recycling bin. Alden didn't list an e-mail address, which would have been my preferred way to communicate, but she did give her telephone number. I let Frenchie sniff around the base of a trash can while I nibbled the edges of a salt bagel. At nine o'clock exactly, I dialed Amber's phone carefully, rehearsing the words in a whisper, praying I'd sound normal. A man answered on the third ring. "Hello?" I almost lost my nerve and hung up. "Hello-oo?"

"Is Alden Langley Chernowitz there?" I asked.

"Who's calling?" asked the man's nasal voice. I could hear kids' voices in the background, which made me feel better. At least I hadn't woken everybody up.

"My name is Joy Shapiro. Alden went to college with my mom."

The man paused. "Hold on," he said. There was a click, and silence, then a woman's voice came on the phone.

"Hello?" The voice sounded puzzled but not unfriendly.

"Hi. My name is Joy Shapiro. My mom is—"

"Cannie," the voice said instantly. "How is she? I was hoping she'd be at the reunion."

"Oh. Oh, I . . . I'm not sure about that." I'd seen the orange-and-black cards and letters arriving all last year. My mom had tossed them straight into the recycling bin. *I'm not ready for that yet,* she'd said. "She's good, I guess."

Alden did not have the kind of voice I'd expected, a snotty rich girl's voice. Instead, her voice was warm and faintly southern, turning my mom's name into "Cann-eh," and "hoping" into "hopin'."

"So what can I do for you?" she asked.

"Um." *Just get it out, Joy,* I told myself. "I read my mom's book?"

Alden didn't say anything, but I thought I heard her inhale.

"And I want to know . . ." *About the sex,* I thought.

"About the earrings," Alden said a little sadly. For a minute I didn't know what she was talking about. Then I remembered page 73 and flipped to it quickly:

My mother dropped me off at Larchmont University with two of everything—two pairs of jeans, two long-sleeved T-shirts, two pairs of shoes. It was a good thing that was all I had, because my roommate Baldwin Carruther's clothes took up all of our remaining closet space and filled the antique armoire she'd placed in our common room, next to the stereo system and on top of the Oriental rug she'd brought up with her from Atlanta. Baldwin was a fourth-generation Larchmontian. Baldwin had fine blond hair that she wore gathered into a ponytail thin as a pencil, and thick forearms from years on her prep school's crew team. While I fussed with my sheets, she set a framed picture next to our bunk beds, a shot of her standing beside her sister in a floor-length gown and elbow-length gloves with a corsage around her wrist. "Was that your prom?" I asked, and she said, "No, my debut." Baldwin had a jewelry box full of strands of pearls, gold bangles, silver hoop earrings, pendants, and charms. "Take anything," she said, waving carelessly at the pirate's chest of treasure.

I never touched her stuff until second semester. I'd been invited to a costume party—really, my entire dorm had been invited—and I was going as Madonna. Baldwin's big gold hoops would be perfect, I thought. I took them out and left a note. When I got back, there was a note on my pillow: RETURN MY EARRINGS, *it said.* THEY ARE HEIRLOOM.

I felt sick as I pulled them out of my ears and put them back on top of her cluttered pile of jewelry: the pearls, the bracelets, the locket engraved with her name. "The rich are different," I said out loud. Then I said, "Heirloom." Baldwin didn't

say much to me for the next two weeks except "good morning"
and "good night," but she clearly hadn't forgotten my trans-
gression. One Saturday night, she stumbled into the room, gig-
gling, with Jasper Jenkins holding her hand. Jasper, my crush
from the school paper, where he was a sports reporter and I was
the copy editor who wrote his headlines and changed his every
"alright" to "all right." I lay there, frozen in place, as she
pulled him up to the top bunk and gave him what was, from the
sound of it, an extremely inept blow job. ("Watch the teeth!" he
hissed more than once.) My hands clenched as I lay there,
equally horrified and aroused, thinking, Note to self: don't bor-
row the rich girl's jewelry, even if she says you can.

"It wasn't earrings," Alden Langley said. "It was a jacket. A
leather jacket. Your mom borrowed it. I got pretty upset."

"Oh."

"But not because it was expensive! It was because it was my
grandfather's. He'd given it to me in his will. It meant a lot to me.
Your mom didn't have any way of knowing that. We had a fight, but
we made up afterward. And I could see . . . I mean, there were girls
like that at Princeton. You know, the rich ones who'd make you feel
like crap about yourself just because you were breathin' their air." She
chuckled again. "You should ask your mama about the girl in our
hall who came to college with her own horses."

"Wow." *No big deal,* I wrote on my Post-it as Alden kept talking.
I wrote *horses.* I wrote, for reasons I didn't understand, *Mama.* "So did
she . . . did she . . ." I couldn't get the words out. *Did she sleep with all*
those boys? Did she walk around with her underwear in her pocket? Was she
really that kind of girl?

Alden chuckled. "Well, it is fiction, honey."

Fiction, I wrote. But just because it was fiction didn't mean
there wasn't truth in there somewhere, glimmering, like coins
at the bottom of a well. *Who was she?* I wondered as I recapped

my pen. *Who was my mother, really? And who am I?* "Hey, is she there?" asked Alden in her honeyed southern voice. "Could I say hello?"

"She's sleeping," I said.

Alden laughed. "Lucky duck. Well, you tell her hi from me, honey. You tell her that I think about her." In the background, a kid whined, "Mo-om," and Alden laughed again cheerfully and said, "Gotta go," and hung up.

FIFTEEN

"Name," said Peter. I was propped against one arm of the couch, and he was facing me with the laptop open and his bare feet in my lap.

"Ooh! Ooh!" I said, waving my hand in the air. "I know that one!"

He looked at me sternly as his fingers rattled over the keyboard. "Dates of birth." More typing as he filled them in. "Address, home phone, work phone, cell phone . . ." He paused. "Occupations."

"Well, you're a diet doctor."

He made a face. "Bariatric physician."

"Yeah, you keep telling yourself that."

"And you?"

I winced. It was Wednesday night. The dishwasher was chugging away, Frenchie was snoozing on her dog bed in the corner, Joy was in her bedroom, and Peter and I were just starting the ten-page application for Open Hearts Surrogate Services. (He'd been the one who'd picked Open Hearts. I, ever the sucker for a good title, had wanted to go with a surrogate and egg-donor business I'd found online called Game Ova.) "Can you just put 'homemaker'? That'll sound good."

He tapped his fingers against the edge of the laptop. "They want to see ten years of tax returns. 'Homemaker' doesn't explain your income."

Good point. "How about 'well-compensated homemaker'? Or 'homemaker who won the lottery'?"

"Candace, it's a very small box." He wiggled his feet. I gave his toes a squeeze, after making sure that Joy was still upstairs. The other night we'd been watching a movie, and when she'd seen me rubbing Peter's feet, she'd given me a look of scorching disgust and walked out of the room.

"Can you do a footnote?"

"What am I, David Foster Wallace?" he asked.

"Can you say former writer? Maybe retired writer?"

"Writer," he said, and typed it in, then stared at me defiantly, as if daring me to tell him otherwise.

When the first copies of *Big Girls Don't Cry* arrived in my mailbox, the hot-pink covers peeking cheekily out of the sober manila envelope, I believed that my whole life was going to change. Years of being a reader, then a reporter, years of dreaming about being a real writer, had trained me to believe that the moment my book entered the world would be the fulcrum on which my life would shift, profoundly and eternally.

The Monday night before the official publication date, Peter took me to Le Bec Fin, where I enjoyed great quantities of wine and told everyone from the coat-check girl to the cheese-cart guy my good news. After dessert, I wobbled down the sidewalk to the Barnes & Noble with Peter's arm around me. I'd stood, swaying and stuffed, in front of the windows, informing uninterested pedestrians, "My book's in there!" (Unfortunately, I hadn't counted on the bookstore still being open, or on the security guard telling me he'd call the cops if I didn't quit smearing the glass.)

The next morning, slightly hungover and extremely nervous, my sister Lucy and I dragged my giant gray suitcase and my tiny daughter (plus her car seat, diaper bag, and assorted food and toddler paraphernalia) to the Philadelphia International Airport for the start of my book tour. We began in Cleveland, where I sat, all dressed up, behind a huge stack of hardcovers. After two hours, I'd managed to sell a grand total of one book. We proceeded to Chicago, where one person showed up at my reading, and I'm fairly certain she was homeless and had just wandered in out of the cold.

In Kansas City, a trembling, white-lipped woman approached me at the podium of a fancy independent bookstore, where they'd had a poster of *Big Girls Don't Cry* in the window, until one of the regulars had complained. "Your mom said she'd kill me if I didn't come, so will you please call her and tell her I was here?" the woman begged. In Miami my nanna shocked me by showing up with her entire bridge club and announcing loudly enough to be heard over the wailing kids in the children's section, "That's my granddaughter the author." Sadly, her pride didn't extend to her urging her friends to pay the $24.95 cover price. "They can take it out of the library," she assured me before leaving a semi-permanent coral kiss mark on my cheek, telling me that my black skirt was "very slimming," and asking my sister whether she'd gotten a real job yet.

In Atlanta, my author escort, the woman my publisher had hired to take me to my events, spent the hour-long trip from the airport telling me all of the details of her husband's death the month before, then got us so abysmally lost that I was an hour late to my own reading. In Milwaukee, an Orthodox Jewish woman in a crooked *shaytel* berated me for having my heroine eat *trayf*. I kept waiting for her to complain about the scene where Allie has sex with a non-Jewish janitor in the synagogue parking lot on Yom Kippur, which had to be more of an affront to the Almighty than the BLT on page 217, but the outrage never came. Apparently, pork was a problem; porking was not.

I buckled Joy's car seat into a different escort's car in a new city every day, driving from bookstore to bookstore to sign copies of my book all afternoon, doing readings every night. After the readings, I'd order a room-service salad, then lie in my hotel bed, on soft cotton sheets, with Joy asleep beside me and my sister rummaging through the minibar, as my thoughts chased around my head. The tour had to be costing a fortune. Except for the night of my nanna's bridge club, attendance at the readings had yet to crack the double digits, which meant that *Big Girls* probably wasn't doing very well. Would my publisher hold me responsible? Would they ask for the advance back? Did that ever happen?

Not that I was particularly surprised. I had expected *Big Girls Don't Cry* to be like a radio signal at the far end of the dial that you could tune in to only on clear, starless nights. I had thought the book would be passed between friends or sisters or mothers and daughters; that my sisters, the unlucky-in-love, unhappy-in-their-own-skin big girls, would find it in the library or on the shelf at a rented summer house, or at a tag sale or a flea market; that they would read it and be comforted. That would be enough for me. I just had to hope it would be enough for my publisher.

I was in Seattle on a Wednesday afternoon, signing copies of my book at the bookstore's information desk and answering patrons' questions about the location of the restrooms and whether I knew the name of a book about love with a red or possibly dark blue cover, when my cell phone trilled and the screen flashed my agent's number.

"Hey, guess what?" I told Larissa, scooping Joy into my arms before she pulled down an entire display of Curious George books. "Five people came last night! And all of them looked like they lived indoors!"

"Never mind that. I am faxing an entire copy of next week's *New York Times Book Review,* which I have obtained with great difficulty and at great expense, to your hotel," Larissa announced.

"Why?" The *Times* rarely reviewed my kind of breezy female-centered book, unless they were romans à clef that cast some thinly veiled Manhattan bigwig as the villain (in those cases, the *Times* would typically hire one of the thinly veiled Manhattan bigwig's lieutenants to write the takedown).

"Just wait! You'll see!"

I bought a sticker book for Joy and a nonfat Frappuccino for my sister, and my escort took us back to the five-star hotel in her SUV, which was so far off the ground that she kept a stepstool in the back-seat for elderly authors. The entire book review, in fax form, was waiting for me at the front desk. I paged through it slowly. The cover piece was a review of a 160-page short-story collection, *Budapest Nights,* by Daniel Furstmann Friedlander, who'd been written up the week before in a ten-page profile in *The New Yorker* that had made much of his boyish good looks and charming Russian accent. Weird. I'd known Dan back in college, when he'd had two names and no accent at all.

On page three, a cultural critic from one of the slim liberal glossies was calling a columnist from a rival magazine an asstard. On page twenty-six, the best-seller column was ignoring the actual best-seller list in order to tout a book currently available only in Germany, in its original German. I was on the verge of calling Larissa to ask what I was missing. Then the best-seller list caught my eye. And there it was: number 11. *A Philadelphia singleton makes the journey from anonymous sexual encounters and family trauma to motherhood,* read the summary. I leaned against the registration desk in shock. "Wow." My sister, who was still going by Lucy back then, snatched the pages from my hand, then squealed in triumph. "Congratulations," said my escort, and she gravely shook my hand.

Peter sent flowers. My publisher sent champagne, which my sister swiftly commandeered. Larissa sent chocolates and a rubber ducky for Joy. *People* sent a reporter, a photographer, and, thank God, a makeup artist to my next tour stop for an interview, which ran with the *People*-mandated picture of Joy and me jumping on yet another hotel bed, above the inevitable caption: "Happy Endings." A New York City magazine, *24/7,* dispatched their star reporter, a terrifyingly thin middle-aged woman with her skin stretched over her cheekbones so tightly that I could see the veins underneath, to do a profile during my three-day layover in Los Angeles. The woman launched into her interview by snapping open her notebook and snarling, "Did you write your book because you wanted people to *like* you?"

"No," I said once I'd caught my breath. "No, that's why I'm pro-miscuous."

My publisher extended my tour to another four cities: Denver, Albuquerque, San Francisco, then back to L.A. By the night of my last reading in Pasadena, I was out of underwear, I'd lost every single one of Joy's Polly Pocket dolls, and I wanted nothing more than to go home, sleep for a week or so, and plan my wedding.

"Someone special's here to see you!" the bookstore manager car-oled, leading me out of her office toward the podium as my sister led Joy off to find the Eloise books.

"Oh?" Maxi, I figured. My movie-star friend had told me she'd be away on a reshoot in Vancouver (which, she swore, could be made to look an awful lot like New York), but maybe she'd made a special trip back. I scanned the crowd hopefully. Twenty people. Not bad. "Hi," I said cheerfully, pushing away my weariness, putting on my meet-the-public smile. "Thanks so much for coming tonight. I'm going to read a little bit from the very beginning of *Big Girls Don't Cry.*" I held up the book, per Larissa's instructions, so that everyone could get a good look at the cover. Not that anyone could miss it, given that it featured big, barely clad breasts on either side of a whipped-cream-topped sundae, with a maraschino cherry sliding suggestively into the cleavage. Not exactly an understated literary look. Daniel Furstmann Friedlander's book had featured a grainy black-and-white shot of a Czechoslovakian castle. *Oh, well,* I thought. *Maybe next time.* "Then, if you have any questions . . ." My voice trailed off as I caught sight of the man hovering by the back row without taking a seat. He wore a dark blue suit and his curly dark hair was shot with silver. Everything about him seemed to gleam: his gold watch and wedding band, his glasses and his teeth. My heart stopped as my father raised his hand.

"Cannie," he said, his voice low and intimate, as if we were the only two people in the bookstore.

I swallowed hard, forcing my tongue to move, my mouth to open. "Hi, Dad."

A murmur moved through the room, probably driven by the people who'd read the book, who'd remembered the horrible father it had described. I forced myself to flip open the cover and began to read, from memory, the words I'd started with long ago.

Of all the men who've fucked me up and let me down, my father was the first and worst. Drew Blankenship was a close second. When I opened my copy of Cosmo, *sucked in, as always, by the promise of dropping a fast ten pounds, mastering the makeup tricks of the stars, and learning some exotic new position that would make him moan and whine and beg like a dog for more, I was astonished to see Drew's byline at the top of a piece titled "Big Big Love."* Drew wrote an article? *I thought.* I was the one who hustled freelance assignments. I was the one who'd kill to have my byline in a national magazine. Up until that moment, I'd thought that Drew's fondest dream was to someday grow a marijuana plant that would appear in* High Times. *It seemed, I realized, scanning the article as my heartbeat sped up and my hands went icy, that I'd gotten it wrong.*

The crowd laughed in all the right places, gasped appreciatively when it was revealed that "Big Big Love" was about Allie's plus-size figure (*God knows it couldn't have been referring to Drew's equipment,* I'd written. *Poetic license will only get you so far.*) As I read, I sneaked glances at my father, who was still standing in the back row, his hands in his pockets, his face unreadable. If that line about being fucked up by a father had bothered him at all, I didn't see it. I turned my eyes back to the page and concentrated, as hard as I could, on my little sister and Joy, safe in an oversize armchair with their backs to the reading. *Keep her away, keep her away, keep her away from him.* Blood roared in my ears, and my hands were slick with sweat. "Questions?" I managed.

A woman in the front row raised her hand. "I've been working on a novel," she began. My mouth moved without my having to think about it as I answered the questions about writing a book and finding an agent and twisting truth until it was fiction. My breath caught in my throat as Joy toddled down the aisle with *Eloise* in her hands, heading right for me. "Excuse me," I murmured. "Lucy?" I said into the microphone. My sister hurried out of the children's section. Fast—but not fast enough. As the crowd murmured, my father bent down and scooped Joy into his arms, and Joy, who usually shrieked at the sight of a strange man—assuming, often correctly, that the strange man was yet another doctor who'd want to stick her with a needle—snuggled against him and flung her arms around his neck. My heart stopped.

"Hi, kitten," my father said.

"Kitten!" Joy repeated, and clapped her hands in delight. I stood there, frozen and numb, unable to move or believe what I was seeing as my father pulled a little silver camera from his pocket and, with a smile, handed it off to another patron who happily snapped their picture. Finally, I got my legs moving. "Joy," I said, holding out my arms.

"Kitten!" Joy chortled.

"Congratulations," my father said. He set Joy gently on the ground. By the time I'd blinked away my tears and picked up my daughter, he was gone, and I was left standing there, heart pounding, legs numb, equal parts furious and bewildered. After all these years, why would my father show up now? I sat down in an armchair and closed my eyes. Never mind. We were leaving first thing in the morning. I could figure it out at home.

The next day we made it back to Philadelphia, to my cozy row house and to Peter, whom I'd missed with a pain that, by the last week on the road, had felt like a permanent stitch in my side. Two of the wheels had fallen off my suitcase. My sister was limping after an injury sustained when she'd tried to climb into Joy's Pack 'n' Play ("I wanted," she explained, with a certain tipsy dignity, "to see if I could fit"). The garden I'd planted before I'd left was choked with weeds;

my baskets of pansies and petunias were dying from lack of water. The book had erased an entire season.

But as the in-print flavor of the week, not to mention the de facto poster girl for every woman size fourteen and up, I did come home to a nice consolation prize: a stack of offers for my consideration, each one weirder than the next. Did I want, for example, to be the new face of Weight Watchers? "But I'm fat!" I spluttered to Larissa, who replied, "I suspect that once they're done with you, you won't be." Did I want to endorse low-calorie cookies, fat-free ice cream, plus-size maternity wear? (No, no, and, tempting, but no.)

My credit-card company upgraded me to the White Card, the rare and fabled instrument that had no spending limits and offered all manner of upgrades and perks. A doctor in Illinois offered me a free gastric bypass. A plastic surgeon in Pittsburgh pledged a gratis nose job. A third cousin whom I'd met twice asked for a loan to start a combination personal training business/smoothie bar. (I told him no but added that if he was interested in having either his nose or his stomach bobbed, I'd be happy to hook him up.)

The strangest pitch came from a company asking if I'd be their on-campus spokesperson for tampons.

"Would I have to visit colleges dressed up as a giant tampon?" I asked Larissa.

I could imagine her behind her antique maple desk, sitting in her padded pink chair, flipping the pages. "I don't think so," she said crisply.

I persisted. "Could I dress up as a giant tampon if I wanted to?"

"Um . . ."

"Does this offer have strings attached?"

Larissa sighed. "Any more period-related humor?"

"Well," I said meekly, "it is a lot to absorb."

And there wasn't much time to absorb it. My publisher had arranged for another half-dozen interviews once I was home. Prior to selling my book, before I'd had my baby, I'd spent years covering entertainment for *The Philadelphia Examiner*. I'd figured that almost a decade of making sausage might have prepared me for my own trip through the grinder. I was sadly mistaken. I'd open the door to my house to my former colleagues—fresh-faced or zit-smattered; harried working mothers with their cell phones buzzing; ambling, long-in-the-tooth good ol' boys who'd bounced from paper to paper and magazine to magazine. I'd show them around my house, tell them stories about the book tour, let them meet Joy. Most of the time it worked out well, even if *Publishing Today* was unimpressed by the contents of my refrigerator (too much butter and not enough fresh fruit for the reporter's taste), and the Chicago weekly's headline had been the regrettable HEFTY GAL IS QUEEN OF MODERN ROMANCE. ("Hefty?" I'd railed to Peter, waving the clipping for emphasis. "Hefty? For the record, 'Hefty' is a trash bag. I am festively plump.")

Then one Sunday morning I'd opened my door and found that the *Examiner* wasn't there. "Did you get the paper?" I called.

Peter shook his head without meeting my eyes. "No paper today," he said. My heart sank. The paper always came, which meant that he must have gotten up early and disposed of it. And I knew why. The week before I'd sat down with the reporter the *Examiner* had hired to replace me, a meek-voiced girl who'd shown up with a gro-cery-store bouquet of carnations. "I love kids," she'd announced upon meeting my daughter. "You know, if you ever need a sitter . . ." I'd thanked her while quietly arriving at the conclusion that the *Exam-iner* wasn't paying her as much as they'd paid me. The interview had lasted all of half an hour and had consisted mostly of questions about how I'd found the time to write a book while working for the paper, how I'd found an agent for the book, and whether my agent might have time to read her book, now that I'd told her how to find time to write one.

Peter stood behind me, his hands warm on my shoulders. I took a deep breath, bracing myself. "How bad?" I asked.

"You probably shouldn't read it."

"Come on. My ex-boyfriend called me fat in *Moxie.* What could be worse than that?"

There was an agonizing pause. "I don't think—" Peter began.

The telephone rang, and I snatched it. "Hello?"

"Why did you tell the *Examiner* that I went to rehab?" my sister shrieked.

My mouth fell open. "Why did I what?"

"Why . . . did . . . you . . . tell . . . the . . . *Examiner* . . . that I went to REHAB?" She sounded angrier than I'd ever heard her. "And if you had to mention it, how come you didn't say that I just did it to meet guys?"

"I don't know what you're talking about. I never told that reporter anything about you!"

My sister's voice got even louder. "Why not? Don't you know I need the press?"

"Hang on," I said, plugging my laptop into the outlet on the kitchen wall and ignoring Peter's urgent head shakes. "I haven't read the story yet." I loaded the page while my sister continued to shriek in my ear. Then I gulped. SPILLING SECRETS, read the headline. HOW FORMER EXAMINER REPORTER CANDACE SHAPIRO TURNED HER FAMILY'S DIRTY LAUNDRY INTO GOLD.

"Spilling secrets?" I said out loud. "Dirty laundry?" The call waiting beeped. "Hang on," I said. "Hello?"

"Candace," barked my brother.

"Josh," I replied as the story loaded. "Are you calling to ask why I told the paper about Lucy going to rehab?"

"No," he said. "I just want to know why you told them I got arrested for violating the city's open-container law when I was fifteen."

"I didn't." I scanned the article. *Candace Shapiro sits on the couch of her posh Center City row house, plump legs not quite crossed, a grin creasing her fleshy face, as if she can't quite believe the good fortune that's fallen into her lap.* "Oh, good God." I kept reading, and there it was: Josh's arrest (he'd been busted on a friend's front lawn with a Merry Berry wine cooler), and my sister's brief stint in rehab. The piece not only reported the amount of my advance, it also printed our street address and the price of our house, something I'd done to only one of my subjects, an Eagles quarterback embroiled in a particularly bitter divorce. " 'A rumpled sundress—size sixteen, Lane Bryant—lies on top of Shapiro's unmade bed, the $399.99 price tag still attached,' " I read out loud. "Okay, first of all, that sundress was $39.99!"

The doorbell rang. "I'll get that," Peter said as my call waiting beeped again.

"Lucy?"

"This would be your mother," said my mother in her sweet, placid voice. "Now, Cannie, you know that I'm happy to provide you with material, but I have to ask whether it was really necessary to tell the reading public that I met Tanya in the hot tub at the JCC?"

"Oh, God," I groaned. "Mom, I didn't—"

Joy's bedroom door swung open, and my daughter, naked except for a tricornered hat and a pair of Ariel underwear with a toothbrush stuck in the waistband, made her way down the stairs. "Pirate Joy!"

"Let me call you back," I told my mother. I hung up the phone and gave Joy a kiss. "Go get dressed, boots. Pants and shirt."

"Scurvy dogs," she said sadly, and padded back to her bedroom.

Peter came back into the kitchen with a wrapped brown-paper package in his hands. "Someone baked you cookies," he said, swiftly dumping the package into the trash can and washing his hands. "I don't think we should eat them."

"Ya think?" I replied, reading the article in cringing snatches, feeling, with each word, a little bit more as if I'd been hit in the midsection by a Septa bus. " 'Neurotic and bitter'? 'Compulsively confessional'? She wasn't around me long enough to know how crazy I really am. And she got Joy's name wrong! It's not Joyce!"

Joy's bedroom door swung open again and she proceeded slowly down the stairs. She'd swapped her pirate's hat for a cowboy hat and had a belt and two plastic six-shooters slung around her naked belly. "Cowgirl Joy!"

"Pants," I said firmly. "Shirt." Usually, we started our Sunday mornings with a walk to Old City for coffee and croissants at the Metropolitan Bakery. Unlikely now, I realized. No way would I be showing my fleshy, possibly crazy face in public.

"Tarnation," Joy said, and wandered back upstairs. I stared at the page, then read out loud, " 'Shapiro's house is crammed with evidence of a three-year-old, from crushed crackers ground into the carpet to a half-assembled plastic shopping cart in the living room. On our afternoon together, her dog, Nifkin, is shedding on the couch, and daughter Joyce is nowhere in sight. Shapiro explained that her mother has been picking up the slack during the publicity explosion. "Sitters, my sister, my mom's girlfriend, the barista at Starbucks, whoever I can get," she laughed, launching into a story about how her fresh-out-of-rehab sister managed to lock Joyce in a hotel room during her book tour.' "

I slammed the laptop shut. Turned out there actually was something that hurt worse than being called fat in print. "I'm a bad mother?" I buried my face in my hands. "I don't get it. She seemed so nice! And how did she find out about my mother and the hot tub?"

"Cannie," Peter said gently, "didn't you tell that story to everyone in the newsroom?"

I hung my head. It was true. I *had* told the story to everyone in the newsroom. I'd usually accompanied it with sound effects I'd make with a straw and a can of Diet Coke. "It wasn't for public consumption." I slumped into a kitchen chair, wincing as something squished underneath me. Best-case scenario: Play-Doh. Worst-case scenario: leftover grape. "And all this stuff about my family!" I squirmed in shame. "She didn't even ask me about them! All she wanted to know was whether I wrote in longhand or on a laptop." I blinked back tears. "Why did she do this?" I asked. "I would never have done this."

Peter raised an eyebrow.

"I wouldn't have," I insisted. "If I had to interview a reporter who'd sold a book, I would have come back, done the story, seethed quietly at my desk, and then gotten drunk to ease the pain."

Peter lifted both eyebrows.

"Well, okay, maybe I would have done this to Bruce," I grumbled. "But he left me! He abandoned me! Pregnant and alone! The man turned my life into a bad country-and-western song, and I deserved to . . . you know . . ." *Have my revenge,* my mind whispered. "Tell my story," I said instead.

"Fair enough," he said. "But then I don't think you get to be angry when people tell stories about you."

"Yes, I do! What did I ever do that was so bad? Who did I knock up and then ditch? When did I ever . . ." I pressed my fists against my eyes. The doorbell rang. Nifkin barked shrilly. "You should get that," I said. "It's probably DFS." I'd said it as a joke, but I could picture it happening—a couple of stern-faced social workers with clipboards and questions and perhaps even a police officer standing at a discreet distance behind them: Had I really entrusted the care of my medically fragile child to my sister, who was no stranger to a late-night raid on a minibar? Had I actually left Joy with a barista? With a stranger? And if I was such a vengeful, ugly monster, how could Peter love me? I groaned out loud, reopened the laptop, and looked down at the picture they'd run in lieu of my author photo: a snapshot from some *Examiner* staffer's going-away party, in which I was standing in front of my cubicle with my mouth wide open, breasts bulging in an ill-advised ribbed sweater, double chin on display, lifting a forkful of frosting to my lips. *The Girl with the Most Cake,* the caption read.

Peter pressed one warm hand to the back of my neck, pulling me close. "Don't worry," he said. "Sticks and stones."

I nodded wordlessly, knowing there was nothing I could do. Sure, I could call up the reporter or the editor who'd handled the piece—one of the legions of short, pasty-pale middle-aged men who comprised the *Examiner*'s middle management, the kind of guy who gave the impression of having spent decades of his life getting sand kicked in his face before rising high enough in the ranks to work out his insecurities on a generation of rookie reporters. I could call him up yelling. I could appeal to his better nature. I could even cry. But it wouldn't matter. I knew what he'd say. *Of course we put in that stuff,* he'd tell me a little impatiently. *It's juicy. It's a good story.* That was what I was now. A good story. All I'd wanted to do was write them. Now, without any intention, it seemed that I'd become one.

"Ignore it," said Maxi, who'd become my counselor on all things fame-related.

"How?" I asked. "My brother's not speaking to me. My sister wants ten thousand dollars for bigger breast implants before she'll forgive me. And when I looked myself up on the Internet this morning, some alternative weekly called Joy my crotch dropping."

"Ignore, ignore, ignore," Maxi chanted in her elegant accent. "Step away from the computer. It's the devil's tool. One, nobody reads past the headlines; two, the people who do don't remember what they read; and three, newspapers don't really matter anymore."

I plopped down on the couch and closed my eyes. Given that I used to work for a newspaper, that wasn't especially comforting.

"Did you happen to see the Akron paper?" I asked.

"Seeing as how I don't live in Akron," Maxi began.

"The reviewer called me frivolous! And ditzy! This from a man who wrote a social history of the Sno-Kone!"

"Honestly, what did you think they'd write?" Maxi asked. "Good things happen to good person? Excellent book is wonderful read? How's that going to sell any newspapers? You should just be glad they think you're worth writing about at all."

I agreed, knowing that she was right. Cynical, but right.

"Water under the bridge," Maxi continued. "Look forward, not back."

"But it's crazy!" I said. "This website's saying that I'm . . . Wait, let me find it." I scrolled through the paragraphs of dense, punctuation-free text (punctuation, I supposed, being just one more tool of the patriarchy). " 'A writer of dangerous sexist piffle a lip-sticked proponent of right-wing family values.' What does that mean? How am I right wing?"

"That is strange," Maxi agreed. "You rarely wear lipstick. Did you get the stuff I sent you?"

"Yes. Yes, I did. Thank you." After one of the Los Angeles week-lies had run my picture at a reading, Maxi had sent me a care package that was embarrassingly heavy on the concealer cream. "I just don't get this. My book is 'hurting America'?" I quoted. "How am I hurt-ing America? I drive a minivan!"

Maxi considered. "Well, you could drive your minivan into someone."

I laughed in spite of myself. "Don't think I haven't consid-ered it."

"Just stop reading it," Maxi said. "Go swimming or something. You have a life, and a beautiful little girl, and a man who loves you. You'll be fine."

I didn't go swimming. I did throw myself into homemaking with a fervor that would have shamed Martha Stewart. I cleaned and scrubbed and sorted; I baked muffins and made cheese from scratch. I planted clematis and roses, chosen as much for their names as their perfume or their blossoms: Silver Star and Double Delights, Day Breakers and Paradise, Golden Showers and Rambling Red, Funny Face and Kiss Me. I wasn't writing, mostly because I wasn't letting Joy out of my sight. I'd load her diaper bag with string cheese and sandwiches and sippie cups each morning, and make the rounds of the zoo, the parks, the playgrounds and spraygrounds, the kiddie concerts and the aquarium and the Please Touch Museum all day long. Maxi's prediction had come true: Nobody I saw ever mentioned the story. Then again, my friends were all too kind to bring it up, and most of the mothers I knew were too busy to even glance at anything besides the headlines, assuming they picked up a paper at all.

One Sunday morning in August, while Peter was sleeping late,

Joy and I were in the living room. Joy was crouched in front of her dollhouse, and Nifkin was curled into his dog bed, keeping watch, when the telephone rang. NUMBER UNAVAILABLE, read the display. I grimaced. Lately I'd been letting Peter answer the phone and the door, and sift through my e-mail, but I didn't want to wake him. *Stop being a wimp,* I told myself, and lifted the receiver. "Hello?"

"Cannie." My father's voice on the telephone was a wondrous thing, rich and silky and resonant. I recognized it instantly, just by the sound of my name.

My own voice was high and wavering. I sounded like a silly girl who'd gotten called on in math class and couldn't begin to guess at the right answer. "Yes?"

"I'm calling to congratulate you." He paused. "Best-selling author," he intoned.

I tried to sound businesslike. "What can I do for you?"

"I'm glad you asked. We didn't really get a chance to talk at your reading." True enough, given the speed with which he'd vanished, along with the added precaution I'd taken of having the manager whisk me out the service entrance.

I got off the couch and started to pace from the front door to the back, with Nifkin clicking along behind me like a tiny, anxious, black-and-white-spotted stenographer, while my father explained. An opportunity had come his way, a chance to increase his income exponentially by joining a partnership with a few other surgeons who were launching their own practice . . .

"How much?" My voice had gone straight past businesslike to flat.

His laughter was startled. "I always did admire that about you," he said. He laughed some more, then the laughter sputtered off into coughing. "You cut right to the chase. Cut right to the quick."

No, that was you, I thought. "How much?" I repeated.

"Now, Cannie," he cajoled. "Is that any way to talk to your old man?"

I said nothing.

"A hundred thousand ought to do it," he said easily, as if asking for change for the parking meter.

I shook my head incredulously. "I don't have a hundred thousand dollars!"

His voice grew truculent. "That's not what I hear. Didn't the *Examiner* say something about a six-figure advance? Didn't your house cost—"

I cut him off. "My advance was split into five chunks. My agent takes a commission, and I pay taxes, and I'm responsible for a child." I shook my head. Never mind the bookkeeping. I didn't owe him anything, least of all an explanation.

As if reading my mind, he said, "You might want to consider where you got your story from. The heroine's life . . . the things she experienced . . ."

"Dad." The word sat like a dead bug in my mouth. "Do not tell me that you think you deserve to be rewarded for abandoning your wife and kids."

"It's hardly far-fetched," he said, as pompous as a professor. "I gave you a voice. I gave you a story to tell."

"You . . . You actually think . . ." I sucked in a deep breath. Joy was staring at me. I forced myself to smile, carrying the phone into the kitchen, away from the couch and the coffee table, spread with the Sunday paper, a slice of toast cut into Joy's preferred triangles, her doll tucked tenderly into its cradle. "You gave me nothing. When I came to see you in Los Angeles, when I was pregnant, you didn't want to know me. And now that I've got money, you want it, because you think you deserve credit for what I've written?"

There was a brief, curdled pause. "Maybe I'll come and see you someday," he said, his voice casual, musing, and not—to the casual listener, to a stranger—threatening at all. But I could hear the menace underneath the silky tone. "Maybe I'll come visit your little girl."

My breath gusted out of me. My courage went with it. "Please," I said. "Please just leave us alone."

I put the phone back in its cradle and sat on the couch with my head in my hands. "Mama?" said Joy. She patted my knees with her hand. "Dolls now?"

"Dolls now," I said, and slid onto the floor, forcing my fingers to move and my lips to curve into a smile for my daughter.

Ten minutes later, Peter came downstairs in his weekend jeans, smelling of soap and the cologne Joy and I had picked out for Father's Day.

"Good morning," he said, rifling through the stack of papers for the crossword puzzle. "Who called?"

I went to him. I wrapped my arms around his waist and leaned against him, my ear to his chest. Then I said, in the inimitable words of boxer Roberto Duran after he'd been beaten to the consistency of steak tartare, *"No más."*

"What?"

"No más. No more. I'm done." It wasn't Bruce writing about me in *Moxie,* telling the world that I was fat. It wasn't the piece in the *Examiner* telling the world that I was the bitter, neurotic product of a dysfunctional family who'd grown up into a bad mother (and was still fat, in case anyone needed reminding). I could survive public humiliation. I'd done it before. A few weeks of carbohydrates and stiff drinks, long walks with friends or my mother, and I'd stop feeling like the whole world was laughing at me. The truth, as I'd learned post-*Moxie,* post-Bruce, was that most people were too caught up in their own humiliation and heartache to spend too much time worrying about a stranger's. It was Joy: Joy, and Peter, and the idea that I'd put them at risk. I'd been angry. I'd written the book because I was angry, because I'd wanted revenge—but it was revenge out of all proportion. It was as if Bruce had lobbed a rock through my window, and I'd responded by dropping a bomb on his entire town, killing everything that lived there, and then, just for fun, salted the earth so that nothing would ever grow again. I'd set out to hurt him, the way he'd hurt me. I'd behaved badly (*like my father,* a voice inside of me whispered) and now I was reaping the consequences. Plus, I knew

how to get over public shaming . . . but how did any daughter survive a long-estranged parent reappearing to treat her like an ATM and threatening to come visit her little girl?

The doorbell rang and I stiffened, thinking again that it would be the social workers from DFS, or maybe just some random crazy who'd gotten my address from the paper, or maybe my father in a black suit, reaching for Joy. What was to stop him from showing up at Joy's summer camp or her nursery school, carrying the photograph he'd snapped, producing his driver's license, showing that he had the same last name that I did? *I'm Dr. Shapiro,* he'd say. He'd call her "kitten," and she'd laugh, leaping into his arms, and then . . . I buried my face in Peter's neck and squeezed my eyes shut. No more. *No más.* I'd risked enough. I was done.

After six weeks of ignoring my agent's telephone calls and e-mails, I finally locked my bedroom door, sat cross-legged on top of my favorite quilt, picked up the telephone, and, with Nifkin curled on the pillow beside me, told Larissa that I was now an ex-writer.

She didn't believe me. "Cannie," she said. "A writer writes. It's what you do. What are you going to do with yourself? Be class mother every day?"

I bit my up. Just lately, I had been spending a lot of time at Joy's summer camp. Last week, the delivery guy had asked me to sign for the paychecks. "Actually," I said, "I have another idea." And just like that, as if I'd reached into the pocket of the winter coat I hadn't worn in months and found a folded fifty-dollar bill, I did.

"Please tell me it's a book," my agent pleaded.

"Sort of," I said, and I laid it out for her. In addition to contemporary fiction, serious nonfiction, and the diet books that typically supported Categories One and Two, my publisher was home to the StarGirl series.

Once upon a time—1978, to be exact—*StarGirl* had been a blockbuster movie. Since then it had spawned an empire of sequels, prequels, comic books, action figures, lunch boxes, board games, bedsheets, birthday party favors, and X-rated fan fiction on the Internet. Valor Press published a line of paperbacks detailing the continuing adventures of the characters the movie had introduced all those years ago.

StarGirl, whose real name was Lyla Dare, had been born between planets on a long-haul cruiser. Her scientist mother had been impregnated the last time her ship had made planetfall—by whom, or by what, and in what manner, Lyla never knew. Her star cruiser was plundered by pirates and crash-landed on a hostile planet (icecaps on one end, desert on the other, plenty of dinosaur-like predators in between). Her mother perished instantly. Baby Lyla was adopted by a tribe of lycanthropes (wolves who could talk and who were, in 1978, truly a triumph of costume and makeup) and raised as one of theirs. When she was twelve, a landing party came to chart her planet and discovered little Lyla, naked except for a loincloth of lion skin, a necklace of teeth, and a rat's skeleton braided in her hair. She'd been tranq'd after she kicked two members of the landing party and bit the pinkie finger off a third. She was cleaned up, given clothing, and taken to an institution on a nameless planet known only as the Academy, where her minders quickly discovered her telepathic abilities and formidable strength. They trained her as an assassin and set her loose to police the galaxy.

Lyla Dare was six feet tall, with blond hair like spun gold that cascaded down to the firm curves of her bottom. She had wide-set violet eyes, a lush mouth, cheekbones that could cut glass, and a body that could start wars (and, in at least three separate adventures, had). She was a telepath who could read minds with a touch and could heal with a kiss. Better still, Lyla took shit from no one. She flew a custom-fitted space cruiser called *Angel* (named after her departed mother) and, for years, had been hopelessly in love with a man who'd taken a vow of celibacy to save his brother's life, a man who loved her desperately but couldn't even kiss her.

It was all very Heathcliff and Cathy on the moors, very Meggie and Father Ralph on Drogheda. Teenagers ate it up, and Lyla Dare, intergalactic ass-kicker, remained a guilty pleasure for a number of grown women who should have been old enough to know better, women who should have, according to the critics, been occupying their minds with some improving piece of literature but preferred Lyla's adventures. When I was a kid, I'd lived for those books, riding my bike to the chain bookstore in the mall the day they were published, retreating to my bedroom to spend a few happy afternoons lost in Lyla's world, where the bad things that happened were completely unlike any bad things that happened to me.

"I want to write StarGirl books," I said.

There was a humming on the other end of the line. When Larissa spoke, her voice was faint. "Please tell me you're kidding."

"Not kidding. Do you think they'd let me?"

"Candace." I could hear the effort it was taking her not to scream, or fly to Philadelphia and hire a pair of strong men who'd hold me upside down by my ankles and shake me until another book fell out. "It's not a question of whether they'd let you. The StarGirl books are all written pseudonymously."

"I know." As far as I was concerned, that was half of the appeal.

"And do you know what Valor pays per book? It's peanuts!" Larissa squeaked. "Do you want your dog to have to go back to eating generic kibble?"

"I'll take it," I told her. "If they'll let me."

Silence ensued. "I'll see," she said at last, "if I can get them to publish them under your name."

"No! I want to be J. N. Locksley," I said, kicking my quilt to the floor and getting to my feet. For the first time in weeks, I could imagine a future that didn't leave me terrified or dizzy with guilt. I could write StarGirl novels. I could work, contribute, keep busy, and do it all without the world finding out, or paying any attention. I scooped up three half-empty mugs of tea and carried them to the kitchen with Larissa sighing in my ear.

"Let me make some calls," she said.

By the next morning, I had a deal. Larissa had even gotten the publisher to pay me the princely sum of fifteen thousand bucks per book, and to extend the normal six-week turnaround time to three months. "Just promise me this isn't forever."

"Of course not!" I said. "It's just until things calm down a little bit."

"Promise," she repeated.

I promised. And so what if I had my fingers crossed behind my back? Just because I'd promised myself—not to mention my husband and my daughter—that I would never put them or me through the experience of publishing a novel under the name of Cannie Shapiro ever again, there was no reason to tell Larissa that very minute. In a few years, or maybe even a few months, she'd find other clients and make them big-money deals. Other books would move to the best-seller list. My father wouldn't bother us. The world would pass me by. We would be safe.

The very next week, a six-hundred-page concordance with background information on all things StarGirl arrived via FedEx, along with a black binder containing a typed two-page outline for the book I was going to write. Beginning, middle, end. How I got from one to the other was entirely up to me.

And that's how it's been for the last ten years. I write four Star-Girl novels a year, books that never get written up, never get reviewed, and sell only a sliver of what *Big Girls Don't Cry* did—but, judging from the letters and e-mails my editor forwards, they keep the fans happy. They keep me happy, too.

Six months after the publication of *Big Girls,* Bruce Guberman returned to the shores of America, and shocked the world (or me, at least) by finishing his doctoral dissertation and marrying the Pusher, whom I eventually learned to call by her real name, which is Emily. Emily Guberman. Goes trippingly off the tongue, I always say.

My father disappeared again. I didn't hear from him again after that August, and I never tried to find him—not online, not in real time. *Let the dead bury their dead* was what I thought, which didn't make sense when I said it any more than it had when Jesus did, given that neither my father nor I was dead, but still, it was what I thought, and it comforted me somehow.

Nifkin, my constant companion all through my twenties and into my thirties, had an easy death when Joy was four. One cold night in November, when the wind blew so hard it rattled the bedroom blinds, he permitted me to carry him up the stairs and feed him a spoonful of cream cheese with his nightly pills buried inside. He curled up on his dog bed by the fireplace, closed his eyes, sighed, and gave one great quiver. His small, spotted body went stiff, and his nails rattled briefly on the floorboards. I sat beside him with tears streaming down my face, patting his head, saying, *Good boy, good boy, that's my good boy.*

When Bruce had been back for a few months, I asked Audrey for a number, screwed up my courage, and called him.

"I think you should see your daughter," I told him.

"That's generous of you," Bruce said coldly.

"I think she'd like that," I said. I took a deep breath and a fast, longing glance at the wine bottle. "I want to apologize," I blurted. "For my book." He didn't answer. "I'm sorry," I said. "I . . . I didn't mean . . . Well, I shouldn't say I never meant to hurt you, because I did at the time, but I guess I never thought, you know, that things would get so crazy."

"My lawyer," said Bruce, "will be in touch."

Two months later, we met at a diner in Cherry Hill, where, over the most uncomfortable plate of pancakes I'd ever endured, we hammered out an arrangement: Every other Sunday, he'd pick Joy up at my house and bring her back two hours later. Over the years, the restrictions have loosened a little. We both attended Joy's sixth-grade graduation, albeit on opposite sides of a large auditorium. It's progress, of a sort.

As for me, the Candace Shapiro who gave interviews and readings, and who posted breezy updates to her website about the time her daughter tried to eat gravel at the playground, is gone. I don't update my website. I don't answer fan mail. I don't do blurbs or book-club visits. Last year I was an answer on *Jeopardy!* ("This author had a plus-size hit on her hands with *Big Girls Don't Cry*." The contestant got it wrong.) I still grow my own herbs and bake my own muffins. I do the laundry and find comfort in the rote motions of ironing shirts and sheets. While Joy's at school, I write about Lyla, out there in the stars. In the afternoons, I'm always available to drive a carpool or sign for a package, to pick up the dry cleaning or peel thirty pounds of potatoes for the synagogue's Chanukah Happening. I don't answer the telephone unless I recognize the number. I don't answer the door unless I'm expecting guests. And I try, with all my heart, to keep my daughter safe from what I wrote, what I did, all those years ago.

PART TWO

Amsterdam

Sixteen

At ten o'clock Saturday morning, my grandma Ann pulled up to the curb in her little hybrid car, which is so covered in political stickers that the bumper's just a red, white, and blue antiwar, pro-environment blur. She honked the horn, waved at my mother through the window, and kissed my cheek after I'd climbed in.

"To what do I owe this privilege?" she asked as I fastened my seat belt.

The real answer was my investigation. What I said was "I miss you . . . and I love your house." My grandmother smiled, turned the radio to NPR, and started to drive.

Grandma Ann used to live in Avondale, a suburb twenty minutes outside of the city, in a big four-bedroom colonial set back from the road by an emerald-green lawn. She lived there with her husband and her kids. Then she got a divorce and the kids moved out, and she was by herself for a while, and then she hooked up with Tanya. They were together for seven years, and even had a commitment ceremony, before Tanya left her for a male plumber she'd met at a weekend retreat for mindful eating. ("Tanya still had food issues?" I'd heard my mom ask Aunt Elle, who'd come over in person to deliver the news. "She couldn't stop eating . . ." Aunt Elle had said solemnly, ". . . cock." My mother had thrown a dish towel at her sister's head. "Little pitchers! Big ears!" she'd hissed, pointing her chin at me.)

Two years ago Grandma Ann met Mona at a Dykes for Peace rally in front of the Liberty Bell. Mona is a law professor at Temple. Grandma Ann used to be a gym teacher ("And now she's gay," Uncle Josh had said at one of the family seders, "which shouldn't come as a surprise to anyone"). Last year Grandma Ann and Mona both sold their houses and bought a brand-new "accessible living" ranch in a development in Bryn Mawr. In the new house, everything is on one level, the doorways are wide, the countertops are low, and all of the bathrooms have steel grab bars around the toilets. ("Your grandmother is settling in for her dotage," my mother told me. "I think we should just put her on an ice floe and be done with it," said Aunt Elle.) Grandma Ann and Mona have dinner parties and go to book clubs, and almost every week they attend a rally or protest somewhere in the tristate area. Mona is very political, and my grandmother is happy to keep her company, even though she usually gets bored at some point during the demonstration and calls to talk to me and my mom while the speeches are still going on. ("What's the demonstration for?" I'd asked during the last phone call. "Hang on, let me check the banners!" my grandmother yelled back.)

The good news is, when I'm at the Accessible Ranch, I can do whatever I want. Grandma Ann is what my mother calls "laissez-faire" and what my aunt Elle just calls "lazy." Usually, when I'm over, she's puttering around in her garden or the kitchen or paying bills on her computer or talking on the telephone to Mona, who has an awful lot of free time to make telephone calls for someone who's constantly telling you how busy she is. I can eat whatever I want for a snack, do my homework while there's music on, and once I rode my mother's old bike without a helmet and my grandmother never said a word.

That Saturday I got out of my grandmother's little car and followed her to the kitchen, where she was making a kosher-for-Passover casserole with matzoh meal, raisins, and goat cheese. " 'Roast, skin, and finely chop one handful of chipotle peppers,' " she read from the cookbook. Her bifocals slid down her nose, and she tossed her head to get them back into position. Grandma Ann has short gray hair that she doesn't dye and that usually stands up around her head in haphazard spikes. Her skin is ruddy. Her eyes are the same green as my mother's, and she's plump, but with skinny legs and arms, which gives her body the appearance of an apple with four toothpicks sticking out. "Do you think I could just use a red pepper?" she asked.

"I guess," I said, thinking that the casserole—which Mona, for some reason, always pronounced "cazzerole"—sounded disgusting and that the bell-versus-chipotle-pepper issue was the least of its problems.

"Do I have a red pepper?"

I looked in the refrigerator. "Nope."

"Green pepper?" she asked without much hope. I shook my head. "Hmm. Well, hand me an onion."

I gave her the onion and watched while she chopped and hummed along to Holly Near.

"Hey," I began. I'd been thinking about this for weeks: what to ask, who to ask. Finding Alden Langley Chernowitz had been good. Talking to Aunt Elle had been useful, too, but Aunt Elle, I'd decided, was what my English teacher would call "an unreliable narrator."

I started with a question. "Did my mom have a lot of boyfriends when she was in high school?"

"Oh, sure," she said. She scraped the chopped onion onto the cooked brown rice in the baking dish. "Football players, soccer players . . ." She squinted at the cookbook, then looked at me. "Hold on. No, actually, that was Lucy."

Figured. "Well, did my mom have any boyfriends?"

"In high school? Just one that I remember." She looked at me sharply through her bifocals. "Do you have a boyfriend?"

For a minute I thought about Duncan Brodkey and how his green shirt had made his eyes look greeny-gold that day in the computer lab, the way he'd pause before answering a teacher's question, like he'd been thinking of something better than algebra or French verbs. "No boyfriends," I said. "I was just wondering about my mom."

"I know she had one who was older," she said. She turned her back, opened the spice cabinet, and started murmuring the word "oregano." "He was someone she met in high school when she was auditing a class at community college. What was his name? Brian? Ryan? Something like that. Either Brian or Ryan."

"Oh." I scanned through my memories of *Big Girls Don't Cry,* but I couldn't remember "Allie" ever being with an older boy in high school. She'd been with an older professor when she was in college, and then she'd had an "encounter" with a police officer who'd pulled her over for driving with a broken taillight, and she'd had lots of boy-friends in college, although "boyfriends" was probably the wrong word for guys she just had sex with.

"They went out for years and years. Her last year of high school, all through college." She flipped her head again. "Or maybe his name was Colin. For some reason, that's ringing a bell."

"She dated him all through college?" That did not line up at all with the book, in which Allie spent four years majoring in Rich Bitches' Boyfriends. That part made me feel sorry for my mother, so I used my Sharpie to scribble over it. I didn't want to feel sorry for her. It was easier when I could just be angry.

"As far as I know," my grandmother said, and held an opened jar out for me to sniff, "he was her first love. Before Bruce. I wish I could remember his name!" Grandma Ann ran one hand through her spiky hair, turned back to her pantry, and pulled out another jar. She held it at arm's length, squinting. "Is this oregano?"

I looked at the label. "Cilantro."

"Close enough," she said cheerfully, and sprinkled it over the chopped onion. I wanted to ask more—about my mother's first boy-friend and about Bruce—but figured it would better to back off and do a little detecting on my own.

I wandered upstairs to the "bonus room," a mostly empty rectangular space with a dusty TV set up in one corner, beige carpets and white walls (in the Accessible Ranch, all of the carpets are beige and the walls are white because Grandma Ann and Mona couldn't agree on any other colors). Heavy-duty plastic shelves lined one long wall, filled with bins of things my grandmother and Mona had brought from their old houses and old lives. There were boxes of report cards and Halloween costumes, photo albums and record albums and even wedding albums from both of their long-ago marriages to men.

I found a cardboard box filled with folded sweaters with blocks of cedar shoved in the sleeves, then a box of tapes labeled TOP 40 COUNTDOWN in Aunt Elle's handwriting. That was good. I liked oldies. I found a dusty radio that played cassettes, plugged it in, popped a tape into the slot, and smiled when I heard my aunt's voice, younger but still the same. "This is Lucy Beth Shapiro, presenting the Top 40 tunes for 1982!" Then Elle announced a Quarterflash song. "I'm gonna harden my heart / I'm gonna swallow my tears," the singer wailed. I turned up the volume and flipped open an album, looking for evidence of what my mom had really been like.

The first book was full of baby pictures, and since my mom and her sister and brother had looked basically the same as babies, I put it aside. In the next book, I found my mother at twelve or thirteen dressed in a flouncy sundress for what must have been a party. *A bat mitzvah?* I wondered, and turned the page to a first-day-of-school shot, with my mom and her brother and sister standing stiffly in front of their old house in brand-new dark blue jeans and striped shirts. Aunt Elle, I saw, had braided her hair into clumsy cornrows. My mom's hair was loose around her shoulders, and when she smiled, she had a gap between her teeth that braces must have erased.

There were pictures from Rosh Hashanah, with my mom and Aunt Elle in pleated skirts and tan panty hose and Uncle Josh in a crooked striped tie. There were Thanksgiving pictures with the five of them gathered around a roast turkey; Chanukah pictures (same table, with a menorah replacing the poultry). Ice skating and ice hockey, Pee Wee Little League and Shooting Stars soccer. My grandfather had curly dark hair that silvered at his temples as the years went on. In most pictures, his eyes were hidden behind dark glasses, and sometimes he clenched a stump of a cigar between his square teeth. He rarely smiled in the pictures, and when he did, it was a hard kind of grin that didn't look happy at all.

I remembered the first time I'd seen his picture, maybe even in this same album, at Thanksgiving at my grandmother's, when I was little. *Who's that?* I'd asked, and pointed. The three of them—my mom and her brother and sister—had come to look over my shoulder. *Dr. Evil,* said Aunt Elle. *Lord Voldemort,* said Uncle Josh. *That's our father,* my mom said, and then she leaned over, her hair brushing my cheek, and turned the page.

I turned up the music and picked up another album, watching time pass. Grandma Ann got bigger, and her hair got shorter and blonder and feathered, then layered, then frosted and straight again, as her kids grew up, but her husband, my grandfather, didn't change much. His beard got a little longer, and his lapels and collars narrowed, and he shaved his mustache once, then grew it back. That was about it.

"Chicago!" Elle's voice squealed through the speakers. " 'Hard to Say I'm Sorry'! Oh God, I love this song!"

I grinned, turning the pages slowly, watching my mother's hair go from a ponytail to a Farrah Fawcett feathered 'do that someone should have told her was a mistake. I watched her boobs and nose grow as Chicago turned to John Cougar, which gave way to the J. Geils Band. Finally, I got to the page I was hoping for—my mother at her bat mitzvah, with her hair cut short and a mouthful of metal, standing in front of the synagogue doors. She wore a long dress—black, sprinkled with pink flowers, with a pink sash and a ruffle on the hem and the sleeves. Tan panty hose again (*such a mistake,* Amber Gross said in my head), black flats, plain gold studs in her ears, and no other jewelry. She looked awful—so bad that I couldn't believe her mother had let her go out of the house like that, let alone to her own bat mitzvah. No wonder she hadn't had a party. Looking like that, she probably hadn't wanted to show her face in public at all.

When the tape ended, I popped it out of the slot, then poked around in the shoe box for more music. There were half a dozen Top 40 tapes from 1982, and then one labeled READING 1974 in narrow, slanting letters, a handwriting I'd never seen before. Curious, I plugged it into the cassette player and pushed play.

" 'Once upon a time, a beautiful but wicked queen was ruler of the land,' " came a deep man's voice. For a minute I thought it was my father I was hearing.

"Don't read the part about the witch!" came a little kid's voice. *My mother?* I wondered.

"How's Snow White supposed to get the poisoned apple if there's no witch?" asked another little kid's voice. I smiled in recognition. *That* was my mother. "If she doesn't meet the witch, she doesn't get to go into the glass box, and then she can't meet the prince!"

"I'll skip that part," the man's voice said soothingly. A thrill ran up my spine as I realized who I was hearing: my grandfather.

"But then it won't make sense!"

"Well, I'll read it quickly."

"*Very* quickly," said Elle.

"Baby," said my mother under her breath.

"Shh," said the man, and he started to read again. " 'The queen had an enchanted mirror, and every night she would gaze into the mirror and ask, "Mirror, mirror, on the wall, who's the fairest of them all?" ' "

"Not 'fair' like 'fair' but 'fair' like 'pretty,' " said my mother in her bossy, self-important way.

"Am I pretty?" asked Aunt Elle.

"Of course you are," their father said, his voice practically a croon. "Both of my girls are beautiful."

I listened to the whole tape, *Snow White* and *Little Red Riding Hood* and *Where the Wild Things Are,* all of the little girls' interruptions. Aunt Elle had lots of questions about whether she'd continue to be pretty as she grew up; my mother seemed more concerned with whether they could have French toast for breakfast. Through it all, the man never lost his patience. He answered every question calmly and kindly. He sounded nice. More than nice. He sounded wonderful.

When the tape ran out, I popped it out of the player and stuck it in my backpack. It was a clue—to what, I wasn't sure yet.

My mother and Grandma Ann were sitting at the table when I came downstairs, their heads together, talking quietly.

"Stay for dinner," Grandma Ann urged, sliding her casserole out of the oven at five o'clock.

"No thanks," my mom and I said at the exact same time. She smiled at me, and for just a second, things felt the way they had when I was little, before I'd kissed a boy and changed lunch tables and looked my mom up on the Internet—before I'd read *Big Girls Don't Cry.*

Then I turned away and my mother said, "Seriously, Ma, it smells like something crawled inside your oven and died."

"Must you be vulgar?" Grandma Ann said. "Mona loves my casseroles."

"Too much information," said my mom. "I'll see you tomorrow." I zipped up my backpack, making sure the tape was still snug inside the front pocket, kissed my grandmother, and walked outside to where the minivan was waiting.

"Seat belt," said my mother, backing down the Accessible Ranch's brand-new extra-wide driveway, lined with stubby little pine trees.

I slid the straps over my shoulders and clicked them closed, sneaking sideways looks at her. What had happened to the man who'd read her bedtime stories? Had my mother ever hated her parents, or stolen some skin cream, or felt ashamed of who she was and who she'd come from? *Who are you?* I wondered as she gripped the wheel in the ten and two o'clock positions with her eyes steady on the road. *Who are you, and who am I?*

"Can we stop at the bookstore?" I asked when we were back in the city.

"Sure. What do you need?"

"*Lord of the Flies.*"

"We've got that at home. I read that one when I was your age." She smiled, obviously hoping I'd smile back. "You know, when dinosaurs walked the earth."

"Ha." *When you were my age,* I thought, *you were already letting the sixteen-year-old at the end of the cul-de-sac stick his hand down your bathing suit bottom—or at least the you in your book was.* "Yours is all marked up," I said. I turned on the radio so I wouldn't have to talk with her, and she didn't say anything until she dropped me off in front of the Barnes & Noble on Walnut Street.

"I'll just pull up in front of the Rittenhouse. Call my cell when you're ready."

I said I would, and I went into the bookstore. *Lord of the Flies* was easy to find, and once I'd paid, I looked out the window. The minivan was nowhere in sight. I tucked the bag under my arm and ran across the street to Kiehl's. The bells on the door jingled, and all three ladies in lab coats looked up. "Can we help you?" one of them asked with a friendly smile. She was young, with pale hair in a bob just brushing the shoulders of her lab coat, and streaks of different shades of pink across the back of her hand.

I took a deep breath. "Um," I started. "I was in here a few weeks ago, and I put this"—I pulled out the tub of wrinkle cream—"in my pocket, and I meant to pay for it, but I forgot."

The woman looked at me coolly. "Nineteen ninety-five," she said. I pulled a twenty-dollar bill out of my pocket. "Plus tax," she said. I added two more crumpled dollar bills. "Sorry," I said, and ran out the door without waiting for my change.

Seventeen

It would have been a perfect question for Ann Landers, if she'd been alive to answer: Where, and with what gifts, do you ask your little sister for the temporary loan of her uterus?

Peter and I had sent in the Open Hearts application, along with our tax returns and our application fee. In the meantime, I'd been privately planning on bringing our search a little closer to home. Elle made perfect sense. She had the right body parts. I had the cash. And having my sister carry a child for us would let us keep things in the family, rather than hiring a stranger. It all made sense, except I wasn't quite sure how to begin the conversation.

Thanks to volunteering at the library and the hospital, I knew a lot about what's known as "the ask," in which you attempt to part the rich person from a portion of his or her lucre. Six years ago, I'd been part of the three-member committee that had made a pilgrimage to a onetime TV star's Radnor mansion to ask him for a breathtaking fifteen million dollars. At least I'd thought it was breathtaking. The former star, by then a magisterial presence in his sixties, with graying temples and a wall full of awards, hadn't even flinched as he'd agreed to write the check. Then again, he'd just been slapped with a lawsuit for fondling PAs on a game show he'd guest-hosted years before, and that check bought him some awfully nice press.

Over the years, I'd asked strangers and acquaintances and friends for their money, for their time, for donations of everything from hamantaschen for the Preschool Purim Parade to thousands of dollars for the children's hospital's new lounge. But I was sure, as I shucked my clothes and pulled on a heavy white robe in the blue-and-green-tiled changing room one of Center City's fanciest spas, I'd never made an ask quite as tricky as this one.

The spa had been my mother's idea. "Take her somewhere fancy, get her relaxed," she'd suggested. Then she'd invited herself along, unwilling to miss a moment of the drama. Getting the spa personnel to swap the standard herbal tea for champagne had been my contribution to the effort. I'd also come armed with wine, chocolate, and my checkbook. At some point between the mint/mojito exfoliating scrub and the warm willow-bark wrap, I'd explain the situation to my sister. Elle would probably be so blissed out that she'd sign up immediately. Maybe she'd even move in with us, I thought, avoiding for the time being thoughts of what Peter would have to say about that. Joy would love it, once she got over the weirdness of her aunt having her parents' baby, which, given the accepting, inclusive, pro-diversity philosophy of her pricey private school, shouldn't take long. I could imagine the three of us taking prenatal yoga and long walks along the paths of Fairmount Park, posing for pictures with my hand on Elle's belly, working side by side in the kitchen to prepare healthy, nutrient-packed meals . . .

My sister's groan of disgust cut through the eucalyptus-scented air. "Mother, for God's sake!" I looked up. The sign above the hot tub said CLOTHING OPTIONAL. My mother opted out, shrugging off her bathrobe. Elle recoiled in horror at the specter of varicose veins, droopy breasts, and sagging belly, covering her eyes as our mother swayed and jiggled into the steaming water and settled herself beneath a waterfall, smiling peacefully. "It's your future, girls," she called. "Embrace it."

"That's Mona's job," said Elle, who was lean as a whippet, tanned and waxed, manicured and pedicured, without a single stretch mark or stray hair.

"Have a drink," I said, shoving a flute of champagne into my sister's hand. Elle scowled, doffed her own robe and slippers to reveal a tangerine-colored bikini and toenails to match, and carried her champagne into the hot tub. Once submerged, she arranged herself as far away from our mother as she could manage and drained her glass. "More champagne?" I asked as my sister placed cucumber slices over her eyes. Without moving her head from her waterproof pillow, Elle extended one slender, bronzed arm. "As you see, so shall it be," she intoned. My mother smiled beatifically. I took a deep breath and ducked underneath the bubbling water.

At some point between her fifteenth high school reunion and the previous Thanksgiving, my sister discovered what she calls, with absolutely no irony, "the meaning of my life." Elle is now a Be-ist. ("A beast?" Joy had asked when Elle had stopped by to make her announcement.)

Be-ism arrived on the scene in 2005, when Jane Myer, a bank teller from South Africa—divorced, down on her luck, fifty pounds overweight, and unfortunately permed—came across an antique self-help pamphlet at whatever they call a tag sale in Afrikaans. The pamphlet contained a primitive version of the power of positive thinking, instructing the poor and needy to simply picture the thing they wanted most. If they concentrated long and hard enough on that image, the thing would be theirs. "See it, be it" was Jane Myer's mantra. Her book of the same title, *See It, Be It,* sold a half million copies its first week out, and that was even before slimmed-down, sleek-haired Jane went on her book tour, beguiling talk-show hosts and TV audiences with her confidence, her accent, her cleavage, and the ineluctable simplicity of her message.

My sister, who'd been through at least half a dozen gurus, self-help movements, and life philosophies by then, bought a copy of the book and began applying its principles immediately. She dropped the name Lucy ("too many unpleasant associations," she'd told us, without saying what those associations might have been). She stayed away from anyone with a drug problem, a drinking program, or weight issues, on the Jane Myer–endorsed belief that mere proximity to the act of overindulging could make you, without the consumption of a single mixed drink or Double Stuf Oreo, overweight and/or addicted yourself. This led to a year's worth of awkward family dinners that Elle would eat leaning as far away from my mother and me as possible, with her eyes half-shut, while the two of us wondered out loud about which she was most hoping to avoid: the fat or the gay.

For the past three years, Elle had insisted that every good thing that had happened to her, from getting the perfect pedicure to landing a recurring role as a homeless woman on *As the World Turns,* had been the direct result of Be-ism. Peter and I privately joked that Elle's version of See It, Be It involved an intermediate step that Jane Myer had never imagined—namely, getting the things she wanted via vigorous and protracted visualization of me paying for them—but neither one of us could argue that, at the advanced age of forty, my little sister had more or less gotten her life in order.

"Shapiro?" called a woman in a crisp white coat, poised at the edge of the hot tub with a clipboard in her hands. I said, "Yes?" My mother started to stand up. Elle pulled off her cucumber slices and scowled. "Keep that under the waterline!" she snapped.

"Now, Lucy," Mom said mildly.

"Are we ready for our massages?" the clipboard lady asked.

We got out of the water ("Me first!" said Elle, shielding her eyes), pulled on our robes, and padded down the hall. My mother slipped into a single room, while Elle and I were led to the couples' room that I'd requested, a candlelit space with two rose-petal-strewn tables set close to the white-draped walls. A fountain tinkled in one corner, and a choir chanted from speakers on the ceiling. I got on the bed closest to the wall.

Elle looked suspicious. "Cannie, what is going on?"

"I thought we could have some time together. You know, we never talk anymore."

"What do you mean? We talk!" This was not untrue. Elle and I did talk a few times a week, and she'd also e-mail me pictures she'd snap on the set of *ATWT* of herself wrapped in a trash bag, with a big, fake, festering cold sore in the corner of her mouth, beneath the memo line I NEED A VACATION.

A man and a woman, identically attired in white drawstring pants and white T-shirts, like nurses at a very hip hospital, walked into the room and greeted us. "I get the guy," Elle announced.

"As usual," I said.

She gave him a cheery wave and flopped facedown (still, I noticed, wearing her damp orange bikini) onto the table. I hung up my robe and lay down beside her. "You're not going to take off your bathing suit?" I whispered.

"Please," she said, wrinkling her nose. "I don't do nudity with other women."

"I'm your sister . . . and you can't catch lesbianism," I whispered.

"They don't know that," she whispered back as my masseuse squirted warm oil between my shoulder blades.

"So what's new?"

"Mphm," my sister said into her pillow. She lifted her head. "Nothing. What's new with you?"

"Not much." I knew how I must look to Elle, with a house in a city she couldn't wait to escape and with a husband and a child, two things she most assuredly had never wanted. Not to mention my minivan. If it was the last car on earth, Elle, I was certain, would walk—or maybe pull off the wheels and try to build herself a sporty little scooter.

"How's the bat mitzvah planning coming?" She pursed her lips. "Are you giving Mona an aliyah?"

"Um." The truth was, I hadn't even begun to figure out what role my mother's partner would have in the festivities.

"And what about Guberman?" Elle demanded. "Is he gonna help pay for it?"

"Well," I said, thinking that I'd ask Bruce Guberman for money at roughly the same moment I'd ask him to sleep with me again. "We'll work something out. It'll be fine."

We lay quietly for a few minutes. "Do you think we're really going to look like Mom?" Elle asked. "All saggy and horrible?"

"Elle," came our mother's mellifluous voice from the cubicle next door, "I can hear you!"

"Mom looks fine," I said firmly.

"Mom does not," Elle replied. "She should have gotten a lift."

"Do Be-ists believe in plastic surgery?" I asked. "Shouldn't Mom just visualize herself getting lifted?"

"It's too late for that for her." Elle herself had gotten her breasts, brow, and chin done before her embrace of Be-ism, not to mention the six-month course of laser hair removal that she'd completed mere weeks before *See It, Be It*'s release.

"And what was she supposed to get lifted?" I inquired.

"Everything!" said Elle. "All of it!"

"I heard that!" our mother called.

"Shh," I whispered as my masseuse raised the sheets draping us and asked us to roll over. "I need to ask you something." I dropped my voice. "It's kind of personal."

Elle lowered her own voice and reached across the space between our tables to grab my massage-oil-slick hand. "Oh, Cannie. Are you having that not-so-fresh feeling?"

I shook my head. Elle ignored me. "You need a woman's advice!" she blared. "Well, Cannie, I'm here to help! Just tell me your troubles! Do you need diet tips? Are you having"—she lowered her voice again, fractionally—"trouble in the bedroom?"

"I don't need your advice, exactly," I said hastily. "I need . . ." And here it was. "I need you to lend me something."

"What?" Elle asked.

"Pardon me, ladies," my masseuse whispered. "It's time for your wraps." I cursed her timing while she explained the procedure: We'd be slathered with willow-bark extract, bundled like baked potatoes in silver space blankets, then left in the room, with the lights down, as our pores absorbed all of the barky goodness. Elle lay back as her guy smoothed lotion on her legs, then her arms, then folded her, burrito-style, into her blanket and draped a padded eye pillow over her face, while my masseuse did the same to me.

Finally, with the lights off and the room quiet except for the crinkling of the blankets and the chorus singing overhead, we were alone, flat on our backs, immobilized. "You don't need me to lend you money," Elle said.

"Nope."

"Clothes?"

Ha. "Uh-uh."

"Accessories? Hair extensions? Back issues of *Vogue*?"

"Peter and I have been thinking about trying to have a baby," I began. "I've got viable eggs, and his sperm is fine, so . . . um. Well. We'd just need a surrogate to carry it." I managed to turn my head toward her, to work one hand free and stretch it across the gap between the tables so I could squeeze her shoulder. "It'd be fun! Maybe you could move in with us until the baby was born—"

Elle sat up fast and almost slid off her plastic-draped table. "You want me to what?"

"I just thought you could maybe think about . . . you know . . . helping us out."

Her eye pillow had tumbled onto the table, and even through the dim light I could see her eyes get wide. "You want me to sleep with your husband?"

"No! God!" I took a deep breath. "It's a simple procedure, really. They'd just inject the fertilized egg into your—"

"What? When? Now?" Elle's feet smacked down on the tile floor, and she struggled against her silvery cocoon. I remembered a little belatedly that the spa shared space with doctors' offices, so the well-tended ladies of Philadelphia could get their Botox or cosmetic dentistry along with their massages and scrubs. Maybe Elle had seen a few white coats as she made her way from the dressing room to the whirlpool and had assumed that the Jacuzzi and the massage were all leading up to some kind of *Rosemary's Baby*–style insemination.

"Calm down!" I whispered.

The masseur cracked the door open and found me on the table, still straitjacketed by my blanket, while Elle was half naked on the floor, kicking her way out of hers, like a naked bird in a hurry to be born. "Ladies, is everything all right?" he asked.

"Everything's fine," I said, hopping onto the floor next to my sister. "Elle, take it easy!"

Red-faced and panting, after extensive convincing, my sister allowed her masseur to rewrap her blanket and hoist her back onto the table. I eased myself back onto mine. "I'll take that as a no," I said.

"No," Elle repeated. "I just— I mean, no offense or anything, Cannie, but I don't think I want to be pregnant. I don't think . . ." She busied herself readjusting the folds of her blanket.

"You don't think what?"

"That any of us have any business having kids. You know. With everything . . ." She flapped her hand in a manner meant to encompass our parents' divorce, our father's defection, our mom's late-in-life lesbianism, the whole mess. "I don't know. I'll think about it."

"You don't have to—"

"No. I will."

"You really should read *See It, Be It*," Elle said for roughly the thousandth time, as I piloted a shopping cart through the produce section of the brand-new organic grocery store that had just opened down the road from the Accessible Ranch. We'd gone there, post-spa, to shop for my mother's traditional end-of-Passover feast, which we'd celebrate with an all-inclusive, politically correct, gender-neutral Seder where God was referred to as the Power, and there were as many mentions of Miriam as there were of Moses.

"Why?" I grabbed a bunch of grapes and a bag of golden-red Rainier cherries, then a container of plump gold raisins for the fruit compote. My mom whimpered as though she'd been stabbed.

"What's wrong?" I asked her. She gestured mutely at the price written on the blackboard. "Ma, they're cherries! I can afford them!"

"Oh, never mind her," said my sister. "Read the book. Maybe if you just, you know, visualized your intended result . . ."

"I appreciate the thought, but I don't know if I can visualize myself a new uterus."

"Well, maybe not," Elle allowed. "Maybe just visualize the end result. A baby."

I picked up a pint of hormone-free half-and-half. My mother gasped. "What now?" I said.

"It's a dollar fifty-nine at the Price Chopper."

"I'm not at the Price Chopper. I'm here."

"You weren't raised like this," she protested.

"No kidding," Elle muttered, tossing a jar of olive tapenade on top of the box of matzoh in the cart. "Three kids in one bed in the Days Inn every summer at the water park."

"You loved the water park!" said Mom.

"Nobody loves the water park for seven summers in a row," Elle said. "Particularly not when they have to share a bed with their brother."

I wheeled the cart to the meat counter, where the dry-aged meat was displayed in a special cooler like jewelry in a glass case. I pointed at a rib roast. My mother clutched her head and moaned.

"If you don't want it, you don't have to eat it," I said. "But I'm not eating casserole." I gathered focaccia, olives, a wedge of sweet Gorgonzola, figs, and salad greens. Elle, meanwhile, was smiling at the white-coated man behind the counter, who seemed to be enjoying the attention. He set the meat on a chopping block, lifting his knife. "You want the bone?" he asked my sister. I rolled my eyes.

"What do you think?" Elle whispered as the guy bent over the counter to wrap the roast. "Gay or just well groomed?"

I looked at the guy. "No idea. Ask Mom."

"Please," Elle said. "She didn't even know she was gay until she was fifty-six. Why would you think she's got any idea about anybody else?" She swished off down the aisle in her short skirt made of tiers of fuchsia satin, a black leotard, a cropped denim jacket, fishnet stockings, a cowboy hat, and hot pink boots. I paid for my groceries, as well as the thirty dollars' worth of stuff (blueberry honey, artisanal marshmallows, twenty-year-old balsamic vinegar) that had mysteriously been added to the haul. At the register Mom snatched the receipt out of my hand, squinted at it through her bifocals, then tottered off toward the café tables. "Get Mother some smelling salts and help me bag," I said to my sister. Elle flipped open a paper sack and began loading it with the stuff she'd picked out. Lemon body wash. An all-natural loofah. A plastic bottle of pink grapefruit juice. Jane Myer would have been proud. I picked up the juice and shook it.

"When I was pregnant with Joy, this was the only thing I had a craving for," I remembered. "I thought I'd want sweet or salty, or pickles and ice cream. Something like that. I just wanted grapefruit juice, though."

"You make it sound so romantic." Elle's face was still faintly flushed from the sauna, and her expression was troubled.

"That wasn't a hint. I was just remembering. It wasn't so bad," I mused, putting the grapefruit juice into a bag. "Once I got through feeling pukey all the time, some days I didn't even notice I was pregnant. And I made some really good friends."

"I have friends," my sister said. "And I think I'd notice if I was covered in stretch marks and waddling instead of walking. Remember how big you got?" She shuddered. "You were like a truck."

I grimaced. I didn't think I had gotten that big, but it was entirely possible that hindsight and nostalgia had improved the view. "A small truck?"

Elle ignored me. "I'd need an entire new wardrobe," she continued. Her face brightened, possibly at the thought of cute maternity outfits. "Pregnancy is actually very hip. All the movie stars are spawning."

I nodded. I was trying to remember how Elle had been when Joy was a baby. She'd stop by every week or two and sit on the floor, amusing my daughter by constructing brown Play-Doh models of bowel movements and leaving them perched on the rim of the toilet seat, taking Joy to Johnny Rockets with a fistful of nickels for the jukebox, or reading her *Us* or *In Touch*. ("Stars," Joy would announce sleepily after I'd sing her "Twinkle Twinkle." "They're just like us.")

"It's a big decision," I said before Elle could start listing which movie stars' bumps had been most vigorously chronicled by the tabloids. "I just wanted to put it out there so you can think about it."

Elle bagged the bread and salad greens. "I couldn't drink, I couldn't smoke . . ."

"You smoke?" asked Mom, who'd reappeared at the foot of the conveyer belt.

Elle scowled. "No, Mother. I've never had a cigarette, Josh has never tried a beer, and Cannie didn't just spend seventeen dollars on cherries."

My mother staggered away again. Elle tapped her finger against her glossy lips, perhaps thinking of the other illicit activities that pregnancy would preclude. The three of us wheeled the groceries outside. I clicked my keys, raised the minivan's trunk door, and played my final card. "We'd pay you."

My sister had been adjusting her hair underneath the cowboy hat. When I said the magic words, her hands froze. "How much?"

"If you're interested—if you're willing to seriously consider it— there are organizations for surrogate mothers, and I'm sure they could tell you what you could expect in terms of compensation."

Elle's tone was casual. "What's the going rate for having a baby?"

I plucked a number out of the air. "Fifty thousand dollars?"

Elle's eyes gleamed. "You know what? I've got this friend, Sarah. She's really nice—I think you met her once, and she loves babies, and I bet she'd be totally into it. Maybe I could call her." She paused and lifted another pair of bags into the trunk. "Maybe I could get, like, a finder's fee."

I leaned against the car. "Elle, I mean, the thing is, if we just wanted to find someone, we could find someone. I was kind of hoping you'd be interested."

She sighed. "I just can't see it." I watched as she shimmied past my mother and hoisted herself into the passenger's seat. "It would be my baby, right? That's how it would feel."

"I don't know," I said. "I don't know how it would feel."

"My baby," my sister said. "So wouldn't I feel like its mother?"

"I don't know." I didn't. How could I ask her, or any other woman, to carry a baby and go through labor and then just give it away, when it wasn't something I'd been able to do myself? I got into the car, put the key in the ignition, and backed out of the parking space. Elle's bracelets rattled as she put her hand on top of mine.

Eighteen

I put the question to Amber's table at lunch the first day after spring break. "Does anyone know how I could get to South Orange, New Jersey, by myself?"

"Steal a car," said Tamsin without raising her eyes from her Earth Sciences book. Unlike the rest of the girls, in pinks and pale blues, Tamsin wore her customary gray hooded sweatshirt. As usual, her hair was hanging in her face, covering everything but the tip of her nose.

"Ha ha," I said. Tamsin had been cool to me ever since my birthday sleepover. I guessed things hadn't gone well when she and Amber woke up in my room together and I wasn't there, but whenever I asked Tamsin about it, she shrugged and said things were fine.

"Why are you going by yourself?" asked Duncan Brodkey.

"It's my cousin's bar mitzvah."

Duncan tilted his head. "Can't your parents take you?"

"It's the other side of the family."

I watched as he considered this, rolling a green apple from one long-fingered hand to the other. "It's the other side of the family for both of them?"

"You could take a train," Tamsin said quickly. That was the great thing about Tamsin: Even when you didn't think she was paying attention, she was. She pulled her laptop out of her backpack. "Let's see . . . SEPTA from Thirtieth Street Station to Trenton, then New Jersey Transit to Metro Park, then a bus to South Orange . . ."

She worked out the times, and I scribbled down everything she told me. If I left Philadelphia by eight o'clock in the morning, I could be there by eleven o'clock, and if I left the bar mitzvah by five, I could easily make it home by eight. I'd just tell my mother I was at Tamsin's. Perfect! Except . . .

I cleared my throat. When that didn't work, I tapped Amber on the shoulder. "Hey," I said when she'd turned around. "What would you wear to an afternoon bar mitzvah in New Jersey?"

On Saturday morning at eight o'clock, I pulled my schoolbooks out of my backpack, slid them under the bed, and replaced them with the navy blue spaghetti-strapped dress Amber had lent me, along with her black ballet slippers, a pair of white athletic socks ("for dancing," she'd explained), and a small canister of glitter-flecked hair mousse.

I walked out the front door, but instead of turning left toward Bella Vista, I turned right, crossing South Street, then Lombard, then Pine. The bus I caught on Spruce Street took me all the way to Thirtieth Street Station. Feeling very small under the soaring ceilings, among the crowds of people pulling wheeled suitcases or pushing strollers over the marble floors, I slid my cash card into the machine and paid for a round-trip fare. Then I ducked into the bathroom and wriggled into Amber's dress and sat on a high-backed curved wooden bench with my backpack in my lap and my eyes fixed on the giant blackboard that hung over the information desk, waiting for the flickering letters to tell me it was time to go.

"Joy?"

I turned around and saw Duncan Brodkey leaning over the back of the bench.

"Hey, were you asleep or something? I was calling your name. Are you listening to music?" He brushed playfully at my hair, looking for earbuds. I felt my whole body flush as I leaned backward, hoping he hadn't seen my hearing aids.

"N-no," I stammered. "Just thinking."

"Deep thoughts," he said, looking impressed, so I tried to look as though I had been thinking deep thoughts instead of wondering whether I had time to get a juice and whether the coffee stand had the kind that I liked. "Are you going to that bar mitzvah?" he asked.

I nodded, tugging my jean jacket closed across my chest, feeling self-conscious in Amber's dress. "What are you doing here?"

"I'm going to see my dad in New York," he said, hopping over the bench and sitting down next to me. He wore khakis with a loose thread trailing from the cuff, unlaced sneakers, and a baseball cap. "Gonna see the Yankees lose." He reached into his pocket. "Mento?"

"Oh, um. Sure!" I took a mint. "So you're going all by yourself?" As soon as that was out of my mouth, I realized how babyish it sounded. After all, I was going by myself, too.

Duncan just nodded. "I do it all the time," he said. "Well, since this year. Hey, you're smart, right?"

I used to be, I thought, but I just nodded as he bent down and pulled out his algebra book. We worked on his homework together until the information board fluttered into life again, and Duncan picked up his backpack, and mine, and led me down the escalator to the train.

An hour and a half later, flushed and flustered, I stepped off the bus, my mascara and lipstick freshly applied, my hair in a chic twist I'd copied from *Allure* (I'd done it with tendrils hanging over my ears to cover my hearing aids), and onto the corner of Gilman Avenue in South Orange. *Duncan Brodkey,* I thought, and then, because there was no one there to hear me, I said it out loud. "Duncan Brodkey likes me." This was going to be the best day. The air was bright and busy with gold pollen and the sound of traffic. There was a gas station to my left and a bakery on the corner across the street. My heart was pounding hard, and I felt exhilarated and a little scared. What if I couldn't find the synagogue? What if I missed the bus, or the train, and I couldn't get home? It took me a minute to figure out which way I was supposed to go, but almost immediately, I saw Beth Israel Synagogue ("A Community of Caring"), resembling nothing more than a gigantic white concrete rowboat sticking halfway out of an invisible ocean.

I was walking through the parking lot when a green station wagon slowed down next to me and the passenger-side window rolled down. "Hi, Joy," said Emily, Bruce's wife, waving one tiny hand out the window. "How'd you get here?"

The hair at the back of my neck prickled. "I got dropped off." Emily nodded. *Our Lady of the EpiPen*, my mother calls Emily, because she's allergic to so many things. *Panic in Peanut Park* is another name, because the thing that Emily and her kids are most allergic to is peanuts. *Trust-fund Trixie* is name number three, because Emily comes from money. Of course, none of these names is ever said out loud when I'm around—I've gotten them from Aunt Elle and from Samantha, listening carefully, reading lips when they don't know I'm nearby. In public, my mother and Emily are polite, the same way my mother is to Bruce. I never would have suspected that Emily might have a more interesting story before reading my mother's book.

In *Big Girls,* "Drew" dumps "Allie," then gets a new girlfriend named "Eva" (whom, of course, Allie instantly nicknames Evil, which is what she's called for the book's last hundred pages). Eva starts dating Drew even though he has a pregnant girlfriend, and when the two of them bump into the pregnant girlfriend, aka Allie, aka my mom, at a Phillies game, Eva trips Allie as she's twisting sideways to go through a turnstile, sending her falling down on the concrete floor, after which Allie's baby, Hope, is born premature, just like me.

Though I'd turned that part of the story over in my mind again and again, I just couldn't imagine Emily pushing anyone in real life. For one thing, she was so tiny and so timid that I couldn't see her working up the nerve—let alone the strength—to go after my mother, who is not tiny or timid. More than one of the reviews of *Big*

Girls that I'd downloaded at school had complained about the book's far-fetched, fanciful plot twists—"Allie's life moves from the implausible to the impossible," one of them said. I figured that the confrontation at the stadium turnstile was one of those instances. Still, it made me look at Bruce's wife differently, the way I'd been looking at everyone differently these days.

I stood awkwardly in front of the station wagon while Emily unfastened Max from his car seat and Bruce and his oldest son, Leo, slammed their doors. Leo's nine. Max is four. (My mother calls them "the producers" when she thinks I can't hear.) Both of them have Bruce's sandy hair, which is my hair, too, but Max's is straight and Leo's is curly. Both of them are pale, like their mother, but Leo is skinny and stern-looking and wears glasses, while Max is round and sweet as a powdered-sugar doughnut. "Joy!" he sang, dancing around me (like his big brother, he wore khaki pants and a button-down shirt, and he'd already spilled apple juice on his tie). "Joy's here! Hi, Joy! Hi there! Hi!"

"Hi, Max," I said, and kissed his sticky cheek.

"How are you doing?" Emily asked, smiling at me.

"Fine." I looked her over, in her floral dress and low-heeled shoes with bows on the toes, her hair held back from her forehead with a matching headband. I think that after he and my mother split, Bruce decided to find someone who was exactly her opposite. My mom is big and tall and busty. Emily is short and small and wears floral dresses with lacy collars, or T-shirts she buys in the boys' department. My mom has brown hair and green eyes and olive skin. Emily has light brown hair and blue eyes. When she laughs, she puts her fingers over her thin lips and coughs out a nervous giggle, as opposed to my mother, who throws her head back and laughs a big honking "ha ha ha" that you can hear across a street or a parking lot.

Then there are Emily's allergies, which earned her most of her nicknames. Nuts. Dairy. Wheat. Gluten. Latex (she can't wear normal Band-Aids). Zinc (she has to wear a special kind of sunscreen). Eggs (no cakes, no pies, no baked goods from the supermarket). Mica (no makeup). Smoke ("It's God's revenge on Bruce," I overheard my mom tell Samantha, who said, "Not really. He'll probably just get high in the basement. Stoners are crazy resourceful that way").

Emily's father is some kind of hedge-fund manager who, according to Aunt Elle, "lives in a palace in Greenwich." Emily's mother does charity work ("She runs the Eye Ball," said Aunt Elle) and grows prize-winning hydrangeas when she's not raising money to battle blindness. Emily doesn't have to work, but she teaches kindergarten at Leo and Max's school. I think she decided to work there so she could personally make sure nobody slipped either of them a peanut or some zinc. Both of them are allergic to everything she is, plus mold and pet dander.

"How's school?" Emily asked me as we started walking across the parking lot.

"School's good."

"I'm in school," said Max, waving his juice box in the air. "My teachers are Miss Meghan and Miss Shannon, and we have easels for painting and a sand table. I like your ball gown! You look like Belle from *Beauty and the Beast*! Belle who likes to read!" Then he started singing in his low, snuffly voice (Max has terrible hay fever all through the spring and summer, straight through the fall, when his mold allergies kick in). " 'Tale as old as time . . .' "

I held Max's hand and led him, still singing, through the synagogue's towering front doors. As soon as we were inside, Emily held out her own hand for Leo's video game, and he grumbled and handed it over. I perched on a bench just inside the foyer to take off my sneakers and jacket, stuff them into my backpack, and slide my feet into Amber's ballet flats.

When I stood up, Bruce kissed my cheek. He smelled like soap and cinnamon gum and was, as usual, blinking too fast. "I'm glad you're here," he said.

"Me, too," I said. Even though I was still nervous, it was true. I had my train and bus tickets in my backpack, and twenty dollars to buy whatever I needed, and the right kind of socks for dancing. Best of all, only a few people here knew me, or my mother, or my history. Maybe this really was another chance to do what I hadn't done back home—to be somebody else. People would look at me and Max and Leo, at how much we resembled one another, and they would think, *Normal family.* I stood up straight in my ballet flats with my head just reaching Bruce's chin, feeling pretty and very grown-up.

The five of us made our way toward the sanctuary behind a mother in a pink tweed skirt and jacket, a father in a dark suit, and a skinny, bird-boned blond girl who looked like she was my age, in a chocolate-brown party dress almost the same as Amber's, and ballet flats. *How did Amber know these things?* I wondered. Then I smiled because, as far as everyone here was concerned, I was the kind of girl who knew them, too.

Bruce shook hands with the man and kissed the wife's cheek. "This is my daughter, Joy," he said. I thought I saw surprise flicker across their faces.

"This is Jessica," the father said. The mother gave Jessica a little push, and the girl stepped forward, smoothing the ends of her blond bob.

"Hi," she said. Her mother and father stared at her expectantly. "Do you want to sit with me?" Jessica asked me.

"That would be great," I said.

Jessica grabbed my arm, said, "See ya!" to her parents, and pulled me through the sanctuary doors without stopping to get a program or a prayer book (I picked them up for both of us).

"There they are," Jessica breathed, and race-walked down to the aisle where there were about thirty kids sitting. "The party's going to be crazy," she said. "I heard there's, like, an entire sushi bar made of ice, and all the kids are getting personalized chocolate gold Amex cards as favors."

"Chocolate gold?"

"Well, chocolate cards in gold foil. They were trying to get platinum foil, but then his mother thought it looked like regular tinfoil. Hi, everyone!" she said. "This is . . ." She looked at me, mouth open in a perfect round O of surprise. "Oh, God, I'm sorry, what's your name again?"

"Don't say 'God' in synagogue," one of the other girls whispered.

"I'm Joy," I said. The other kids slid over to make room, and I took my seat, one more girl in a dark, tight dress in a row of girls in dark, tight dresses. The sanctuary ceiling soared as high as the one in the train station. The only bar and bat mitzvahs I'd attended had been at the Center City Synagogue, which made this by far the biggest, fanciest synagogue I'd ever been in. There must have been two hundred people in the room, and we barely filled a quarter of the seats. *Oh well,* I thought. At least the prayer books were the same. "Page sixty-two," said the rabbi, a tall man whose silver hair matched the silver thread on his tallis and went nicely with the silver fringe on the bimah, the podium where Tyler would read from the Torah. I wondered whether they'd hired the rabbi because he matched the building so well.

Jessica opened her prayer book the wrong way and stared at it in confusion.

"Here," I said, showing her. "Like this."

"Oh, yeah. Thanks," she whispered as Tyler, who'd been sitting like a ventriloquist's dummy in a tall wooden chair next to the ark that held the Torahs, looking like he was going to throw up or pass out or both, got to his feet and made his way unsteadily across the stage. He wore a dark blue suit and a blue-and-silver tie, with a blue satin yarmulke clipped to the top of his frizzy mop of curls. When he leaned in to the microphone, it squealed like it was afraid of him. Laughter rippled through the crowd. The rabbi bent down, murmured something in Tyler's ear, and adjusted the microphone. Tyler fiddled with his bobby pin. I saw his throat working as he swallowed and started again.

"Please turn to page sixty-three and join me in reading responsibly," he squeaked. More laughter bubbled up. His Adam's apple bobbed again. "Responsively," he said, and launched into the *Ashrei.*

I opened my book and chanted along, figuring it was good practice, as we did the *v'ah hafta.* *You shall love the Lord your God with all your heart, with all your strength, with all your mind, with all your being.* Jessica didn't even bother trying to read the transliterated Hebrew or the English. An entire paragraph before Tyler was done, she closed her book and started whispering urgently to the girl on her other side. I caught the word "Zach" a lot.

Tyler wobbled through the blessings—the prayer saying that there was only one God, the prayer of mourning for the dead, the prayers, the rabbi told us (a little sternly—I figured he could hear the whispers and giggles from where he was) that Jews around the world were reciting this Shabbat, as Jews, throughout their long, sad history of persecution and displacement, had chanted every Shabbat. That shut Jessica up.

The congregation held its breath as the rabbi lifted the Torah—a five-hundred-year-old parchment that, he explained, had been destined for a Nazi museum to a dead religion. After Germany's liberation, that Torah, and dozens of others, were rescued by British soldiers, then restored, then sent to congregations around the world. The rabbi's arms trembled as he lifted the parchment, wrapped around two heavy wooden scrolls, up over his head. "This is the word of God, passed down to us from Moses on Mount Sinai . . ." The rabbi set down the Torah. Everyone exhaled. Tyler cleared his throat, touched his tallis to the parchment, then raised it to his lips and kissed it to show his reverence for the word of God. His voice cracked as he began to laboriously chant the Hebrew words of the week's portion from the book of Numbers. I followed along, wincing as Tyler stumbled through the syllables, silently promising myself that I'd do better.

Beside me, Jessica flipped her Pentateuch shut. She reached into her purse, opened her cell phone (it had a leopard-print, rhinestone-studded case) to look at the time, then pulled out a water bottle. She spun off the cap, lifted the bottle to her lips and sipped, then passed it to me. A sweet, eye-watering smell filled the air. "Peach schnapps," she whispered. "Want some?"

Adventure, I reminded myself, thinking of Duncan's raggedy khakis, the curve of his chin in the flickering light from the train window, the feeling of the sun on my bare shoulders as I'd crossed the parking lot. I lifted the bottle to my lips and took a tiny sip, then braced myself, expecting the stuff to burn going down, but all it did was tingle a little. It actually tasted delicious.

"Thanks," I said, and handed the bottle back.

"No prob," Jessica whispered, sliding the bottle back into her purse.

I leaned back against the padded seat and fumbled with my prayer book. Tyler finished chanting and bent low to kiss the Torah again. Then his parents, my cousin Bonnie, and her husband, Bob, climbed onto the stage to stand on either side of him. Bonnie looked like she was going to cry as she said, "Tyler, my oldest son, your father and I are so proud of you today." She pulled him against her, crushing his face against her bosom. Tyler's bobby pin gave up the fight, and his yarmulke slid to the floor.

Jessica snorted. I giggled, then blushed when an old lady at the end of our row turned sideways and glared at us. Standing between his parents, with his sister, Ruthie, next to him, Tyler smiled and seemed to be breathing normally. I shut my prayer book and watched him while the rabbi talked and his mother sniffled and the kids along my row whispered. The girls' skirts rustled over their knees, the boys fiddled with their ties, and I thought, *Who would be up on the bimah with me?* My mother and father, but what about Bruce? If Grandma Ann got to say a blessing over the Torah, what about Grandma Audrey? And how was I going to convince my mom that if I wore the kind of dress she liked, I would be the laughingstock of Philadelphia?

Jessica reached into her purse again, and when she offered me her water bottle, I didn't even hesitate.

• • •

In the country club down the street from the synagogue, the walls glowed in the sunshine that came streaming through the skylights, and the voices of two hundred well-dressed guests and about twenty little kids bounced and echoed off the floors. Behind a waist-high countertop made of ice were the sushi chefs Jessica had promised, slicing fish and wrapping rice and setting the finished products on smaller blocks of ice that had been carved to spell out my cousin's name. There was a man in a chef's hat tossing pasta, and another one filling pancakes with Peking duck. There was an authentic New York City hot-dog cart in one corner and, on the table right next to it, paper cones of Belgian frites lined up on a metal rack with six different kinds of mayonnaise to dip them in. Waiters in white shirts and black ties offered bite-size hamburgers, miniature Reubens, lamb chops, and little phyllo-dough bundles full of what the waiter said was mushroom duxelles.

I saw Tyler standing behind a table draped in fringed blue velvet, next to a braided loaf of challah for the *motzi,* the blessing over bread. I watched him looking proud and relieved and a little sweaty, accepting kisses and congratulations.

The boys who'd been sitting in our row during the service climbed up to the balcony to flick mints from commemorative TYLER tins at the servers who were setting the tables down below. Jessica gathered up the girls, beckoned to me, and walked over to the bar.

"What can I get you ladies?" the bartender asked.

"Daiquiris for everyone." Jessica grinned. "Make them doubles."

"Funny girl," the bartender said, and poured frothy white liquid out of a pitcher into the empty blenders lined up in front of him. I hated banana. I would have picked any other flavor. The menu said there was peach, and raspberry, and lemon-lime . . .

Too late. Jessica handed me a drink with a chunk of pineapple stuck to the rim of the glass and a piece of banana skewered on a toothpick, floating inside. "Step two," she said. We followed her around a corner into an empty hallway, where she pulled a bottle, this one flat and glass, out of her purse. She looked around to be sure we were alone, then poured some of the brown liquid into each of our glasses. "Cheers!"

I clinked my glass and held my breath and took a sip, which was all I needed to decide that I liked the peach schnapps a lot better than a banana daiquiri. The other girls twirled their straws and clustered together, their black and dark brown and dark blue strapless dresses making them look like a funeral bouquet. I took another sip and put down my glass and plucked a miniature hamburger off a platter. I ate it slowly and drifted toward the corner, toward Tyler.

When the burger was gone, I wiped my fingers on a dark blue paper napkin with Tyler's name engraved in rabbi-hair silver on the corner and made my way to the table. "Hi, Tyler."

He looked at me blankly. Up on the bimah, when he'd said *Today I am a man,* Jessica had crossed her skinny legs and said, "Doubt it," but looking at him now, in his dark blue suit, I wondered whether it was true, whether he actually had changed.

"It's Joy," I reminded him.

"Oh, hi. Sorry. You look different."

I smoothed my dress. "You did really great."

His cheeks turned pink. "I screwed up my haftorah."

"I couldn't tell," I lied.

Tyler was already looking past me, over my shoulder, where the next guests were waiting. "It's going to be an awesome party," he said. I sidled back to my corner and watched him standing between his parents, with his face crushed into his mother's bosom every time she hugged him, and his father's hands gripping his shoulders, until the lights flashed on and off and the waiters walked through the room ringing bells, telling us it was time to go inside.

It took my eyes a minute to adjust to the darkness of the ball-room, where thirty tables draped in silver and blue stood in rows, filling the room. Each one had a towering centerpiece made of different sports equipment, which made no sense: As far as I knew, Tyler hated all sports equally, except for professional wrestling. I stared up at the centerpiece at the kids' table: a dozen footballs and a Jets jersey with Tyler's name suspended in the air. How had they gotten the shirt to float? Was it strung up on invisible thread? Stuffed full of balloons?

I sank into my seat between Jessica and another girl. "Enjoying the refreshments?" Jessica asked, smiling as she handed me another daiquiri—strawberry this time. I took a gulp, letting the icy sweetness melt over my tongue, as a waiter set a plate in front of me: sushi, and a tiny salad topped with candied nuts, and something baked in puff pastry.

Jessica looked down at her food unhappily. "I totally should have gone for the hot dogs," she said. "Why are the appetizers always better at these things?" She poked the puff pastry. "What is this?"

"Um . . ." I took a nibble. "Quiche, maybe?"

"It's a savory goat-cheese tart with garlic coulis and frizzled leeks," said the girl on my other side, whose curly hair was sticking up on top of her head.

"Frizzled leeks," Jessica repeated, her face wrinkled in disgust. She poked at her plate again. The other girl took a bite. She was wearing a dress with puffy sleeves and a blue satin sash.

"*She* kind of looks like a frizzled leek," I said to Jessica. I'd meant to say it softly, but I saw the girl with the curly hair turn her face away.

Jessica laughed. "Frizzled leek!" she said.

I bent my head over my plate. My lunch swam in my vision, and for a minute there were two goat-cheese tarts. *Okay, so it was mean,* I thought. At least I hadn't said she looked like garlic coulis.

I made myself sip a glass of water. The waiters cleared our plates. Jessica grabbed my daiquiri glass and sneaked it under the table, and when it reappeared, it was brimming again. "Drink up," she said, and raised her straw to her lips. The lights went out, and an instant later, the music from *Rocky* blared through the building so loudly that our silverware trembled and the floor shook. In a circle of dazzling blue light, Tyler emerged, held aloft on—I blinked, and yes, it was true. My cousin was being carried into his bar mitzvah reception on the shoulders of actual real-life Jets cheerleaders. Four of them carried him, and the other eight whisked their silvery pom-poms and smiled their bright white smiles. "Come on!" Jessica screamed in my ear, and she grabbed my hand and pulled me up out of my seat and onto the dance floor.

The party started at one and lasted for hours. There were line dances and the limbo and Tyler Trivia, where kids won sweatshirts and CDs and gift certificates. I remembered a raspberry-peach dai- quiri that I gulped down during the endless candlelighting ceremony ("I never met you, and we would have had fun / so in memory of Grandpa Hyman and Grandma Marcia, I'll light candle number one"), and a banana-pineapple daiquiri that I drank while the bar mitzvah boy danced with his mother. I danced with two boys named Jack and three boys named Noah and even with the elusive Zach. After I noticed that my head had started to feel too heavy for my neck, and that my hands didn't feel like they belonged on my arms at all, I told Jessica I had to pee, and we slipped out of the strobe-lit, booming ballroom into the cool, dim lobby. I hustled her past my grandmother ("Joy! Honey!" she said, waving, but I knew I couldn't risk talking to her until I'd eaten a box or two of personalized Tyler breath mints). At last we escaped into the deliciously chilly, pale pink ladies' lounge. "Best . . . party . . . ever!" Jessica hiccupped, slam- ming the door of her stall. The door bounced back open, which made her laugh, and it took the two of us three tries to get the door shut.

I slipped off my shoes and leaned my cheek against the cool metal stall door. My face was flushed, my head was pounding, and my mouth, in spite of everything I'd had to drink, was dry as straw.

"Hey, did you see the chaperones in the coatroom?" Jessica called. "You know why they're there?" She hiccupped again. "Because at Ainsley Kiernan's bat mitzvah, one of the girls was, like, giving a guy a blow job in the rabbi's study, and her parents found out, so now the temple makes everyone have chaperones."

"Ew," I said. It sounded like a scene out of *Big Girls Don't Cry.* I flushed the toilet, walked to the sink, splashed water on my hot face, smoothed on some lip gloss, and had just stepped into the lobby when I saw Emily pulling Bruce toward the front doors and heard her say my name.

"Party!" Jessica whooped.

"I'll meet you in there," I said. As soon as she was gone, I crept through the emptied room after Emily and Bruce, ducking down behind the melting, half-dismantled sushi bar so I could hear them talk.

". . . didn't even know she was coming."

I held my breath and slid down so that I was entirely hidden by the soy-sauce-splattered tablecloth. Peeking through a gap between the tables, I could see Emily and Bruce standing by the wall. She had her tiny hands balled on her hips. He was slouching away from her, eyes on the floor, looking like a boy who'd thrown his baseball through a window.

"Maybe she just forgot to tell me."

"Maybe her *mother* forgot to tell you," Emily said.

"Well, what's the big deal?" Bruce asked. His normally high voice was even higher than usual, and he was blinking faster than ever. "She's here, there's a place for her at the table. What's the problem?"

"The problem," Emily squeaked, turning on one heel, "is that this is embarrassing to me. Do you think I enjoy this? Your family staring at her, staring at me? Aunt Lillian telling everyone, 'Oh, and that's Bruce's daughter from his previous relationship'?" She raised her voice to an old-lady warble. " 'No, no, not another wife, just a girlfriend. She's a—what did they used to call it?—a love child.' With Candace. *You* remember. That book?"

I cringed back against the wall, feeling dizzy and sick. I'd been so busy being embarrassed by my mother that it had never occurred to me that I could be a source of someone else's shame.

"That book," Emily said bitterly. "And what about Max and Leo?" I squeezed my eyes shut, feeling my heart clench, thinking of how stupid I'd been when we'd been walking together, the five of us, and I was imagining that this was what it must feel like to be part of a normal family.

Bruce tugged at his tie. "I'm not happy about this, either," he said quietly. "I know you're uncomfortable, and I'm sorry."

"Uncomfortable!" Emily squawked.

"She's my daughter," Bruce said. "She's got as much right to be here as anybody."

That's right, I thought, my head throbbing, the daiquiris rising up in my throat. *That's right, you tell her!*

"But I'm sorry," he said, and reached for Emily's shoulders. "I know this doesn't put you in a great position."

Emily turned her face away. "I wish . . ." My head was pounding harder than ever, and I felt my lips trembling. I couldn't hear or see what else she said, but I could take a guess. *I wish she wasn't here. I wish she'd never been born.* Crouched behind a dripping block of ice that smelled like fish, I wished for the same thing.

I waited a minute. Then I stood up, steadying myself with one hand on the softened ice. Even in ballet flats, I was taller than Emily. "Excuse me," I called. She and Bruce turned as I walked toward them, their bodies flying apart. Emily cringed. Bruce blinked triple-time. "I want to apologize," I said in what I thought was a perfect high, breezy Amber Gross voice. "For ruining your day."

Emily's face was horrified. "Oh, honey, I didn't mean—"

"Obviously, you didn't want me." I was looking at her, but I was talking to both of them, and I was sure that Bruce knew I was talking about more than just today, more than just his cousin's kid's bar mitzvah.

"Of course we want you," Bruce said. "We—"

I cut him off. "I have to go now. My mom's here," I said, and turned and snatched my backpack off the coat hook where I'd hung it. I pushed the doors open and stood for a minute, dazzled by the sunlight.

They both came after me. I ignored them, which was easy to do once I'd slipped my hearing aids out with tears clouding my vision. *Keep moving, keep moving,* I chanted in my head, and I started walking fast across the parking lot, Amber's ballet flats slapping the pavement, sunshine sparkling off the windshields. Bruce called my name, but I just kept going, as if I'd find my mother's blue minivan idling at the curb. At that minute, I thought I would have given anything if she had been waiting there, if she'd taken me into her arms and said, *Never mind him and never mind her and never mind what I wrote. Of course I wanted you, I wanted you more than anything.*

I kept my head high and didn't turn around even though I could hear Bruce calling my name. *Probably they're glad I'm going,* I thought, and brushed a tear off my cheek. *Probably now they'll have fun.*

My train pulled into Thirtieth Street Station at seven-forty-five. I changed my clothes in the bathroom, but I still thought my day's adventures would show. Not on my breath, because I'd chewed an entire pack of Tyler mints on the bus ride from the train station back home. Not on my face, because I'd scrubbed away the makeup and shoved my hair back into a bun . . . but somewhere. When I got home at just after eight-thirty, the house smelled like the chili that was bubbling away on the stove. Bright blue and gold pottery bowls filled with chopped avocados, sour cream, and grated cheese sat on the table, along with a place mat and napkin for me. I found my parents in the office, huddled in front of the computer, which my mom snapped shut as she pushed her chair back from the desk and spun around to face me. "How was your day?" she asked.

"Did you and Tamsin get a lot done?" my father prompted. I felt the urge to laugh surging inside of me. It tasted like peaches. I opened my mouth and a wall-rattling burp emerged.

"Nice!" said my mother. Her fingers were drumming on top of

the laptop, like she couldn't wait to flip it open again. She got like that sometimes when she was writing, but that didn't explain what my father was doing beside her. Usually, when she and Lyla Dare were on the plains of Saidith Khai or wherever, he left her by herself.

It took me too long to realize that my father wasn't even looking at her. He was staring at me. "Joy, are you feeling all right?"

Uh-oh. "I think I might have a stomach bug," I mumbled, and went upstairs, where I locked myself in the bathroom and sat on the toilet with my head cradled in my hands. A few minutes later, there was a knock at the door.

"I'm indisposed!" I called.

"It's just me." My father's voice was very deep and soothing.

"One second," I called. I swished a gulp of Listerine around my mouth and opened the door. My dad was standing there, tall and familiar in his jeans and blue sweatshirt, with a bottle of Tylenol and a glass of grape-flavored Gatorade in his hands. I remembered being sick a dozen different times, with earaches or fevers or bronchitis, and how he'd take care of me, brewing his special tea (chamomile plus secret ingredients), bringing me extra pillows in crisp pillowcases, and soft scrambled eggs and toast, sitting with me while I watched TV.

I gulped back tears and another burp, feeling wretched with regret and shame. I should have invited him to the blended-family bar mitzvah thing, not Bruce. I should have looked like him, with his dark hair and dark eyes, instead of Bruce, who didn't even want me. Bruce, who I embarrassed.

"Try to sip it," my dad said, handing me the purple drink. I guzzled half the glass, then burped once more and slumped onto the fuzzy pink bath mat. He pulled a towel off the rack and folded it behind my shoulders. "I'm going to assume," he said in his low, slow voice, "that you've learned an important lesson and that there's no need to tell your mother about what you may or may not have been drinking, because you won't be doing this again."

I nodded, not even trying to come up with a lie about bad cheese or sushi. There was a lump swelling in my throat. I wanted to have him hug me or take me to a matinee or an Eagles game. I wanted to be a little girl again, a girl who loved ice cream and the color pink and always wore her hearing aids, a girl who didn't lie or steal or sneak around. I opened my mouth, not sure what would come out of it: whether it would be about peach schnapps, or Bruce and Emily, or where I'd gone and where I'd been all day long. "Amber Gross has a boyfriend," I croaked.

My father considered this. "Do you want a boyfriend?"

I laughed. I could just picture my mom and dad spreading a big net full of video games and buffalo wings across South Street, waiting patiently until a boy who looked right wandered into their clutches. I laughed even harder as I imagined them rolling up the net and dragging it back home. *Honey, we've got a live one!* my mother would say. Or *Throw him back, he's not a keeper!*

"Am I in trouble?" I asked.

My father shook his head, then pulled off his glasses and polished them on the tail of his shirt. Behind them, his eyes looked soft and tired, with lavender pouches underneath. "Let's not let this happen again," he said. I made myself smile, even though I felt like crying. "You think you could manage some toast?" he asked, and I told him that maybe I could.

Nineteen

"I don't know," I told Peter, fidgeting on the chair beside him. "This feels weird. Immoral. It's like we're picking out a prostitute or something. Ooh, she's cute!"

Joy had sipped a cup of chicken broth and nibbled a piece of toast, then gone to her bedroom at nine-thirty. Ten minutes later, Peter and I had put a pot of coffee and shortbread cookies on a tray and tiptoed into my office. I'd gathered up my latest StarGirl outline while Peter had logged on, and we'd spent the next hour huddled together in front of my laptop, scrolling through the classified ads at the Open Hearts website, which I'd insisted on calling Moms.com. We'd been conditionally approved by the agency, which had sent us an access code so we could browse the pictures and biographies of the surrogates while we waited for our home visit, and we'd been looking at the profiles with a mixture of horror (mostly mine) and interest (largely his).

"Check her out," I said, feeling vaguely pimplike as I pointed to a picture of a sweet-faced brunette posing on a porch with two beaming little boys. She was squinting into the sunshine, a hand on one of her son's shoulders, the other hand brushing her bangs out of her eyes. "She even kind of looks like me."

Peter studied the picture. "I don't see the resemblance."

"We both have brown hair," I said. His eyebrow went higher. "And we're both female." Peter gave me an indulgent smile.

212

"Oh, c'mon," I said. "You would totally hit that."

"Is that how we're talking now?"

"Well, isn't that kind of the point?" I replied. "If we're looking for a woman who's going to carry our child, shouldn't she be, you know, someone you'd theoretically want to sleep with?"

"I guess." Peter, agreeable as ever, stretched his long legs out in front of him. "But because it's my sperm and your egg, shouldn't it be someone you'd want to sleep with, too?"

"Huh." I looked at the surrogate's picture. "That does put things in a different light."

The creases bracketing his lips deepened as he smiled. "Hey. Cannie. Are we really doing this?"

I felt as reckless as if I'd drunk a dozen espressos, jittery and excited and deeply disconcerted. "It seems that we are." My fingers flew over the keyboard. Dozens of women's faces and screen names zipped by. I stopped and laughed at one posed in a T-shirt that read WILL BREED FOR FOOD. Then I scrolled back to the first woman I'd picked. "Twenty-nine years old, brown hair, brown eyes, and she's done this before." I scrolled down through the ad and read out loud. " 'My first surrogate experience was fantastic! I gave birth to a beautiful, healthy nine-pound, two-ounce baby boy without complications or pain meds . . .' " I pushed my chair away from the computer so my husband wouldn't see how the words "beautiful" and "healthy" and "no complications" had pierced me. He did see, of course, and he put his fingers under my chin, turning my face toward his.

"You okay?" he asked.

"I'm fine!" I said. I must have sounded convincing, because Peter rested his elbows on my desk and peered at the screen.

"She says she'll travel for the transfer."

I shuddered. "God. Is that what they call it? The transfer? It sounds like we'd be picking up a package or something. Hang on." I located the glossary. "That's the transfer of the fertilized egg. Oh," I said, scrolling down the page to the next ad. "Oh dear." HELLO I AM A TWENTY-THREE-YEAR-OLD WHITE FEMALE. THAT LIVES IN DENVER,

MOTHER OF TWO. I HAVE BLOND HAIR AND BLUE EYES AND BOTH OF
MY CHILDREN HAVE BIG BLUE EYES AFTER ME. DO NOT SMOKE OR
DRINK AND HAVE NO DESIRE TO DO SO. WHILE I AM NO LONGER
WITH THE FATHERS OF MY CHILDREN, I DO LEAD A STABLE LIFE
STYLE AND AM VERY EAGER TO HELP ANOTHER FAMILY BRING A
NEW LIFE INTO THE WORLD.

"Sheera," I read. "Her name is Sheera. Don't women named
Sheera automatically have to be strippers?"

"I guess not," my husband said.

I got to my feet and walked over to my bookshelves, studying the
framed pictures: me and Peter at our wedding, Nifkin and Peter and
Joy on the beach, Nifkin with a miniature Frisbee in his mouth, Joy
with a stripe of sunblock on her nose. "I don't know. It's just too
weird! Paying some woman, some stranger, someone who doesn't
have as much money as we do—it'd feel like we were, I don't know,
hiring a maid or something. And it shouldn't be that way. Having a
baby isn't just doing the laundry or the dishes. I know." I wiped at
my eyes, not even trying to pretend that I wasn't on the verge of losing it. "I remember."

Peter got up and put his hands on my shoulders. I turned away
from him, toward the window, and stared out into the darkness.
"And who's to say she wouldn't change her mind?" I plopped myself
back down in front of the computer, reading out loud. "This one says
she'd let the IPs make a decision about termination if the quad screen
or the amnio looked bad. 'It would bother me but it is the IPs' decision and not mine.' What's an IP?"

Peter clicked one link, then another. "IP," he said in his low,
rumbling voice. "Intended parents."

"Intended parents," I repeated, and pressed my hands together in
my lap. I imagined being twenty-three in Colorado, with two blue-
eyed babies, working and going to college while my mother took
care of my kids, and getting a call or an e-mail from a much wealth-
ier, older couple two thousand miles away, seeking to rent out my
body the same way they'd lease a unit in one of those U-Stor-It places

they advertise on billboards on I-95. Would I love the baby I was carrying? Would I resent the couple I was carrying it for? I straightened up in the chair. "Whoever we pick, whatever they're asking, I think we should double it."

Peter looked at me cautiously. "Why?"

"Because they're not asking enough!" I swept my arm toward the screen. "None of them are! For what they're doing, it isn't enough! To give up a child—"

"But it would be our child. Biologically," he said.

"Biologically." The word didn't signify. A baby was a baby, and I couldn't believe that a woman could carry a baby for nine months and feel like it wasn't hers. I shook my head, remembering, in spite of myself. The doctor who'd come to my room to tell me that I was now minus a uterus had worn a white lab coat with a coffee stain on the sleeve, and he'd had kind, tired eyes. *We're sorry,* he'd said. *We did everything we could.* I'd stared up at him from my hospital bed, still foggy from the drugs and feeling like my insides had been scooped out by God's own melon baller. *No more babies?* I'd asked in a faint voice. *We're sorry,* he'd said again. I hadn't realized how much I'd wanted to be a mother until the minute I'd learned that I wouldn't be able to do it ever again.

"And what if she has complications? Like I did?" My voice cracked. "How do you compensate someone for never being able to have another baby?"

Peter reached over my shoulder and shut the laptop. "Let's take a break."

I sighed and folded my hands on the laptop, thinking about time and how little of it we had left for this.

"Cannie, it's all right," Peter said. "We don't have to decide anything tonight. Maybe your sister will change her mind. Maybe . . ."

I nodded in all the right places and let myself imagine Sheera in Colorado. I put her in an apartment like my old one, on the leafy, tree-lined street around the corner: two bedrooms, one for her and one for her boys. I added music—the *Annie* sound track, which Joy had always loved—the sounds of the washer and dryer eternally running, the smells of diaper cream and apple juice and macaroni and cheese. That had been Joy's favorite when she was a little girl. She'd had a little china dish with a gold rim and a pink bunny painted on the bottom, and a stepstool with her name carved into the top, a gift from Grandma Audrey. I'd let her stand beside me on her stepstool and dump the cheese powder into the noodles. The stepstool and the bunny dish were still in the basement, along with boxes of Joy's nursery-school finger paintings, the clothes she'd outgrown, her tricycle and training wheels, the things I couldn't make myself let go.

The words of the first ad I'd looked at surfaced in my mind like a bright banner snapping in the wind under a cloudless blue sky. *A beautiful, healthy nine-pound, two-ounce baby boy . . .*

Peter studied my face. I did my best to make it look normal as I pushed myself away from the desk. "I'm just going to clean up a little. Not tired yet."

"Okay," he said. "See you upstairs."

I did the dishes and wiped off the kitchen counters, listening for his feet on the stairs and the sound of the water running. After half an hour, I tiptoed back into the study. The desk lamp was still on, and the laptop flared into life when I tapped the keypad. I hit *sort surrogates,* grabbed a notebook and a pen, and started scrolling through the names and faces and cities, searching for the woman who could make our dreams come true.

"Stand, huntress," hissed the voice that came from the darkness. My fingers flew over the keyboard. I leaned forward, mouth slightly open, teeth unbrushed, hair uncombed, sprinting down the homestretch of Lyla's latest adventure, happily lost in her world.

> *Lyla bit back a groan as she staggered to her feet and ran her hands along her sides. Ribs bruised, maybe broken, a front*

tooth snapped to a jagged edge. Her whole body sobbed with pain, but she made herself stand tall, shoulders back, feet planted, like a soldier, the way she'd been trained.

The voice in the darkness laughed at her. "Such a brave girl," it said. "Foolish but brave."

Lyla bent as if seized by a sudden cramp. Her boots were still on her feet. The knife was still in her boot, the blade warmed by her skin. She fumbled it free, imagining she could see the steel flash in the darkness, as the voice said—

The telephone rang, startling me out of my space traveler's trance. "Shit," I said, sighing, and saved my document. I usually remembered to turn off the ringer when I was working. I glanced at the caller ID before lifting the receiver. "Hi, Sam," I said. "Aren't you out with a Jew? Who may or may not be for you?"

"I am indeed," my friend said faintly. "We're at Lacroix. The walls are a lovely shade of pumpkin."

"Be right there," I said, snatching my car keys off the desk. "Pumpkin" was our safe word, the one we'd agreed on when I was single, too, the word that meant "Rescue me." I'd used it only once, when the guy I'd met in line at the video store had asked me out for dinner, then, over appetizers, asked whether I was into swinging. I'd smiled politely, run to the restroom, called Sam, and said the magic word. Ten minutes later, she'd arrived at the restaurant in a taxi with its engine running and a story about a death in the family.

I drove to the Rittenhouse Hotel as fast as I could and pulled up beside the fountain, tossed the keys to the valet, hurried through the doors, and almost smacked into Samantha, who was waiting by the elevator bank, looking unhappy.

"Cannie!" She grabbed my arm and held on to it like the last life jacket on the *Titanic*. "Oh, thank God you're here, you're not even going to believe—"

"Hey!" We turned around. The elevator doors had parted to reveal a furious-looking gray-haired man in a white nylon windbreaker with a to-go bag looped over his wrist. He walked over to Sam, who turned to face him, the epitome of regal disdain. Toe to toe, he was eye level with her nipples. He squinted up at her furiously, waving what appeared to be a check in the air. "Thirty-four ninety-five!" he said.

I watched as my friend extracted two twenty-dollar bills from her wallet and held them out to him, pinched between her fingertips. "Keep the change."

The man snatched the money. There were flecks of white stuff crusted in the corners of his mouth. "You know," he hissed, as I wondered whether the white crud was toothpaste, food, or something indescribably worse, "it's an actionable offense to misrepresent yourself on the Internet."

My heart sank as I realized that I was witnessing the moment I'd long feared: a blind date calling Sam on her failure to be Brooke Shields.

"Oh, really?" Sam said coolly. "That would be an interesting lawsuit from a man who claimed to be five-eight in his profile."

"I am five-eight!" the man insisted. Sam raised her eyebrows and looked at me. I made the universal face of *not getting into it,* even though if that guy was five-eight, I was a size two.

He glared at Samantha for what felt like an eternity before snorting and stomping past us, with his doggie bag in one hand and Sam's forty bucks in the other. Sam sank onto one of the hotel's plush tasseled couches, almost displacing a display of lilac and hydrangeas on her descent.

I sat down beside her. "Do you want to talk about it?"

She shook her head.

"Was it worse than Foreskin Man?"

She grimaced, remembering the date she'd been on long ago with a man who'd launched into an impassioned speech about how he'd been psychologically scarred by his circumcision some thirty-eight years previously.

"Or the guy with one eye?"

The guy with one eye had been mine, and technically he'd had two eyes, but one of them had wandered. One of them had focused on me while I went through my first-date patter; the other one had stayed locked on our waitress's ass.

Sam sighed. "What's to say? He seemed completely normal on the Internet."

"Don't they all."

"Divorced. Two kids. Works as a corporate litigator."

I stared out the doors, watching the man's back get smaller as he stomped across the park. "Does he represent the Lollipop Guild?"

Sam shook her head and got to her feet. "I want to go home. There's no place like home."

"Okay, Dorothy," I said, and led her to my car.

After all our years as friends, after all of our bad dates, after a hysterectomy (mine) and a needle biopsy (hers, and thank God, a false alarm), Sam knows my kitchen as well as her own. She pulled plates and mugs out of the cupboard while I bent in front of the refrigerator, pushing past the carrots and skim milk to find the good stuff. I fixed a plate of Brie and crackers, grapes and fig jam, figuring we'd hang out in the bedroom, eating and watching the *E! True Hollywood Story* on Liza Minnelli that I kept permanently on my TiVo. I picked up a basket of laundry while Sam took the food and followed me up the stairs.

"So do I get to see this notorious dress?" she asked as we walked down the hall past Joy's closed bedroom door.

I flung open my closet door dramatically and pointed at the offending garment.

Sam lifted it from the rod and slipped off the plastic. "Wow," she said. Sadly for me, her reaction wasn't disgust; it was appreciation. "Say what you will about your sister, girlfriend's got great taste."

"It's beautiful," I acknowledged. "But it's way too old for Joy."

Sam ran her fingers along the skirt's shimmering fabric. "I don't know, Cannie. I bet she looks amazing in it."

"But that's not the point! It's a religious ceremony! The point isn't to look amazing, it's about tradition, and Judaism, and . . ."

"What does Peter say?" Sam asked.

"Peter's a guy." I spread the dress on the bed and sat down beside it. "First time he saw it, he thought it was for me."

"God bless that sweet, sweet, clueless man," Sam said, raising a brie-slathered cracker in a toast.

"And the synagogue has rules," I said. "No spaghetti straps, no bare shoulders."

"Doesn't the dress come with a wrap?" Sam asked innocently. I groaned out loud. Those words would be the death of me. They'd engrave them on my tombstone. They'd show up in my obituary. *Candace Shapiro Krushelevansky, 42, died after a short illness brought on by a wrap.* "The dress wouldn't bother me so much if Joy wasn't being so awful."

"Do you think she's on drugs? Does she have a boyfriend? Is she a secret bulimic?"

I shook my head, but I wasn't as certain as I would have liked to be.

Sam got to her feet, eyes sparkling, looking more lively than she had since I'd picked her up at the hotel. "Is she being cyber-bullied? Stalked by older men on MySpace? Can we go through her Internet history?"

"Joy isn't on MySpace, her school just had a seminar on cyber-bullying, and no, we cannot go through her Internet history."

Sam wasn't giving up. "Can we get an ultraviolet light so we can see if there's semen on her bedspread?"

I stared at her. "How do you even know about that?"

"*CSI,*" she said. "*Excellent* TV."

"We can't invade her privacy."

"You're her mother. Invading your kid's privacy is part of the job description. Besides, it's not invading her privacy if we just decided that it was time to flip her mattress over, which you're actually supposed to do every six months." Before I could stop her, Sam had trotted down the hall, opened Joy's door, knelt in front of her bed, and shoved her hand between Joy's mattress and her box spring. "Bingo!" she said.

My breath caught in my throat. A diary? Condoms? A box full of joints and crack rocks?

Worse. Sam pulled out some printed pages, a printout of a ten-year-old newspaper story. SPILLING SECRETS, I read. My heart sank. "Oh," I managed. "Oh, shit." With numb fingers, I flipped through the pages. There I was, giddy and beaming and oblivious, stuffing my face with cake. I flipped through the story slowly, remembering every sordid detail: my mother in the hot tub, Josh's arrest, the allegations of my neglectful parenting and unhappy childhood, and how my sundresses came from Lane Bryant.

"I don't get it," I said. "Why dig this up? Why does she care?" A worse fear seized me. "Do you think she's read the book?"

Sam rolled her eyes. "Um, duh."

I shook my head. "I don't believe it."

"Why not?"

"I read an interview once with Erica Jong's daughter, and she said she read, like, ten pages of *Fear of Flying,* and then she just wasn't interested."

Sam cocked an eyebrow. My heart sank. "Oh, fuck," I said softly, and flipped the pages over. "Maybe it's homework. Maybe she's doing a family tree or something."

"A family tree that she's keeping underneath her mattress?"

I hung my head, silently acknowledging that this seemed unlikely.

"You should ask her about it."

"How? Tell her I just happened to be snooping through her room?"

"Tell her you were flipping her mattress," Sam said.

"She'll kill me." I groaned. I smoothed the pages and slid them back underneath the mattress. "She'll hate me worse than she already does."

"Tell Peter," Sam suggested. "She'll talk to him."

"We shouldn't have done this. I shouldn't even be in here." I smoothed Joy's comforter and pointedly stood by the opened door until Samantha shrugged and followed me out into the hallway.

TWENTY

"So here's what we picked for table linens," said Amber, flipping the page in the special album that her party planner had put together. "I really liked the embroidered silk toppers layered over the linen, but they were special-order from India, and we weren't sure they'd get here in time. These are the Chinese lanterns . . ." She flipped the page. Sasha and Tara and Sophie and I oohed and aahed over the globes of scarlet and peony-pink that would dangle from the Four Seasons' ceiling next month, while Tamsin ate her Zone chicken salad without lifting her eyes from her book. "And the favor bags . . ." Amber pointed at a picture. "Of course, that's just a sample. They'll be monogrammed with my name. We're just finalizing the fonts."

More oohing and aahing. I stifled a yawn. Amber turned another page. "Dress for the service," she said, pointing at something long-sleeved in pale blue. "Dress for cocktails." That one was hot pink, with a poufy skirt. "And the ballgown for the party."

"Oh my God," Tara squealed while I stared at the page.

"Is that a wedding dress?" I asked.

"Bridesmaid's," Amber said smugly. "Vera Wang. Hey, when are you meeting with your personal shopper again?"

I ducked my head. I'd already told the entire lunch table the saga of the dress from New York: how beautiful it had been and how my mother had said no, and how the dress was now hanging in my mother's closet, waiting for my personal shopper, who they didn't know was also my aunt, to pick it up and return it. "God, your mom's a bitch!" Amber had said, and I'd said, "She's totally clueless."

"Clueless," Sasha had repeated.

"Totally," Amber had said.

"God, yeah, totally," Tamsin had said from behind her book. I couldn't tell whether she was being sarcastic or actually trying to sound like the rest of the girls.

"My personal shopper's booked, so I'm going to the mall with my mom this afternoon," I told them.

"I really hope you hurry," Amber said. "Some of the stores are already starting to get their fall stuff in. You so do not want a fall dress."

"Totally," Tamsin muttered again from underneath the tent of her hair. I ignored her, munching my celery with peanut butter while Amber and Sasha reviewed the many reasons why I so did not want a fall dress, which seemed to boil down to an issue of navy and neutrals, which were fine for New Jersey, versus jewel tones, which was what Amber's occasion required.

The bell rang and I packed up my lunch. "See ya," Amber said. Tamsin said nothing, just shoved her empty milk carton into the trash can and hurried out of the cafeteria so fast that there was no chance of my catching up.

Today was early dismissal for a teacher in-service. I stopped in the bathroom to wipe off my lip gloss, then walked through the doors. Outside, my mom's minivan was parked at the curb underneath the gray, humid sky. I took my seat next to my mother, who was talking quietly on her cell phone. "Call you later, Sam," she said as I clipped the specially installed five-point harness-style seat belt in place. "Iced coffee?" my mother offered, pointing at the fresh cup in the cup holder, next to a still-wrapped straw. I shook my head. "Restorative dark chocolate?" she asked, waving a candy bar.

"No, thanks."

"How was your day?" my mother asked as we pulled away from the curb.

"Fine."

"How'd the science test go?"

"Pretty good."

She looked at the road with her own seat belt slipping up over her bosom toward her chin. "Listen," she said.

My body tensed as she drove the car back to the curb and parked there. I sat perfectly still, wondering what she wanted, what she'd say.

"If there's ever anything you want to ask me about, or talk to me about, you know that I'm here."

Like I could miss you. I pushed my lips together and said nothing.

"About boys, or drugs, or your family . . ."

"I'm not doing drugs."

"I don't think you are," said my mother. "But I don't think you're fine. I'm concerned about you, Joy. Your grades worry me."

"I told you, I'm in all these honors classes, and they're just a lot harder."

"If you're having trouble with your classes, we can get you a tutor, or we can talk to your teachers. This is important, Joy. Junior high grades matter for high school, and high school matters for college. This is your life we're talking about! Real life!"

"I don't need a tutor. I'm fine."

"I just want you to know," she said, her voice rising, "if you want to talk about anything, school or friends or anything— anything at all—I'm here to listen."

"Fine," I muttered.

"I love you, Joy," she said, her voice cracking, and I winced at how completely sappy it was . . . and how my eyes filled when she said it.

"Love you, too," I said in a tone that let her know I was saying it only because I had to. She sighed and shook her head, but at least she got the car moving again, out of the city and onto the highway, toward the mall.

When we pulled up at a traffic light, she reached over to smooth my hair, and I let her. Then her hand stopped moving.

"Joy," she said. "Where's your hearing aid?"

I froze. I'd pulled them both out that morning, the way I did every morning, but I'd forgotten to put them back in. "I . . ." *Think of something, think of something, think of something quick!* "I . . ."

The light turned green, and the car behind us honked. "In my pocket!" I said triumphantly, remembering Amber Gross's Rules for Lying to Your Parents. *Keep it as simple as possible. Stay as close to the truth as you can. And keep it short. The more you say, the more chances they'll have to find out you're snowing them.*

I pulled the hearing aid for my left ear out of my pocket and showed it to my mother. "It wasn't working." I congratulated myself because this, technically, was true. Of course, it wasn't working because I hadn't turned it on, but I wasn't going to tell her that.

"Did you get it wet?" my mother asked. "Is the battery dead?" She sighed. "Joy, those things are—"

"—very expensive," I recited. "It just wasn't working. I don't know why."

"Huh." My mother pulled into a parking spot in front of Macy's and studied the hearing aid in her hand. "Do you think that maybe it's not working because you didn't have it turned on?"

"Really?" I sounded as innocent as she sounded sarcastic. "Oops."

"Oops? Joy." I watched as she did something I'd only seen described in books: She flung her hands in the air. "What is going on with you?"

"Calm down," I said, swinging my door open. "It was a mistake. It's not like you've never made a mistake, right?"

She stared at me strangely. "What do you mean?"

"Never mind," I muttered. Finally, she heaved herself out of the car and stared unhappily at the entrance to the King of Prussia Mall. As she got out, I pulled the right hearing aid out of my pocket and stuck it in my ear. I slammed my door. My mother held out her hand, then quickly dropped it back to her side as I tried not to groan out loud. I am thirteen years old, and she still thinks I'm supposed to hold her hand when I cross a parking lot.

My mother took a deep breath. "All right!" she said, as enthusiastic as a cheerleader on pep pills. "Let's go!" I followed her into the store. We threaded our way through the makeup and perfume counters and took the escalator up. I started walking toward the designer gowns on one side of the floor. My mother headed toward juniors on the other.

"Mom."

"What?"

"Aunt Elle said I'm a four and I'd do better in straight sizes."

"Straight sizes? As opposed to gay ones?"

"As opposed to juniors," I said, trying not to roll my eyes.

"I think we should at least take a look here."

"Nothing's going to fit."

"Just a look," she coaxed.

I sighed and plodded after her. She pulled a knee-length linen dress off the rack. "This is pretty."

I looked at the dress. It was unbelievable. "Mom," I said slowly. "I have that dress already. You bought it for me for Class Day last year."

She frowned. "Really? Huh. Well, it's cute." She looked at me hopefully. "Does it still fit?"

I leaned against a pillar and said nothing. The dress has cap sleeves and a full skirt and looks pretty much like the dress Julie Andrews wears when she's leaving the convent in *The Sound of Music.*

"I need a party dress," I explained. "A dressy dress, with sparkles and spaghetti straps . . ."

"Oh, no," said my mom.

"With a *jacket,* or a *wrap,* which I will *wear* when I'm in the *synagogue,* obviously, so that nobody faints because they can see my *shoulders.*"

"Let's watch that tone," said my mom. Her own voice was pleasant, but I could hear the warning underneath. She grabbed something off a sale rack: a brown tweed jumper that had a round-collared white blouse underneath and a short, pleated skirt, with a matching brown velvet beret pinned to its sleeve. "What do you think of this? I mean, maybe not for a bat mitzvah, but isn't it cute? For a school dance or something?"

I stared at the dress in horror, then at my mother's face, waiting for her to wink or smile or say that she was kidding. Except, apparently, she wasn't.

"No," I said. "Just . . . no."

A saleslady in tight black jeans and pointy-toed shoes wandered over. "Start a dressing room?" she droned over the thudding of the rock music they blasted in the juniors department.

My mom rummaged through the sale rack (I could imagine Aunt Elle screaming in horror) and pulled out a long-sleeved forest-green dress in too-shiny satin, then handed it to the saleslady.

"It's too babyish," I said.

"Just try it on," she coaxed.

"I don't like it."

"Just for the size."

"One," I said, lifting one finger, "I already know my size. Two, the theme of Amber Gross's bat mitzvah is Hollywood, not *Little House on the Prairie.*"

My mother sighed. "All I'm asking is for you to try it on. If it fits, then we'll at least know we're in the right ballpark, and if we're not, we'll move along."

"It's all wrong. Completely wrong," I said. "I know what kinds of dresses girls wear. I've been to these parties—" I closed my mouth. Not fast enough.

My mother looked at me. "When have you been to these parties?"

My heart jumped into my throat as I scrambled for my second big lie of the afternoon. "Well, I went to Todd and Tamsin's, and I hear all the girls talking about them, and I know the kind of dresses they're wearing. Party dresses," I said, and then hurried to the dressing room. The faster I could demonstrate the green dress's absolute wrongness, the faster I could get out of here. *Some fun,* I thought, kicking off my shoes and yanking off my jeans. Oh, we were having some fun now.

The dress slid smoothly over my hips, but the zipper stopped about halfway up my back and wouldn't go any farther. As I looked in the mirror to see my breasts bulging up toward my chin in a way that reminded me, horrifyingly, of my mother, it didn't take me long to figure out why the zipper wasn't moving.

"Joy?" My mother knocked on the door.

"It doesn't fit."

"Just let me see!" she said.

"It doesn't fit."

"Honey . . ." She actually started turning the doorknob of the dressing room, as if it would pop open just because she wanted it to.

I slammed the door open and stood in front of her with my arms hanging at my sides and my boobs squashed against the satin. "See? Do you see now?"

My mother cleared her throat. "Okay," she said. "Maybe we can try another size. Or maybe a different bra would help."

She reached toward my chest, probably to adjust the straps of my bra. I slammed the door and stood in front of the mirror, flushed, breathing hard. The zipper wouldn't move up or down, and I hated the sight of myself, hair sticking up, breasts quivering, one hearing aid sticking out of my ear.

"Joy . . ." My mother's voice was sweet as honey. I could see her hand coming over the top of the door, dangling a pink dress with puffy sleeves. I yanked the green dress over my hips, hearing it rip before I threw it over the door.

"Just . . . leave . . . me . . . alone." I punctuated each word by tossing a piece of clothing onto the floor: my pants, my shirt, my left shoe, my right shoe. Then I sank down on the pin- and price-tag-covered floor in my bra and underpants and sat there with my head in my hands. Her fault. It was all her fault. Her fault I was so big on top, her fault that my family was so abnormal, her fault that I would spend my whole life being a freak who would never sound right or look right, who couldn't even disguise her freakishness with the right dress.

"I'm sorry," she said through the door.

"You don't listen to me," I said. "You never listen."

"Okay," she said quietly. "Let's go to the designer dresses. Or maybe we should try another store? Nordstrom, Neiman's—"

"Forget it," I said without opening the door, or looking up, or moving. And then it hit me: my revenge. "You know what? Let's go shopping for you."

There was silence from the other side of the door.

"Come on! Neiman's, Nordstrom . . ." I pulled on my pants and yanked my shirt over my head.

"I've already got something."

I didn't even have to fake being horrified. "You were going to wear something you already have to your only child's bat mitzvah?"

"Well, there's my black dress. You know, the one I wore to Tamsin and Todd's."

I made a face.

"And I have a really nice suit."

"A suit," I said sarcastically. "You're going to wear a suit to my bat mitzvah."

"It's a beautiful suit, and it's practically new. I only wore it once."

"Where?" I shoved my feet into my shoes and opened the door.

She dropped her gaze. "The *Today* show."

"So it's ten years old, and everyone in the world's already seen it? I bet it's black. Is it black? It's black, isn't it?" I glared at her until she gave a sheepish nod. "Save it for a funeral. Come on." I dragged my mom toward Nordstrom, where the plus-size department was called Encore (why, I have no idea).

My mother headed immediately toward the back wall, which was covered with an array of black suits. "I don't think—" she began.

I ignored her and flagged down a saleslady just the way Aunt Elle had in New York. "Hi, there. I'm becoming a woman. My mom needs a dress."

"Oh, how nice," said the saleslady, who was short and plump, with a broad, rosy face and bright red lipstick to match it. Was it a law that salespeople in the fat-lady department had to be fat ladies themselves? "What were you thinking?" she asked my mother.

"I don't know." My mom picked up the sleeve of the dress closest to her and ran her fingers over the sequins like she was blind and they were braille and were going to tell her something important.

"Let me take a peek," the woman said, and disappeared around a corner.

My mother pulled the horrible red-and-gold sequined dress off the rack and held it up against her. "What do you think?"

I studied her carefully. "It looks like God ate Mexican food, then threw up on you."

"Thank you, Joy." She hung the dress up without looking at me. "That's delightful."

The saleslady came bustling back with her arms full of clothes. I saw something that looked like black satin with a big glittering rhinestone belt, and a black jersey dress with a jacket attached. Black. All black. Black with shoulder pads. Like my mother needs shoulder pads. Like anyone my mother's size needs shoulder pads. "Here we are!" she said.

My mother snatched the outfits out of the woman's hand and disappeared into the dressing room, leaving the saleslady and me to stare at each other for about three seconds, until she spotted some other clueless large lady wandering through the sportswear and bustled off to help her. I knocked on my mother's dressing-room door. "How's it going in there?" I asked sweetly.

"Fine," my mother called. Her voice was muffled. Probably she was pulling one of the dresses over her head, slipping the shoulder pads into place.

"Are you going to come out, or stay in there all day?"

"I don't know, Joy. I think the suit I have is perfectly—"

I twisted the door handle. Locked. "Cut that out!" my mother said sharply.

I leaned against her door, examining my fingernails. "You know what you should wear? That red dress you wore to the premiere of Maxi's movie." I'd seen pictures of the red dress. It had long, full sleeves and a gathered neckline, and my mother had had her hair curled and piled on top of her head, and she'd looked—not beautiful, exactly, but radiant and happy.

"I don't have it anymore," my mother said.

"You don't?" She was lying, I bet. She never threw anything out. The dress was probably still zipped up in a garment bag and stuck in the back of her closet, somewhere near the perfect silvery-pink dress she'd taken away from me. "That's too bad. It was pretty."

She opened the door and stood there, dressed the way she had been when we'd first walked through the door. "No keepers."

I smirked. "Maybe you need a different bra."

She shook her head again, then squared her shoulders, heaved another epic sigh, and led me back toward Macy's. Over the next two hours in the designer-dress department, she turned down a beautiful ivory dress (too short) and the perfect purple dress (too revealing), and we couldn't find a single thing to agree on except that she was probably just as sick of me as I was sick of her.

We rode home without a single word. My mom pulled into the garage and closed the door behind us, and we sat there in the dim space that smelled like motor oil. Our bicycles leaned against one wall, alongside an old sled that had been my mother's when she was little, and had her name written in Magic Marker on one of the wooden slats. It was propped up in the corner, with cobwebs hanging like lace off its rusted runners. I thought I recognized the sled from the pictures I'd seen at Grandma Ann's: my mother and Aunt Elle in matching snowsuits at the top of a hill; their father behind them, waiting to push. I remembered his voice on the tape, crooning, *Both of my girls are beautiful.*

I followed my mother into the kitchen, watching as she pulled things out of the refrigerator: a cut-up kosher chicken, carrots and celery and fresh dill, all the ingredients for chicken in a pot. It was one of my favorites. I imagined her spending the afternoon shopping, planning a special meal to celebrate the purchase of my special dress, thinking about how happy I'd be.

I swallowed hard. "Mom." It was hard to push the word out of my mouth. I hadn't been calling her "Mom" much lately, not even in my head. I'd been thinking of her just as "She." *She said. She did. She won't let me. She embarrasses me every time she opens her mouth.*

She pulled the blue-and-white Dutch oven from its drawer next to the stove, then took onions and garlic out of the pantry. "The way I see it," she said without looking at me, "you get to hate me for three years. Four years, tops. And I'd seriously recommend you saving some of them for high school and college."

I blinked at her. "What?"

"Four years," she repeated.

"Did you hate your mother?"

She gave me a tight smile. "Two years in high school, about a year and a half in college, a year in my twenties, and then for about three weeks when I was twenty-eight."

I did the math. "That's over four years."

"You get extra time if your mother falls in love with a woman she meets in a hot tub at the JCC." She bent down beside me and pulled her chopping board out of its drawer. "Don't get your hopes up."

She put the carrots on the chopping board and began peeling an onion. "Do you hate your father?" I asked.

She handed me a bowl of pistachios and paused for a long time. "I don't really think about him," she said. "He wasn't a very nice guy."

I pulled a pistachio shell apart, thinking that this was exactly what Elle had said, and how it didn't line up with the kind voice I'd heard on the tape in the bonus room of the Accessible Ranch. "Did he ever want to meet me?"

She paused again. I chewed the pistachio into paste, watching as she spooned matzoh meal on top of the eggs, whisked in oil, then covered the bowl with waxed paper and set it in the refrigerator.

"I used to think that he would," she finally said. The late-afternoon sunshine came through the window, casting squares of the kitchen floor in shadow and light. My mother looked tired as she adjusted the flame underneath the pot.

"But he never did?"

I watched her as she thought about it, her face soft and unguarded, the way it usually was at night. She put the lid back on the pot, wiped her hands, and shook her head. "No, honey. He never did."

TWENTY-ONE

There is something wrong with me. Seriously wrong. But isn't recognizing that you have a problem the first step toward solving it? I admit that I have a problem. I can recognize my behavior as aberrant, even compulsive. In the clear light of day, I can look at the situation objectively, acknowledge that what I'm doing is unhealthy, and promise that I'll stop.

I just can't quite manage that last part. The stopping.

The night after Joy and I had our disastrous shopping trip—the night I'd lied to her about my father, figuring it was a white lie, a lie told to protect her, and a mother's lie, born out of love, was hardly a lie at all, was something more akin to a prayer or a blessing—I woke up at one-fifteen in the morning and eased myself noiselessly out of bed. I tiptoed down the hall and paused in front of Joy's room. I wanted to go in and straighten her covers, reassure myself that she was still breathing, but I dug deep for some unknown reserve of restraint and settled for just looking at her—her hair spilling over the pillow, one foot sticking out from under the quilt, pale and perfect in the glow of the streetlamp. I stared for a long moment, wishing her secrets would reveal themselves: that there was a diary I could read, that I could snoop through her e-mail and find out whom she'd been talking to and what she'd been saying.

"I think Joy read my book," I'd whispered to Peter the night Samantha found the *Examiner* article underneath her mattress.

"Did you ask her about it?" he asked. I bit my lip and confessed that I hadn't. "It shouldn't surprise you. You had to know that someday she'd want to read it."

I shook my head in frustration, unwilling to give him my Erica Jong story, because he'd probably laugh at me, too. "She's probably got a million questions. About the book . . . and Bruce . . . and my family."

"So tell her what she wants to know," he said, which sounded like a perfectly rational response, except I didn't know what Joy wanted to know. I didn't know what she was looking for. For the first time in her life, she was in trouble, and I couldn't fix it.

I bent down and brushed her hair away from the curve of her cheek. "I love you," I whispered. "I love you so much." Joy sighed in her sleep and rolled onto her back, and I crept out of the room. Maybe it would seep into her subconscious, and she'd wake up happy.

Then I eased myself down the stairs, retrieved my bar of dark chocolate with raspberries from the cabinet where I'd stashed it behind the flaxseed and soy-fortified oatmeal, and sat down at my desk in front of my laptop. I began with the big-girl news. None of it was good. Here was an AP story about a sorority in Indiana that had pared its membership from twenty-five girls down to two. The national chapter president insisted that it was mere coincidence that all of the girls who got the boot were fat, bespectacled, and/or minorities. Here was a brief about a girl who hanged herself after being teased by her classmates about her weight. Police arrested her mother. The girl weighed 325 pounds at the time of her death. Her mother was being charged with neglect for, presumably, not putting her on a diet.

I shook my head, minimized the screen, leaned forward in anticipation, and pointed and clicked to the surrogacy website. This is what I do at night while my husband and my daughter are sleeping. I sneak downstairs in my bathrobe and bare feet, eat dark chocolate, and stare at pictures of young women on the Internet. I am sure there is some significant way in which that makes me different from your run-of-the-mill male porn addict; I just haven't quite figured out what it is yet, unless it's that the women I look at are, for the most part, fully clothed, except for a small and surprising minority whose members have decided that posing in bikinis will somehow improve their chances of being picked as a potential parent.

I began with BETSY82, one of the first women I'd seen, the one with two boys who I'd claimed looked like me. Betsy lives in Horsham, which is close but not too close. She's been married for seven years, and she and her husband both work. Betsy has a nursing degree, works part-time, has already gone through one successful surrogacy for a married male couple (gay-friendly! open-minded!). *I loved being pregnant. I loved how I felt and how the world responded to me. I felt as if I were in bloom.* (Me, too, I thought, taking a bite of chocolate and absently wiping my eyes. Oh, Betsy, me, too.) *I even loved my hideous maternity clothes! LOL.* Those three little letters might be a deal-breaker. Could I entrust my genetic material—not to mention Peter's—to someone who used cutesy abbreviations on the Internet? We'll see. I'd already nixed all the candidates who had animated emoticons in their profiles or referred to frozen embryos as "snow babies." A girl's got to draw the line somewhere.

I'd read Betsy's profile so many times that I knew each word by heart, had stared at her pictures for so long that I could probably draw each one from memory. In one shot, she and her boys were at a pumpkin farm. They were dressed in jeans and jackets, and each one was holding a pumpkin—small, medium, and large. Betsy's dark-brown hair was pulled back in a clip. She wasn't a knockout, but she was pretty in her plum-colored cords and tan coat, with her husband standing beside her and her skin glowing with good health. Or maybe her skin was glowing from the pint of cheap vodka she'd chugged before getting behind the wheel, and she'd mowed down an entire kindergarten class on her way to the pumpkin patch. How was I supposed to know?

It was the second picture that broke my heart. In that one, Betsy was in a hospital bed, looking pale and drained and exultant. There was a plastic bracelet around her wrist and a baby bundled in her arms with his eyes closed and a pink-and-blue knitted cap pulled down to his eyebrows. On either side of the bed, framing her and the newborn, were two beaming men. They wore matching platinum wedding bands, and each of them had stretched out a pinky for the baby to grasp.

She had done it once. She wanted to do it again. *I will work with you and your partner to make your dreams come true* was the last line of her profile, and for the last month I'd been a perpetual ten seconds away from writing to her and asking whether we could meet.

But not tonight. My e-mail chirped: There was a letter from my editor, Peyson, who didn't normally write in the middle of the night. DID YOU SEE THIS? read the memo line, and the missive had been marked with a red "urgent" flag. Curious, I clicked on the link, which led me to one of the Internet's most lively gossip websites, then jerked back in my chair as if I'd been slapped.

IS CANDACE SHAPIRO J. N. LOCKSLEY? screamed the headline on Groklt.com. My heart jumped into my throat when the cover of *Big Girls Don't Cry* appeared above my old head shot—my hair longer and lighter and more elaborately styled than it had been in years, the corners of my eyes crow's-foot-free. *An anonymous—but very convincing—source tells us that the author of* Big Girls Don't Cry *has been writing Lyla's adventures for Valor Press for the last nine years. Calls to Valor and Lyla Dare Enterprises for confirmation have so far gone unanswered.*

"Holy shit!" I blurted, then shot a panicked glance toward the stairs. All quiet. I turned back to the computer, staring at the screen as if expecting it to start talking. "Guberman?" I muttered, before rejecting it instantly. Bruce had no idea what I did for a living. No interest, either, as far as I knew. But if not Bruce, then who'd done this? There were only a handful of people who knew that I was J. N. Locksley: my husband, my daughter, my mother and my siblings, my agent, of course, and my editor and publisher in New York. Could Peyson have leaked my name, or Patsy Philippi herself, as a way of yanking my comfortable carpet out from underneath me so that I'd have to give the people at Valor Press the novel they wanted?

I groaned and shoved myself away from the computer, knowing I'd never get back to sleep, trying to figure out how this had happened, whether I'd lose my job, my livelihood, and whether I could get it back again.

Twenty-Two

O n Thursday morning, I got up as usual, took my shower, styled my hair, got back into my nightgown, and lay in bed, waiting for my mother to show up. I waited until seven-twenty, then got dressed and went down to the kitchen, where my mother was sitting at the table, staring at her laptop.

"Hey, Mom? How come you didn't wake me up?"

She didn't say a word. She was still in her pajamas, with bruised circles under her eyes, looking like she hadn't slept at all. My dad was standing behind her with his hands on her shoulders, staring over her head at the screen. "It's not the worst thing," he said, his voice a low, comforting rumble.

"I'm going to lose my job," my mother said bleakly.

"So you'll be free to do other things," he said.

"What?" I said. "What's going on?"

My dad pointed wordlessly at the computer screen. I leaned over my mother's shoulder. STARGIRL SCANDAL! read the headline of the page she'd pulled up. *Wondering why StarGirl Lyla Dare's been obsessed with the size of her thighs? Wonder no more! GrokIt can EXCLUSIVELY report that the Philadelphia-based author CANDACE SHAPIRO* (Big Girls Don't Cry) *has been writing as J. N. Locksley for years.*

I could hear the click in my throat as I swallowed. "What happened?"

"Somebody leaked the story," said my mom. Her cheeks were pink, her lips were white, and it hit me that she didn't look angry. She looked scared.

Which made me scared, too. "Who?"

She looked at me for so long that I started to squirm and feel guilty, even though I wasn't. Finally she shrugged. "I honestly have no idea. But I think this is the end of the road for me and Lyla."

"Why?"

Her fingers clattered over the keyboard as she opened up a Lyla Dare fan message board. I squinted and read the first comment: *If it turns out that no-talent pink-book-writing pus-hole Candace Shapiro is writing Ly, I swear I'll never buy another book!*

"See, the thing is, these books are supposed to be written by J. N. Locksley, and J. N. Locksley didn't write *Big Girls Don't Cry*," she said.

I scanned through the messages. None of them sounded too happy about the prospect of my mother writing Lyla Dare's adventures. My father bent down to wrap his arms around my mother's shoulders, and she made a sad little whimpering noise and leaned back.

"Who?" she asked. "I just can't figure out who'd want to do this to me."

I pulled my lunch out of the refrigerator and stood there, waiting for someone to notice that it was a school day and I needed a ride. Finally I cleared my throat.

"Can you take a cab?" my mother asked faintly. She didn't look at my hearing aids to make sure they were turned on. She didn't peek into my backpack to make sure I'd remembered my lunch. She barely looked at me at all.

I swallowed hard, wondering if she thought that I was the one who'd spilled the beans. Then I zipped up my backpack and stood in front of the door with my hand on the knob. "I'm sorry," I said. Neither of them answered. I walked outside, realizing, with a sinking feeling, that maybe I did know what had happened, and maybe it was actually my fault.

I paid the cabdriver, ran through the play yard, skipped my lip gloss application/hearing aid removal, and caught up with Amber Gross on the way into homeroom. "Hey," I said.

She turned around with her usual smile in place. "Hi, Joy!" She had on a light blue button-down, jeans, and a narrow blue satin belt. A matching satin headband held back her smooth hair, and she had pale blue elastics in her braces. She didn't look like a girl who'd lie or steal or tell her mom that she was babysitting when she was really at a high school party with Martin Baker, but I knew for a fact that she was that girl, that she'd done those things, and maybe worse.

I cleared my throat. "Hey," I said. "Did you, um, by any chance, happen to mention to anyone that my mom . . ." I chanced a look up. Amber was staring at me, eyes wide underneath their sparkly shadow, not looking guilty at all. "That she writes the StarGirl books?" I whispered.

Amber shook her head. "Nope."

One-word answers, I heard her say in my head when she'd been talking to the lunch table about how to tell a lie. *Don't give them anything to hold on to.*

"Look," I said, feeling a little panicky, remembering my mother's white lips, the hurt on her face at the table that morning. "If you did, I won't be mad. It's just that . . . it's kind of a big deal. For my mom, you know? She really has to keep it a secret."

Amber's hair swished against her shirt as she shook her head no.

"Okay," I said, turning toward my own locker. "Okay."

Tamsin and Todd walked past us, heads bent together, talking quietly, Todd in a perfectly pressed shirt, Tamsin in her gray sweatshirt.

"So listen," said Amber. "How did it go yesterday at the mall? You seriously have to get something soon, you know."

"I know," I said, easing myself away from her. "I'll see you at lunch." The first bell had just rung. There was time for me to catch up to Tamsin and Todd at their lockers.

"What's wrong?" Todd asked when he saw my face.

I told them both while we put away our backpacks in our lockers and walked to homeroom.

"I don't want to be the one to say 'I told you so,' " said Tamsin. "But Amber? Is a big fake bitch."

Just because she doesn't like you, I thought.

"She's a big fake bitch and a gossip," Tamsin said, flipping her hair off her cheeks. "Can we please stop sitting with her at lunch now?"

"Seriously. I miss you," Todd said. My throat tightened. I missed him, too. I missed the three of us together, and how easy it was for me to tell them everything. I just wasn't sure I missed it enough to give up sitting with Amber, and with Duncan Brodkey.

"Maybe it wasn't Amber," I said. "She said she didn't do it."

Tamsin made a face. "Oh, please. You think she's going to tell you the truth?" she sneered. "She lies about everything."

"She's got a great look," Todd acknowledged, smoothing the cuffs of his shirt. "But she's kind of a bitch."

"A major bitch," said Tamsin. She tugged her sweatshirt hood up over her head and yanked the drawstrings: first the left one, then the right. "So who's it gonna be, Joy? Them or us?"

My insides twisted. "That's not fair," I said. Tamsin and Todd were my best friends, but I wanted to go to Amber's bat mitzvah—except Amber had blown off my friends and sold out my mother. Unless she hadn't.

"I don't know," I muttered. The second bell rang, and I sank into my seat, wondering what was going to happen, whether my mother would really lose her job, whether it was really my fault.

Usually, when I come home from school, the kitchen smells good. My mom makes bread, or she snips herbs from the garden and hangs them up to dry. There's always some smell: peppermint tea, toast from breakfast, a breath of sweetness from the roses in a vase on the table where they stay until they've shed all their petals on the table and the floor. Today the kitchen smelled like nothing. My mother was sitting exactly where I'd left her that morning, at the kitchen table, staring at her laptop. She wore a shirt on top, but her legs were still covered in her red-and-green pajama bottoms, and her feet were bare.

"Hi," I said, edging toward the table.

She lifted one hand in a halfhearted wave and said nothing. I got a glass of juice and carried it over, unsure what to do next. "Do you want some?" I finally asked.

She shook her head. "I'm sorry I was so out of it this morning," she said. I took that as a sign that I could sit down at the table across from her. "It was kind of a shock. Maybe it shouldn't have been. My publisher's been after me to write something else, something under my own name, and I think maybe someone there decided that this"—she gestured toward the screen—"would be a push in the right direction."

"Oh." I was thinking about Amber's face, the way she'd looked at me when she'd shaken her head no. I swallowed hard as my mother stared at me.

"You don't know anything about how this happened, do you?"

"No! Of course not!"

She stared at me again, then shrugged.

I forced myself to ask, "What happens now?"

"I have to wait and see if anyone else picks up the story."

"What if they do?"

"I'll just say no comment, but you can only cover your tracks so well. I guess it's all a question of how much it ends up mattering . . . how much truth people can handle about who's been writing their science fiction."

"I'm sorry," I said.

"Yeah. Well . . ." She shrugged and tried to smile, then pushed herself back from the table. I waited for her to ask if I wanted to make cookies or help with dinner, if I needed help with my homework, if I wanted to go for a walk or go to the bookstore. Instead, she just turned away and walked slowly down the hall, to her office, and for the first time that I could remember in my life, she closed the door behind her.

TWENTY-THREE

"*D*on't think of it," said Lyla Dare, grinning, with the heel of her boot *digging into the soldier's filthy neck.* I was midway through my latest manuscript, and Lyla was doing what Lyla did best: kicking ass and taking names. It felt, I had to confess, wonderfully cathartic to imagine the neck beneath her boot heel as belonging to whoever had betrayed me.

> *The soldier twisted his head and spat at her. Lyla gave a small, untroubled smile, bent down, and swiftly disarmed him, pulling the taser and the curved knife from his belt. Then she yanked him to his feet, twisting his arms behind him. He lurched forward, trying to shake her off. She jerked his hands higher, her grin widening as both of his shoulders were wrenched out of their sockets with a satisfying pop.*

I grinned, my own teeth bared, leaning forward, imagining that it was me doing the damage.

> *"Reconsider," Lyla whispered, so close that her lips almost brushed his dirt-caked ear. There was blood on her teeth, he saw, as the world wavered in front of him, and he fell to his knees, moaning.*
>
> *"Mercy, sister," he cried as tears and blood mingled with*

the sweat and dirt on his face. "Mercy, huntress. Are we not the
same?"

"Hardly," I muttered as a car honked outside my window. I
snapped my laptop shut, looking at the clock. Ten-fifteen A.M., which
gave me an hour and forty-five minutes to get my house in order. I
looked out the window. Bruce had bought yet another new car.

"Joy!" I yelled. "It's your . . . It's Bruce!" The bathroom door
slammed, and my daughter came clomping down the stairs, her hair
gathered in a ponytail, lipstick that I wasn't supposed to notice on
her lips. I beckoned her close, and she sighed noisily. I looked in both
of her ears to make sure her hearing aids were there and turned on.

"Is it okay if we go shopping?" she asked, waving at Bruce
through the window.

"Sure," I said. "Call if you're going to be past four."

She gave me a look suggesting that I'd sustained major brain
damage at some point after breakfast. "I won't be home until dinner.
Bruce is dropping me off at the Ronald McDonald House. For my
mitzvah project, remember?"

"Right." That worked out perfectly. I'd have time to clean the
house, get through the home visit, then unstraighten things again.
Peter and I had decided not to tell Joy anything about the possibility
of a baby until we'd passed our home inspection and found a surrogate who'd work with us. I wasn't used to keeping secrets from my
daughter, but this, I figured, was for a good cause. With everything
else that was going on—her moodiness, her grades, the hearing aids
she couldn't remember to turn on, the article I'd found under her
mattress, her mother's looming lack of employment—why give her
something else to worry about until we knew one way or the other for
sure?

"Kiss," I said. Joy groaned out loud but let me kiss her cheek and
accidentally on purpose swipe some of her lipstick off with my sleeve.
"Have fun! Be careful! Call if you need me!"

Joy waved impatiently and ran out the door. As soon as Bruce's brand-new car pulled away from the curb, I shut down my laptop and sprang to my feet, straightening stacks of magazines on the coffee table, stashing shoes and umbrellas in the closet, lighting candles, sliding an apple pie I'd prepared and frozen the previous weekend into the preheated oven to give our house that homey, nostalgic, cinnamon-and-nutmeg smell that spoke of solid morals and steady love—or at least regular access to homemade desserts.

"Peter!" I called.

My husband, still unshaven and in his weekend wear of rumpled khakis and a paint-splattered T-shirt, ambled down the stairs. "Home visit, remember?" I said.

He grinned at me. "Bagels purchased. Fruit platter procured."

I followed him into the kitchen. Half a dozen bagels were perfuming the air from their bag on the counter, and he'd remembered to get low-fat and regular cream cheese, the fresh-fruit platter I'd ordered from Whole Foods, and half-and-half for the coffee. "Have I mentioned that I love you?" I asked. He nodded. "Have I mentioned that you need to shave? And can you run the vacuum over the living room rug?"

"I'm on it."

I followed him into the living room. "You're on it, or the Roomba's on it?" Sure enough, the vacuum was still in the closet, Frenchie was cowering in the corner, and the little robot vacuum disc was whirring over the carpet. "You know I don't trust that thing."

He put his hand on my neck. "Candace. We've had the Roomba for ten years, and it has never, quote-unquote, turned on us."

"That doesn't mean it won't." I stared at the Roomba suspiciously. "In fact, as far as I'm concerned, that means it's overdue."

"I'm going to shave," Peter announced.

"You do that," I said, and went back to the kitchen to slice the bagels, brew the coffee, distribute the armful of pink and yellow tulips, lilies, and peonies between three different vases, and pour fresh orange juice into a cut-glass pitcher we'd gotten for our wedding. "Champagne?" I called. "Do we want Remy Heymsfeld to think we're the kind of people who drink mimosas?" Peter and I hadn't been able to determine whether Remy Heymsfeld was male or female, so we'd spent the two weeks since we'd gotten our home visit date referring to him/her simply as Remy Heymsfeld.

"Maybe we should all do tequila shots," Peter said as he came back downstairs ten minutes later. "It'll be a good icebreaker." There was a dab of soap on his earlobe and a tiny piece of toilet paper stuck to a cut in the center of his chin.

I could use a shot, I thought. I was a nervous wreck. I poured cream into a pitcher and set it on a tray alongside cups and the sugar bowl and the silver spoons and the napkins I'd gotten up at six o'clock to iron. Once that was done, I trotted up the stairs. *Hot rollers, hot rollers, where were my hot rollers?* I rummaged underneath my sink: blow dryer, jumbo bottle of conditioner, dusty bag of free-with-purchase lipstick and foundation, both in the wrong colors, and nary a single hot roller. I slammed the cabinet shut and dashed into Joy's bedroom. Her backpack was unzipped on the floor. As I passed by, I saw her math book and her English folder and, between them, a familiar flash of hot pink.

My heart sank. I sat down on her bed, dry-mouthed and dizzy, before dipping my hand into the backpack and extracting a battered paperback copy of *Big Girls Don't Cry.*

I flipped through the pages slowly, my dismay giving way to confusion. Sentences, paragraphs, entire pages had been inked over in black. Every curse word and sex scene had been redacted. The pages bristled with Post-it notes. *Ask Elle?* read one. *No way,* said another. A third said simply, *Amsterdam.* On the inside cover was the address of Princeton's website, a phone number with an area code I didn't recognize, and a string of words like haiku: *Horses. Mama. Fiction. No big deal.*

"Cannie?" I jumped off the bed as if I'd been electrocuted, and shoved the book into Joy's bag. Then I wobbled to the staircase. Peter was staring up at me from the foyer. "You're not dressed yet?"

My voice was faint. "We may have a problem."

"What's wrong?"

"Joy . . ." I shook my head. There was no time. I'd have to deal with this later. "Never mind. I'll be down in a minute." I ran back to the bedroom for the skirt I'd collected from the dry cleaner's the day before, along with a pink cashmere twinset and Samantha's strand of pearls.

Five minutes later, I was back in the kitchen, standing in front of Peter for his inspection. "Well?" I asked. "Do I look young and vital?" Peter, in khakis and a crisp blue cotton shirt, looked perfect now that his face had stopped bleeding. I'd helped him pick out his clothes the night before, after Joy had gone to sleep: the pants, I thought, said, *I will take a child to the playground without even having to be asked,* while the shirt proclaimed, *Gainfully employed with good health insurance.*

He looked me over. "I'd say either the necklace or the heels. Not both."

"Too much?"

"You look like it's a costume party and you're going as June Cleaver."

I slipped the pearls into my apron pocket and smoothed my hair. The pie smelled delicious, and the coffee was perking. On the mantel above the fireplace in the living room were a charming array of freshly dusted family photographs in frames of silver and polished wood. My sullen thirteen-year-old would be out of the house for hours, and I had the rest of the night to talk to her about what she'd read. It wouldn't get better than this.

Remy Heymsfeld, it turned out, was a twenty-five-year-old male social worker ("Remy is short for Jeremy"), enthusiastic as a golden retriever puppy, with fresh comb tracks in his damp brown hair and pinchable pink cheeks. He devoured two bagels slathered with cream cheese, spooned sugar into his coffee, admired my garden, petted Frenchelle, and asked how we liked Philadelphia. Then he opened a folder (our names, I saw, were typed very officially on the tab) and started asking us page after page of questions. How long had we known each other? How had we met? How would we describe our marriage? (I said "stable." Peter said "fun.") How would we characterize our relationship with Joy? (I thought "fraught" but crossed my fingers behind my back and said "warm and open." Peter said "loving.") Remy wrote it all down. I let myself wonder briefly whether there was any couple in the world who couldn't feign normalcy for the duration of a home visit. Even if your true intentions were to keep the child in a chicken-wire cage in the basement before selling her kidneys on eBay, you could probably keep it together long enough to impress a stranger for an hour or two.

"Would you mind showing me around?" Remy asked. We got to our feet. Our instructions from the agency had told us that this would be part of the deal. The week before, Peter and I had relocated the treadmill from the office to the basement and given the walls a fresh coat of buttermilk-colored paint. When Joy had asked what was up, I'd told her a version of the truth: that I needed to keep busy until my work situation was resolved. When she was in school, I'd gone up to the attic, opening the cedar boxes labeled INFANT/WINTER and TODDLER/SUMMER and BLANKETS and TOYS. I hadn't gone so far as to retrieve my old rocker from the basement, or put any of the blankets or tiny knitted sweaters in the dresser, but I'd washed them all, using Dreft and the gentle cycle, and folded them carefully back into their boxes, just in case.

Remy pulled out a digital camera. He took pictures and measurements to see how far the theoretical baby's room would be from ours, from the bathroom, from the stairs. He noted the number of bathrooms, photographed the fire alarms, and listened to our lengthy reassurances that Frenchelle was so placid and well trained that she'd barely notice a new baby in the house, let alone attack one. Then he ate a slice of apple pie and lingered in my office, taking in the stacks of StarGirl books and the top shelf, with all of its versions of *Big Girls Don't Cry.*

"Your books?" he asked.

"My books," I told him, half shy, half defiant. No point in denying it now, I figured. Plus, if Remy Heymsfeld spent ten seconds on-line, he'd find it all out anyhow. "Writing's a really great job for a mother," I said enthusiastically, leaving aside the question of whether it was a job that I had anymore. "The hours are very flexible. When Joy was little, I'd write when she was napping." Remy nodded and wrote something in our folder. I leaned closer—like any ex-reporter worth her salt, I could read upside down—but couldn't make out the words.

"Thank you both for your time," he said after he'd tucked our folder back into his briefcase. "I can't say anything official until after the review, but . . ." My heart stopped. Peter squeezed my hand. "You two seem like ideal candidates," Remy concluded, his unlined face wreathed in a cheerful smile. I felt myself relax as Remy extended his hand for Peter, then me, to shake. "I don't think you've got anything to worry about at all."

Twenty-four

"Hi," I said to the lady sitting behind the desk. It was three-thirty on Sunday afternoon, and I was standing in the hallway of the Ronald McDonald House, which smelled like potpourri and Lysol and, underneath, very faintly, like pee. "I'm Joy Krushelevansky? I'm here to volunteer? For my mitzvah project?"

The lady held up one finger, then pointed at the telephone. "Sure . . . uh-huh . . . the social worker will be in touch." Then she pulled off her headset. "Hi!" she said, smiling at me with her big red wet-looking lipsticky mouth. "I'm Debbie Marshall, one of the house coordinators." The telephone rang. She frowned at it, pushed a button, and got to her feet. "Here, why don't you hang up your stuff? I bet we could use you in the kitchen!"

She showed me a closet, where I set down my coat and my shopping bag, then led me to a kitchen that smelled like disinfectant, with a linoleum floor and a gigantic stainless-steel refrigerator and an eight-burner stove. There were two more big refrigerators along one wall, two dishwashers, and two sinks, both filled with breakfast dishes. I saw crusts from toast and floating soggy Cheerios in a puddle of milk at the bottom of a blue-and-white bowl.

Debbie sounded apologetic as she said, "Do you mind? We're at capacity right now. Six families. People are supposed to clean up after themselves, but . . ."

It took me a minute to figure out what she wanted. "Oh, no problem." I found a pair of yellow rubber gloves and pulled them on. I opened one of the dishwashers, turning on the hot water, finding the sponge and the dish soap. Doing dishes was better than what I'd been worried I'd have to do, which was talking to sick children, or the families of sick children, because what in the world would I say to them?

I thought of the shopping bag in the closet and smiled. It had been easy. So easy. Today had been the first time I'd seen Bruce since our scene at Tyler's bar mitzvah, and he'd treated me like I'd break at the first hard look or sharp word. When I got into the car, he asked what I wanted to do instead of telling me what our plans were. When I asked to go shopping, he agreed and drove us to the Cherry Hill Mall. "Joy," he'd said after pulling into the parking lot. "I want you to know that in spite of what happened between me and your mother, or what you might have overheard, or what you might have read—"

I cut him off. "It's okay. It's totally fine. I'm fine." I hadn't missed the look of relief on his face.

"Are you sure?" he asked, bending over to unbuckle Max from his booster seat. "Because look, the truth is—"

I so did not want to know the truth, especially not his version of it. "It's fine," I repeated, and took Max's hand. "Can we have money for a snack?"

Bruce did what I knew he'd do, what he always did: pulled his wallet out of his pocket and flipped it to me. "Help yourself." His wallet was a mess, bulging with old ATM receipts and business cards and credit cards and three expired driver's licenses. I pulled out five dollars. Then I pulled out a MasterCard, looking up quickly to see if Bruce was watching, which he wasn't. I stuck the card in my pocket. I took Max on the kiddie train, and when the boys asked if they could go see a movie, and Bruce looked at me with his eyebrows raised, I said, "Why don't you go ahead. I can just look around here."

"Are you sure?" he asked, clearly relieved, and I said that I was. The movie lasted an hour and a half, which was more than enough time. The dress I found wasn't exactly the same as the one I'd bought with Aunt Elle—the pink was a shade or two darker and the beading on the straps and hem was different, but it was close enough, and I didn't even flinch as I slapped Bruce's card on the counter. *Let him pay,* I thought. *He should pay. I'm his daughter.* I waited for him to ask about the bag when he picked me up in front of the Build-a-Bear workshop, but Max was whining and Leo was pestering Bruce about some music he'd wanted to buy, and it was the easiest thing in the world to shove the credit card into the backseat pocket of Bruce's brand-new car on our way out of the parking lot.

I was rinsing glasses and stacking them in the top rack of one of the Ronald McDonald House's dishwashers when a girl in overalls and pink rag wool socks wandered into the kitchen. I followed her out of the corner of my eye as she pulled up a chair at the kitchen table, which was round and had enough room for ten. She sat there, watching me wash dishes. *Say something? Say nothing?* Finally, I turned off the water and pulled off my gloves. "Hi," I said. "I'm Joy."

She looked me up and down. "Do you work here?"

"I'm a volunteer." Did I look old enough to work here? To work anywhere? The girl had light brown skin. Her hair was in two puffy pigtails, she had big round brown eyes, and she wore a pink-and-white-striped shirt under her blue overalls. I thought she was maybe ten or eleven, so maybe I did look old enough to her.

"You talk funny," she said.

"I do not!"

"Yes, you do," said the girl. "Your voice is all . . ." She dropped her own voice until it was a low, raspy growl. "Like this."

I did a quick check to make sure my hearing aids were still in place. Then I folded the dish towel I'd been using and hung it neatly over the oven handle. "For your information," I said, taking care to say every syllable precisely, "I just have a husky voice. I do not talk funny."

"You got hearing aids?"

I smoothed my hair down tight against my cheeks, frowning.

"My grandmother has them, too."

Great. "Are you sick?" I asked. If she was sick, if she had cancer or something awful, if all that puffy brown hair was a wig, then maybe I'd cut her some slack, but if she wasn't, I was going to march right back to Lipstick Debbie and ask for another assignment.

"Not me," said the girl. "My brother. He's doing chemo."

"Oh."

"Probably he'll die," said the girl.

"Oh," I said, and tugged at my hair again.

Lipstick Debbie stuck her head around the corner. "Cara? Did you finish up your homework?"

"Yeah," said Cara, only she sighed it more than she said it.

"And the dishes are all done," I said.

"Great! Thanks!" I could tell that Debbie was trying, and failing, to remember my name. "You know what?" she said. "I never gave you the tour!"

"I'll show her around," Cara volunteered.

Debbie raised her eyebrows. Out in the hallway, the telephone rang again, and I heard the front door open and close. "Well, if you're sure."

"Sure I'm sure," said Cara. Then she muttered, "It's not like I've got anything else to do." She padded down the hall toward the staircase, and I followed her.

"Dining room," said Cara, pointing at a room with a long table and kids' artwork in colored plastic frames on the wall. "Den," she said. This room had a collection of couches that didn't match, a big TV set mounted on the wall, and more works in crayon and finger-paint. I also saw a few plaques on the wall, probably to thank the people who'd donated the couches or the TV. "Bathroom." The bathroom had a chemical smell, and there were stainless-steel grab bars around the toilet. A red plastic trash can with a sign that read BIO-HAZARD stood in the corner next to the regular trash can, and there was a printed notice about handwashing taped up next to the mirror. "Playroom." This was a room with high windows, and more couches, and window seats. There was a little puppet theater in one corner, next to a cardboard trunk of ratty dress-up clothes, beanbag chairs, and shelves full of books, a low table with three small chairs covered in construction paper and little-kid scissors, and on a metal desk in the corner, a computer. *Where are Cara's parents?* I wondered. *Why is she here all by herself?*

Then I looked at the computer, and I had another idea. "Hey," I said casually. "Do you know if that's online?"

She gave a combination nod/shrug.

"Do you think I could send a quick e-mail?"

Another nod/shrug. Cara plopped down on a red beanbag and stared at me as I sat on the wheeled chair and tapped the mouse until the computer's screen came alive. I was thinking about Bruce, the way he'd kissed Max's forehead after putting him back in his car seat. I was thinking about Tyler, standing on the bimah with his mother squeezing him against her chest and his father's hand on his shoulder. I thought about the sled in our garage, my mother's name written along one of the wooden slats in a stranger's handwriting, and the voice I'd heard on the tape.

I erased the Ronald McDonald House home page, decorated with a slide show of happy, healthy-looking families, and opened my account.

Cara watched from her beanbag. "Who are you writing to?" she asked. "You got a boyfriend?"

"Ha. No." I opened another window and plugged in my best guess at the address that would lead me to my mysterious grandfather. The Beverly Hills Surgical Centre had a very fancy website, with video downloads of its most popular procedures and podcast interviews with the surgeons. I didn't bother with any of that. Dr. Lawrence Shapiro had his picture on the "Our Physicians" page. With his curly white hair and silvery beard, he looked like an older version of the man I'd seen in Grandma Ann's photo albums. He didn't look like someone who'd force his daughter to stand on a scale in front of her family, or throw an ice skate at her, or moo when his wife bent over. He looked like the man I'd heard on the tape, kind and patient with little girls.

Click to e-mail our physicians, said the link. I clicked and wrote, *Dear Dr. Shapiro, my name is Joy Shapiro Krushelevansky. My mother's name is Candace, and I think she may be your daughter.*

I stared at the words as the cursor blinked. Then I backspaced over "may be" and typed in "is."

My bat mitzvah is in November, and if you are my grandfather I would like to invite you. It will be at the Center City Synagogue at 10 A.M., *with a luncheon to follow. If you send me your address I will be happy to send you an invitation.*

I typed my name and my e-mail address. *Not a very nice guy,* my mother and Aunt Elle had said. But maybe they'd been wrong. Maybe the tape I'd heard told the real story. Maybe time had changed him. Maybe I could introduce him to everyone at my bat mitzvah. "This is my grandfather." Not *This is my, um, Bruce* or *This is my father* and then, later, having to explain that Peter wasn't really; or *This is my grandmother's partner, Mona,* and watching people get weird or way too friendly. Just something nice and simple and true: *This is my grandfather.*

P.S., I wrote. *If you aren't the Dr. Shapiro who is Candace Shapiro's father, I'm sorry.* I hit send, feeling almost cheerful, then turned back to Cara. "So what do you want to do?"

"Why do you talk funny?" she answered.

I pushed myself away from the desk and sat down on a yellow beanbag, opposite from hers. "I was born two and a half months early, and the nerves that carry sound from my ears to my brain didn't develop enough. But I don't talk funny. People can understand me fine."

"Huh." There was a hole in Cara's pink sock. The two of us stared at it for the minute it took for her to work her big toe through it. "Do you go to school while you're here?" I asked.

"I have a tutor."

"Oh." I watched for a minute while Cara wriggled another toe through the hole in her sock. Her toenails were long and ragged-looking, like nobody had cut them in weeks. "Hey, maybe you shouldn't do that," I said.

She shrugged. "I got more socks."

I glanced at the clock on the wall. Four-thirty, which meant another hour and a half of this. "Do you like it here?"

Another shrug. "It's okay."

"Do you miss your friends?"

"I guess."

"Do you want to do something?"

She looked at me. "Like what?"

"I don't know. What's there to do around here?"

"Well." Cara got to her feet. She didn't exactly look enthusiastic, but at least she was moving. She pointed to a stack of board games, their cardboard boxes softened by overhandling, stuck together with silver tape. "There's Candy Land. Chutes and Ladders. Boring. Origami," she said, pointing at the squares of brightly colored paper, brilliant orange and pink and green. "We can make cranes. Which I've already done about a million times. Want to watch a movie?"

"Are you allowed to watch movies?" In my house, whenever I asked about watching a movie on a Saturday or Sunday afternoon, my mother asked if I wouldn't rather go for a walk or on a bike ride. Then she'd offer to go on the walk or the bike ride with me. I don't even ask anymore.

"Joy." I was startled when Cara said my name, surprised that she knew what it was, until I remembered that I'd told her. "Nobody here cares what I do."

If I was an actual grown-up, I would have said something like *Of course people care* or *Your parents care* or maybe even *I care what you do.* But I hadn't had my bat mitzvah yet, so I let myself off the hook. "Are you hungry? Do you want to make popcorn?"

I asked Debbie's permission—she was on the phone again, and gave me a quick thumbs-up without missing a word of her conversation. We found popcorn in the kitchen, kernels in a jar, not the mi-

crowave kind. Cara studied the jar suspiciously, unscrewing the top
and sniffing it, then taking out a kernel and rolling it between her
fingers.

I took the jar back and read the directions out loud. "We'll need a
big pan with a lid . . ."

"I got that." Cara pulled a pan out of a drawer with a flourish and
a bang.

"Oil . . ."

"Top cabinet. I can't reach."

I stood on my tiptoes and got it. "Salt and butter."

"Here and here," she said, slamming the first and setting the second down on the counter beside me. I poured oil in the pan, flicked
on the burner, and waited for it to get hot while Cara stood beside
me, bouncing impatiently from foot to foot.

"I did popcorn like this one time, at camp last summer, only that
was in a pan over a fire," Cara said.

"Did it work?"

"Yeah, it was really good."

When the oil was spitting, I let Cara toss one kernel into the pan.
She squealed when it popped out and flew right at her face. "Ow!
Hot," she said, brushing at her cheek.

"Be careful," I said. I made her wear an oven mitt to pour the rest
of the kernels into the pan, and then I found a stool so she could stand
in front of the stove, holding the handle and shaking it. I melted butter in the microwave, dumped the popcorn into a bowl, and poured
the butter on top. Cara shook the salt. I found paper napkins and a
pitcher of some kind of juice and a tray to put everything on. We carried it all into the den. Cara rummaged through a stack of DVDs and
found *The Little Mermaid,* which I'd watched when I was little, and
we sat down on one of the couches with the bowl between us. Ursula
the sea witch was just starting her big number when Cara spoke.

"Harry."

"Huh?"

"That's my brother's name. Harry."

"Oh."

"Now I admit that once or twice / Someone couldn't pay the price / And I'm afraid I had to rake 'em 'cross the coals," Ursula sang.

"It's totally stupid," Cara said. Her eyes were still focused on the TV, the blue glow of the movie flickering across her face, her hand dipping automatically into the popcorn bowl and lifting fistfuls of kernels to her mouth. "He doesn't even have any hair anymore." I turned my head away because I thought she might have been crying, and I thought there should have been something for me to do about that, but I couldn't think of what.

And then I did. "Hey," I said. "Do you want to try on the most beautiful dress in the entire world?"

TWENTY‑FIVE

By the first Friday in June, the weather had turned freakishly cold. Some kind of low-pressure air mass had blown down from Canada overnight, dropping the temperatures from the eighties down to the fifties, half killing the petunias in my window boxes. Green leaves skittered down the sidewalks and iron-gray clouds scudded across the sky. I could already feel the beginnings of a cold—the scratchiness at the back of my throat, the dull ache behind my eyes. I chugged down a pint of water and a mug of rose-hip tea, popped vitamin C tablets, and looked up my beef stew recipe. If I hustled, I could get a piece of chuck at Chef's Market, a baguette and salad greens and a blueberry tart for dessert, get the stew simmering, then pick Joy up from school.

I tucked a basket of clean clothes against my hip and carried it up to Joy's room, noticing as the door swung open that, angry as she was, she was at least keeping her bed made and her clothes off the floor. That was good. Not good enough to offset the fact that she'd barely spoken to me in the past two weeks, but still, not nothing. I'd tried to bring up the topic of *Big Girls Don't Cry,* telling her that if she ever wanted to talk to me, if she ever had any questions, if there was ever anything that concerned her . . . I'd let my voice trail off, and I'd waited, tense, barely breathing, as Joy looked at me blandly and told me everything was fine.

I set a stack of folded underwear and shirts on the bed and opened her closet to hang up her jeans, and there it was. Pink. Spaghetti-strapped. Sparkly. Except the dress was gone. The week before, Elle had picked it up and brought it back to New York.

I stared for a minute, trying to make sense of what I was see-ing—how the dress, like the cat of the old children's song, had come back. When I lifted the hanger off the metal bar, I realized that this was actually a different dress, not from Bergdorf's but from Macy's, an almost identical version in pink with silver sequins.

It took me about thirty seconds to figure out what had hap-pened, another ten to find the telephone. Bruce Guberman didn't answer his office line or his cell phone. Emily answered at his home.

"It's Candace Shapiro. Is Bruce there?"

"What is this regarding?" asked Emily.

Oh, the night your husband and I had sex on the basement stairs while his parents put Passover dinner on the table was right on the tip of my tongue. *You know, the good times!* I managed to restrain myself, man-aged, even, to cut short the memory of how, for years after, the taste of *charoset* made me horny. "Joy," I said. "It's about Joy."

Another minute passed, and then Bruce was on the line. "Can-nie," he said. "What can I do for you?"

Bruce Guberman and I had loved each other once. Then we'd done our best to destroy each other: him with his magazine article, me with my book, hurling words as if they were arrows with deadly poison at their tips. What we had now was the thin crust of good manners laid over the bittersweet mess of our history . . . and Joy. We had Joy.

"Sorry to disturb you at home," I said formally. "But we need to talk about this dress you bought Joy."

"I didn't buy Joy a dress." He sounded confused. Then again, Bruce frequently sounded confused.

"At Macy's? Last Sunday? There's a dress in her closet with a price tag on it. You took her to the mall. She had to have bought it there. And Bruce, this dress is completely inappropriate."

"I don't know anything about a dress. Joy went shopping when I took the boys to the movies—"

"You left her alone?" I asked sharply.

Bruce sighed. "For ninety minutes in a shopping mall. We were right across the street, and she had a cell phone with a GPS locator."

Never mind that for now, I told myself. "She must have bought the dress while you were at the movies."

"Does she have a credit card?"

I forced myself to breathe. "No, Bruce, my thirteen-year-old daughter does not have a credit card." *You stupid pothead,* I thought . . . except I guess I said it instead of thinking it, because Bruce replied in a very dignified voice, "I haven't smoked pot in more than ten years."

"Wow. Congratulations." Not that I believed him. If Bruce had truly given up weed, the entire East Coast's black-market economy would have collapsed. Dealers would have been wandering the streets, rending their garments and weeping. "But that doesn't explain how Joy got the dress. If I didn't pay for it, and you didn't pay for it . . ."

"You think she stole it?"

I squeezed my eyes shut. No. There was no way. I looked at the dress, and my heart unclenched. "There's a receipt in the bag. She used a MasterCard. You definitely didn't give her a credit card?"

"I gave her five bucks so she could get a pretzel and take Max on the train. I . . ." He paused. "Hang on a minute."

He set the telephone down. I sank onto my bed with my eyes closed. A minute later, Bruce was back on the line, and his voice was grave. "I think she might have taken one of my cards."

"No way," I said reflexively. "Joy wouldn't . . ." I swallowed hard.

"My MasterCard is missing from my wallet."

"And you're just noticing now?" *Idiot,* I groaned in my head. "Why don't you call the company to see if there've been any recent charges? If there were—if that's what happened—I'll speak to her. See if I can figure out what's going on."

"Okay." Bruce paused. I sat there, burning with fear and with shame. How had my beautiful, solemn, good-hearted little girl turned into a thief?

Bruce cleared his throat. "I was hoping I wouldn't have to tell you, but Joy may have overheard something at Tyler's bar mitzvah."

"Overheard . . . at . . . Wait, she wasn't at Tyler's bar mitzvah!"

Bruce sighed. "We weren't expecting to see her there, and Emily didn't react very well. We were having a discussion at the party—"

I spoke slowly and clearly, so that there was no chance that he could miss a word or mistake my meaning. "Joy wasn't at Tyler's bar mitzvah!"

"She was," Bruce said. Now he was the one to sound bewildered. "I thought you dropped her off."

"She told me she didn't want to go." My hands were gripping her sheets so hard that I could feel my fingernails through the fabric. *Joy,* I thought. *Oh, Joy.*

"Huh," said Bruce. "Maybe she took the train. Or got a ride with someone. Or—"

"I'll call you later," I said, and hung up the phone and sat there, stunned and sick and not very surprised when Bruce called me back to say that, yes, there was one new charge on his card, from Macy's. "Hey," he said, not unkindly. "I'm sorry."

"Me, too," I croaked, and told him I'd find his card and call him back.

They say that nothing is more delicious than food cooked with love. My beef stew that night would have proved them wrong. I got out my cutting board and my heaviest cleaver and decimated an onion, three carrots, three potatoes, and an entire can of plum tomatoes. I rocked the blade of my knife over garlic cloves until they were pulverized to a paste. I wrenched the lid off a frozen container of beef stock that I'd yanked out of my freezer, jerked the cork out of a bottle of wine, hacked the beef into oozing red ribbons. I browned the vegetables, deglazed the pan, dredged the meat in flour, and adjusted the seasonings, flinging brown sugar, bay leaves, molasses, and more garlic into the pot. Then I slammed on the lid and sat at the table, fuming, trying to figure out how and when my daughter had turned into a stranger. Joy stealing credit cards! Joy on the train! By herself! Without anyone knowing where she was! *Anyone could have talked to her,* I thought. *Anything could have happened.*

At two-forty-five I got behind the wheel. Driving up Lombard Street while the wind whipped against the windows, I rehearsed arguments in my head—only where would I start? With the dress? With the train trip? With her lying to me about not wanting to attend Tyler's bar mitzvah?

I sneezed twice, wiped my eyes, and pulled up to the curb, searching for Joy's face among the crowd of kids clustered around the gates. I raised my hand and waved at Tamsin, who gave me a brief wave back, then tucked her chin into her chest and marched past me. No Joy. Strange. Usually, wherever there was Tamsin, there was Joy. I got out of the car and scanned the play yard. There was a group of big boys squabbling over a basketball, a row of girls in gigantic pink and purple backpacks so heavy they looked as if they would tip their owners over, and there was my daughter, huddling in the school doorway as if trying to keep warm, with her sweater pulled tight around her.

"Joy!" I yelled. She turned around and smiled, the sunny, open little-girl smile that I hadn't seen in months, and she beckoned to me, just the way she had when was three and my sister had bought her a DVD of *Willy Wonka and the Chocolate Factory.* "Come with me! And you'll see!" Joy would say in her husky rasp. "See the world of pure imagination!"

"Hi, Mom! Guess what? I got an e-mail from your father!"

"We'll talk about that later," I said before her words had a chance to register. *My* father? Surely I'd misheard her. Maybe she'd meant Bruce.

"Later?" Joy repeated incredulously. "Mom, this is, like, a huge big deal! He's your father!"

"We have other things to discuss," I snapped.

Joy recoiled. "He says he wants to see me," she said softly.

The words were out of my mouth before I could stop them. "Why, does he need money?" I asked.

Her eyes got huge, and her mouth fell open. I rubbed my temples, wishing I could take it back. I changed the subject instead. "Did you take Bruce's credit card?"

Joy lifted her chin and said nothing. I climbed behind the wheel, and she got into her seat.

"Did you go to Tyler's bar mitzvah?" I asked.

She turned toward the window without answering.

"Why?" I asked. "Why lie to me? Why keep it a secret? If you wanted to go, that would have been fine!"

She didn't answer. I stared at her profile: honey-colored hair, cheeks rosy from the wind, Bruce's straight, narrow nose, and Bruce's rounded chin, only smaller and finer. *A grown-up,* I thought, and on the heels of that thought came another one: *A stranger.*

"You stole Bruce's credit card," I said, a judge reciting the charges, "and you bought the exact same dress you got with Elle."

"It's not exactly the same," she muttered.

"Close enough for government work."

"What does that mean?" she asked.

I blew out an exasperated breath. "You lied to me," I said. "You've been sneaking around. You've been stealing. You went out of the state without telling me or your father where you were going."

"You lied, too," Joy said so softly I almost didn't hear her.

"I beg your pardon?"

"You told me my grandfather had never even seen me. You said he never tried to meet me." She reached into her backpack and pulled out two sheets of paper. The first was indeed an e-mail from Lawrence Shapiro at the Beverly Hills Surgical Centre. I scanned it fast: *Sadly, your mother and I have been estranged for years due, I believe, to my ex-wife's attempts to poison my children's minds against me . . .*

I threw the paper down in disgust. "Oh, please." I shook my head. "Joy, he's lying. Grandma Ann didn't have to try to poison us against him. We didn't need poisoning. All we had to do was see what he did to us! He abandoned us, he never wanted anything to do with us, he wouldn't pay for our educations . . ."

Her voice was small but implacable. "You told me he never tried to see me, but he did."

My stomach clenched, and I thought for a minute I'd be sick. I chose my words carefully, as if picking my way across a swollen river, looking for the stones that would support me. "Joy, what is going on with you? Why the sudden interest in my father?"

My daughter extracted another piece of paper from her backpack. I knew what was coming even before I saw it: a ten-year-old snapshot from that long-ago bookstore in Los Angeles, a picture of Joy tucked into my father's arms.

"He says he came to a reading and took that picture," Joy said.

"He did." My mouth was so dry it was as if it had been stuffed with straw. "That's true. He showed up at one of my readings, and he . . ." I forced myself to breathe again. "Look. I can see that you'd like a grandfather in your life, and I'm sorry to disappoint you, but other than that reading, the only time he ever got in touch after you were born was to ask for money."

"You said," Joy repeated, "that he'd never tried to see me. But he did. So you lied."

I swallowed hard, feeling even more dizzy and sick. Had she somehow decided that a reunion with my father was the key to her happiness? My father, who'd never cared about her, never asked about her, had been interested in me only for my money? A man who'd never called, never sent her a birthday card, never asked for a picture, an update, anything at all? "I . . . I only . . ." I shook my head and reached for Joy's hands, which she had folded primly in her lap. I should have told her the truth, I realized, even if it hurt her. I should have told her that he was no good. "Joy. Talk to me. I can't help you if I don't know what's—"

She cut me off. "You lied," she repeated calmly.

"Joy . . ." The word wrenched itself out of me.

"Stop saying that!" she cried.

"Stop saying what?"

"My name! My stupid name! *Joy,*" she spat. "Like I made you so happy. Like you even wanted me in the first place."

"What? What are you talking about?" My voice sounded high and frightened. "Where did you ever get that idea?" I knew the answer. She'd gotten the idea from my book, of course, my angry book, the one that was never meant for my daughter's eyes, the version of the story she was never meant to believe. "Of course I wanted you! You do make me happy!" I reached for her shoulder. She flinched and wriggled away. "Honey, I'm sorry if I—that I—that I lied to you. But the thing about my father—"

" 'He's not a very nice guy,' " she recited.

"I know him better than you do. I know what he is. I'm your mother. I just want to keep you safe." My voice was shaking. "That's all I ever wanted. Just to keep you safe." I gulped. "Is this about something you read?" I gulped again. "My book? Because you should know, Joy—"

"Take me home," said my daughter. And that was all she said until we pulled into the garage, at which point she marched past me, up to her bedroom, and closed the door. I heard the lock click into place, and I stood there wringing my hands, wanting to knock, to call her name again, to say something, even though I wasn't sure what I would say that would do either of us any good. "Listen," I said at last, addressing the blank surface of the door. "If you want to meet him—your grandfather—then I'll try to find him. If it's important to you, then that's what we'll do."

I thought that I heard the word "liar" drift out from under the door, but as long as I waited, as hard as I knocked, Joy wouldn't open the door or say another word.

PART THREE

Certain Girls

TWENTY-SIX

I ignored my mother until she gave up and clomped back down the stairs. I turned off the lights and lay on my bed with my pillow pressed against my ears, trying to ignore what was outside my door: my mother, my father, the telephone ringing, more knocking. Then silence.

Some time later, there was another knock at the door. "Go away," I yelled, not very nicely.

"Joy?" The sweet, calm voice didn't belong to my mother or my father. It was Grandma Ann. I'd forgotten that she was coming over for dinner. "Can I come in?" she called, loudly enough so that there was no chance of me pretending not to hear.

I rolled out of bed, flicked on the light, unlocked the door, and stood there, glaring at my grandmother, who stared placidly back at me.

"Oh, honey," she said, and reached out to hug me. I jerked away and stalked back to my bed, brushing angrily at my eyes. Grandma Ann sat down at the foot of the bed. I breathed in her smell, a little like sugar cookies, a hint of Bengay. "You heard from your grandfather," she said.

"Mom lied to me," I croaked. Grandma Ann merely nodded. "About everything," I continued. "My father . . . her father . . . everything's a lie."

My grandmother sighed and tucked her legs up until she was sitting Indian-style. "Parents make mistakes," she said. "I did, and your mother did, and you will, too. But I can promise you that everything your mother did was with your best interests at heart."

My best interests, I thought. As if my mom had any idea what those were. As far as I could tell, she'd done everything for her own interests, to make herself look better: the good mother, the pillar of the community, not a slut who'd written a scandalous, embarrassing book, a stupid slut who'd gotten pregnant by accident and never even wanted a baby.

"Your mom didn't have it easy," Grandma Ann said. "After Bruce left, it wasn't easy for her. And as far as her father goes, I think she was just trying to keep you away from someone she felt wasn't the kind of person you'd want in your life."

"Why does she get to be the one to decide who I want in my life? I'm thirteen years old, I'm going to be bat mitzvahed, it's not her choice—"

"Joy, she did the best she could."

"Well, she did a sucky job!" I shouted, loud enough so that my mother could hear me. My face was hot, and my head felt like it was going to burst. "She made my father take off for years. I've got a grandfather who doesn't know me, even though he wanted to."

"I don't fault your mother for that," said Grandma Ann a little coolly. Her voice surprised me. I'd expected her to fall to pieces when she saw that I was crying, to do whatever she could to comfort me. It didn't look as if that would happen. "Your grandfather broke her heart."

I wiped my face. "What do you mean?"

"I mean," she said, "that she was his favorite, from the time she was a little girl until she was maybe twelve or so."

I sat up, blinking. Parents weren't supposed to have favorites, and if they did, they definitely weren't supposed to talk about it.

"So what happened?"

"He loved her because she was smart and sharp, but then, I think, when he saw her struggling with the same things he'd struggled with—"

"Like what?"

The bed shifted as my grandmother rearranged herself, tugging at the cuffs of her loose-legged cotton pants. I could tell from her face that she was thinking hard about what to say and how she'd say it. "Her looks," she said. "Fitting in. Making friends. None of that came as easily to her as schoolwork did, and I think . . ." She paused and recrossed her legs. "I think that it brought back lots of memories for him. Not good ones."

I winced. If parents never talked about having favorites, they absolutely didn't talk about being ashamed of their kids or being reminded of their younger, unhappier selves.

"And then he left," she said. "Which wasn't a picnic for any of us."

"But she told me he never wanted to meet me . . ."

"And as far as I know, that's the truth," she said. "As far as I know, the only time he ever tried to get in touch with her was at that reading, and then to ask her for money. Not after you were born, not after she got married, just when he thought your mother might be worth something to him."

I scrubbed at my eyes again and stared at her. Picking favorites among your kids was bad. Being embarrassed by one of them was worse. But ignoring a kid except when you wanted money? That was awful. If it was true. And I couldn't make that behavior line up with the picture of the man holding me in his arms at the bookstore, or the voice I'd heard on the tape, the voice promising his daughters that he'd skip the part about the witch and make French toast in the morning. How did I know who to trust or what was true anymore?

"He's really . . ."

". . . not a nice guy," I finished wearily.

"Oh, he was worse than that," Grandma Ann said.

I sniffled. "Worse how?"

She just looked at me. "That's for your mother to tell you. If she wants to. The only thing I'll say is that no parent is ever perfect, and every mother tries her best. Which is exactly what I did when I had children, and exactly what you'll do, too."

"I'm never having children," I muttered. My grandmother ignored me. She went into my bathroom and came back with a washcloth that she'd wet with cool water. I used it to wipe off my face.

"Mona's downstairs. Oh, and Bruce called."

I sighed. "Tell him I put the credit card in the back pocket of his car seat. It's probably still there."

"I think you need to tell him that yourself." She kept looking at me with her soft blue eyes and her silver hair pulled back into a nubbin of a ponytail that made her look, Aunt Elle said, like George Washington.

"I'll return the dress," I grumbled. "It's not like she was going to let me wear it anyhow."

She nodded again. "Your mother made stew."

As if I could eat. As if I could ever eat again. But I said okay just to say something, and I let her say all the things that any grandmother would say, about how this would blow over and work itself out and everything would turn out fine.

TWENTY-SEVEN

"This is nothing," said my mother, draping her towel over the handlebars of the treadmill. "Absolutely nothing. Remember when Elle ran off with that man who had no teeth?"

"He was a hockey player," I said wearily. "He didn't have no teeth, he just had fake teeth."

My mother pressed the buttons to increase speed and incline and started to walk, swinging her arms vigorously with each stride. "Josh didn't speak to me for a year and a half. He said his braces hurt too much for him to talk. And you . . ."

"Oh, what'd I do?"

"Hmm." She walked and thought it over.

"Nothing, that's what. I never do anything. I just sulk for a few years, then write a book. And I'm not the point! The point is Joy!"

"How can I help?" she asked. It was Saturday morning. I'd sentenced Joy to a day in the company of the ever righteous Mona. They'd go to the bead store, then to Macy's to return the dress, then shopping for art supplies in preparation for a fun afternoon making signs for an upcoming peace march in Washington.

Meanwhile my mother had taken me to the Avondale Jewish Community Center for a restorative workout. We were walking on adjacent treadmills, me in my Philadelphia Academy sweatpants and one of Peter's shirts, my mother in her LOVE MAKES A FAMILY tie-dyed tank top with her tufted gray hair sticking up over and under a rainbow-colored sweatband.

"This is motherhood for you," said my own mother. "Going through life with your heart outside your body."

I plodded along, thinking about Elle and how much grief she must have given my mother with the parade of inappropriate guys and temporary jobs, before Be-ism, or simply time, finally calmed her down. "I don't know what to do," I said, thumping along at four miles an hour. "What am I supposed to do?"

"Give her time, Candace," my mother intoned. "Give her space. Give her love."

I snorted. *Give her money* was the only thing missing from the litany, and that, as far as I was concerned, was the only concrete action I'd taken that had actually helped my sister. Then again, Mom had given Elle time and space and love. She'd also turned a studiously blind eye to my sister's more outrageous adventures, including the time Elle had worked as a stripper and tossed her see-through thongs and a bra with cutouts for the nipples into the household hamper (my mom, if I remembered right, had merely washed them, dried them, folded them, and stacked them without comment on Elle's bed).

"Joy is falling apart," I complained, loudly enough to earn me an interested look from the ninety-year-old gentleman turtling along on the treadmill on my other side. "She's falling apart, and I'm just supposed to stand around and watch it happen?" I wiped my sleeve against my forehead. "And what am I supposed to tell her about Dad?"

"Tell her the truth," my mother said calmly. "Tell her your father is still in Los Angeles. Tell her he got divorced again."

I whipped my head around sideways to stare. "How do you know that?"

"My lawyer keeps track."

I sighed. After all these years, my mother still clung to her quixotic, costly hope of someday recovering a portion of the tens of thousands of dollars of alimony and child support my father had never paid her in the 1980s and 1990s. In all that time, she'd been through three lawyers and outlived two judges and hadn't gotten enough money out of her ex-husband to buy a decent purse.

"What happened?"

She shrugged, then went back to pumping her arms. "I have no idea. His second wife had a prenup, though."

Good for her, I thought, but didn't say.

"Is he in touch with . . ." It took me a minute to recover the names of my father's second round of children. For years Elle and Josh and I had referred to them exclusively as the Replacements. "Daniel and Rebecca?"

"I don't know," she said.

I shook my head again. "The part I can't figure out," I said, "is why. Why even answer Joy? Why pretend that he's this wonderful grandfather who's been shut out of her life because of . . ." I quickened my pace and hooked my fingers into air quotes. " 'Parental estrangement'? Does he need money?"

"I don't know," said my mother. She shook her head and sighed. "I'm sorry about this."

"Yeah," I said. "Yeah. Me, too." I hopped off the treadmill, red-faced and panting, and bent down to retie my shoe. "And now she's got some kind of reunion all set in her head."

"Maybe you should let her," my mother said.

"What?" I snatched the flimsy towel off the handlebars and wiped my face, hearing my heart beating too hard in my chest, my blood pounding in my ears.

"Let her see him," she said calmly, her Mona-made bead earrings bobbing as she walked. "Joy's not stupid. She'll see him, and she'll see what he really is."

I straightened up, shaking my head. "He can be pretty charming when he wants to be. What if she decides that he's right and we're all wrong?"

"She knows you," said my mother. "She knows us. She's got a good head on her shoulders."

Not lately, I thought. "She read my book," I said slowly. "And a bunch of articles. She knows . . ." My voice trailed off. *She knows what I am,* I thought. Or at least she knew what some reporters had made of the old public version of me—or of Allie, who'd been the bastard child of all of my years' worth of rage. I pictured myself twelve years ago, after my father had left and Bruce had left and I'd pushed Peter away, hunched over my notebook in Joy's bedroom, scribbling so hard that I could see the outline of each word on the page below, thinking, *They'll be sorry . . . they'll pay.* I couldn't blame that girl for what she'd done, but still, what mother would ever want her child to see that version of herself, so fucked up and furious?

My mother had the nerve to sound amused. Her eyes crinkled as she smiled and stopped her own treadmill. "You could just say it was fiction. That's what I've been doing for years!"

I shook my head wordlessly. Allie wasn't entirely made up. The sex was all hers—well, almost all hers—but the anger was all mine, and surely, being that angry was at least as embarrassing as sleeping with strangers.

"But you should probably tell her you never had sex in the parking lot at Emek Shalom," my mother urged. "The rabbi hasn't looked me in the eye since the book came out."

I twisted the towel in my hands and said nothing.

"Well, I'm going to tell her that Tanya and I met at the hardware store instead of in the hot tub," she said, and led me toward the ladies' locker room, where she stood in front of her locker and began the leisurely process of removing her shoes, then her workout wear.

"But you and Tanya did meet in the hot tub. Tanya told me about it."

My mother hung up her T-shirt and looked at me innocently.

"*All* about it," I said.

She shook her head, smiling, wrapped a white towel around her chest, and opened the door to the sauna. Steam whooshed out, obscuring her face. "At least tell her the truth about your father," my mother said as I sat down on a tiled bench beside her. "If you don't, you're only increasing his allure."

"What allure?" I asked. "What's alluring about a man who never wanted the first thing to do with her?"

"The allure of the unknown," my mother said. "It's like with junk food or Disney princesses. The more you tell a kid she can't have something, the more she wants it."

I wiped my forehead again as steam poured out of the vents. My mother smiled serenely and closed her eyes.

Twenty-eight

"**M**other!" I called. It was Friday night. I'd finished my homework and had planned on spending the hour before bedtime doing research for my d'var Torah, the speech I'd give at my bat mitzvah explaining what my Torah portion meant to modern-day Jews in general and me in particular.

"I'll be right down!" she called. "Just give me a second!" She sounded overjoyed to hear my voice. I hadn't been talking to her more than I absolutely had to, which was making her crazy. In the week since I'd gotten my grandfather's e-mail, she'd tried to start about a hundred conversations, offering to take me out for coffee, or a walk, or tea at the Ritz. Once she'd even dropped a fresh copy of her horrible book on my bed. *I guess it's time we talked about this,* she'd said. I'd curled my lip and said, *I don't have time to read anything that's not on the list for school, and believe me, they don't want us reading that.* Her face had gone pale, but she'd just picked up the book and walked out of my room.

"What do you need?" she called from the top of the stairs.

"I need to get online." Reasons I hate my mother, number seventeen: She's put so many blockers and parental controls on the Internet in our house that the only places I can surf are the websites for Nickelodeon shows. I think my mother really believed that if I accidentally wandered onto a porn website, my head would explode.

"Just go to the start-up menu and hit 'disable'!" she called. "I'll be down in a minute!"

Lie. She was picking up my father, and they were going out to dinner, which meant she'd have to spend at least twenty minutes on her makeup, during which time she was guaranteed to practically blind herself with her eyelash curler. "Never mind!" she yelled. "Just log in as me!"

"What's your password?"

"Nifkin!"

Frenchelle, turning in circles in preparation for a nap on her dog bed, raised her head and growled. I typed in *Nifkin* and the screen flashed into life. My mom's screen saver was my most recent school picture. In the upper-right-hand corner, a dancing Thin Mint informed me that there were 243 days until Girl Scout cookies went on sale again.

I rolled my eyes and checked out her favorites. Lyla Dare fan site. Gossip website. A headline reading GIRLIE BOOK AUTHOR EXPOSED! and a comment underneath my mom's picture: *I thought the chicks who wrote those books were at least supposed to be good-looking.* I winced and clicked to an online store that sold shoes for people with foot arthritis . . . then a news story about parents who'd had their newborns implanted with silicon chips in case they got kidnapped or lost. I opened up a Google search and typed in *bat mitzvah* and *Jacob* and *Esau.* Then I glanced upstairs, made sure the water was still running, opened another window, and hit "history." Immediately the computer regurgitated all the websites my mom had visited in the last week.

There were a hundred different Lyla Dare fan sites that my mom had viewed in the last forty-eight hours. I cringed, knowing she must have been looking for her name, still trying to figure out what had happened. At least GrokIt.com had dropped her as a topic for the time being and was instead bashing a TV reporter they'd decided was too fat to be delivering the news. My mom had been browsing on websites about bar mitzvahs and blended families, and she'd been shopping for evening gowns online. But the place where she was spending the most time was the website for the Open Hearts Surrogacy Service.

I squinted at the home page. *Please enter your password,* said the text. I typed in *Nifkin* again. An instant later a smiling, brown-haired woman's face filled the screen. "Hello, CANNIEGIRL70. BETSY82 has posted an update." I clicked on BETSY82, who, according to the website, was a happy, healthy mother of two who was ready, willing, and able to make an infertile couple's dreams come true.

"Joy?" My mom was standing behind me, barefoot, with her hair dripping on the shoulders of her bathrobe. She squinted at the screen. "What are you—"

"What is this?" I asked, pointing at the woman's picture. My voice bounced off the walls and windows, buzzing in my hearing aids. I felt monstrous, enormous, like my feet were too big for my shoes and my body had grown too big for my clothes.

Her hands fumbled at the lapels of her bathrobe. "What are you . . . how did you . . ."

I couldn't let her change the subject. "What's going on?" I demanded, and shut off the computer before she could figure out that I'd been looking at her Internet history. "Are you and Dad going to have a baby?"

"I . . . well . . ." She sat down in the armchair in the corner of the room. It was piled high with books and papers. She didn't seem to see them or feel the big black Lyla Dare binder underneath her. "Your father and I weren't planning on discussing this with you until we were a little further down the road," she said, and at that moment it was like I could hear something click into place. This was real. It was actually happening. They were going to have a baby together, a baby they'd wished for, a baby they wanted, a baby who would be the exact opposite of me.

"You're getting a surrogate." I felt dizzy and sick. I remembered the first passage I'd inked out in *Big Girls Don't Cry,* in which Allie takes a pregnancy test. *Heads, I win; tails, I lose. One line, please, God, one line. One line, I'm saved; two lines, my life is over.*

That was the truth, right there on the screen. No matter what she said and how she called me her joy, she had never wanted me. And now she was going to have another baby, a wanted baby, a baby with the man she loved.

"Nothing's final yet," she said, but I knew that was a lie, one more to pile on top of the rest she'd told me. *Your grandfather never tried to get in touch. Of course I wanted you, Joy.*

I got to my feet. My mother blinked at me miserably. She'd curled and put mascara on only one set of eyelashes, and she looked like a lopsided raccoon.

"I don't have to stay here, you know." I said this casually, as if it had just that minute occurred to me.

She looked up at me, shocked. "What?"

"I could go live with my father. Bruce. My real father."

Her eyes got very wide. She twisted her hands in her lap with her head bent. I wished I could take it back, but I couldn't. So I said, "He always says I can stay with him whenever I want to. I could go to the same school as Max and Leo. I'm going to call him right now."

She gave a wry smile. "Don't you think you'll miss peanut butter?" I just stared at her coldly. She sighed. "Joy, I wish I could sit here and explain everything to you. About that website; about my father. But I can't miss this dinner. It's really important. I need to—"

I cut her off. "Fine. Go." I blinked as she bounced up out of her chair and stood there, her hair still dripping. The world seem to blur out of focus. That wasn't supposed to happen, and that wasn't what she was supposed to say. She was supposed to say *No* and *Absolutely not*. She was supposed to say *I won't let you* and *You're grounded* and *We're your parents* and *You belong here*. She was maybe even supposed to cry, to reach for me, to ask me over and over again what was wrong until I told her.

Instead, she twisted her hair around her hand and wiped underneath her made-up eye with one fingertip. "I . . . I have to go now," she said. "I have to go. I have to meet your father. I have to . . ." Her eyes, as she looked past me to the clock at the top of the stairs, were almost frantic, and her lips were trembling. "There's food in the fridge. Those spicy string beans you like. Your dad and I will be back by ten, ten-thirty at the absolute latest, I promise, and we can talk. I'll explain everything." She shot another desperate look past me, then started moving, walking fast, taking the stairs two at a time, thighs jiggling underneath the terry cloth.

I stared with my mouth hanging open. I waited for her to come back down and apologize some more, to give me all the details about the baby, if there was one. Instead, twenty minutes later, she hurried back downstairs in a lacy white skirt and a pink top. I watched as she checked her lipstick in the mirror and picked up her purse. Again, she repeated, "Your father and I will be home, and we'll talk about everything."

She bent down to put on her shoes, picked up her purse, gave me one more desperate look, then picked up her keys and practically ran out the door, leaving me sitting there as shocked as I'd ever been. She'd started leaving me alone in the house only when I turned thirteen, but she'd only done it twice before, and before she did, she'd go through about three dozen questions before setting a single foot out the door: *Do you have your cell phone? Are your hearing-aid batteries charged? Are you hungry? Thirsty? All set with your homework?* I went to the window, positive she'd turn around. But she just kept walking, not even turning back to look at me, moving quickly down the sidewalk, then around the corner, until she disappeared.

I stood there in the empty office, in the empty house, hearing nothing but the thunder of my heartbeat in my ears. Then I spun on my heels and ran up the stairs. Grandma Audrey had bought me luggage for my last birthday, a pink zippered suitcase and a little carrying case for makeup. I opened the suitcase on my bed and started throwing stuff inside: jeans, underwear, my copy of *Big Girls Don't Cry,* a picture of me and Tamsin at Sesame Place on my sixth birthday, all the steps of the Jon Carame program, plus my flat iron and my toothbrush. I was panting by the time I zipped the suitcase, and of course Bruce wasn't answering his phone. I didn't leave a message. *Bump bump bump* went the suitcase as I dragged it down the stairs. *I don't care, I don't care, I don't care,* I chanted in my head with each step.

TWENTY-NINE

I power-walked the entire thirty-two blocks from our front door to the Hospital of the University of Philadelphia, so rattled that I barely realized where I was, so miserable that I almost didn't notice when the blister that had risen on my right heel burst and started bleeding, or that I got on a service elevator instead of the regular kind and wound up riding up to my husband's office next to what I was pretty sure was a corpse. The plan was for me to meet up with Peter. We'd spend a few minutes going over our list of questions for the potential surrogate, then head to the restaurant.

"Are you having a medical emergency?" the sweet young thing behind the desk at the weight and eating disorders center asked as I limped through the door with my shoes in my hand. The concern on her face told me better than any mirror just how bad I looked.

"No," I said, twisting my hair into an impromptu bun. "No, no emergency, I'm meeting Dr. Krushelevansky."

She looked dubiously at the schedule spread in front of her. "He's running a little late . . ."

Great. Figured. "I'll wait," I replied. "Tell him it's Cannie." I asked for a Band-Aid, stuck it over the oozing patch on my heel, and plopped myself into one of the clinic's new chairs (armless, for the plus-size patient's comfort—a sign of progress if ever there was one). There was a limp year-old issue of *Ladies' Home Journal* on the table. I fanned myself a few times, then started reading recipes for cakes that looked like Easter eggs.

The woman spilling over the sides of the chair across from mine frowned at me. "You here to see Dr. K.?"

I nodded.

"He's running late," the woman said.

"He gets busy," I said.

"Oh, sure. I know that." The woman stretched her legs out in front of her, rotating her ankles. "Don't worry, I'm done. Just waiting for my daughter to get me. I wouldn't see anyone else anyhow. Dr. K. saved my life."

"Did he?" The armless chairs were a step in the right direction, but that stupid poster—TAKING IT OFF, ONE DAY AT A TIME—was still there, a relic from my own trip through the weight-loss drug trial I'd signed up for all those years ago. The skinny model on the sun-faded poster romping through the field full of wildflowers was looking decidedly dated in her leotard and leg warmers. How many times had I told Peter that fat ladies would not find that image encouraging? No matter how thin one gets, I'd said, one has a hard time imagining a situation in which one would don a leotard and appear in public, and under no circumstances would one run in public unless one were being chased.

"Oh, yes," said the woman. She put down her right foot and lifted her left. "I had that lap-band surgery?" She dropped her voice. "In Mexico? My insurance wouldn't cover it here. They said I wasn't obese enough. Not obese enough," she said, looking ruefully at her belly. "Can you imagine? I told them to give me a month and a few boxes of Krispy Kremes, and then let's talk."

"Uh-huh," I said. I pulled my phone out of my purse to see if I'd missed any calls. I hadn't. I wondered where Joy was. At Thirtieth Street Station? On a train to New Jersey? Knocking on Bruce and Emily's front door?

"So I had the band put in down in Puerto Vallarta, and I'm on a plane back home, and everything's fine, you know. My ankles were swollen a little, but I figured that's just normal . . ."

I nodded. The GPS locator put Joy in our living room, probably sitting right where I'd left her. Or maybe she was on the phone, pouring her heart out to Bruce, begging him to rescue her from her monstrous mother and reunite her with her no-doubt-loving grandfather who'd been so cruelly kept from her for her entire life. I pressed my eyes shut, willing myself not to cry, willing myself into stillness even though I wanted to spring up from the chair and race down the staircase, out to the street, and back home. But I couldn't. We'd just get dinner as fast as we could without offending our guest. Maybe we'd pick up a quart of lemon water ice from Rita's. That was Joy's favorite. I'd take her to the living room and explain everything calmly, whether she wanted to listen or not: about the surrogate, about the possibility of a baby, about my sex life or lack of same in high school and college; the truth about who Allie was, and who I'd been, the truth about my father. So I'd been a nerd, I thought, and insecure, and unhappy, and bigger than the average mother. So my sister had been to rehab, and my mom had had illicit congress in a hot tub. So my father had hit me up for a six-figure loan and her biological father had dumped us and run off to Amsterdam. We'd all survived. We'd all come through. Surely that had to count for something!

". . . I wake up, and I'm in agony. 'Call 911!' I say to my husband. The poor guy's white as a sheet. He never wanted me to get the surgery in the first place. 'Why don't you just eat a little less, exercise a little more?' he says to me. Ha. Like that's gonna work. So he calls 911, and the ambulance comes, and the next thing I know—"

I nodded and sighed in all the right places as she unfurled her story of sepsis, necrotic tissue, and the lifesaving surgery that my husband had performed.

"So it's working now, I guess," she said. "I mean, they say slow and steady, but the band people go to the same support groups as the bypass people, and it looks like they're having a lot more luck. I'm thinking about a revision."

Peter popped his head out of his office door. "Mrs. Lefferts? What are you still doing here?"

The south-of-the-border-surgery-happy Mrs. Lefferts told Peter that she was waiting for her ride. Peter nodded, then smiled at me. "Are we all set?"

"All set." I got to my feet.

Mrs. Lefferts looked from Peter back to me. "You two know each other?"

"In a manner of speaking," I said.

"We're married," said Peter, and looked at me sternly.

Mrs. Lefferts looked me up and down. "Lucky you," she said, and picked up her purse, waving through the window at her daughter.

Five minutes later Peter and I were on a corpse-free elevator, and I was filling him in on the latest with Joy.

"I don't think she's serious about going to the Gubermans'," he said as we hurried down Thirty-fourth Street, surrounded by throngs of disgustingly young students in the beaded leather sandals everyone under thirty was wearing that spring. "I told her she'd miss peanut butter." A cyclist whizzed within inches of us, calling "On your left!" "We need to get her a therapist. Or maybe send her to one of those tough-love boot camps in Wyoming."

"I think those are just for kids with substance-abuse problems." A cab pulled to a halt at the curb in front of us. Peter held the door, and I scooched over toward the window while he gave the driver the restaurant's address.

"Stealing credit cards and leaving the state without your parents' knowing has to count for something. I'm finding her a therapist. First thing in the morning. She should be talking to someone."

The cab bumped and jolted past the Oriental-rug shops and cafés and brick row houses with painted doors and bright flower boxes. When we crossed Twenty-third Street, I made myself ask the question: "Do you think I was wrong to not tell her about the . . ." I couldn't bring myself to say "baby" yet. "The surrogate? About my father? To say that he'd never seen her? No, I wasn't," I said before

Peter had a chance to answer. "I wasn't wrong. My father's nuts. He shouldn't have anything to do with her."

Peter reached for my hand. "If getting her a therapist would make you feel better, then by all means, we should. But this is going to be fine. She's being a teenager. It's what they do."

We zipped across Broad Street, passing beneath the big red University of the Arts sign that curved around a building on the corner. Peter looked at his watch, then squeezed my hand in both of his as, one by one, the streetlights flared to life.

"So what can I tell you?" BETSY82, whose real name was Betsy Bartlett, smiled at us from across the white tablecloth. Candlelight lit her rosy cheeks and gleamed off the thin gold necklace in the hollow of her throat. She had curling brown hair, longer than it had been in the pictures online, a high forehead, and an easy smile.

I lifted my glass of sangria, trying hard to shake the feeling that the two of us were on a date with this easygoing, forthright thirty-two-year-old nurse/surrogate mother. After much discussion, Peter and I had decided to take Betsy to Uno Mas, one of my favorite tapas places in the city. We'd exchanged pictures of our kids (I'd come equipped with an old one of Joy in which she was smiling), and we'd talked about the weather (unsurprisingly humid, with thunder threatening every night), the presidential campaign, and the latest scandal involving a pantyless starlet having sex in public. Then we'd ordered a carafe of white sangria with slices of peach and raspberries floating on top, and half a dozen little plates: deep-fried olives, tiny veal meatballs, warm fava and lima-bean salad, slices of cheese, glistening white and ivory, with spoonfuls of honey and jam. Betsy had nibbled bites of this and that, exclaiming that you couldn't get food like this in Horsham.

I asked the waiter for more flatbread. Betsy smiled, leaning forward. "I bet you have a lot of questions."

I'd come with three typed pages' worth, but the first one that came to mind was, simply, "How'd you get into this?"

"I wanted to give something back," she said. "I've been really lucky—healthy, good marriage, great kids. We don't have a ton of money, and with an eight-year-old and a six-year-old, I don't have a lot of free time to volunteer, so I decided that this would be my contribution."

"And what was it like?" I asked. "How did it feel?"

"It was a little strange," she said. "With the first one—that was Eli—I was never sure how much to tell people, how much of it was their business. Of course, my boys kind of took care of that for me." She smiled and raised her voice to a child's falsetto, and in her expression I could almost glimpse her son's face. " 'Mommy's got a baby in her belly that belongs to someone else!' "

"Did people just accept that?" Peter asked.

She shrugged. "If they thought anything about it, they never said so to my face."

"What about after the birth?" I asked. "Was it hard when it was time . . . I mean, when you had to . . ."

"Give the baby up," she said, and shook her head. "You know what? I thought it would be, but it wasn't. I felt . . ." She toyed with an oyster shell on her plate. "I guess I felt more like an aunt than a mother, if that makes any sense. It wasn't quite like being a babysitter, even though I've heard other surrogates describe it that way. It was more like I'd been entrusted with the baby for a finite period of time, and that when that time was over, the baby would go with his parents, and I'd go and be with my kids."

"The fathers must have been very grateful," said Peter.

"They cried," Betsy said. I looked down in my lap, and she reached across the table to grab my hand. "Oh, no. They were happy tears! Everyone in that room was crying! When I saw the look on his dads' faces . . ."

I dabbed at my own eyes with my napkin. "Sorry," I croaked. I was remembering when the nurses had handed me Joy, how I'd been too foggy and bewildered to do much more than open my arms and hold her, a package I hadn't signed for, a gift I had never expected.

Betsy squeezed my hand. "You know," she said shyly, "I wasn't sure I should tell you this, but I read your book."

That stopped the tears. "You did?"

"Uh-huh. When I was in high school. My parents were going through a divorce, and then my older sister came home from college with a girlfriend. My father didn't handle it very well. I'd never read a book about stuff like that. I thought I was the only one who'd had someone she loved just, you know, wake up one morning and say, 'Hey, guess what? I'm totally different than what you thought!' " She lifted her sangria. "I felt like I couldn't tell anyone. Your book came along at just the right time for me."

"Wow. Thank you. I'm . . ." I reached for my own glass. I never knew what to say when people wanted to talk about the book. "That's nice to hear."

Sensing my unease, Peter filled Betsy's glass, then mine. "So what can we tell you about us?"

While they talked, I smoothed my napkin back over my lap and thought that if this was like a date, I had a feeling it would turn out to be a successful one, where none of us would be sitting at home fretting and waiting for the phone to ring and knowing that it wouldn't. A *baby*, I thought. A little boy, because somehow, I thought that was what we'd get. My eyes filled again as I remembered the sweet and singular weight of a newborn baby in my arms, the smell of soap and warm cotton, the feather-light touch of a tiny fist against my cheek. One perfect boy to go with my perfect, if troublesome, girl.

THIRTY

I sat on the couch with my suitcase between my feet and my cell phone in my hands. It was eight-twenty-seven. My mother had left two hours before.

I could have just taken a taxi to the train station and gone to Bruce's house, the way I'd threatened, except Bruce wasn't answering his phone and I wasn't about to show up in New Jersey in the middle of the night with nowhere to sleep. I groaned and flipped my phone open. There was no one I could call. My life was ruined. My mother was a liar, my parents were secretly plotting to have another baby, and Amber Gross's bat mitzvah was the very next morning and I didn't even have a dress to wear.

I stared at the telephone's blank screen. Aunt Elle? Samantha? My grandmother? None of them seemed right. "I want to run away," I said out loud to the empty room. "I want to run away and join the circus." My telephone buzzed in my palm. I looked down and saw MOM on the screen and stuck the phone in my pocket without answering. My father had taken me to the circus once. I could remember the smell of popcorn and sawdust, the beautiful aerialist in her spangled pink-and-silver leotard hanging over us, glittering like an angel as she twisted and spun.

A plan—hazy, confused, maybe completely impossible, but a plan anyhow—was starting to form in my mind. I walked to the foot of the stairs, then back to the couch. I'd need money . . . plane ticket . . . but oh, if it worked, I could make my mother so scared. I could make her sorry. Maybe I could even get some answers on my own, right from the source, the story that nobody wanted to tell me. *You will be your own responsibility,* the blended-family bar mitzvah lady had said, and if I could pull it off, this would be the ultimate example of being an adult, going out in the world and getting what I needed for myself. Plus, it would be in the family tradition. My mother, or "Allie," had run away to Los Angeles. Bruce had run to Amsterdam. I could run, too.

I ran into my mother's office, rummaging through her desk until I found what I needed. I grabbed my suitcase, locked the door behind me, and walked fast down the sidewalk toward South Street, where I could get a cab.

Ten minutes later I held my breath and pressed my finger against the Marmers' doorbell. If it was Mrs. Marmer, that would be bad. If it was Tamsin, that would be even worse. But luck was with me, because Todd was the one who opened the door and looked at me.

"Avon lady?" he inquired.

"Can I come in?" I whispered.

He raised his finely arched eyebrows. "Are you on the lam?"

"I don't know what that means," I said. "Is Tamsin home?"

Todd opened the door, lifted my suitcase, and gestured toward the staircase, which felt about a mile long as I made my way to the top. Tamsin's room was at the end of the hall. The door was closed. I held my breath and knocked. "It's Joy," I said before she could answer. "Can I come in?"

For a minute there was silence, and I was sure she was going to say no, or nothing. But after a minute I heard the squeak of bedsprings, then the door opened up and Tamsin stood there staring at me.

"Hi," I said. She was wearing an old white shirt and pajama bottoms. I looked down and saw pink polish glittering on her toenails. When had she done that? I wondered. Was she trying to look like Amber, secretly, in a way nobody would notice? Those pink toes shining above her long white feet made my heart feel like it was breaking.

"What do you want?" Tamsin asked.

I looked at her, trying to think of how to answer, when she sighed, opened the door wide, and plodded back to her bed.

Tamsin's room is small, and it feels even smaller because every inch of the wall is plastered with pictures: blow-ups from her graphic novels, drawings of regular girls mixed with superheroes. Some of them I recognized from the books she read: *Summer Blonde* and *Plain J.A.N.E., Fun Home,* and *Ghost World.* Some of them she'd drawn herself. There was a drawing of her and me and Todd, sitting in a row on a bench with our lunch bags in our laps, and one of me and Amber Gross, looking like twins, walking down the Philadelphia Academy hallway with our flat-ironed hair flying out behind us, twice as big as we were in real life.

Tamsin saw where I was staring and tried to stand in front of the picture. I pointed at it. "I look like Lyla Dare or something." I wasn't quite sure how to say what I was thinking, which was that Amber and I looked almost menacing, tall and strong and pitiless, like we'd stomp on anyone who stood in our way.

Tamsin tilted her head sideways in a gesture that wasn't quite a shrug. "What's with the suitcase?"

"I'm running away," I said. I hadn't known it was true until the words were out of my mouth, and once I'd said them out loud, there was no going back.

"You're going to miss Amber's bat mitzvah."

"I don't care," I said.

Tamsin turned toward the wall, toward her drawings. "What's wrong?" she finally asked. "Why are you here?" Her voice did not sound very best-friendly. "Did Amber break up with you?"

"No," I snapped. "You know what? Never mind." I reached for my suitcase handle. "I shouldn't have come here," I muttered, and I was almost out the door when Tamsin said, "What do you need?"

She sat down on her bed. Last summer we'd sewn different-colored patches to the pink-and-red-patterned quilt, trimmings from jeans we'd outgrown, pieces of our old show-choir robes.

"A favor. A big one." I sat down on the bed across from her.

"What?" She yanked up her sweatshirt zipper and flipped her hair back over her shoulders, all business.

"If I wanted to get to Los Angeles by myself, without my parents knowing, do you think I could?"

"Did you get invited to another bar mitzvah?" she asked.

"No, it's . . . It's something else. It's my grandfather. My mother's father. I e-mailed him, and I want to go and meet him."

Her laptop was folded on her bedside table, next to the lamp that she'd decorated with red and gold bottle caps, glued in rows to its base. She reached for it and opened it up. "Where will you stay? With Maxi Ryder?"

"No! No, she can't know. Nobody can know. I'll stay in a hotel." I rolled my suitcase back and forth with the tip of my foot. Excitement was building inside my chest, making my fingertips tingle.

"Do you have enough money for that?" Tamsin asked.

"Nope. But I have this." I reached into my pocket and pulled out the thing I'd taken from my mother's desk, a credit card she'd never used, never even activated, still in its heavy cream envelope, attached to a square of paper with WELCOME TO WHITE CARD written on it in gold script. I handed it to Tamsin, who stared at it, then at me.

"You've got a White Card?"

"It's my mom's, but it's never even been activated. It probably won't work. I just—"

"Hang on." Tamsin grabbed her laptop. Her slender fingers danced over the keyboard. "Checking Wikipedia . . . Okay, it says here that White Cards are never supposed to expire. They have unlimited periods of usage and no credit limits, they entitle you to automatic upgrades on seventeen international airlines, sixty-three hotel groups worldwide . . ."

"How do I activate it?"

"You'll probably need your mother's social security number and her date of birth."

"I've got those."

Tamsin stared at me. "You know your mother's social security number?"

I smiled smugly. "Check it out." Finally my mom's paranoid overprotectiveness was going to pay off. In the front pocket of my backpack, where my mother had insisted I carry it for years, was my Medical ID card, with my name, date of birth, address, health conditions, insurance information, and all of that for both my parents, including their dates of birth and social security numbers. Tamsin stared at it for a minute, then shook her head. "Wow. It's a good thing you never lost this. It's, like, an engraved invitation to identity theft."

I waved away her concerns.

"You might need something else," Tamsin said. "Something nobody else would be able to know, like her pet's name or her mother's maiden name."

"I could guess." My heart was rising in my chest. *Nifkin,* I thought. The magic word was "Nifkin."

"Then you just dial the number on the back, get the card activated, and according to this . . ." I heard her fingers clattering over her keyboard. "You'll be connected to your personal concierge."

"Good," I blurted. "Great. Thank you, Tamsin, seriously, thank you so much!"

Todd brought us the telephone, ceremoniously carrying it to the room and laying it on the bed between us like a totem, before returning to his regularly scheduled *Project Runway* marathon. Tamsin and I sat facing each other, cross-legged, me with the White Card in my lap, Tamsin with her back against the wall and, in her lap, a list of things I might need to know: previous addresses, social security numbers, Grandma Ann's last name, the word "Nifkin."

I called the toll-free number and plugged in my card number. I'd expected a computer, but a live woman with a smooth voice answered my call. "Good evening, Ms. Shapiro. My name is Riley. How may I be of service this evening?"

"Hi! I, um, I never activated the card," I said.

"The card was activated when you signed for it with our messenger," Riley said. "However, for security purposes, can you please verify your home telephone number and social security number?"

I rattled them off, glad for once that I had a deep voice, because it would make me sound older than I really was. Tamsin, who was reading the numbers over my shoulder, gave me a thumbs-up.

"Your date of birth?"

My heart hitched in my chest as, for one panicked moment, I couldn't find the right dates on my medical card. Tamsin pointed them out and I read them off, exhaling after Riley accepted the number without comment.

"How can I assist you this evening?"

"I need to make arrangements for my daughter, Joy Krushelevansky, to travel to Los Angeles tomorrow morning."

"Unaccompanied?" Riley asked.

"That's correct."

"She's thirteen?"

"Yes." *How'd she know that?* I mouthed to Tamsin, who shrugged.

"We can ticket her as an unaccompanied minor if you like. Most airlines give it as an option for travelers thirteen or under."

Could it really be this easy? I wondered as she rattled off the possible times that I could fly in the morning. I booked a one-way ticket, leaving the next morning at ten A.M. I'd figure out how I'd get back to Philadelphia once I was there.

"Of course, the ticket will qualify for an automatic upgrade," said Riley. "Will you be needing any tickets?"

It took me a minute to sort out that the "you" she thought she was talking to was my mother, not me. "I . . . um . . . no, I'll be fly-

ing to Los Angeles later in the afternoon. I have a script out there that
I'm . . ." There was a word for this. What was the word for this?

"Doctoring!" Tamsin whispered.

"Doctoring!" I said. "So the ticket's just for Joy. Also, she needs
to be able to check in to the hotel by herself, because I'm not sure
what my day will look like. I'll give her the card, of course—"

"Will she be meeting you there?" Riley interrupted me smoothly.
"The reason I ask is that, unfortunately, most hotels won't let minors
check in by themselves."

"Um . . . well, I'll be there eventually."

"I'll make a note in the file and call the hotel to follow up. Is
there a number where you can be reached?"

I gave Tamsin's number.

"And does Joy have ID?"

"I have . . . I mean, I have for her a passport. I have a passport
for her." Tamsin was making frantic throat-cutting motions. Oh,
boy. Maybe Riley would just think that English wasn't my first
language, or that I'd had some kind of head injury since I'd gotten
the card.

"I'll call the hotel to let them know." Riley paused. "I'm sure, of
course, that Joy is a responsible young lady?"

"Very," I assured her.

"Will you be needing anything else? A car and driver to meet Joy
at the airport?"

"Sure," I said giddily. "Sure, why not?" And find my grandfather,
too! Maybe the White Card people could do that. Maybe they could
do anything.

"My pleasure."

I hung up the phone and grinned at Tamsin, who dropped her
head without meeting my gaze.

"What?" I asked.

"I have to tell you something."

I stared at her and waited. Finally she said, "You know that Internet story about your mom writing the Lyla Dare books?"

I nodded, with a dawning idea about where this was going. Tamsin paused. "Well, I was the one who told them."

I stared at her. "You did? But why?"

"I was really mad at you," Tamsin said miserably. "You kept blowing me off for Amber. So I found a website where you could send an anonymous tip . . ." Her voice was almost a whisper. "I thought you'd think it was Amber and then you'd be my friend again."

"But I was always your friend!" As soon as I'd said it, I knew that it wasn't true—or at least I could see how Tamsin wouldn't believe it.

"What about Amber?" Tamsin asked.

"She's okay. You know, if you like talking about dresses and tablecloth colors."

Tamsin laughed a little. Then she looked at me. "I'm really sorry." She sighed. "Probably I should tell your mom, too."

"Never mind her right now." I bounced off the bed and over to my suitcase. "We've got to talk about tomorrow." I tucked the card carefully into my backpack. Then Tamsin and I went to pull Todd away from the TV for a fashion and packing consultation, to print out addresses and maps, to make sure I had everything I needed for my quest.

Thirty-One

"Gone?" Bruce's voice was impassive, but I imagined I could hear disdain lurking somewhere in that single word. I was pacing in front of the Four Seasons at six o'clock on Saturday night with my cell phone pressed against my ear, feeling frantic enough to hurl my body into traffic, throwing myself in front of strangers' cars and taxicabs, wrenching open their doors, and screaming, "Where is my daughter?" Throngs of partygoers, men in tuxedoes and women in gowns, streamed past me and down the red carpet that stretched toward the doors bracketed by a pair of ten-foot-tall inflatable gold Oscars. Half a dozen photographers—instructed to act like paparazzi, I figured—fired off shots and shouted the names of the teenage guests. "Madison! Madison, this way, please!" "Give us a smile, Gavin!"

I hoisted my hip onto a planter filled with petunias and shouted over the din, trying to explain the situation: "I thought she might be at your place." Peter and I had come home from dinner the night before to an empty house. Joy had informed us, via a terse message on the home phone, that she was spending the night at Tamsin's. I'd called the Marmers. "Yep, they're upstairs watching *High School Musical* again," Shari had cheerfully confirmed. I'd asked her to have Joy call me in the morning, but I hadn't been terribly worried when I hadn't heard from her. Amber's bat mitzvah was slated for ten A.M.

Maybe Joy had overslept and needed to hustle to get there, and of course she knew enough to turn off her cell phone in the synagogue.

I called her at noon and was sent straight to voice mail, where I left a message asking her to call. I'd called again at one and two. Still nothing. Her GPS feature had been disabled, but that was to be expected if her phone was off. At two o'clock I'd called the Marmers. "Nope, sorry, she left first thing in the morning," Shari said.

Unease rose in my throat as I asked to speak to Tamsin.

"I haven't seen her since this morning," Joy's best friend said.

"Do you have any idea where she might be?" I asked. The worry had been just a tickle before. Now it was more palpable, a living thing taking a slow tour of my intestines, making me feel panicked and queasy.

"Maybe with Amber or Tara or Sasha," Tamsin said. "Then she's got the party tonight."

Amber. Tara. Sasha. I scribbled down the names and rummaged through my desk for the class directory. From three until four-thirty, I sat in my office and called everyone's numbers: mothers, fathers, stepmothers, stepfathers, cell phones. Nobody answered at Amber's. Tara said she hadn't seen Joy at services but that there were "like, sixty kids there, so maybe she was just sitting somewhere else." There were three Sashas attending the Philadelphia Academy. My daughter wasn't at any of their houses, and the third Sasha—the right one— hadn't seen Joy at the bat mitzvah, either.

I sucked in air through a windpipe that felt narrow as a pencil. Then I turned to Peter, who was standing in the doorway with his hands crammed into his pockets, frowning. "I think we should call the police," I said.

"She's been missing for, what, six hours?" he said. "I'm not sure they'll take that seriously."

"She's thirteen," I said. "I will make them take it seriously." I stared at him, waiting for him to say *Let's not panic* and *This is normal.* I almost collapsed in gratitude when he said, "Tell you what. The party's at six. We'll go to the Four Seasons and watch until we see her."

"Oh boy, she'll love that," I grumbled, imagining the look on Joy's face when she saw her parents loitering outside the hottest bat mitzvah party in town. "But she deserves it," I added hastily.

I spent the next three hours rearranging a china cabinet that didn't need rearranging, transplanting lilies in the garden, putting on lipstick and running a straightening iron through my hair, figuring Joy would be embarrassed enough when she saw us and that I didn't need to ratchet her shame up to mortification by looking like a slob.

At six on the dot, we were in position across the street from the hotel. By six-thirty, all of the tuxedoed and evening-gowned guests had made their way inside, the fake paparazzi had packed up their cameras, and we hadn't caught a glimpse of Joy. "Be right back," Peter said. I watched, my heart hammering, as he trotted across the street. A minute later he was back, frowning, with something in his hand: a tiny reel of film with Joy's name on the front. "Her place card," he told me without spelling out what that meant—Joy wasn't here.

I rocked back and forth on the ledge of the planter with my arms wrapped around my chest. Then I pulled out my cell phone and called Elle. Nothing. I called Josh. Ditto. I dialed my mother's number.

"Hello, you've reached Ann and Mona Shapiro-Pasternak," my mother's calm voice said in my ear. I shook my head as a late arrival, a girl in a skintight gown with cutouts at the hip and back, hopped out of a cab and raced through the doors. When had the two of them decided to hyphenate? "Neither one of us is available to take your call." The voice mail offered a number of options. I could press one to leave a voice mail for Mona. I could press two and leave a message for Ann. I could press three and leave a voice mail for both of them. I could press four and send a message to the White House about dignity and respect for same-sex households. Instead of pressing anything, I hung up and called my mother's cell phone.

"Have you heard anything from Joy?" I could hear chanting in the background.

"What?" my mother yelled.

"JOY!" I shouted above the racket of the activists. "JOY IS MISSING!"

"Hold on, I need to get somewhere quieter." There was a muffled thump—my mother putting the telephone in her pocket, I supposed. I dug my fingernails into my palms.

"Hello? Cannie? Can you hear me? I'm in a coffee shop."

"A coffee shop where?"

"In Washington. Mona and I are marching for justice."

Justice for what? Never mind. "Joy slept over at Tamsin's house last night. She was supposed to call me by this morning and she didn't, and she was supposed to be at this bat mitzvah party and she's not here, and I don't know where she is!"

"Oh," said my mother. "Well, let's think. She's not here with us, and I haven't heard from her today. Where do you think she could be?"

"I don't *know*," I said.

"Hmm," said my mother. She paused. "Do you think this has anything to do with your father?"

"I already called Bruce, and he said—"

"Not her father," my mother said. "Yours."

My skin went icy. "There's no way," I said, but as soon as the words were out of my mouth, I realized that I wouldn't have believed Joy had been capable of getting herself to New Jersey or stealing credit cards, and she'd pulled off both of those tricks quite nicely.

When my mother spoke again, her voice was gentle. "I think I'll go home and see if I hear from either one of them. Or do you want me to come over?"

I leaned against the minivan, feeling sick. "Do you have a phone number for . . . for . . ."

"I have his lawyer's number," my mother said. "I don't know if I'll be able to reach him on a Saturday, but I'll try."

I promised to call as soon as I learned anything, then hung up.

Peter looked at me expectantly. I shook my head and dialed Bruce's number again.

"Guberman residence."

"Hello, Emily," I said as nicely as I could. "It's Candace Shapiro. Is Bruce there?"

"Is Joy still missing?" she asked.

"May I speak to Bruce?" I repeated.

I heard Emily sigh before Bruce got on the line. "Candace?"

"Have you heard anything?"

"Not yet." When he spoke again, his voice was softer. "What should we do?"

Tears rose up, scalding, in the back of my throat at his unexpected kindness and the unbidden memory of how the two of us had once been "we."

"Have you two been fighting?" Bruce asked. "Is there something going on?"

"She's angry," I said, without mentioning any of the reasons why. "Listen, if you could just keep your cell phone on, you know, in case Joy calls you . . ."

"I will." He paused. "Hey, Cannie, I'm really sorry about this."

I brushed at my eyes. "It's not your fault. I'll call as soon as I hear anything."

"Same here."

I shoved my cell phone into my pocket. Peter dropped me off at home and went to check Joy's school, the coffee shops in our neighborhood, the bookstore, the Ronald McDonald House. I opened Joy's class directory and started calling every family with a kid in her class, asking if they'd seen her, if they'd heard from her, if they knew where she could be.

Thirty-Two

I walked off the plane, down the jetway, and into the bright, bus-tling Los Angeles airport, my suitcase handle clutched tightly in one sweat-slippery hand, still not quite believing that I'd pulled it off, that I was really here.

My plane, scheduled to leave at ten A.M., had taken off two hours late, and I'd spent each of those hundred and twenty minutes in the waiting area feeling as if I would jump out of my skin, as if, at any moment, my mother would come storming around the corner, or I'd get picked up by the police. Finally, they let us board the plane. I took my seat and fastened my seat belt and sat there, staring straight ahead, as the man in the aisle seat looked at me, amused. When his Bloody Mary was gone, he set down his empty plastic glass and tapped my shoulder. "I've heard of nervous fliers, but what's your story? Nervous take-offer?"

"Something like that," I said, and forced my hands to relax on the armrest while the rest of the passengers filed past us. We'd been stuck on the runway for another twenty minutes, and every time the captain came on the speakers to announce another delay, I was convinced it was because my mother had found out where I was and where I was going.

I'd left Tamsin and Todd's house at eight o'clock that morning, before Mr. and Mrs. Marmer were awake, and caught a cab to the air-port, dressed in the outfit that Todd had picked out from Mrs. Marmer's closet. While Tamsin stood at the bedroom door, keeping watch, Todd had flipped through his mother's dresses and skirts and sweaters. He'd selected dark-rinse straight-legged jeans ("Boot cut is too trendy"), a plain cream-colored T-shirt and dark brown cardigan, along with a necklace of silver beads ("I can't take your mother's jewelry!" I'd protested, and Todd had rolled his eyes and said, "A, it's costume; B, she'll never know; and C, yes you can"). My shoes were my plain brown school shoes. My hair was loose and wavy around my ears ("Not to criticize, Joy, but that stick-straight look is kind of played," Todd had said). He'd made me swap my backpack for his mother's brown suede hobo purse ("Kids carry backpacks, ladies carry purses"), but, in my favor, he'd approved my pink wheeled suitcase ("Next time, though, ask for leather. Much more versatile").

He'd loaded me up with different tops and extra underwear and helped me tiptoe past his sleeping parents' closed bedroom door, down the stairs, and out to the street. As I headed back toward South Street, pulling my suitcase behind me, looking over my shoulder to make sure Mrs. Marmer hadn't noticed that I was carrying her purse and wearing her clothing, Tamsin had come sprinting out the door.

"Here!" She handed me a brown-and-white polka dotted scarf and a pair of gigantic white plastic sunglasses. "Todd says to put the scarf in your hair. He says it's very Sienna Miller meets Edie Sedgwick. I have no idea what that means, but here you go. Oh . . ." She pulled her phone out of her pocket. "Trade me. So your GPS will still say you're here." I handed her my phone, shoved hers in my purse, and raised my hand for a cab.

As soon as the cab was moving, I tied the scarf into my hair and put the sunglasses in the purse, next to my copy of *Big Girls Don't Cry* and the printed-out e-mails my grandfather had sent me. In the book, there's a scene where Allie leaves Philadelphia and flies out west. *I watched the world tilt underneath me, then vanish as the plane ascended through the clouds, and I felt my heart lift. I pulled the tight seat belt even more snug around my waist, thinking, Maybe I'll find what I'm looking for, the thing I can't name, the thing I need.*

Whether Allie or my mother had found what she needed, I wasn't sure, but maybe I could find my own version.

At the airport, my heart had almost stopped after I'd swiped the stolen credit card through the machine to get my boarding pass and the screen read PLEASE SEE GATE AGENT. Maybe my mom had found out somehow. Maybe she'd already called the airport, or even the police. But when I went to the gate agent, all that happened was they gave me my ticket and a pin reading UNACCOMPANIED MINOR that I stuck on Mrs. Marmer's sweater, then slipped into my pocket as soon as I'd run my shoes and suitcase and borrowed purse through the X-ray machine.

I pulled the seat belt tighter and stared out the window, letting my breath fog the scratched plastic, listening to my heartbeat thundering in my ears. "We're number three for takeoff," said the pilot. "Flight attendants, please take your seats for departure."

My breath whooshed out of me. The businessman gave me an amused look. "See? No worries. Everything's fine."

I nodded, using the sleeve of my borrowed sweater to wipe the condensation off the window as the voice invited me to sit back, relax, and enjoy the six-hour flight to Los Angeles. "I'm going to see my grandfather."

"Oh yeah?" The man had opened up his *Wall Street Journal.*

"Yep." I nodded and ran my fingers through my hair.

When we'd been in the air for a while, the flight attendants served lunch to the first-class people, our choice of salad or steak. I had a chicken Caesar salad, soup, and a roll. The tray came with tiny shakers of salt and pepper, real glasses for wine and water, and cloth napkins, but the silverware was all plastic. "Nine-eleven," grunted my seatmate. "The security people confiscated my toothpaste, and I'm eating my steak with a spork. Score one for Al Qaeda."

I nodded, slipping off my shoes and resting my feet on the pink suitcase that I'd stowed underneath the seat in front of me. Maybe I'd be discovered in California. Maybe someone would see me and decide that I was just the girl they were looking for. I could move in with

Maxi, I could get a tutor to finish school, I could turn into somebody else, somebody better. I could rewrite my own history. I could tell people that my parents had been married and they'd loved me very much but unfortunately had died in a car accident, and everyone would believe me because I'd change my name to Annika and there wouldn't be anyone around to tell them otherwise.

I used my own spork to eat the chocolate cake for dessert. Then I fumbled around until I found the button that reclined my seat. I'd planned to close my eyes for just a minute, but I guess I was more tired than I'd thought, because the next thing I heard was the thump of the landing gear, and when I looked out the window, we were descending through a thick brown cloud into Los Angeles, where the temperature was seventy-two degrees and the local time was two-forty-five P.M.

"LAX," said the spork man, accepting his suit jacket from the flight attendant. "God help us all."

I grabbed my purse and suitcase and walked through the airport, ignoring, for the time being, the buzzing of Tamsin's cell phone.

"Ms. Krushelevansky?" The driver was unbelievably handsome: square-jawed, dark-haired, with sparkling blue eyes, waiting at the base of the escalators with a sign with my name on it, just the way Riley had said he'd be. I wondered why he wasn't a movie star. I wondered if maybe he was trying to be, if the driving wasn't just to keep him busy until his big break came. "I'm Kevin. We're going to the Regent Beverly Wilshire?" he asked, taking my suitcase.

"Yes, please," I said, and put my sunglasses on. We'd flown through a cloud of brown smog, but the sky above looked perfectly blue, and the palm trees that lined the road leading out of the airport were waving in the warm breeze. I rolled the window down, thinking the air would smell like the seashore, but I got a faceful of exhaust instead. It didn't bother me. All of a sudden I was happy . . . and hungry enough to eat the copy of *Fortune* folded into the seat-back pocket.

"Um, excuse me? Kevin? Can we maybe stop for a snack?"

He pulled the car smoothly off the road and into the parking lot of an In-n-Out Burger, which I'd had before, when I'd been to California with my mom to visit Maxi (Maxi always got her burger wrapped in lettuce leaves). I ordered and devoured a cheeseburger and fries. Then I got back in the car with milkshakes for me and Kevin, and we drove for half an hour before we pulled through the ornate wrought-iron gates and up the cobbled drive of the hotel.

Inside the lobby, it was all cool beigey-pink marble. A towering arrangement of lilies and forsythia stood in the middle of the room on a round gilded table. Fancy people glided through the sweet-smelling air. There were men in uniforms standing beside the heavy glass doors, asking if they could hail a cab or help with shopping bags. I spotted a bowl of green apples on the counter, and I took one. Then, feeling very competent, like Joy Krushelevansky, Girl Reporter, or Girl Detective, or Girl Solver of Family Mysteries and Unraveler of Secrets, I checked my suitcase at the bell desk and went to the ladies' lounge, where I locked myself in a stall, flipped open Tamsin's phone, and called her house. When Todd answered, and got his sister on the line, I said, "Operation Eagle Soaring Free is a success!"

"That's great," Todd said. "But I think you should call your mother and tell her that you're okay. She's already called our house five times."

"I'll call her later." I crossed my legs and thought about it. "Or maybe you could tell her that I forgot my phone at your house but that I borrowed someone's phone at Amber's bat mitzvah and called you from there."

"I think she knows you weren't—" Todd started.

I cut him off. "Just call her. You don't have to say that you know where I am or anything, just that you've heard from me, and I'm okay, and I'll call her by . . ." I looked at the time and did some quick math. "By midnight, okay?"

"What if she thinks you've been kidnapped?" asked Todd.

"Kidnapped?" I repeated. Why would anyone think I'd been kidnapped? Who would want me? "I don't know. Make her pay you ransom money, I guess."

"We'll call her right now," said Tamsin in the background. "Call us, like, every hour, so we know you're okay."

I promised I would. I studied myself in the mirror to make sure I looked all right, that my hearing aids were in place, and that the credit card and my list of addresses were safe in my pocket. I went back outside, where my car and driver were waiting.

The address I had for Dr. Lawrence Shapiro was on Linden Lane—a bungalow, I thought that kind of house was called. It was a little building with lots of right angles and a low-hanging porch that set the front door in shadows. In front of the house was an iron gate, painted blue. A walkway led up to the gate, then past it to the front door; there was an orange tree in the front yard. Nobody answered when I rang the doorbell. No dog barked, and I didn't hear anyone inside. I went back to the car. "We might have to wait awhile," I told Kevin, but fifteen minutes later, a little white car zoomed up the driveway and a lanky woman with short blond hair wearing pink scrubs got out with her keys in her hand. "I'll be back soon," I said. I walked across the street, through the sweet-smelling, balmy air, and jogged onto the sidewalk, then over the lawn, right by the painted door. The grass was crunchy underneath my feet, strange and different, L.A. grass. Six or seven oranges had fallen off the tree and were rotting on the ground. I could see something that looked like black liquid streaming over one of them—ants, I thought. "Excuse me," I called.

The woman's face looked tired and guarded as she turned toward me. "Yes?"

"Mrs. Shapiro? Christine? Is Dr. Shapiro here?"

She had a backpack over her shoulders, and as I watched, she tugged it closer. "Mrs. Bloom," she said. "I'm Mrs. Bloom now."

"But you were Mrs. Shapiro? You were married to Dr. Shapiro?"

She squinted at me through the hazy twilight. "You're the youngest process server I've ever seen."

"I'm not a process server," I told her. I didn't even know what a process server was. "I'm Joy Shapiro Krushelevansky. My mother is—"

"Oh God," the woman said unhappily. "Candace."

"Yeah. So listen, I'm sorry to bother you, but I'm wondering if you know where my grandfather is now."

"Right now? No idea," she said. She turned toward the house, reaching into her pocket, probably for her keys. In the book, my mother had described "Allie's" father's new wife as slender, and maybe this woman had been once, but at some point she'd crossed the line from slender to skinny and looked pretty close to emaciated, like one of those actresses whose pictures they show under the words EATING DISORDER??? on the covers of supermarket magazines. The ex–Mrs. Shapiro had a corded neck and scrawny arms. The short-sleeved V-necked pink scrubs revealed the cracked skin of her elbows, the bony plate of her chest.

"You don't know where he is?" I asked. "Do you have another address or a phone number?"

"I don't," she said sharply. She shot a scornful glance at the car. "Traveling in style, huh? Is your mother in there?"

"I'm here by myself," I said. "I don't want to bother you or anything, but I'd really, really appreciate any information you have about my grandfather."

She slid her backpack off her shoulders and thumped it down onto the grass. "Let me tell you about your grandfather. He left. He owes me money. Lots of money. Me and my kids. And I can't exactly write a best-selling book about it." She bent down stiffly, like her back hurt, and picked up her backpack. Then she grabbed the blue gate, like it was helping to hold her upright.

"I just wanted to give him something."

"Can't help you. Sorry." She didn't sound sorry. Her fingernails on the hand clutching the gate were ragged, like she'd bitten them. "We're divorced. Three years ago. I'm remarried now." She flung the words at me nastily, like a fistful of sharp-edged stones. Probably she was hoping I'd go away. Except I wouldn't. *I flew three thousand miles to a place where there are palm trees and the air smells like suntan oil and ambition,* my mother had written. *I flew away from the twisted wreck of my past and toward the bright edge of the sea.* I was, I figured, at the bright edge of the sea right now, and whatever I found out, whatever happened, it had to be better than what was waiting for me back home.

"I came all the way from Philadelphia," I said. I couldn't tell whether she'd heard me, but her back stiffened, just like Tamsin's did when she was mad. "I just want to give him something." The bat mitzvah invitations my mother and I had picked out on the Internet hadn't arrived yet, so, the night before, in Tamsin's bedroom, I'd written out a pair of invitations by hand on Tamsin's stationery. "Here," I said, and shoved one at her. "Here. It's for my bat mitzvah. I invited him already, but this is official. If you hear from him or find out where he's living now, I'd really appreciate it if you could give it to him."

She curled her hands into fists. The invitation fluttered to the concrete. "You don't want him at your party," she said. "You don't want him in your life. Believe me. He's a jerk." She gave a tight, horrible smile. "For a long time, I thought he was just misunderstood. His wife was gay, his kids were brats, whatever. But it wasn't that. It wasn't them. It was him." She bent her head and muttered something that I could tell by reading her lips was *abusive asshole.*

"If you could just—"

"Go home," she repeated, then turned away, a too-thin woman in a too-big pink shirt.

I picked up my invitation as she walked inside the door. I heard the click of the lock turning in place. "You should pick up your oranges!" I called toward the closed door. "They're all rotten!" No answer came. I made myself count to twenty, saying "Mississippi" in between. Then I bent down and slipped the invitation through the mail slot. The brass door of the slot clicked shut, and I imagined I could hear the envelope sliding onto the floor.

• • •

"Dr. Shapiro?" The lady behind the reception desk at the Beverly Hills Surgical Centre had glossy black hair pulled into a twist and creamy skin, but when I said my grandfather's name, her almond-shaped eyes looked dubious. "He's not on call this weekend."

Great. Not at home, not even living where I'd thought his home was, not at work. This wasn't going well. "Can you do me a favor?" I asked. "My name is Joy Shapiro. I'm his granddaughter. He isn't expecting me, but I came all the way from Philadelphia to see him."

The woman looked at me with her heavy-lidded eyes. "Do you have his phone number?"

"Not a current one," I said. The only number I'd found was for the house on Linden Lane, and clearly, wherever he was living, it wasn't there.

She looked at me for another minute without blinking. "Hold on," she said. "I'll see if I can reach him." She disappeared behind a door set almost invisibly underneath the word "Centre." I stood in front of her empty desk for a minute, fidgeting, then I wandered through the waiting room. There were fat couches covered in gold fabric, and round tuffets that had fringed skirts, piled high with glossy magazines. The walls were hung with poster-size photographs of the doctors who worked there. I looked until I found my grandfather's picture, the same Santa Claus one that I'd seen on the website. I was standing underneath his picture when the beautiful receptionist came back. "He's on his way."

In person, my grandfather's hair was almost entirely white, and he was short and barrel-chested, with stocky legs in blue jeans that sagged beneath his belly. I watched as he waved an electronic key fob at the door and stomped inside, looking out of place against the pale pink carpet and cream-colored walls. He wore a thick leather belt with a horseshoe-shaped silver buckle and a plaid shirt. His face was lined, and his cheeks were ruddy, and his eyes behind his glasses were watery brown, threaded with red.

He said something to the receptionist before he walked over to me. "Joy?" His voice was low and gravelly, and I felt a thrill of recognition spike my blood. I realized that it was a version of my own voice I was hearing.

"Hi." I ducked my head, shy, unsure what to call him, whether I should hug him or shake his hand. He solved the problem by smiling even more widely. He had beautiful teeth, gleaming and even and white. "Did you get my e-mail?" I asked.

"I did, but I wasn't expecting a visit. What a nice surprise," he said, and I heard the voice from the tape, warm and welcoming, rumbling through his chest. "Welcome to California." He paused while we looked each other over. I was reminded of Frenchelle in the dog park, the way she'd cautiously approach a new dog, sniffing delicately, trying to figure out whether it was friend or foe. "There's a coffee shop downstairs. Can I buy you something to drink?"

"That sounds good," I said, relieved. I hadn't made any plans beyond actually seeing him, and this sounded perfect: We'd be in public, and Kevin and the car would be nearby.

"Your mother with you?" he asked casually as we walked into the hallway.

I shook my head. "Not right now," I said, which was enough of the truth to work for both of us.

He held the door of the coffee shop for me, and we ordered drinks at the counter: something frozen and blended with whipped cream and chocolate syrup for me, an espresso for him. Then we carried our cups to a table by the window. I waved at Kevin, parked in a space up front, while my grandfather poured sugar into his cup.

"So," he began. "What brings you to our fair city?"

"I'm just visiting, but I wanted to make sure you knew about my bat mitzvah. You know. Officially. I left an invitation with your—I guess your ex-wife?"

"Christine," he said shortly. I waited for him to say something else, to maybe apologize for her behavior and say that she'd been sick or she was crazy, but he didn't.

"This was the first time I was ever on a plane by myself," I told him, even though he hadn't asked.

He raised his eyebrows. "Oh yeah?"

"Well, I've been on planes before. Just never by myself. I usually go places with my parents. We go to Florida sometimes, and I've been to California with my mom and with Aunt Elle . . ."

A crease appeared between his eyes. "Aunt . . ."

"Oh. That's Lucy. She changed her name."

His teeth gleamed when he smiled. "Did she change her ways, too?"

Huh?

"Probably not," he said, continuing to smile. "There was never much potential there. Now, your mother was a different story."

I stared at him, speechless, then looked down at my drink. How could he say Aunt Elle had no potential? Aunt Elle was beautiful!

I lifted my eyes to look at him. My grandfather had a cell phone and a beeper tucked into his breast pocket, along with a crumpled pack of cigarettes. *Cigarettes?* I thought. *Would a doctor smoke?*

He pulled off his glasses and massaged the bridge of his nose with two fingertips. "Big success," he said, "your mother."

"I guess," I said.

"How is she?"

"She's good."

"Just good?" He folded up his glasses and set them on top of the napkin dispenser. " 'Good' doesn't tell me anything. A useless word."

My stomach cramped. Was he saying that I was useless? "Busy!" I finally said. "She's very busy."

"Oh yeah?" He sounded bored.

I tried to change the subject. "So . . . um. I'm almost done with seventh grade. I go to the Philadelphia Academy. Do you know it?"

He didn't answer. "Wait here," he said. I watched through the window as he walked back to his car, pulled a book out of the trunk, and came back, setting the book on the table. I recognized it instantly: It was a photo album, a sibling of all the ones I'd seen in Grandma Ann's bonus room. "I thought you might like seeing this," he said.

I watched as he flipped the book open to the first page, which was a picture of a bald baby with its mouth wide open, wrapped in a pink-and-blue blanket.

"Your mother," he announced. He flipped to the next page, and there was Grandma Ann, her short hair brown instead of silver and her skin unlined, smiling with the bald baby on her shoulder.

I looked at the baby. "That's Aunt Elle. Aunt Lucy, I think."

"Nope. Candace." He tapped the photograph with one finger. "See, Ann hadn't gotten fat yet."

I swallowed hard.

"Thirty pounds with each kid," he said. "If you can believe it. Probably a good thing your mom stopped with one."

I said, "Oh," because I could tell that he expected me to say something. My feet tapped against the floor, faster and faster.

"You've got a genetic tendency to put on weight," he lectured. His bloodshot brown eyes looked me over critically. "You'll have to be careful."

I wanted to tell him that I was careful. I wanted to tell him that my mother was careful: that everything she served me was organic and all-natural and hormone-free, that I had the healthiest lunches and snacks of any kid I'd ever seen, that I hadn't even tasted soda until I was ten years old. Instead, I wiggled my straw around the whipped cream in my drink, then took a big swallow.

He shrugged and turned the page. "Your mother," he said again. There she was, in a bathing suit with a frog appliquéd on the tummy. Her hair was wet and curly. She'd been running under a sprinkler set up on the lawn. I could see the strands of water at the far end of the photograph. She was grinning, her sturdy round legs planted on the grass, her belly sticking out proudly. "Four years old, but she could already read. I read to her every night. Poetry. Shakespeare. Every night."

"That's nice," I said quietly, remembering the tape I'd heard. Oh God, I wanted to get out of here so badly. The man who'd made those tapes, who'd sounded so kind, was gone. Coming here had been a huge, huge mistake.

"I taught her to read," he said, and flipped the page. My mother again, with Aunt Elle, the two of them in snowsuits and ice skates on the bumpy, pockmarked surface of a frozen pond. Underneath the ice, I could glimpse the black water. "Taught her to swim." Flick. Grandma Ann again, heavier and tired-looking, her brown hair threaded with gray, another baby in a blanket in her arms. My grandfather quickly flipped past that shot—Uncle Josh, I guessed. "Taught her everything, when you come right down to it." The pictures passed by in a blur: first days of school, birthday parties, and bar mitzvahs. Flick. High school graduation, my mother in a shiny cap and gown, standing behind a podium, her face set in familiar lines, sullen and shy and ashamed. She looked bigger underneath her black cap and gown.

I toyed with my straw. My grandfather pushed the book across the table. "Take a look," he said.

I flipped back to the beginning, then paged through the pictures more slowly, trying to find something that looked familiar, an echo of my own face in these faces. There was Uncle Josh with a buzz cut, holding a fishing pole, and my mother again, stretched out in front of a fireplace, frowning over a book. I shivered, goose-bumpy in the air-conditioning of the coffee shop. There wasn't anything scary about the pictures, except that nobody ever got any older in them. On these pages, under the plastic, the children stayed children. They never grew up.

About halfway through the book, the pictures gave way to clippings. Some were from what looked like a high school newspaper. One or two were poems. Then the real newspaper articles began. The first batch had my mother's byline. *School Board Postpones Budget Hearing,* I read. *Science Fair Instructs, Delights. New School Lunches Cut the Fat.*

"You see?" he asked. His voice was half kind, half gloating. "I always knew she'd be a writer."

I flipped slowly through the pages. The stories with my mother's byline ended in 1999. There was a three-year gap, when I was born, in which there was only a handful of columns from *Moxie* magazine, including one she'd written, called, like Bruce's first column had been, "Loving a Larger Woman." *I will whisper in my daughter's ear. Our lives will be extraordinary,* I read. My throat felt like it was closing, and my eyes began to burn.

I turned the page. The next bunch of stories weren't written by my mother anymore; they were about her.

PHILADELPHIA AUTHOR LANDS BIG BOOK DEAL, I read. QUEEN OF THE BIG GIRLS: HEFTY GAL CANDACE SHAPIRO PENS TRIUMPHANT TALES FOR HER PLUS-SIZE SISTERS. There were copies of best-seller lists from around the country, cut out and neatly glued to the blank pages. Then came the one with my picture in it from *People* magazine: me and my mother, jumping on a bed, our feet in the air, hair flying, mouths open, laughing. It was just the picture—the story itself was on the next page—but I remembered what the headline had been, and said it out loud.

"Happy endings." *Oh, Mom,* I thought.

"I ordered it from the magazine," my grandfather said, pulling the cigarettes out of his pocket and thumping them on the table. "They'll send it to you if you pay them. They don't even care who you are."

He spread his hands on the table. He wore a heavy gold watch on one wrist and a chunky gold ring on his pinky. "She never wrote anything else," he said. "No more books."

"Maybe she didn't want to," I said. "Maybe she didn't have to."

"I guess not," he said. His voice sounded loud and angry. "That Philadelphia Academy's a private school?"

I nodded.

"Must be nice," he said. "Never believed in that, myself. Public education was good enough for me. Good enough for all of my kids."

I nodded.

"I'll bet you take nice vacations," he said.

"We go to the beach in the summer."

"I took my kids to the beach. Your mother probably never mentioned that." He tapped the pack of cigarettes on the table.

I nodded and sneaked a look out the window, making sure Kevin was still there.

"Nice vacations," he said. "Nice school. Nice life. Well. She never was very generous with family . . ."

"She is. She takes care of me." I stuffed my hands in my pockets and lifted my eyes, telling him something that I'd never in a million years tell her. "She's a good mother."

"That's a surprise. You know, she didn't have the best example." I thought he meant himself, but then he started talking about Grandma Ann. "I should have known what she was when I married her," he said. "Nineteen sixty-eight, though. Who knew what a lesbian was back then? I don't blame myself."

I swallowed hard. My knees were bouncing up and down; my feet were jittering on the floor. "I should probably get going."

"I don't blame myself," he repeated. "I've been the victim. The victim of a fraudulent marriage, then an adulterous one. Have you read any Shakespeare?" he demanded. I didn't need my hearing aids to tell that his voice had gotten louder. People were staring at the two of us.

"A little. We did *Romeo and Juliet* in—"

" 'How sharper than a serpent's tooth it is to have a thankless child,' " he quoted. "That's your mother. That's all of them. Thankless."

"She's not." My tongue felt shriveled; my teeth felt like they'd been coated in sawdust. "She's not," I said again. I remembered the pictures from Grandma Ann's, from when my mother was older, how she'd always looked like she was cringing. I remembered how my mother would take me swimming in the ocean when I was little, staying close to the shore, letting me hold her shoulders as she kicked and paddled, how I'd floated above her back and felt like I was flying. I remembered what she'd said to Hope, the baby she'd had but hadn't wanted, on the last page of her book. *I will love you forever. I will keep you safe.*

"I made her who she is." My mother's father gave me a sly, smug smile. "Read to her. Taught her to swim. Gave her all of her material. The story she told. And she made a fortune off it, didn't she? Where would she have been without me?"

"Happy?" The word was out of my mouth before I knew it. His face contorted, and for a minute I thought he was going to do something: yell or pick up his coffee cup and hurl it on the floor, or at my face.

I got to my feet. "I should go."

"Why'd you come here?" His voice was cold, mocking. "Did she send you here? Did you come to gloat? Tell her next time she can come and gloat herself. Come see the old man. Get a good look. See if that makes her . . ." His voice filled with spite. "Happy."

"I wanted to see you," I said. "That's all." My voice trailed off. "I left an invitation at your house." Then I was moving, and my chair had fallen to the floor, and I snatched my purse and practically ran out the door, through the parking lot, diving into the backseat of Kevin's car, where I sat with my head in my hands, shaking so hard that I could barely pull out the telephone, could barely make my fingers press the button that would connect me to home.

Kevin acted as if this was all perfectly normal. "Back to the hotel?" he asked as the phone started ringing.

I nodded. My eyes caught a flash of motion in the rearview mirror as the coffee-shop door swung open. "Hello?" said my mother. "Joy?" The car pulled smoothly out of the lot and into the street, but not before I saw my grandfather step, blinking, into the waning light.

"Joy?" my mother yelled in my ear. "Where are you?"

"I'm in California," I said. "I want to come home."

Thirty-three

When Joy was four years old, she started having headaches. She'd sit on the sofa with her head in her hands, pale and drawn, and nothing helped—not cool washcloths or Tylenol, not lying down in a dim room, not chamomile tea. "It hurts," she'd cry, tears streaking her cheeks. "It hurts and it will never stop hurting!"

We made the rounds from the pediatrician to the ophthalmologist to the otolaryngologist, ruling out ear infections and sinus infections and run-of-the-mill migraines. Finally, the neurologist proposed a night in the hospital and a series of tests, including an MRI of Joy's brain. "You think she's got a brain tumor?" I said, keeping my voice light, waiting for the inevitable *Of course not,* for the doctor to tell me that there were only so many medical problems one little family and one little girl could be expected to endure. Instead, he'd flipped the pages of her chart and told me that actually, his concern was a tumor in the paranasal sinus.

I stared at him, waiting for the punch line. None came. Two days later, we checked Joy into the hospital. I sat outside the chamber where the MRI was performed and watched Joy's prone, gown-clad body slide into the mouth of the machine. Her tiny, pale feet, with the remnants of red polish on the toenails, were almost more than I could stand, but I made myself lean forward, at the technician's urging, made myself speak into the microphone and say in a voice that did not tremble and did not crack, "Don't be afraid, baby. Mommy's right here."

"Don't be afraid," I said into my cell phone the next morning, remembering how I'd spent those twenty minutes offering God everything I could think of, up to and including years of my life, if only Joy would be safe and well. A few hours later, we had our diagnosis: stress headaches. She'd grow out of them. She'd be fine. "I'm on my way."

Joy sighed and said nothing.

"What were you thinking?" I blurted. I shoved my carry-on into the overhead compartment and buckled myself into my seat.

A wordless hum filled my ears. "Joy Leah Shapiro Krushelevansky—" I began.

"I went to see my grandfather," she muttered. "It was a big mistake."

I felt my breath whoosh out of me even though, at some level, I'd known that was where she'd gone. I'd known as soon as my mother had mentioned it.

"You were right," she said. "He isn't very nice."

Oh God. I swallowed hard, with my father's greatest, hardest hits playing on a loop in my head: calling me ugly, calling Elle stupid, telling Josh that he was a mistake. "What did he say to you?"

"Not much." She gave an unhappy giggle. "Nothing, really. I don't think he wants to come to my bat mitzvah, is all."

"Oh, honey." I remembered the day she came home from kindergarten, closemouthed and red-eyed, and how I'd finally pried it out of her that one of the other girls (Amber Gross? The name rang a bell) had said that Joy couldn't be her friend because she wore things in her ears. I'd delivered a politically correct speech about tolerance and understanding and how every kid was different, meanwhile entertaining a brief but vivid fantasy of figuring out which girl had hurt my daughter and drop-kicking all thirty-five pounds of her across the Philadelphia Academy's parking lot.

Joy sniffled. "I'm okay."

"Just hang on. I'll be there soon," I said.

Her voice was tiny. "I took your credit card. Your White Card. Am I in trouble?"

"Oh. Um." It took me a minute to recover myself. "Yes. Yes, you are, Joy, you're in a world of hurt!"

She giggled, because *in a world of hurt* was what I said to her, or to Peter, as a joke, something we'd been saying for years. "I'm sorry," she said. "I'm sorry about everything. I'm sorry I went to Tyler's bar mitzvah and that I lied to you."

"It's okay, it's okay," I crooned into the receiver, imagining rocking her when she was a baby, twining her curls around my fingers with her sweet weight in my lap. "It's okay. I'll be there soon. We'll figure it out. We'll be fine."

THIRTY-FOUR

"Joy!"

I ran down the driveway in front of Maxi's white-shingled beach cottage (she called it a cottage even though it had five bedrooms, two additions, and a cook's kitchen as big as the one at the Ronald McDonald House) as my mother got out of the taxi and let her sweep me into her arms.

"Don't ever do that again," my mom whispered into my hair. I could tell that she was crying, and for a minute I thought I'd start crying, too.

"I'm sorry," I said. She ran her hands over my hair, touching my ears lightly, then my cheeks, inspecting me the way she used to when I was little to make sure I wasn't hurt.

"Are you all right?"

I nodded, then hung my head.

"Come on," she said as the taxi turned around in the driveway and pulled back onto Maxi's steep street. She pulled a sheaf of tickets out of her purse. "We'll fly back tomorrow morning." She raised her eyes to Maxi, who was waiting by the white-painted gate, thick with ruby-colored roses, in a polka-dotted sundress and matching wide-brimmed hat. "If that's okay?"

"Fine," Maxi said, and smiled. "I'm glad for the company."

My mom turned back to me. "Do you still have that credit card?"

I pulled it out of my purse and shamefacedly handed it over. "Good," she said, sliding it into her wallet. "I thought that maybe we'd do a little shopping."

My eyes widened. I'd been expecting any number of things: getting yelled at, getting grounded, having my bat mitzvah party canceled. A shopping trip wasn't one of them.

My mom smiled at my expression. "You're still in trouble, though. When you get home, you're grounded, and no TV privileges for a month, and you have to give me your cell phone when you're not at school."

I nodded, probably too eagerly, because her forehead wrinkled. "No allowance, either."

"Fine." And then, because no one was looking, I reached up and hugged her again.

Forty-five minutes later, my mom and Maxi and I walked into the Badgley Mischka boutique on Rodeo Drive, a street that I recognized from many viewings of *Pretty Woman* with my mother. "Thank your father for this," my mother said as a man in a uniform held the door open. "This was his idea, not mine." We stepped onto the thick ivory carpet, into the icy air-conditioned room, where the dresses were displayed like exhibits in a museum, ten of them hung on mannequins. I looked at each dress, gold and cream and silver and bronze, getting more and more panicky, until my mother tapped my shoulder and I turned around to find a salesgirl smiling at me with the pink-and-silver gown in her arms.

I followed as she hung the dress in a mirrored cubicle, along with the matching wrap, and a shoe box with a pair of silver sandals. "Thanks," I said. Then I looked at my mom. "Are you sure?"

"If it's what you want," she said, only a little reluctantly. "I still think it's very adult."

"I," said Maxi, "think it's lovely."

"And you're not being rewarded for running away," said my mom as she sat down on a stool in the dressing room opposite mine. "Just so we're clear on that. Your father thinks you should have the kind of dress you want. And on his head be it," she muttered as I shimmied the dress up over my hips, then stepped out of the dressing room with my back to my mom so she could zip me. She rested her hands on my shoulders, and for a moment we stood in front of the mirror: her with her eternal ponytail (neat, at least, today), me with my curls, her in her black shirt and khaki pants, me in that dream of a dress. My mother sighed and wrapped her arms around me. "Is it what you want? Does it make you happy?"

I nodded. She draped the wrap over my shoulders and turned to the manager, who was waiting behind us with his hands clasped. "We'll take it," she said.

The next morning, we were on an eight o'clock flight back home. After takeoff, my mom pulled out a book. I lifted the Badgley Mischka dress bag out from under the seat in front of me, where I'd tucked it, then slid it back. We'd reached our cruising altitude of thirty-two thousand feet when my mother stuck her book into the seat-back pocket, turned to me, and said, "I think we should talk."

"About what?"

She smiled. "Oh, I don't know. Maybe what made you decide to go to Los Angeles and hunt down your long-lost grandfather?"

I shrugged. "He was . . . pretty awful." There weren't words for what he was, I realized. Maybe that was why my mom and Aunt Elle and Grandma Ann all used the same ones. *Not a nice guy* didn't even begin to cover it. *Scary* was a better word. *Pathetic* worked, too. And *old.* He was an old, mean man with a book full of pictures of kids who'd grown up and didn't know him anymore. "He showed me all of these pictures from when you guys were kids," I said.

My mom seemed surprised. "Really?"

"You and Aunt Elle and Uncle Josh, and his other kids, too, I guess. And reviews of your book. And stories about you."

She didn't seem happy to hear it. "I wonder why."

"I found a tape of him at Grandma Ann's."

"A videotape?" She looked even more puzzled.

"No, a tape recording. You guys were kids. He was reading to you."

She nodded slowly. "He did that. When Aunt Elle and I were little girls." Her face softened at the memory.

"I don't know. He sounded so nice on that tape . . ." A lump was growing in my throat. "He sounded like my dad. But you were right. I should have listened. He wasn't very nice."

"He used to be," my mother said. She pressed her lips together, maybe remembering something tender: her father taking her ice skating, or teaching her to swim. "He used to be fantastic. That was the worst part of it," she said slowly. Her voice was shy, soft, even girlish. "He wasn't always awful, you know? He was a wonderful father for the first little while. He'd read to us and take us places. He'd teach us things."

"How to skate," I said. "How to swim."

"Yep. And he loved us . . ." She blinked and turned her face away. "He loved us so much before . . . Well, I don't know. Maybe what happened was chemical, or just a really bad midlife crisis. But I remember when he'd tell me that he was proud of me, it was the best feeling in the world. Because it was so rare, you know?" I could tell she was having a hard time finding words for this—my mother, who had something to say about everything, who'd tell me that words were her tools. "Grandma Ann was always proud of us, and we always knew she loved us, but with him, you didn't always know. So when he said it . . ." She crumpled an airplane napkin in her fist. I looked at her, then looked away. Peter told me how proud of me they were all the time. He read me books, he took me places. I never doubted for a minute that he loved me, or that my mother did, even if her love sometimes felt like a straitjacket. Even Bruce loved me, I thought. Even though he'd run away to Amsterdam. He'd come back, and done the best he could.

"I shouldn't have lied about him," she said heavily. "I'm sorry for that. It wasn't a good decision, but I thought it would be better for you to think he didn't care than to think that he cared for the wrong reasons. I thought that maybe later, when you were older, I could tell you the whole story. If you were interested."

I thought for a minute. Then I figured, *In for a penny, in for a pound,* which is something else my mother always says. I bent over and pulled my copy of *Big Girls Don't Cry* out of Mrs. Marmer's purse.

"Oh God," my mom said miserably. "That. Okay," she began, taking a deep breath. "Before you say anything, in my own defense, I wrote it when I was twenty-eight, and I'd been through a very bad breakup. Things in there were exaggerated for comic effect."

"Like how many guys Allie slept with?"

She winced. "Especially that. And, um, the angry and insecure thing. And thin-skinned and petty. All of that. All made up." Her lips curled upward, almost in spite of herself. "Except the fat part. That, sadly, is true." She thought about it. "Also thin-skinned. But as far as you're concerned, I was a virgin until the day I got married." She thought it over. "Well, until the day I met Bruce. Which, by the way, was when I was much, much older than you are." She sighed and bent down, reaching for her book. "What else?" she asked.

"You're a good mom," I said.

Her hands froze on her tote bag. "You think so?"

"The best," I assured her. From the way her shoulders were shaking, I thought she might be crying, but she pulled herself together and opened her book. "Can I just ask about one thing?"

"Sure." Her voice was a little wobbly.

"When you went to Los Angeles, in the book."

"When Allie went to Los Angeles," she corrected with a little smile.

" 'To escape,' " I quoted. " 'To escape and be reborn.' "

My mother rolled her eyes. "Boy, didn't I think I was the writer."

I ignored her. "The thing she was running away from . . ." And here it was, the root of it, the heart of my journey. "It was me, wasn't it?" I whispered. "You didn't want to have a baby."

Her eyes filled with tears. "Oh, Joy." She pulled me close to her, rubbing her hand against my curls. I rested my head against her chest, close enough so her breath rustled my hair when she whispered, "You were the thing I was running to. I just didn't know it yet."

Somewhere over Virginia, I told her about Tamsin, how she'd been the one to spill the beans on my mother's career writing Lyla Dare. She was just as shocked as I'd been. "Tamsin?" she said. "Tamsin Marmer? Your BFF?"

"She was mad at me," I admitted. "That's why she did it."

"Great," my mother muttered, and heaved a long, bosom-shifting sigh. "Oh well. Nothing to do about it now, I guess. Cat's out of the bag. Water under the bridge. When God closes a window, he opens a marriage."

"Huh?"

"Door," she said, shaking her head. "It's actually 'When God closes a window, He opens a door.' "

"Why would God open a marriage?"

Her cheeks were pink. "It's a joke," she said. "Old joke. There was this rabbi in Cherry Hill who had his wife murdered, and then he told his mistress that when God closes a window, He opens a door, only Peter and I would always say that when God closes a window, He opens a marriage. Anyhow. If it wasn't Tamsin, it probably would have been someone else eventually. It'll work out."

"So . . ." It seemed impossible, but I asked it anyway: "Are you grateful to Tamsin?"

She gave me a crooked smile and a shrug—not a yes, but not a no, either.

"Are you grateful to your dad?" I asked.

The captain came on the loudspeaker to announce that we were beginning our descent into Philadelphia. My mother was quiet for so long I wasn't sure that she was going to answer. Finally, she said, "The thing is, I got everything I wanted, you know? Eventually, I did. A husband and a wonderful daughter, and a beautiful home, and friends I love, and work . . ." Her voice trailed off. "When you get everything you wanted, I think maybe you do have to be a little grateful for the people who got you there . . . whether or not they thought they were doing you any favors at the time."

I must have winced, because she squeezed my shoulder. "Don't worry," she said. "Oh, and before we land, there's something else we need to discuss." She pulled open her tote bag. Underneath her book and her wallet and her bottle of water was a folder with a stack of printed pages and a photograph of Betsy, the woman from the website. "So listen," said my mom. "How would you feel about being a big sister?"

THIRTY‑FIVE

"**I** don't know." I stared down at my lap, draped in a white hospital gown with a blue pattern of snowflakes, and stretched my legs toward the bottom of the bed. "I feel weird that I don't feel any weirder. Does that make sense?"

Peter shrugged. He was sitting in a chair beside my bed, where he'd been since I came out of the procedure room. There was a pitcher of ice water on the bedside table, and an arrangement of flowers that he'd brought, tulips and daffodils. "I don't think there's any one way to feel," he said.

I yawned. The harvest had been scheduled for the revolting hour of six A.M., which meant we'd been up since four. Outside, the sky was hazy and gray, with dark thunderclouds massed in the distance. I was glad my doctor had ordered me to spend the rest of the day in bed. Back at home, the central air would be keeping things delightfully chilly. "Nine eggs. That's pretty good, right?" I said. In fact, nine eggs struck me as a kind of middling total. I'd read online about women my age who'd gone through the regimen of hormones shot and swallowed and wound up with only two eggs. I'd also read about egg donors in their twenties who'd produced a whopping twenty‑four eggs in a single cycle.

"Nine should be plenty," Peter said.

"Then my work here is done," I said, and shifted my weight, wincing at a cramp. My nine eggs would be whisked off to a labora‑

tory, where they'd be combined with the best contenders from my husband's early-morning sample of washed and spun sperm. The best-looking sperm plus the best-looking eggs would, with any luck, equal a few nice-looking eight-celled embryos, which would be threaded through a catheter and injected into Betsy's chemically primed uterus. Then we'd wait.

Peter lifted my hand and kissed it. "Are you feeling all right? You're not uncomfortable at all?"

"I feel fine. It's just a little unnerving. Brave new world, right?"

He squeezed my hand. "So what now?"

I shrugged. "We wait, I guess."

"And what about you?"

I looked at him curiously. "What about me? I'm going back to bed."

"Have you thought about your writing? That other novel Valor's been after you for?"

I turned my face away and sighed. The Monday after I'd gotten back from L.A., I'd gotten the call from Larissa I'd been dreading. After careful review of the salient facts, Valor had decided that I could no longer function effectively in Lyla Dare's universe. "But that's not such a bad thing," Larissa had told me. "Now you can clear your plate for your next novel!" "Sure," I'd said softly, and hung up the phone.

"Honestly, I haven't been thinking about books. I've been thinking about how fast my eggs are deteriorating, and how to keep my daughter from leaving the country without my knowledge."

"I'm serious," Peter said. He looked at me steadily. "You wrote StarGirl for how long?"

"A while," I allowed. It had been nine years, and I would have written those books forever, I thought, if things had worked out differently. Lyla's world had been such a comfortable hiding place. By the end, her skin had been so easy for me to slip into, her body and her emotions so easy for me to inhabit, even if both were worlds away from my own.

"Maybe what happened was a good thing," he said. I bit my lip and said nothing. He put his hand on the back of my neck and rubbed. "I just wish you weren't so afraid."

"What am I afraid of?" I demanded. "I'm not afraid. I'm fine."

He wasn't giving up. "You should write another book. A real one."

"I liked my fake ones," I said.

Peter was undeterred. "I think," he continued, "that you have a purpose, and you need to live up to it."

I rolled my eyes. "Did you hit your head, then watch *Oprah*? Can I have some pain pills now?"

"Are you in pain?"

I looked at his face in the too-bright hospital light, the planes of his cheeks, his straight dark brows and warm brown eyes, and remembered how, the first time I'd met him, I hadn't thought that he was handsome—all I'd been able to see was that he wasn't Bruce, and I'd overlooked the kindness in his expression; the way, more than anyone else, he saw me, really saw me, and was not fooled by all my sass and poses or the names the world had called me.

"I do have a purpose," I said. "I take care of Joy."

"Joy's thirteen," he pointed out. "She'll be in high school soon. You've done your job, as well as any parent can."

"Some job," I said, looking down at my lap. "Except for her running three thousand miles away, I've done just great."

He ignored me. "I think there's something else you're supposed to be doing."

"My purpose," I repeated. "Like a divine purpose? From God?"

Peter didn't smile. "Maybe," he said. "And if it is, you shouldn't ignore it. Remember what happened to Moses when he ignored God?"

I struggled to recall my Hebrew-school lessons. "Are you saying that my editor's going to appear to me as a burning bush? Because that would be cool." I thought it over. "Different, anyhow."

"You should write another novel."

"You," I said, "should lay off. Anyhow, if we have a baby, don't you think I'll have my hands full? What with the diapers and the middle-of-the-night feedings and the sleep deprivation and the cracked nipples and all?"

"You won't be breast-feeding."

"I'll have sympathy cracked nipples," I explained.

"You wrote the first one when you had Joy," he pointed out.

"I was young!" I said. "I was young and I needed the money and nobody wanted to take naked pictures of me! I didn't know what was going to happen." I looked back into my lap and said, half to myself, "I can't go through that again. I can't put you guys through it again."

"We all came out fine," he said patiently. "People survive worse things than having a writer in the family."

"I won't," I began. He looked at me calmly. "I can't," I said. He continued to watch me with a smile on his face. I flopped back onto the pillow. "Agh. Go harass one of the doctors about her divine purpose. Or go see how our embryos are doing. Do you think it's too early to give them names?"

He got to his feet, then bent down and kissed me. "I love you."

"Yeah yeah yeah."

He kissed me again, and I kissed him back, one hand on his cheek, the other on the soft down at the back of his neck, pressing him toward me. "Love you, too," I said.

THIRTY-SIX

"You missed last Sunday," Cara said. I'd been at the Ronald McDonald House for forty-five minutes, and she hadn't said a word to me. She'd just followed me into the kitchen and sat at the table with her arms folded across her chest, staring at me with her eyes narrowed while I did the dishes and put away the cereal boxes and sponged the counters clean of what looked like the aftermath of oatmeal cookies.

"I had to go somewhere," I said, and tossed her a sponge. "Hey, do you want to help me out with this?"

"Not really," she said, tilting her chair back on two legs.

"Don't do that. You're going to fall."

"So what?" she asked. "I hear there's a good hospital right nearby."

"Ha ha ha." I squirted more cleanser on the countertop and went back to attacking the dried-on brown sugar with my sponge. When the counter was as clean as it was going to get, I folded the dish towel next to the sink. "I'm sorry I wasn't here last weekend."

"Whatever," said Cara.

"How's your brother?" I asked. She shrugged. "How are your parents?"

She shrugged again. "They're at the hospital. They sleep there most nights."

I dried my hands. She tilted back in her chair, farther than she had before, staring at me, before she thumped back to the floor.

"Do you want to go outside?" I asked.

She looked out the window at the thick green leaves of a chestnut tree waving gently in the wind, and didn't answer. "You'd be doing me a favor. I'm grounded. I'm not allowed out of the house except to go to school, and my bat mitzvah lessons, and to come here. So if we went out . . ." I looked out the window, making calculations about time and money and how much of each I had. "We could go to the coffee shop, or we could go to Cereality, or we could look at clothes at Urban Outfitters."

"Why are you grounded?"

I pulled up a chair beside her. "I stole my mother's credit card and went to Los Angeles."

Her chair thumped down on the floor. "No way! What did you do? Did you see any movie stars? Did you go to Disney World?"

"Disneyland," I corrected her. "Disney World's in Florida."

"So did you go? Did you go to Universal Studios? You went on an airplane all by yourself? I've never been on an airplane." She stared up at the ceiling. "I guess I'll get to go on one soon, though."

"Really?" It seemed like an odd time for Cara and her family to be planning a trip.

"Well, maybe. You know, those Make-A-Wish people. Stupid Harry'll probably ask to go to Sesame Place. You can drive there," she said. She lifted her legs off the floor. Her chair tilted sharply backward. I jumped up and grabbed her before she hit the floor, surprised by how small she was, how light her body felt.

I set her chair onto the floor. "See?" I said. "I told you that was going to happen!"

She inched back toward the table. "So what'd you do in Los Angeles?"

I sat down again. "I went to meet my grandfather."

Cara's eyes were shining with interest. "What happened?"

"Not much," I said. "He's kind of a jerk."

She pulled a ponytail holder out of her pocket and wrapped it around and around her index finger. "Oh." She bent her head and mumbled something.

"Huh?"

"My brother," she said. "I'm supposed to go see him."

"Oh." I got to my feet and started wiping a counter that I'd just wiped. "Are your parents coming to get you?"

"I guess I could wait for them." She tilted her chair back on its legs again, and this time I didn't stop her. "Maybe you could . . ."

"Could what?"

"Take me to the hospital. It's visiting hours now."

I felt my palms go cold. I hated hospitals. I had ever since I was a kid. Hospitals were where bad, painful things happened. "Don't you need an adult to take you?"

She pursed her lips and pouted. "You went all the way to California all by yourself, and you won't even walk me across the street to go to the hospital?"

When she put it like that, there was no excuse. Plus, I couldn't be a baby forever—not with my bat mitzvah coming up. I told Deborah at the front desk where we were going. I got my backpack out of the closet, stuck my cell phone in my front pocket, and walked Cara across the street.

The hospital stood on a corner, a big building that stretched the length of an entire block, with ambulances lined up in front of the entrance and people clustered by the doors, smoking (some of them were in wheelchairs, with lit cigarettes in their hands and IV bags dangling from poles over their shoulders). Cara walked ahead of me with her head down and her arms swinging at her sides. "It's the sixth floor," she said.

"Wait," I said. "Hang on."

She stared up at me. "You don't have to be scared," she said. "It's not catching or anything."

"No, I . . . I just . . . Wait." There was a fruit cart across the street. I waited for the light to change, then crossed the street and bought three oranges, better versions of the fruit that had dropped onto my grandfather's lawn. For years I'd watched my mom go to the hospital to visit people, sick friends or ladies who'd just had babies. *It's always nice to bring something,* she'd said.

We walked through the revolving doors into the lobby. Cara signed us in at the desk and got us stickers that said VISITOR and our names. We walked down the wide white hallways, over scuffed tile floors with empty gurneys parked on the sides. I took one of the oranges out of the bag and sniffed it, then held it in my hand, thinking that the world was like an orange, that I could split it open with my thumbnail and find a whole different world, the grown-up world, the secrets underneath the skin.

The elevator doors slid open. I followed Cara's pink shirt down the hallway to room 632. A little boy sat in the bed wearing a hospital gown and a Phillies cap. He had an IV in his arm and dark shadows under his eyes. His parents sat on either side of him, and there were cards spread over his lap. They were playing Concentration.

"Hi, Harry!" Cara sang out. I blinked in confusion, wondering where this cheerful, beaming little girl had come from as Cara crossed the room and kissed her brother. I smiled and said hello when she introduced me to Harry and her parents, who looked more tired than I'd ever seen two people look and still be awake. I sat quietly, perched on the edge of a radiator, thinking how maybe there were faces we only ever wore in front of our families, the ones who'd known us the longest and loved us the best.

"It's nice to meet you," Cara's mother said to me, trying for a smile. "We've heard a lot about you. Let me find you a chair."

"I'm okay here," I said. I lined the oranges up on the windowsill. Someone had tied balloon Bert and Ernies to the curtain pulls, and there was a bouquet of daisies wilting in a vase. I filled the vase with fresh water. I untangled the strings of the balloons. Then I perched on the windowsill and watched them play cards under the fluorescent lights while nurses came in and out to check Harry's temperature or peer at the screen on his IV. I stayed with them until the sun went down, until my oranges were the brightest things in the room.

THIRTY-SEVEN

I'd been digging in the garden when the call came. It was an unreasonably hot Sunday morning. Peter and I had slept late, then he'd gone to the office to catch up on paperwork, and I'd spent the morning outside, cutting back the roses, fertilizing the hydrangeas, replanting sweet peas and stargazer lilies.

It had been a quiet weekend. Samantha was in Pittsburgh at her brother's wedding, which she'd finally, reluctantly, decided to attend on her own. "How bad can it be?" I'd asked, helping her carry her bags to her car. "Don't ask that if you don't want the answer," she'd said. I'd hugged her and told her to call if she needed me.

I was on my knees, up to my elbows in dirt when the phone started ringing. "Joy, can you get that?" I yelled toward the house. No answer. The phone kept ringing. I wiped my forehead on my shoulder. "Joy!" I shouted. Nothing. Maybe she'd left for the Ronald McDonald House. She'd already done her six weeks of bat mitzvah–mandated service and had just kept going. "What do you do?" I'd asked her, and she'd shrugged and said, "Dishes, mostly. And I listen to people, if they want to talk."

I jogged over to the little table next to the gas grill. I had time to glance at the caller ID as I lifted the receiver to my ear. U OF P HOSP, it read, but it wasn't Peter's extension.

"Hello?"

"Ms. Krushelevansky?"

"Yes?" I said.

"This is Dr. Cronin at the University of Philadelphia Hospital. I'm calling from the emergency room. We need you to get here as quickly as possible."

I was detached enough to think, even as I sank onto a white wicker chair next to the koi pond, that on some level I'd been waiting for this call for over thirteen years. In a voice that didn't sound like mine, or even human, I heard myself asking, "Is it my daughter? Joy Krushelevansky? Did something happen? Is she—"

The voice—young, female, harried, worried—cut me off before I could finish. "We have a Peter Krushelevansky here. In the emergency room, ma'am, and it's urgent that you come as soon as you can."

I said, "Oh my God." I said, "Yes, of course." From my knees, on the bricks, where I'd somehow landed, I turned my head toward the doors and screamed my daughter's name. No answer. I scribbled a note: *At hospital, call cell.* I told myself as I whizzed along Front Street, then up Lombard, that it could have been a mistake or a mix-up. Peter sometimes saw patients in the emergency room. He could be with a patient. It could all be a big misunderstanding. But as I turned the car onto Twentieth Street, then onto Walnut, I knew that hospitals didn't make that kind of mistake. I knew it in my breath, in my bones, with every step I took through the shocking cool of the lobby and into the emergency room, as the doctor, who had blue eyes and freckles and the kind of lovely alabaster skin you have only, if you're lucky, until you're thirty, took my arm and led me to a chair beside the window.

It was a cardiac event. It was quick.

"So he's . . ." I swallowed hard. It felt like my mouth was full of cold caramel. "Peter's dead?"

Dr. Cronin patted my knee. "I'm so sorry. So very sorry." I could see her hand on my knee, could observe its movements, but I couldn't feel anything. It was as if I'd left my body, had floated up to the tiled ceiling and was looking down without feeling anything at all.

"Event," I repeated. "That makes it sound like a party." I laughed. "Was it catered?"

She stared at me. I wondered whether young Dr. Cronin had had a lot of experience with the bereaved, whether I was the first person she'd ever had to tell that a loved one had died in her care, and whether, for the rest of her working life, she'd expect every brand-new bereaved person to be my particular brand of spacey and strange. "I want to see him," I added.

"Of course," she said, not even trying to hide her relief. *Was it catered* was confusing. *I want to see him* she could deal with. "The nurses cleaned him up."

"So you tried—"

"I'm so sorry," she said again then repeated what she'd said before. It was a cardiac event. It was quick. He was dead by the time he'd gotten to the emergency room, and no, there were no symptoms, and no, there were no signs, no way of knowing, no way of telling. He'd had a stomachache, his administrative assistant, Dolores, had told them, and he'd put his head down on his desk, and when she went to check on him to see if he wanted some water or Alka-Seltzer or just to lie down, he was unconscious. Dr. Cronin said *cardiac event* again, until I just wanted to shake her and say, *Heart attack, just call it a heart attack!* She said *quick.* Her voice was like a radio station fading out of range as I drove away. *He didn't . . . Such a wonderful . . . All of us who worked here . . .*

I watched from my perch on the ceiling as my body got up off the chair and lurched down the hallway. I observed my hand pushing back the curtain and my legs crossing the green-and-white tiled floor over to the bed where my husband lay.

Someone had pulled a white sheet up to his chin. His eyes were closed, and his hands had been folded on top of the sheet, on his chest, and whatever tiny spark of hope that still existed—that this was all some monumental mix-up, that maybe my father had come back to

Philadelphia and that it had been Dr. Shapiro, not Dr. Krushelevansky, who'd had the cardiac party—guttered briefly and then went out forever. Peter looked like he was sleeping, but when I bent closer I saw it wasn't like that at all. His body was still here, more or less the same, but Peter, my husband of eleven years, the love of my life, was gone.

"Oh no," I heard. "Oh no." The voice came from the doorway. I turned and saw Dolores, who'd baked him biscotti every December since I'd known him. She stood at the edge of the room with her hands bunching up the neckline of her blouse. "Oh no, oh no, oh no."

"It's all right," I said, and patted her arm before going back to the bed. My hands, as I smoothed the sheet over his chest, were dirty; the back of my wrist was bleeding from where I'd gotten slashed with a thorn. I bent over him, then knelt in front of his bed, the way I'd knelt in front of the roses.

My cell phone rang. I yanked it out of my pocket with nerveless fingers and let it clatter to the floor. "Cannie?" asked Samantha's disembodied voice. "Can you hear me? Listen, you won't believe it! I met a guy. Here! In Pittsburgh! At the wedding! There's some kind of magicians' convention at the hotel . . ."

Dr. Cronin must have picked up the phone from the floor where I'd dropped it and carried it outside. I don't know what she told Samantha. I don't know where Dolores went. I didn't hear anything, couldn't see anything, except my husband's body on the table, my dirty hands, grimy fingernails on the clean white sheet, my mouth warm against the cool curve of his ear. "Peter," I whispered low, so that only he could hear. "Cut it out. You're scaring everyone. Wake up. Come home."

"Mrs. Krushelevansky?"

Someone took me by the shoulders and guided me into a chair. *Wake up,* I whispered again, knowing that he wouldn't, that this wasn't a fairy tale, that no kiss, no wish, no amount of love could bring him back to life. *Peter. Oh, Peter,* I thought . . . and then, *How will I tell Joy?* I pressed my fist against my mouth, tasting dirt and salt as I started to cry.

Cannie.

I groaned and rolled over with my eyes still shut. I had been having the sweetest dream about Peter, the first time we'd slept together, in his old apartment.

Cannie.

"Five minutes," I muttered with my eyes still shut. Not fair. Not fair. Did I really want to live in a world without him? Oh no. No, indeed. *No más.* Maybe I'd just stay in bed.

Cannie, wake up.

Fuck that, I thought. *Fuck that noise.* I had a black satin eye mask with ALMOST FAMOUS written on the front in sequins—Maxi had given it to me as a joke, years before. I had blackout blinds on the windows. I had frozen pizzas and frozen waffles and frozen vodka in the freezer, money in the bank, and many pairs of comfortable pajamas. I could stay up here a long, long time.

I heard a door opening, then shutting. Snatches of conversation, female voices. *Do you think* and *Should we try.* I yanked the comforter over my head. Peter wasn't dead. We were together in his apartment. There was light streaming through the blinds, dust motes dancing in the air. He was sitting on the couch, legs spread, leaning back. *Let me see you,* he'd said. *Take me dancing first,* I'd said. I could hear his breath coming faster as he'd said, *I'll take you wherever you want, but I want to see you right now.*

Cannie?

I squeezed my eyes shut. I was in Peter's old apartment. I was twenty-eight years old, three months postpartum, half out of my mind with anger and desire. He was on the couch and I was standing above him, thumbs hooked into the waistband of my jeans, bra still on but unhooked in the back, hair bed-tossed, lips swollen and parted. He was looking up at me like I was the most beautiful girl he'd ever seen. If I tried hard enough, if I blocked out everything, I could feel the way the temperature changed as I leaned closer to his bare chest, I could see a trace of my lip gloss on his shoulder, I could will myself back to that apartment and stay there as long as I had to. I could stay there and never come back.

Rise, huntress.

I opened my eyes on the bone-white sands of the plains of Said'dath Kahr. A hot wind blew my hair into my eyes. I sat up, blinking, brushing grains of sand from my palms. Lyla Dare stood over me with her back to an empty firepit, smoke curling into the darkening sky behind her.

"So you've come," she said.

I looked around at Lyla's desert, an ocean of white beneath the twinned moons. There were the caves, and there the oasis, just the way I'd imagined them for the last ten years. Everything was where I'd left it. A thousand stars, pinpricks of light in the darkness, wheeled in the sky. Lyla sank onto the ground beside me, twisting her hair into a careless knot at the nape of her neck. "Will you stay?" she asked.

It was a thought. To live here forever, to go with Lyla on her adventures through the cosmos, to kick ass and take names and never look back and never go home.

Lyla gave me a slanting half-smile and pulled a skin bag from her shoulder. I watched as she poured the wine into embellished gold cups. I recognized them from my own bat mitzvah. They were the gift that my congregation's Sisterhood had given me for when I'd celebrate Shabbat in my own home, light my own candles, pour my own wine. If I lifted one and ran my thumb underneath it, I would feel my own name engraved there.

"Drink with me," she said.

I hesitated. I knew if I drank what she gave me, I would stay here forever. It was my mind's version of Persephone's pomegranate seeds, the curse that lived inside each happy ending, each act of magic. I could stay here, but I'd never see my child again.

Lyla held the cup, her eyes black shadows in the darkness, her lovely face expressionless.

"You don't understand," I said.

She tilted her head.

"He saved me," I said. My voice was a croak. "He saved me."

"We only save ourselves," said Lyla. "You know how, don't you?" Her hand was steady as she held out the wine.

"It isn't fair," I said.

"No," she agreed. I watched as she poured the wine on the sand, which instantly absorbed it, erased it.

I pressed my hands against my eyes, and when I took them away, Lyla leaned close. I could feel her lips moving against my forehead as she whispered, "Then I set you free." She kissed my forehead with a tenderness I'd never guessed at, had never written about. When she spoke again I heard the warrior's voice I'd only ever heard in my head ringing across desolate plains and down dungeons' depths. "Now wake up!"

"Wake up," said the voice. "Mom, you seriously have to wake up!"

I opened my eyes in my own world, in my own bed. Joy was standing over me, her eyes red and swollen, her face pale. She was wearing her Class Day dress, unzipped, with two mismatched shoes in her hand.

"Mom?" she said. Her voice was shrill. "My dress won't zip, and I can't find my shoes."

"Okay." I threw back the covers and sat up. My head felt heavy and my mouth was as dry as if I'd spent all night in a desert. Where to begin? "What day is today?"

She stared at me, looking panicked. "Tuesday," she said. "Daddy's funeral's in two hours. Grandma Ann and Aunt Elle and Aunt Samantha are all here already. You have to wake up!"

"I'm up," I said a little grumpily, and I patted the bed beside me. "Come here."

Her eyes widened.

"Just for a minute," I urged her. "When you were little, you used to love to come in here. You'd stand by the edge of the bed, and you'd say . . ."

". . . can I be the middle girl?" said Joy. There wasn't any of the old familiar exasperation in her voice. Her lips trembled. No Peter on the opposite pillow. She'd never be the middle girl again. Joy dropped her shoes on the floor and climbed in beside me and let me hug her.

"See, that's not so bad," I murmured into her wet hair.

When I looked up, my sister was standing at the doorway. "Are you awake?" she asked.

"Obviously."

Elle walked across the room, kicked off her heels, and got into the bed next to Joy. "Fancy," she said, wriggling back and forth. "Is it a pillow top?"

"I think so."

"Can I have it?"

"Can you have it?" I repeated.

"Well, you'll probably want a new one. You know. The memories."

"No, Elle," I said with exaggerated patience. "You cannot have my bed."

"She wants the memories," said Joy. Her voice was muffled by the pillow. Peter's pillow.

"Who wants what?" This was my mother, standing at the door, with Samantha looking over her shoulder.

"Your daughter's already making a play for my earthly possessions," I said.

Elle sat up indignantly to defend herself. "I read that after a long marriage sometimes the surviving spouse dies, like, a few days after. You know, from the grief. And all I'm saying is that if you haven't made plans—"

"She's not going to die," said Joy.

My face felt strange. It took me a minute to realize that I'd smiled. "Doesn't that usually happen with old people?"

"Like I said!" said my sister, rolling her eyes at me.

"I'm not that old, and you can't have the bed."

"Good. I always liked it. Scooch over," my mom said to my sister, and climbed aboard, displacing Joy and Elle, who recoiled in horror.

"Ew! Stop touching me! You know I don't like to be touched!" Elle complained.

"Well, it's getting crowded, is all."

"Ladies," said Samantha. I stared at her expectantly. She sighed, shrugged, and perched one hip on the very edge of the bed—a symbolic gesture at best, but one that I appreciated.

"Okay," I said. "Leaving the nest now." I swung my feet onto the floor. For a minute I could imagine the sands of an alien desert drifting from my palms onto the floorboards. *Philadelphia,* I told myself sternly. *Tuesday. Peter's funeral in an hour and a half.* I turned to Joy. "I think you can wear a gray skirt and a nice blouse. Your sandals should be okay. They're in the closet downstairs." I slid my bare feet along the floor. *One step. Two steps. Okay. Breathe.* I'd brush my teeth, comb my hair, find my black *Today* show suit, the one Joy had told me would be perfect for a funeral. I'd get the two of us dressed and out the door, even though all I wanted to do was curl up on my bed and howl into my pillow. I would get through this, and the next day, and all of the days that came after that, days that would pile up endlessly, empty, because I didn't have the luxury of falling apart or departing for some imaginary desert. When you're a mother, you can't. I raked my fingers through my tangled hair. *Oh, Peter,* I thought. "Come on, baby," I said to Joy. "Let's go."

Goldstein's Funeral Home on North Broad Street was filled to capacity with our friends and Peter's colleagues, my family and what was left of his. I saw Dolores weeping into a wad of Kleenex, and Dr. Gerlach, the head of his department, who squeezed my shoulders in a half-hug and told me what a terrible loss this was, for the hospital, for Philadelphia, for all of us.

Two rows were taken up by Peter's large ladies, including Mrs. Lefferts and her daughter. Three rows in the back were crammed with Joy's classmates. The boys looked uncomfortable in the button-down shirts and ties they'd undoubtedly purchased for their classmates' bar and bat mitzvahs; the girls, in skirts and heels, were wide-eyed and whispering as Maxi, in a wide-brimmed black hat, made her way down the aisle and came to sit beside me.

"Up here," Elle murmured into my ear. "In front." Her dress was black and tight but not indecently short or low-cut. Her shoes were closed-toe, with a sensible heel, and she'd cried off her eye makeup. My brother Josh was there, pale and somber in a gray suit. My mother wore a loose cotton dress and clutched Mona's hand. Joy sat next to her, and I sat next to Joy, and Samantha slipped in the row behind me, reached over to squeeze my hand, and wiped her eyes.

I patted her shoulders, looking around. "Is your guy here?" I whispered.

"In the back," she replied, sniffling.

"Some first date," I said, and craned my neck until I saw him, a man in a navy suit with reddish-blond hair, affixing a yarmulke to his head.

There must have been prayers, though I can't remember them. I'm sure there was a eulogy, but I can't remember that, either. I remember thinking, midway through the kaddish, the mourners' prayer, that maybe someone had found the notes I'd taken about Peter's demise, and there'd be a flaming funeral pyre and someone to sing "Many Rivers to Cross" once we got to the cemetery. I held Joy's hand. I dispensed Kleenex along the length of the aisle. I didn't cry at all.

Then Joy and my mother and Elle and I got into the back of a rented Town Car (rented when? by whom? I had no idea), and it drove away. "You know, he didn't want this," I remarked to no one in particular as I climbed out of the car. "He wanted to lie in state at the Apollo." I hummed a few bars of "Many Rivers to Cross."

Joy stared at me. "What?"

"Never mind," I said. "It was just a joke we had. Just something silly." Out the window, the leaves on the trees burned brightly against the perfect blue sky. Cars zipped down the highway on their way to normal places: the school and the supermarket, the drugstore and the post office, and inside of them were people going about their business, singing along to the radio and enjoying the sun. "It was before your time."

Rabbi Grussgott stood at the head of a rectangle dug in the dirt and chanted the kaddish, and I was fine. The coffin went creaking into the ground on canvas straps. Still fine. Then, in a ritual I remembered from Bruce's father's funeral and hadn't seen since, the rabbi handed me a shovel.

Uh-uh. No way. "I can't," I said, handing it back.

"It's okay," she said quietly. She held it in her hands. It was just a regular gardening tool with a worn wood shaft and a rust-flecked spade. She looked at us. My mother made a small moaning noise in her throat and stepped backward. Elle took the shovel and looked a question at me. I shrugged. Joy stepped forward and took the shovel in her hands.

"I'll love you forever, Daddy," she said, scooping dirt from where it had been piled by the side of Peter's grave and sprinkling it on top of the wood of his coffin.

The kitchen and the dining room were filled with flowers, and every countertop held an assortment of trays from the Famous Fourth Street Deli, where the three of us had eaten so many meals. "Deli equals death," I told Sam. I wadded up the plastic wrap I'd pulled off a platter of cookies and tossed it into the trash can.

"Would you please sit down?" Samantha asked me for roughly the hundredth time since we'd gotten home. "It's sitting shiva, not running-around-the-kitchen shiva. You're supposed to let us help."

"I want to keep busy," I said. "It helps." That wasn't actually true. It wasn't helping. I felt as numb as if I'd been wrapped in six inches of gauze, yet somehow I was functioning, finding plastic cups and extra toilet paper for the powder room and the monogrammed ice bucket one of my Cleveland cousins had given us for our wedding. Every time I turned around, I thought I'd see him walking through the door, sitting on the couch with a crossword puzzle in his hands and his long legs stretched out in front of him, and every time it felt like being hit with something heavy. *Oh,* I would think as the vision dissolved. *Oh, Peter.*

I made myself go to the sink and start loading the dishwasher, even though Sam and my mother tried to shoo me away. "How did that happen? Do you think the Chinese take-out industry's pissed? Or the fried-chicken people? How come fried chicken didn't get to be the universal food of Jewish grief?"

"We can get you fried chicken," Sam promised. "We can get you anything you need."

"Do you remember my bachelorette party?" Because I was preparing to wed a diet doctor (*Bariatric physician,* I heard my husband say in my head, *please!*), we decided that instead of a party that celebrated a farewell to flesh and included a trip to the local version of Chippendale's, we would instead have a Farewell to Trans Fats, which, I'd sadly told my friends, would probably never be permitted to darken my cupboards again. Six of us had gotten all dressed up and gone restaurant-hopping for deep-fried mozzarella sticks, biscuits with honey, macaroni and cheese, McDonald's french fries, fried chicken, and fried ice cream. Then, I remembered, we'd gone to see the strippers anyhow. I'd gotten home at two in the morning, reeking of grease and tequila and whipped cream (the last acquired at the strip club), with my high heels in my hand and a lei made of condoms around my neck, swearing to myself that it would be nothing but salads and All-Bran until the vows were said.

I hope it was worth it, Peter had called from the bed, and I'd giggled and crawled in next to him, fully dressed except for my shoes. He'd told me I'd smelled like a zeppole. *You know it turns you on,* I'd said.

"You know what the moral of this is?" I asked. I was in the kitchen. There was the table where we'd had thousands of meals, played hours of Candy Land and dominoes when Joy was little and Scrabble when she was big (even though I should have been the family champ, Peter would usually eke out a victory by dint of some obscure medical term that always sounded made up). There was the stove where he'd make his chicken cacciatore, and it was so delicious that I'd never complain about the way he'd use every pot and pan we owned to make it, and I'd wind up washing all of them. The refrigerator still held half of a six-pack of Yuengling and the skim milk he'd poured on his oatmeal. On the door was a Rocky magnet with a picture of the two of us on the museum steps underneath it. "The moral is, eat whatever you want, because it doesn't fucking matter. You're gonna die anyhow."

"Come on." Sam gripped my shoulders briefly, then steered me toward the pantry. "Language. And we need more napkins. Just tell me where they are."

"Napkins. Right." Around my waist was the gingham apron I'd bought to impress Remy Heymsfeld from Open Hearts. I guessed I'd need to call him soon, him and Betsy both, to tell them what had happened, to see what could be done. There was a magnetic pad on the refrigerator, and I scribbled down CANCEL BABY before rifling through the shelves. The only napkins I could find were left over from our Fourth of July barbecue. Their red, white, and blue stripes would probably give the proceedings an incongruously patriotic feel. *Ah well, I* thought, and piled them next to the platters on the table and looked at my watch, wondering when I could go back to bed.

"How can people be eating?" Joy demanded with her hands on her hips, staring at the spread: corned beef and pastrami, turkey and tuna and egg salad, smoked fish and Swiss cheese and cream cheese, rye bread and bagels, kugels studded with raisins, platters of sugar-dusted linzer tortes and chocolate-chip cookies. "How can anyone be hungry?"

"Life goes on," I said. It was the worst cliché, and possibly the most true.

Joy curled her lip in the scornful manner she'd perfected over the last nine months. Her hair hung in ringlets around her face. "Well, I think it's disgusting." She brushed at her swollen eyes and walked out the back door.

The doorbell rang. "I'll get it," Sam said, wiping her hands on a dish towel tucked into her waistband. A minute later, she came back, leading a little girl and her mother. The girl introduced herself as Cara.

"From the Ronald McDonald House," said her mom. "She was wondering if she could say hello to Joy."

"Sure, honey," I said, and I led her into the garden, where Joy and her friends were sitting. Sam's guy was doing card tricks for them, and they were doing a good job of making a dent in the cookie trays.

I stood on the steps as Joy looked up. "Hi, Cara."

"My mom saw about your dad in the paper," Cara said. "Is it okay that I came?"

"Sure it's okay," said Joy. My heart swelled as I watched Joy pull up a chair for the little girl, introduce her to Tamsin and Todd, and ask about someone named Harry. "He has hair now," the girl said, and smiled, and Joy smiled back at her. "That's good," my daughter said. *Today she is a woman,* I thought, and turned away so Joy wouldn't see me cry.

Maxi handed me a handkerchief, a crisply ironed monogrammed linen square. I wiped my face, then smoothed my apron and went back to the kitchen. Through the windows beside the door, I could see a station wagon parked at the curb with its blinkers on and six feet of Bruce Guberman standing next to the driver's door.

"Oh my God," I whispered. "Guberman."

"That's him?" Maxi whispered back, peering at the car. She beckoned for Samantha, who took in the scene with narrowed eyes.

"Do you want me to tell him to leave?" Sam asked hopefully.

"No," I said. Then a horrible thought struck me. "Oh my God, you guys. What if he thinks that every time someone dies, I'll have sex with him?" I started laughing as the passenger-side door swung open, and Emily, dainty as a doll, exited, then opened the door behind her and extracted one of her sons. My fingernails dug into the meat of my palms.

"Let me handle this," Samantha said, stepping past me.

"No," I said. "No, it's okay. They're here for Joy. It's okay."

I stood there and watched as Bruce took his wife's elbow and steered her (or maybe "dragged her" would be more apt, although I could have been projecting) up the steps toward my front door. Then I made myself walk down to meet them. "Cannie," he said.

"Bruce," I answered.

"I'm sorry," he said.

"Sorry," I said, like a parrot.

Emily detached herself from Bruce's side.

"I'm so sorry for your loss," she said quietly. "Boys," she said, bending down (short as she was, she didn't have far to go). The older boy put his video game in his pocket, and the younger one, the spitting image of Bruce, looked up at me and said, "Sorry."

Two little boys. Two perfect boys. Oh, Peter. My throat closed again, but I managed to say, "Joy's in the garden." I wiped my eyes and stood aside to let them pass.

Three days later, I made myself play the forty-seven messages on our voice mail. I sat in the living room, a glass of wine in my hands, with Peter's blue bathrobe belted around my waist, and let the words wash over me. *We were so sorry to hear . . . such a terrible shock . . . if there's anything we can do.* I wiped my eyes. I could push through the days, but the nights were terrible. I kept seeing him. That was the thing. Coming out of the shower with a towel around his hips. Walking up the stairs with the newspaper, folded in thirds, in his hand. Pulling a sun-warmed tomato off the vine in the backyard, slicing it and salting it and giving me half. Standing in front of the refrigerator with the door open, like he was hoping the contents would change if he just stared at them long enough. *Don't you be putting my butter back in there*, I'd say as I walked past, and saw him eyeing the butter I kept on the counter, and he'd say, *If you want this entire family to die from botulism, I suppose I shouldn't stand in your way.*

Come back, I would try to tell him. *Don't leave me. Don't leave Joy. Come back to us. Come home.* Sometimes I'd get a word or two out. Then he'd be gone.

If you need anything . . . if we can help . . . I wrote down names and numbers with one of Peter's University of Philadelphia pens. The writing on the page didn't even look familiar. It was like a stranger had stolen my hands.

The forty-second call was from a woman with a high, sweet voice that sounded almost giddy. "Hi, guys!" she said. *Didn't get the message,* I thought . . . her, and messages 22 (a guy trying to sell "Peter Krushel . . . Krushla . . . um, the gentleman of the house" a subscription to the *Examiner*) and 30 (a computer asking if we wanted to switch our car insurance). "It's Betsy!" *Betsy,* I mouthed. It took me a minute to remember who Betsy was, and when I did, I groaned out loud. "Listen," she said, "I know I'm not supposed to home-test, and it's not official until your doctor confirms it, but . . ." She paused. I held my breath, staring at the wall, clutching the pen and the pad, thinking, *Oh yes,* thinking, *Oh no.* When I looked sideways Peter sat at my desk, smiling at me. "Wait," I whispered as he turned toward the window. "Oh, please, wait . . ."

"Congratulations, Mom and Dad!" said Betsy.

THIRTY-EIGHT

"I t doesn't always work on the first try," my mother said.

I gave her a look to tell her that she was being ridiculous. "You had somebody implanted with a fertilized embryo, and now you're surprised that she's pregnant? Did they not have health class in your school?"

"Well, when you put it like that," she murmured, and ran her hands through her hair. She was wearing her own clothes—she'd made a big deal out of getting dressed every morning—but on top of her outfit, she wore my father's terry bathrobe, the way she did whenever she was at home. Every time I saw her shuffling down the hall with her hands in the pockets and the hem dragging on the floor, I wanted to cry.

"We'd been prepared to do three rounds, and then, if nothing happened . . ." Her voice trailed off. On the stove, the teakettle whistled. My mom ignored it, so after a minute, I got up and poured boiling water into her mug and brought it to her, along with the sugar bowl and the pitcher of milk. We were almost out of milk. *Milk,* I wrote on the notepad on the refrigerator. The words "crackers" and "shampoo" were still there in my father's handwriting. I wondered if we'd just leave that page up there forever, or if someday I'd come home from school and it would be gone.

I poured myself juice and sat at the table across from my mother. My hair, still damp, was in a ponytail; my hearing aids were in my ears. I wear them all the time now. I don't ever want to miss anything again. "So what are we going to do? If we don't take the baby, does Betsy get to keep it?"

"I'm not . . . I mean, we can't . . . Well, it's a baby," my mom said, as if this was a news flash. "It's not a dress. You can't just return it, or not pick it up at the store."

I nodded and sipped my juice, watching her.

"We have to be sure, though," she said. "It's such a big thing. A baby. We have to be certain. It's forever, you know?"

"Forever," I repeated. The steam from her teacup curled toward her face, and she used the heel of one hand to wipe at her forehead. There were purplish crescents underneath her eyes, lines I'd never noticed at the corners.

I sat there, looking at her for a minute, waiting for her to say something else. When she didn't, I flipped to a fresh page of the shopping list. *Bottles,* I wrote. *Bibs. Blanket. Crib.* "Do we still have my old crib?"

"Huh? Oh, yeah," she said, and nodded vacantly. "In the basement. I saved . . ." She stared over my head. "I saved everything. I don't know why. I just did."

Get her back on track, I thought. "Is that the safest kind?"

"Safest?" She blinked. "I'll check."

"*I'll* check," I said, and made a note. *Check on crib safety ratings. Stroller. Car seat. Diapers. Rocking chair.* "Hey, Mom? What do they call those slings ladies use to carry babies on their chests?"

She thought about it. "Slings," she said. Then she said, "I should probably get a job."

I wrote down *Job.* Then I looked up. "Do we need money?"

"We'll be okay. But I should have something to do. Your father thought . . ." She lifted her cup, then set it down without drinking. "I don't know. Maybe I'll try to write something."

"You have to take care of the baby," I pointed out.

"In my spare time," she said. "In my spare time, I could write."

I wondered whether she was lying about the money, whether

we'd have to sell our house, whether I'd have to drop out of the Philadelphia Academy. "I can take care of the baby after school. You can work then."

She nodded. "Maybe."

Pajamas, I wrote. *Books. Educational DVDs.* I'd probably get some money for my bat mitzvah. I could use it to buy things the baby would need. "We'll be okay," I told her. She gave me a watery smile. Then she blew into her cup of tea and sipped from it, staring out the window. The leaves outside our window were still dark green. Soon they'd be crimson and gold, falling in drifts to the sidewalk under the bright blue fall sky. People would put pumpkins on their stoops, then wreaths on their doors, and by May the trees would be budding again, the boughs bright and heavy with cherry and dogwood blossoms. I tried to imagine me and my mother pushing a stroller down the sidewalk, one of those fancy ones with big rubber wheels and bright canvas hoods, but all I could think of was my father, walking with me to Rita's to get a water ice or to TLA to rent a video, his hand warm around mine. In the winter, we'd take my mother's old sled to Fairmount Park. He'd pull me up the steepest hill, then run down to wait for me, crouching in the snow, his arms outstretched. *Don't be afraid,* he'd say, and I'd dig my heels into the snow, balancing for an instant before tilting forward and sending the sled over the lip of the hill, knowing that he'd catch me. He would always catch me. A sob wanted to push its way out of my throat, but I wouldn't let it. *Snowsuit,* I wrote. *Hat. Scarf. Mittens.*

THIRTY-NINE

We sat shiva for a week. Then I threw out all of the picked-over deli trays, uncovered the mirrors, and took Joy shopping for summer camp. I cried after the bus drove her off to the Poconos, but I did it in my car, with the windows rolled up and the radio playing, telling myself that I'd be all right, that women survived worse things, war and famine and horrible illnesses, that I could deal with widowhood and two weeks in an empty house. On the first Monday after Labor Day I drove Joy to the Philadelphia Academy, the way I had so many times before. "If you want to come home, just call me," I said as I pulled the minivan up to the curb.

"I'll be okay," she said.

She went to school, and we went to services together for Rosh Hashanah and Yom Kippur, sitting side by side in the Center City Synagogue, chanting the words of the *Ashamnu,* the recitation of sins.

Ashamnu, we sang. *We have been guilty. Bagadnu. We have betrayed.* We curled our hands into fists and joined the rest of the congregation in striking our chests symbolically with each word. *Gazalnu, we have stolen. Dibarnu dofi, we have lied.*

Peter, I thought, holding on tightly to the back of the seat in front of me with my free hand, dizzy with hunger from the daylong fast, dizzy with grief. What had he done? What had he stolen? Whom had he betrayed? Why did God take him before he could even see

Joy's bat mitzvah, let alone his own biological child? I looked up toward the bimah and the Torahs and Rabbi Grussgott, dressed in white. No answers came, only the ancient words of the chant, the melody in a minor key, the sounds of hundreds of fists thumping hundreds of chests as we prayed to be inscribed in the Book of Life for another year, please God.

Ni'atznu. We have been scornful. Well, God only knew I had. Maybe it was all my fault. *Saranu.* We have been disobedient. Maybe Peter had been right. I'd been running from my divine purpose. I was supposed to . . . What had he said? *Write something real.* And I hadn't. I'd been too afraid.

Ta'inu. We have gone astray. *Ti'tanu.* We have misled others. *Sarnu.* We have turned away from You.

"Forgive us, pardon us, grant us atonement," Joy said beside me. I bent my head and prayed for the two of us, that things would work out, that I'd find the courage I needed to do the things that had to be done.

We broke our fast at Samantha's, and once we'd cleared away the blintzes and the bagels, she'd offered to come over and spend the night, but I told her I thought we'd be fine. After we got home and Joy was asleep, I went through our closet, spreading Peter's ties out on the bed. I'd give a few of the nicer ones to Josh and keep my favorites—the orange-and-gold one with frogs that I'd bought him for his birthday, the cream-and-gold one he'd worn to our wedding. Maybe I'd sew them into a quilt someday, or use them to line a little purse for Joy, something she could carry at her own wedding. The suits I'd already sent to Goodwill, along with his good wool winter coat, but I'd kept some things: the Penn sweatshirt he'd worn on the weekends, the mug Joy had made for him in nursery school that read WORLD'S GREATEST DAD, where he'd kept his dry-cleaning receipts and movie-ticket stubs and spare change.

I sat cross-legged and leaned against the headboard in the big, empty bedroom that would, I feared, always feel big and empty to me now. I rolled the ties into tie-balls and put them in a paper shopping bag. Then I got off the bed and sat down at the small wooden desk against the wall. Peter had used the desk for his work and to pay the bills. I'd never written a word there, not even my signature on a check. *You remember how,* Lyla had told me, but at that moment, in the darkness, with the empty bed stretched out beside me and the empty years looming before me, I wasn't sure.

Okay, I thought. *You can do this.* I turned on the light, retied the belt of Peter's bathrobe, and took out a notebook and a pen. *Once upon a time,* I wrote, just to get myself started, and then the world fell away as I leaned into the pool of lamplight over the desk and began again.

FORTY

"Honey?"

My mother was standing at the bottom of the stairs, wearing the red dress I remembered from pictures of Maxi's movie's premiere, the dress that my father had loved. "What do you think?" she asked, smoothing the skirt, tugging at the sleeves. "Too much?"

I shook my head. "It's pretty," I managed. "Where'd you find it?"

"Closet." She pulled at the top uneasily. The dress was cut to leave her shoulders bare, and her skin was tan and gleaming. *You look beautiful,* my father would have said if he'd been there, and maybe he would have kissed her, too, if he thought I couldn't see. And if she thought I wasn't listening, she would have said, *You know, you don't have to flatter me. I'm a sure thing.* Then he'd whisper something in her ear, and she'd duck her head, blushing, pleased.

"Well, at least it still fits," she said, and watched me carefully, poised to grab me and catch me as I wobbled down the stairs. With me in my new not-too-high heels, my mom and I were exactly the same height. I'd overheard her on the phone with Rabbi Grussgott about three weeks after the funeral. "Do we reschedule?" she was asking. I'd stood at the kitchen door, holding my breath. I knew what the rabbi would tell her, which was that in Jewish tradition, you don't cancel a *simcha* because of a tragedy. Not a wedding, not a bris or baby naming, not a bar or bat mitzvah. You don't cancel, because in the midst of life we are in death, and we find joy in the midst of sorrow.

"Joy in the midst of sorrow," I said. She reached out and smoothed my hair, tucking a curl behind my ear, giving my hearing aid a friendly tweak (or maybe just making sure it was still there). "No black suit?" I asked her.

She shook her head. "I've worn that black suit enough for the rest of my life, and I thought . . ." Her eyes filled with tears, but she blinked fast, so they didn't ruin her makeup. "I thought I'd wear something that I'd worn with your father. I don't know. Maybe it's silly."

I hugged her, careful not to wrinkle her dress or mess her hair. "It's not," I said. "I like it. It's good."

Two hours later I stood in the synagogue lobby in my pink dress with the thin straps and the silvery beaded skirt; the dress that I'd bought with Elle, then returned, and bought with Bruce's credit card, then returned, and finally bought with my mother and Maxi, after I'd lit out for the territories, after I'd been lost, then found again. I wore pearl earrings that had belonged to my great-grandmother, silver sandals I'd found with Tamsin and Todd, and a pink-and-silver shoulder-covering tallis that Emily had made for me. Aunt Elle had taken me to get my hair and makeup done that morning. ("Subtle!" she kept saying. "Sheer! Clean!" Meanwhile, she'd pulled up a chair right beside me and used the makeup lady's tweezers and glue to affix gigantic long fake eyelashes to both her upper and lower lids.)

I stood in the lobby, watching as my friends walked in: Tamsin and Todd, Amber and Martin, Sasha and Audrey and Tara and Duncan Brodkey, and Cara with her parents, looking grown-up in a black dress. My family gathered in the little foyer by the front door, by the blue prayer books stacked on a table next to the programs. Beams of sunlight made their way through the high windows, and the wooden floors shifted and creaked underneath us as Rabbi Grussgott gave us last-minute instructions, going over the order of the aliyahs and where everyone would stand when we passed the Torah down through the generations, from my grandparents to my parents then to me. My mom stood on my left side, and Bruce was on my right, in a dark blue suit and a blue-and-white tallis. For a minute the thought jumped into my head that this was what I'd wanted, this was *normal*: a mom and a dad, and not some weird, confusing, hard-to-explain situation, just a regular mom and dad who loved each other, or could at least look that way in synagogue on a Saturday morning. I'd wanted that so badly, and now, of course, I'd give anything to have my old, freakish family back again, anything in the world to have my father standing there with me.

The rabbi smiled at me and slipped into the sanctuary, leaving just the immediate family in the foyer: my mom and Aunt Elle and Uncle Josh and Grandma Ann and Bruce. "Please join me in reading responsively," I whispered. I heard "responsibly" in my head, and I smiled a little. Tyler was in the audience. He'd grown about six inches since his bar mitzvah and had done something to tame his hair. I thought I'd noticed Tamsin looking at him appreciatively on her way in, and I reminded myself to introduce them at the party. Then I flipped through my prayer book, glancing at the passages I'd highlighted, the pages I'd dog-eared: *Baruch atah adonai, elohainu melech ha'olam . . . Blessed are you, oh Lord our God, ruler of the universe, who sustains us and has brought us to this joyous day.*

"Are you ready?" my mother whispered, and just as I nodded, the front door eased open, and a man with close-cropped white curls, in an immaculate black suit, shining black shoes, and black sunglasses, slipped inside.

"Joy," he said.

My mouth fell open. Behind me, Elle whispered something you are definitely not supposed to say in synagogue.

My grandfather smiled as he walked toward me. "I hope I'm not too late." He reached into his pocket and pulled out a soft zippered bag of blue velvet. A tallis bag, holding the traditional blue-and-white fringed prayer shawl. "This was my father's," he said, and handed it to me.

"Th-thank you," I stammered. My numb fingers worked at the zipper. My mother stood behind me, her hands still on my shoulders. I could imagine her glaring at him, or trying to drag me out of his sight, but instead, she said, so softly I almost couldn't hear her, "Thank you."

"All set?" asked Rabbi Grussgott, sticking her head back through the door. "It's time."

"One more thing." My grandfather reached into his pocket and pulled out something round and silver. I heard my mother suck in her breath. I remembered the silver dollars from her book. Her father would toss them into the deep end of the swimming pool, and Allie and her sister would dive for them. They got to keep the money after. Dorrie would spend hers on candy and magazines, but Allie—my mother—had saved every one.

"For you," my grandfather said, and pressed the silver dollar into my hand. "For luck." He pulled off his glasses and looked at all of us: Grandma Ann and Mona, Uncle Josh and Aunt Elle, and then, finally, me and my mother. "I'm proud of you," he said. My mother started to cry. I remembered after Tyler's bar mitzvah, when I was sick in the bathroom and my father had said the same thing to me. It was weird to think of my mother being a daughter the same way that I was, and how she might have been comforted by those words the same way I had been.

"Joy?" Rabbi Grussgott stared at me, then at my grandfather, looking puzzled. I nodded.

As we filed into the sanctuary, down the aisle toward the bimah, I looked over my shoulder for my grandfather, thinking that he'd slip into a seat toward the back, and I could call him up for an aliyah, let him drape the tallis over my shoulders . . . But by the time I'd climbed the stairs, stood behind the podium, and opened my prayer book, the faces in the audience seemed miles away, and no matter how hard I looked, I couldn't find him anywhere.

· · ·

"For my first aliyah, I'd like to call Grandma Ann and Grandma Audrey." I read their Hebrew names, then stood back and waited as they climbed the three steps onto the bimah, touched the spines of their prayer books to the Torah, and kissed them. For one endless, horrible moment, I couldn't remember the words to the blessing, or the tune, even though I'd been singing it for six years of Hebrew school. *Barchu et adonai h'am vorach* . . . And there it was, like a piece of candy tucked under my tongue. I opened my mouth and started to sing.

Baruch atah adonai le'olam va'yed, the crowd—or at least the Jewish people in the crowd—chanted back. Tamsin was in the front row, with her glasses off and her hair down around her shoulders, her features less pointed than delicate, her face a pale oval above her dress. Todd was sitting next to her, perfect and elegant in his suit and pink-and-silver tie.

I picked up the silver pointer, in the shape of a small hand with the index finger extended. I touched it to the parchment gently, like Rabbi Grussgott had told me. The words were in my head—I'd listened to them so many times on my iPod that I knew every sound, every syllable—and as I chanted and slid the pointer over the Hebrew, my nervousness fell away.

By the end, there was a crowd gathered around me of everyone who'd been called to the Torah for an aliyah: both of my grandmothers, Aunt Elle and Uncle Josh, Samantha and Maxi, my mother and Bruce. Now it was time for my speech, my message, the thing that I wanted to tell them.

"We read today from Genesis," I began. "Abraham was Isaac's father. When Isaac was forty years old, he married Rebecca. His wife was barren, and Isaac pleaded with God for her sake."

Behind me, I felt my mother stiffen.

"God granted his plea, and Rebecca became pregnant. But the children clashed inside her, and when this occurred, she asked, 'Why is this happening to me?' She went to seek a message from God. God's word to her was 'Two nations are in your womb. Two governments will separate from inside you. The upper hand will go from one government to the other. The greater one will serve the younger.' When the time came for her to give birth, there were twins in her womb. The first one came out reddish and as hairy as a fur coat." Someone— maybe Todd or Duncan Brodkey—snorted. I kept reading. "They named him Esau. His brother then emerged, and his hand was grasping Esau's heel. Isaac named him Jacob. Isaac was sixty years old when Rebecca gave birth to them." I paused, then said, "Which, in my opinion, was totally unfair. I mean, he'd be, like, seventy-eight when they finished high school."

My mom laughed. I bent my head back over my typed pages. "The boys grew up. Esau became a skilled trapper, a man of the field. Jacob was a scholarly man who remained with the tents. Isaac enjoyed eating Esau's game and favored him, but Rebecca favored Jacob. Jacob was once simmering a stew, when Esau came home exhausted from the field. Esau said to Jacob, 'Give me a mouthful of that stew! I'm starving!' Jacob said, 'I will, if you sell me your birthright first.'

" 'Here I'm about to die!' said Esau. 'What good is a birthright to me?' 'Make an oath to me right now,' said Jacob. Esau made the oath, and sold his birthright to Jacob."

I looked down at the three pages spread in front of me on the dark red velvet covering the bimah. The words swam in front of my eyes. What had I meant to say? What did any of it mean? I blinked and could make out individual words: "obligation" and "responsibility" and "traditions of our people." I felt my mother's hand on my shoulder, and I knew that people were staring, but all I could think, all I wanted to say, was *I miss my dad.*

I blinked again, hard, and looked at the pages. "I'm supposed to tell you about what I've learned this year as I got ready to become a bat mitzvah," I said. "And I had a speech like that all written. It was about my Torah portion, and the idea of obligation, and how if you do something wrong then you have to make it right, but really, the truth is, what I learned this year is that life is hard."

My mother's hand tightened on my shoulder.

"Good people die for no reason. Little kids get sick. The people who are supposed to love you end up leaving." A lump grew in my throat. I swallowed hard and kept going. "I imagine how Esau must have felt. It wasn't his fault he was hairy, and it wasn't his fault he was hungry, and it probably wasn't his fault that his mother liked Jacob better. Jacob was sneaky, but he's the one who got his father's blessings. He's the one whose descendants are supposed to be numbered as the stars in the sky." I looked down and managed another breath. "But Esau kept going," I said. "He didn't get his father's blessing. He had to live by the sword. But he at least got to live. Isaac told him that the fat places of the earth could be his dwelling, and he could still have the dew of heaven to drink."

I folded up my pages and pressed my hands on top of them. "When you don't get what you want, you take what's left and make the best of it. The Torah tells us that Esau had two wives, and maybe they helped him out. I know that my mom and my grandmothers have helped me a lot this year. And my aunt Elle and uncle Josh, and my . . . and Bruce. Even when I did the wrong thing or made the wrong choice, my family stood with me. What I learned this year is probably what Esau learned, even though in Jewish history, he's just the other brother, the one nobody talks about much. Bad things happen. Stuff doesn't work out." I looked down at the sheet of paper, the important words I'd written down. "Everyone has sorrow. Everyone has obligations. Everyone keeps going. You lean on the people who love you. You do the best you can, and you keep going."

I folded up the pages again and tried to stuff them in my pocket before I remembered that my fancy dress didn't have one. Rabbi Grussgott raised her eyebrows with a look that very clearly said, *What happened to the speech we worked on?* Then she gave a little nod and gestured to my mother, who looked like she was going to start bawling as she stepped up to the microphone with her red dress rustling.

"Joy, my daughter, my darling," she began. Behind me, I heard Grandma Ann start to cry. "I am so very proud of you today, as you stand here before us, reading so beautifully, looking so beautiful and so grown-up."

My mom wasn't crying. Her eyes were sparkling, and I thought it was because she was happy, even impressed with me, as if I'd turned out to be just as special, just like she'd always said I was.

"I know how proud your father would be, too. I know how proud you always made him. You were—you are—the most wonderful daughter anyone could ever ask for, and even if you drive me crazy sometimes . . ." I smiled a little, and she did, too. "And I drive you crazy a lot of the time . . ." She wiped underneath her eyes carefully, with just the pad of her forefinger, like Elle had shown her. "You're the best thing I've ever done. You're the best thing I could have ever hoped for. And I know that you will be, as the Torah says, a woman of valor, like Sarah and Rachel and Rebecca and Leah, your namesake. I know that even if you don't get exactly what you want exactly when you want it, you'll be strong and you'll be smart and you're already beautiful, and I know that you're going to have a wonderful life, because I know you've already learned one of the most important lessons of all."

"Close your eyes," I said as we walked into the ballroom of the College of Physicians, and I held my hands over my mother's face to make sure she couldn't see. I walked behind her, guiding her into the ballroom. "Okay . . . now!"

For a minute she didn't say anything, and then she started to cry. "Oh, Joy," she said, and clapped her hands. "You didn't!"

I did. All of my years building scenery for a dozen different Philadelphia Academy plays and musicals had finally come in handy, and my friends had helped. We'd been able to transform the big ballroom into a *Sound of Music* wonderland in celebration of the sappiest musical of all time, which of course was my mother's favorite. Each of the tables was one of "My Favorite Things." There were raindrops on roses (Tamsin and I had worked for an entire Sunday making papier-mâché flowers, then gluing round crystals to them) and whiskers on kittens (that was the kids' table; we'd bought a pile of stuffed animals, and each kid could take one home). There were bright copper kettles (Aunt Sam knew a party planner who'd gotten a bunch of them on loan from Fante's in the Italian Market) and warm woolen mittens (Grandma Ann and Mona had spent the last three weeks speed-knitting). The favors were in brown paper packages tied up with string, and for dessert there were crisp apple strudels, even though I'd drawn the line at serving schnitzel with noodles for lunch, because I didn't know what it was and thought it sounded disgusting.

" 'Girls in white dresses with blue satin sashes,' " my mom recited. Tamsin twirled proudly and beamed.

" 'Snowflakes that stay on my nose and eyelashes,' " I recited, and led my mom to the head table, where there were a dozen different snow globes as the centerpiece (each one had a different Philadelphia scene at its center and a blank space for guests to slide in a picture that the photographers would take).

" 'Wild geese that fly with the moon on their wings'?"

"Um. The banquet manager nixed that. You can't have wild live-stock in a public place for the purposes of . . . you know . . . enter-tainment."

"Well," she said, "I have no doubt that you tried."

Todd strolled over, wearing a silver suit, pulling a skateboard with a spool of rope on top of it. "See if you can get it," he said.

She only had to think for a minute. "Are you 'So, a needle pulling thread'?"

"You see?" said Todd, turning to his sister. "It's obvious to any-one who knows the musical."

"I still think the lederhosen looked better," she said.

Todd handed the skateboard to his sister and pulled me toward the empty dance floor. "Come on, Joy," he said. "Let's dance."

It wasn't as fancy as Tyler's party, or as big as Tamsin and Todd's, but all of my friends had fun. There was a chocolate fountain for des-sert, which the caterers shut down after Max tried to jump inside it. There was even a small scandal when my mom hauled Aunt Elle into the lobby and whisper-yelled at her for dirty-dancing with Jack Corsey ("The boy is thirteen years old, Elle!" she said, and Aunt Elle smirked and said, "Today he is a man").

I danced with Todd. I danced with Bruce. I held Max under his armpits and let him balance his little black loafers on top of my silver sandals. I even danced with Cara for a minute, before she sniffed and said, "Stupid," and went back to her table. When Duncan Brodkey tapped my shoulder, saying, "Hey, you wanna?" I smiled at him and took his hand, feeling my skin, my whole body, lighting up when we touched.

After the cake-cutting and the candle-lighting and the speeches, when the music was just starting to wind down, I sat on a bench in the medicinal herb garden, thinking about my father. We'd go to the Franklin Institute and walk through the giant heart, or to the Academy of Natural Sciences to look at dinosaur skeletons. We would ride our bikes on the towpath from Manayunk all the way to Valley Forge, and my mom would meet us there with a picnic lunch. We'd go to the Reading Terminal for blueberry pancakes and turkey bacon at the Dutch Eating Place, and buy whatever looked interesting (a leg of lamb once, and another time a guinea hen), and bring it home and figure out how to cook it for dinner.

The bench creaked as my mom sat down beside me. "Are you all right?"

I nodded. *I miss my dad,* I wanted to say, but it was as obvious as the air around us, the ground underneath my feet. So instead I said, "My . . . your, um, father. He didn't stay for the service?"

She sighed. "I think he took off. At least, I didn't see him."

I pulled the silver dollar out of my purse and handed it to her. My mother turned it over in her hand. "He used to throw these in the swimming pool, and we'd dive for them," she said.

"I know," I said. "It was in your book."

She sighed and nodded.

"It was nice of him to come, I guess," I said. She said nothing. "So maybe he really was okay. Right?"

"Nobody's just one thing or another," my mother said. "Nobody's just bad or just good." She sniffled and wiped her eyes. "It was nice that he came."

"It was," I said, and for a minute I leaned my face against her shoulder and let her hold me up.

When I got home I hung my beautiful dress in my closet. I'd never wear it again, I knew. Maybe I'd give it to Cara, and she could wear it someday—except probably the fashions would change in the next three years, and she'd have her own ideas about what was beautiful.

I took the silver dollar out of my purse and my jewelry box off my bookshelf. The box had been a birthday present from Maxi when I turned eight. Inside was a plastic ballerina; she spun and played "Beautiful Dreamer" when you wound the knob on the back. There wasn't much in there: a silver bracelet my father had given me for my last birthday, two twenty-dollar bills from a babysitting job, and a picture of Duncan Brodkey that I'd taken from the yearbook office's pile of discards. It was better than nothing, I thought. A silver dollar that my mother had once dived under the water for, an *I'm proud of you.* A mother who loved me, maybe more than I wanted her to sometimes. A father who'd loved me, then died. It was more than a lot of kids got.

I ran my fingers along the bottom of the box until I found what I was looking for: my old silver baby rattle, engraved with JOY. It could work for another baby, I thought, and I slipped it in my pocket and went downstairs to look for the silver polish.

FORTY-ONE

As the days piled up into weeks, and the weeks turned into months, and fall slid into winter, I realized one of the great truths about tragedy: You can dream of disappearing. You can wish for oblivion, for endless sleep or the escape of fiction, of walking into a river with your pockets full of stones, of letting the dark water close over your head. But if you've got kids, the web of the world holds you close and wraps you tight and keeps you from falling, no matter how badly you think you want to fall.

Frenchie scratched at the screen door, and I let her out, and when she whined, I let her back in. Joy outgrew her shoes, so I took her to the mall to get another pair, plus winter boots and a new winter coat. When she drank all the milk, I would go to the supermarket, just like a normal person, and buy more . . . and if anybody noticed that I was wearing a men's blue bathrobe under my long winter coat, none of them said a word. I cooked dinners, ran the dishwasher, emptied it, then cooked some more and filled it up again. The leaves fell, and I swept them off the sidewalk. The snow fell, and I shoveled it and salted the front steps, trying not to cry when I pulled the shovel out of the closet, trying not to remember the way Peter and I would tease each other about whose turn it was.

December was awful. I avoided the stores full of tinsel and carols and holiday lights, the happy hand-holding couples lingering in front of the jewelry-store windows on Sansom Street, the crowds of families at the mall, but eventually, I had to go to Target to pick up Tupperware and paper towels, washcloths and diapers and wipes. I was doing fine, piloting the shopping cart around the perimeter of the store, avoiding the video and music section, where Peter and I used to linger, when the bread-machine display stopped me in my tracks.

I groaned out loud, remembering. *We should get a bread machine,* Peter had said. *Fresh bread would make the house smell good.*

But the bread always comes out gummy, I'd said.

It's good when it's toasted, he'd replied.

I'd told him that we didn't have the counter space, and he'd said that maybe we could consider relocating the cappuccino machine because, honestly, how often did we use it? And I'd said the cappuccino machine was more aesthetically pleasing than a boxy plastic gummy bread maker. Then I'd go home and make a frothy, noisy cappuccino, and he'd sigh and give up until the next time we walked past bread machines in a department store, when he'd look at them wistfully, as if they were a row of girlfriends who'd gotten away. Sometimes he'd run a finger down one of the digital displays and heave a sigh, and I'd say *Forget it* and keep pushing the cart toward the toilet paper and the juice boxes.

On the speakers overhead, Mariah Carey's "O Holy Night" gave way to "Grandma Got Run Over by a Reindeer." I leaned against the Crock-Pots and started to cry. Why hadn't I just bought the damn bread machine? It would have made him happy. It would have made the house smell good. And even bread-machine bread was good when it was toasted. What was wrong with me? Why hadn't I—

"Ma'am?"

I wiped my eyes. A clerk in a red polyester pinny was staring at me. I pulled a package of tissues out of my pocket (these days I never left home without them) and pointed at the Crock-Pots.

"I thought they were on sale," I said weakly. The clerk led me to what must have been the break room, a cheerless white-tiled windowless space with red plastic tables, a refrigerator, and a microwave.

"He's never coming back," I said to myself. Or I'd meant to say it to myself, but the clerk must have heard me.

"Ma'am?" he said. "Are you sure you're all right? Do you have anyone I can call?"

"I'm okay," I managed, and hurried to the cash register, then my car, where I could cry in peace.

Time passed. I read the copy of *See It, Be It* that my sister had given me, and tried to visualize my desired end results: not just looking normal but feeling that way, too. In March I baked hamantaschen for the Preschool Purim Parade, because I always did that, and I hadn't called the synagogue to say that I wouldn't, because I couldn't stand the thought of explaining to the stranger who might answer the phone that they'd been my husband's favorites, only now my husband was dead. In April I planted purple and yellow pansies in our window boxes so that ours weren't the only empty ones on the street. I cut back the roses. I watered the hostas. I swept and weeded, keeping up appearances, thinking that I could fake normal, could fake happy, even if I never felt that way again.

I went on walks with my mother, out to brunch with Samantha, to New York to visit my sister, and I talked to Maxi on the telephone. I sat on the sidelines at Joy's softball games and tried not to stare at Peter's replacement as first-base coach, a man I'd never seen before, with reddish hair and twins in the outfield. I found a therapist for Joy—a man, at her request—and I dropped her off every Wednesday and didn't ask questions when I picked her up, even though I could tell from her swollen eyes that she'd been crying in there. She had to cry somewhere, I figured. At home she was making lists, doing price comparisons of diapers in bulk on the Internet, printing out articles about educational toys and signing the as-yet-unborn child up for music appreciation, which began at the unbelievably early age of three months.

At night, when I couldn't sleep, I wrote, imagining that I was a young mother again, with a mug of tea cooling next to my laptop and Frenchie snoozing on a pillow by my side, dressed in my husband's sweatshirt, the one that still held a hint of his smell. Sometimes, when I woke up, I would imagine that I could smell him, that he was still there, that I would open my eyes and see him, his head on the pillow, eyes open, lips curved into a smile, saying my name.

Betsy called every week or so. She e-mailed pictures from the twenty-week ultrasound, pictures of her belly and her boys patting it proudly (but not, I noticed, pictures of her husband—maybe it was just that he was always the one behind the camera, or maybe there were more deliberate editorial choices going on).

By the end of January, I had a rough draft of the book I'd started the week of Peter's funeral, and I shyly presented it to Larissa. It was called *The Family Way,* about a man in the suburbs, a judge, wealthy and stable and secure, who at fifty fell in love with a much younger woman, married her and started a family, in spite of being married with children already. It was told from the perspective of the dead man, in heaven; the first wife; and the first wife's oldest daughter, who referred to her mother as Original Style and his father's young bride as Extra Crispy. It was, I supposed, an attempt to make sense of a version of my own father's life, to take a man like him and crack him open like an oyster, solve his puzzles, make him both similar to and different from my own father, to make sense of things.

Maybe it was a real book, or maybe it was just 350 pages of throat-clearing, the gunk I needed to get out of my system before I could do the real work again. I couldn't be objective. I'd have to wait and see. Either way, no matter what the pages turned out to be, they had comforted and sustained me, had given me something to think about other than how much I missed Peter, something to do besides cry. For that, I would always be grateful.

On the Friday night before Valentine's Day, at ten o'clock at night, the telephone rang. I talked to Betsy, then sat cross-legged on my big empty bed, the telephone in my hand and the silence of the house pressing down around me. "We did it," I said softly, and sat there and hoped for an answer. When none came, I cried for a few minutes, clutching a pillow to my midsection, wishing that for once

I could have gotten things in the right order: a husband and then a baby. *You get what you get,* I told myself, the way I used to tell it to Joy when she was little, when I'd cut her grilled cheese into rectangles instead of the preferred triangles, when I put on her sneakers instead of her beloved green rubber rainboots, and she'd cry. *You get what you get, and you don't get upset.* Soon, I supposed, I'd be saying it again.

I washed my face, combed my hair. I walked down the hallway, imagining I could see Peter standing in front of the linen closet, looking for his wool blanket, carrying a basket of laundry to the washing machine. Then I tapped on my daughter's bedroom door. "It's a boy," I said.

Forty-two

My mother steered the minivan down South Second Street, where the bare tree branches arched above our heads, turning the pavement into a tunnel of flickering shadows. We drove past the Wawa, and the little Chinese take-out place that had caused such a stir when it opened and some of the neighbors had passed out leaflets complaining that the restaurant would attract the wrong element. "Which is what, exactly?" Samantha had demanded, tossing the flyer onto the kitchen counter for my mom to see. "Jews?" I smiled at the memory.

My mom turned onto Delaware Avenue, then onto the highway. The day had been warm and breezy, a hint of spring in the air. Now the night sky was cloudless, illuminated by the moon. The car seat was snug in the backseat, and I'd double-checked the diaper bag for everything the baby book said we would need: diapers and wipes and ointment, burp clothes, bottles and formula, a change of clothes, a soft fabric ball lined with snippets of ribbon, each one a different color and different texture, which was a good developmental toy. I'd found it in a box in the attic. I think it used to be mine.

"Are you doing all right?" my mother asked. It was only a two-hour drive, but she'd packed a cooler with snacks for us: string cheese and crackers and apples and juice.

"Do we have a name yet?" I replied.

"It will come to me," she said with her eyes on the road. "That's how I named you. The name just came to me."

I didn't say anything to that, but I thought I saw a smile flicker across her face when I pulled the *1001 Baby Names* book out of my backpack. "Not Peter," I said, half to myself. My mom shook her head. I read down the list of P names. "Pablo. Pace. Padriac. Patrick. Paul. Pax. Paz."

"Pace?"

" 'From the Latin word for peace,' " I read.

"Then it would be Pah-chay."

"Okay," I said. Thinking, *No way will I let her name an innocent child Pahchay.*

"What do you think of Charles? With Peter as maybe a middle name?"

"That's good, I guess."

"We could call him Charlie. His Hebrew name could be Chaim. Life."

"Charlie Krushelevansky," I said, trying it out. "It sounds good. We'll see. Maybe he won't look like a Charlie." I ran my finger down my list again. "Maybe he'll look like a Padriac."

My mother snorted. I rested the top of my head against the cool glass of the window, and I must have dozed off because when I opened my eyes, she was parking the car underneath a haloed streetlamp in a big parking lot. Then we were inside, smelling that familiar hospital smell.

"Maternity?" she asked at the front desk.

"Fifth floor," said the woman, and she gave us both VISITOR stickers (I stuck mine on the leg of my jeans; my mother, of course, put hers proudly on the uppermost swell of her bosom).

We rode up in the elevator, and as the nurse at the desk on the fifth floor buzzed open the heavy swinging doors. You could smell urine and vomit, eye-watering disinfectant, and fear—but on this floor, you could also smell flowers. Every room we passed, I glimpsed a bouquet out of the corner of my eye, lilies or roses or a bunch of pink or blue balloons bumping against the ceiling.

At 514, my mother stopped so abruptly that if I'd been behind her instead of at her side, I would have walked right into her back. "Oh," she said softly. "Oh."

Betsy was in bed in a striped cotton bathrobe, smiling at us. "Hey, guys!" There was a plastic bracelet around her wrist, a blue-and-white-wrapped bundle in her arms. The baby had a dusting of dark hair underneath a knitted blue-and-white cap, a crooked little nose, skin so pale that I could see blue veins tracing their way on his eyelids and his cheeks. I tiptoed closer to the bed. I thought I recognized the shape of my mother's eyebrows, my father's forehead and chin. One of the baby's tiny hands was tucked into the blanket. The other hand was doing a kind of spazzy wave in the air. His fingers opened and closed, opened and closed, and it seemed like the most natural thing in the world for me to stretch out my hand and give him my pinkie to grab. He held it tight.

"Charlie," I said. "He looks like a Charlie."

"Want to hold him?" Betsy asked. She looked exhausted, as drained as if she'd been up all night running on a treadmill, but she also looked happy.

"Is it okay?" I asked.

"Sure, big sister," said Betsy. I crouched down, and she shifted the baby into my arms without his letting go of my finger.

My mom stood with one hand against the doorway, like she was afraid to come inside. Betsy looked at her. "Are you all right?"

"Fine," she said faintly. Then she shook her head and seemed to collect herself. "Better question: How are you?"

My mother pulled up a chair, and the two of them talked about labor and Apgar scores and episiotomies. As soon as I heard the word "placenta," I closed my ears and walked the baby over to the window, thinking that he didn't need to hear about any of that. "Check it out," I said, bouncing him lightly in my arms, aiming his face so he could look out at the night sky. He looked at me with eyes that were a muddy grayish-brown. "Charlie," I said experimentally, and cuddled him close to my chest. I felt my mother's hand on my shoulder and saw her face reflected in the window, her expression tender as she looked at the baby in my arms, her eyes shining as she kissed me and then the baby's forehead; her secret face, the one she's only ever shown to me.

ACKNOWLEDGMENTS

This book would not have been possible without the hard work and stewardship of my agent, Joanna Pulcini. I am grateful, as ever, for her unflagging enthusiasm, painstaking attention to detail, and for her inadvertently hilarious failure to get the dirty jokes or X-rated references in any of my books.

My editor, Greer Hendricks, is, as ever, worth a price above rubies for her patience, kindness, and good humor.

I'm grateful to Joanna's assistants, Elizabeth Carter and Trinh Truong, and to Greer's assistant, Sarah Walsh, for their attention to detail, and to Suzanne O'Neill and Nancy Inglis for their careful work on the manuscript. I'm also lucky to have found an assistant as fabulous, indefatigable, and good-hearted as Meghan Burnett.

Judith Curr at Atria and Carolyn Reidy at Simon & Schuster have always taken the best care of me and of Cannie, as have all of the people at Atria: Gary Urda, Lisa Keim, Kathleen Schmidt, Christine Duplessis, Craig Dean, and Jeanne Lee.

I'm grateful to Jessica Fee and her team at Greater Talent Network, and to Marcy Engelman, Dana Gidney, and Jordana Tal, my NYC PR miracle workers.

Curtis Sittenfeld was a perceptive and generous reader.

In researching this book, I was lucky enough to be invited to the bar mitzvah of Charlie Sucher and the bat mitzvahs of Samantha Wladis in Cherry Hill and Abby Kalen in Simsbury, Connecticut, where absolutely NOTHING untoward happened. I thank Charlie, Samantha, and Abby and their parents, friends, and families for being so gracious and welcoming.

My friends and family, far and wide, are still supplying me with love, support, and material. Jake and Joe Weiner are not only my brothers, they do an excellent job with my business on the coast. Molly Weiner is a constant source of inspiration and fun. I'm grateful to Faye Frumin, Frances Frumin Weiner, and Clair Kaplan, for all of their help and encouragement, for laughing with me and, occasionally, being willing for me to laugh at them.

Finally, on the home front, Wendell is still the king of all dogs. My husband, Adam, is still my traveling companion and the person I'd most like to watch *The Big Lebowski* with. My daughter Lucy Jane is the light of my life, and her new little sister Phoebe Pearl demonstrated unflagging courtesy by keeping the kicks and rolls to a minimum while I wrote this book. My love and thanks to all of them . . . and to all of the readers who've come with me this far.